Please return/renew this item
by the last date shown.
Items may also be renewed by
Telephone and Internet.
Telford & Wrekin Libraries
www.telford.gov.uk/libraries

ALSO BY NATALIE K MARTIN

Together Apart

love you better

NATALIE K MARTIN

LAKE UNION
PUBLISHING

This is a work of fiction. Names, characters, organizations, places, events, and incidents are either products of the author's imagination or are used fictitiously.

Text copyright © 2015 Natalie K Martin

Published by Lake Union Publishing, Seattle

www.apub.com

Amazon, the Amazon logo, and Lake Union Publishing are trademarks of Amazon. com, Inc., or its affiliates.

ISBN-13: 978-1503946439
ISBN-10: 1503946436

Cover design by Najla Qamber

Printed in the United States of America

love you better

1.

'Welcome to the family.'

Effie followed Oliver as he led her to the dance floor with applause echoing around them and her new father-in-law's words in her ears. She placed a hand on Oliver's shoulder, and the new platinum band on her finger sparkled.

She looked up at him. 'Are we mad?'

'Maybe.' Oliver grinned. 'But it's too late for you now – you're stuck with us.'

There was no 'maybe' about it. Just shy of four months after meeting, they'd exchanged vows, sealed them with a kiss and laughed, clutching hands under a shower of rice.

'You make it sound like a prison sentence.'

'It is.' He pulled her closer and dropped a kiss on her lips. 'A life term in the weird world of the Barton-Coles.'

Effie peeked over at the faces smiling back at them as the lights that had shone down on them during the wedding toasts softened, and the music started. Despite its size, The Lancing Hotel felt cosy and intimate with its stylish, understated furnishings, and the fragrance of the Calla lilies around the room filled the air with sweetness.

'They're not so bad.'

'Ah, the innocence. You haven't met Aunt Grace yet.' He nodded over to a woman with a perfectly coiffured grey bob and a string of pearls around her neck, stroking the arm of a man no more than half her age. 'When she corners you and starts raving about the time she smoked a joint with Andy Warhol in '68 and actually *inhaled*, you'll think differently.'

Effie laughed as Oliver buried his nose in her hair. By the sound of things, his aunt Grace would fit right in with her family. She cast her eyes around the room again, looking at the sea of intricate fascinators, pastel dresses and dark three-piece suits.

She looked back up at him and frowned. 'Do you think they like me?'

'Of course they do. What's not to like?' He laughed and shook his head. 'Izzy adores you. She always used to say she wished I'd been a girl so she'd have had a little sister, and now she has you. As for Mum, she's just glad someone's finally pinned me down.'

His mum had congratulated her for doing what no other woman had been able to, and Effie had laughed, saying it was nothing to do with her. She'd thought it would sound like a compliment, telling her how charming her son was, how when he'd swept her off her feet, she'd been unable to resist. Instead, Celeste had scowled, telling her it was a skill he must have got from his cheating swine of a father. Effie had almost died from shame. The ink was barely dry on their marriage certificate, and already she'd made a faux pas. She looked over at Giles, her father-in-law.

'And your dad?'

Oliver sighed. 'Dad's just Dad.'

Although Giles had never been anything other than perfectly polite, his speech was less than enthusiastic. She could see he wasn't the type to get overexcited and sing from the rooftops, but saying that they'd have as *good a chance as any*?

Oliver tucked a finger under her chin, tilting her face up towards him. 'Don't.'

'Don't what?'

'The way he parades Anna around, it would have been downright hypocritical of him to say any more than he did.' Oliver scowled. 'Frankly, the sooner they bugger off back to Berkshire, the better, and they can take the twatty twins with them.'

Effie frowned and kissed his lips. 'Shh. Not today. Today's about us.'

Oliver had barely spoken to Rosie or Henry all day. They were his half-brother and half-sister, but Effie knew that if he'd had it his way, he wouldn't have invited them at all. Maybe this was what normal family life was really like. Fights, feuds and seething silences. For a fleeting second, she was grateful to be a second-generation only child.

He nodded back to the guests. 'No regrets? You're part of it all now.'

'Not even one iota.'

'It's a shame about your mum, though. I was rather looking forward to meeting her.'

Effie burrowed her head into his shoulder to hide her grimace. She couldn't think of anything worse. She tried to picture her mum mingling with the other guests. No doubt she'd have turned up in some hideous hemp excuse for a dress, and her low, husky voice would have carried all kinds of inappropriate stories. If Oliver's aunt Grace thought smoking a bit of weed was risqué, Penny Abbott's stories of dancing with top DJs at Glastonbury, under the influence of LSD, would have made her eyeballs pop out on stalks. Effie cringed, thinking about what Oliver's family would've thought of her if they knew the way she'd been brought up. For once, her mum's lack of interest in her life seemed to be a good thing.

'It doesn't matter,' she said. 'She's missed out on an amazing day. It's her loss.'

'And my gain. You've made me the happiest man alive.' He leaned down and softly pressed his lips against hers.

With the scent of his aftershave under her nose, one hand on her cheek and the other in her hair, Effie's stomach flipped. When he pulled away, he held in front of her face a grain of rice between his index finger and thumb, with an amused grin.

'Bloody stuff gets everywhere.' She laughed, shaking her hair to get rid of any stray grains.

'Everywhere?'

She grinned. More than a few grains had found their way inside the bodice of her dress. '*Everywhere.*'

'I say we duck out and de-rice ourselves then. I want to get you all to myself.'

His fingers trailed their way down her back, and someone, probably one of her friends, let out a long wolf whistle. With a hundred and twelve pairs of eyes on them, heat flushed her cheeks. She nodded at the MC, who declared the dance floor open, and the space around them slowly filled. Finally, she could relax. She wrapped her hands around Oliver's back as Al Green asked them to stay together. She had every intention of doing so.

∽

'How's it going, *Euphemia*?' Mickey laughed, and Effie whacked his arm with her cream clutch bag.

She slid into a chair next to him at the table, closely followed by Oliver. After going to each table, accepting congratulations and more glasses of champagne from Oliver's distant relatives and acquaintances, it was a relief to finally sit with her own friends.

'Don't,' Effie warned. 'I've never been called Euphemia in my life.'

'One must use one's full name now one's part of the jet set.' Mickey winked.

Effie looked at her best friend, Lou, as she shook her head and jabbed Mickey in the ribs. Lou looked beautiful. Effie had refused to opt for a sickly pastel number for her chief bridesmaid, and as a result, Lou's strapless black dress provided a classy contrast to Effie's ivory gown. She'd been a rock all day, from pouring Effie a nerve-busting shot of rum before the ceremony to circling the room and making friends with everyone, including Rosie and Henry.

'What jet set?' Oliver said. 'I'm not a millionaire – not even close. All this is the old man's doing. I'd have been happy nipping down to Wandsworth Town Hall.'

Effie looked at him and grinned. With his public schoolboy demeanour, it was easy to imagine him being a spoiled brat, but he'd been considerate of the fact that, unlike his side, her guests weren't bankers, magazine editors or captains of industry. His dad had insisted that they choose a hotel befitting what was expected of a Barton-Cole wedding, and Oliver had obliged only after Effie had turned down his suggestion of eloping to Gretna Green. There was no way she could pass up the chance of having the fairy-tale wedding of her dreams.

'You have to admit, though, it was a laugh at the ceremony. Oliver William Barton-Cole. Definitely need a plum in the mouth for that one,' Lou said, grinning at Oliver.

Effie laughed. Lou could make fun of Oliver's name all she wanted, but the award for most embarrassing name of the day was unquestionably hers. Euphemia Willow Abbott. Willow. How many other people were named after a bloody tree?

'Oh, I plan on sticking a plum tree in the garden for the wifey to start practising on.'

Mickey sniggered as the word *wifey* dropped from Oliver's mouth. With his polished accent, it didn't have quite the right ring to it.

Lou shook her head and waggled her finger at him. 'Sorry to disappoint you, mister, but I got there first. She might have your name now, but I hold the wifey rights. I've got ten years of her on you.'

Oliver held his hands up in mock horror. 'I'd never dream of coming between you two.'

'Good.' Lou winked back. 'It's been such a lovely day. Bet you can't wait for the honeymoon.'

Effie grinned. 'It's going to be so good. I've always wanted to go to Thailand.'

'Bit too far for me,' Mickey said. 'I hate flying.'

'He's such a wuss.' Lou laughed. 'He practically cried the whole four hours to Crete this summer. It was like travelling with an infant.'

Mickey silenced her with a kiss, and Effie grinned. They were so perfect together. They always seemed to laugh with each other, constantly winding each other up. Their kiss was interrupted by beeping from Mickey's phone, and he frowned, reading the screen. Lou leaned over to look at it and quickly shook her head at him.

'What's up?' Effie asked before taking a sip of her champagne.

'Oh, nothing. Especially not anything to worry about today.' Lou took a box of cigarettes from her bag. 'Fancy one?'

Effie looked at Oliver. It was clear that he was struggling to keep the disapproving frown from his face. He hated smoking, and she didn't intend on spending their honeymoon surrounded by a puff of smoke, but their flight wasn't until tomorrow morning. And as amazing as the day had been, the idea of five minutes to bask in it all without an audience was way too alluring to pass up.

'I thought you were going to quit?' he asked, taking her hand and rubbing it with his thumb.

'It's only one. And today's the last day.'

'Promise?' asked Oliver.

She smiled and crossed her heart with her fingers. 'Hope to die. Don't get eaten alive by Mickey.'

She pecked him on the cheek and looked across at Mickey, flashing him a warning look. Lou was bad enough, but she had nothing on him.

∽

Ten minutes later, having made it to the other end of the hall, she stepped outside. It was like an obstacle course, being stopped at every turn to receive a hug or boozy cry of congratulations. It had been a perfect day, and she tilted her head up to the obsidian sky, taking in a gulp of the cool, bonfire-scented air. Guy Fawkes's night was one of her favourite holidays – second only to Christmas. Choosing the fifth of November as their wedding day couldn't have been any more romantic. The moon shimmered over the River Thames at the far end of the gardens and over on the south side of London, the red sparkles of a firework sprang out in the sky.

She walked down the steps and onto the perfectly manicured grass, her heels sinking into the soft ground. She wriggled her toes in her ridiculously high Saint Laurent shoes. She practically lived in trainers, and her feet were aching from being in heels all day. How did Lou do it? And where was she anyway? Effie scanned the gardens, but there was no sign of her. It had taken so long for her to get outside that Lou had probably already been and gone. Grateful for a few minutes alone, she lifted the hem of her dress and slipped her feet out of her shoes, almost purring as she closed her eyes, letting the cold grass send relief to her feet.

'Looks like congratulations are in order.'

7

The deep voice cut right through to Effie's core, and she impulsively shivered at the sound of it. She'd recognise it anywhere, but she kept her eyes firmly shut. There was no way it was him – it simply wasn't possible. Maybe she was hallucinating. Or maybe she was drunk.

You've had six glasses of champagne over the course of the whole day, and you're as sober as a judge.

It was true. Despite her glass never being empty, the alcohol had taken no effect on her whatsoever, which meant that it really *was* him standing so close she could practically hear him breathing. She swallowed and opened her eyes. Slowly, she tracked her gaze up from the black Converse on his feet, over his trouser-covered legs and his close-fitted, sky-blue shirt. Her heart skipped as she looked at the tattoos etched into his arms, exposed by his rolled-up shirtsleeves, the cold air apparently having no effect on him at all. The breath was knocked out of her when she looked past his coat of stubble and up into the pair of grey eyes staring back at her.

Smith.

'Lace always did suit you.'

He looked her up and down, his eyes trailing a blaze over the intricate dress hugging her body, and then stuffed his hands in his pockets. The only lace he'd ever seen her in before had always been hidden under her clothes. It was all she could do not to run away. Or reach out and touch him – she wasn't sure which. She gripped her tiny clutch bag, just in case.

'What are you doing here? You're supposed to be on the other side of the world.'

He looked out at the river and shrugged. 'Money ran out.'

She'd forgotten what a great profile he had, with his beautifully straight nose and strong jaw. His top shirt button was undone, and she looked at the strand of brown leather around his neck, tapering off to hold a horn-shaped pendant. She looked back at the doors she'd just come through and prayed nobody would come outside. She didn't want anyone to see him standing there. In fact, she wanted him to disappear altogether, like he had five months ago, because now that he was standing in front of her, her stomach was fluttering and her pulse was racing, the way it always had with him – the way it hadn't for a long time. Before, it would have been a pleasurable feeling, but now all she felt was sick. His leaving had made her life a whole lot easier and happier, and she didn't need him to come back and wreck it all over again.

'So, who's the lucky guy?'

Why did the sound of his voice make her skin bloom with goosebumps? She rubbed her arms, demanding they go away, and squared her shoulders as she jutted out her chin.

'Why does it matter?'

He smirked, and she had to restrain herself from wiping it off his face. 'The old crowd in there?'

'Some.'

'Mixing with Hoorah Henries . . . I guess things really have changed.'

Effie sighed with irritation and shook her head. Oliver wasn't a Hoorah Henry, and Smith had no right to call him that.

'You don't look pleased to see me.'

'That's because I'm not. You attract trouble like shit attracts flies.'

'Ouch. What, are you worried I'll screw up your happy day?'

'Why else would you be here? You always screw things up.'

He shrugged. 'I was curious. I wanted to see what was so great about whoever he is that had you skipping up the aisle so quickly.'

She scowled. 'It wasn't that quick.'

He raised his eyebrows. 'Less than a month after I leave, I hear you've got with someone else, and now you're married. Hardly taking your time, is it?'

'So? Why do you care? What do you want me to say? That I'm sorry?'

'Only if you mean it.'

She studied the trees behind him, lit up with fairy lights, fighting to keep her breath steady as anger pulsed through her. She'd been euphoric all day, but just a few moments with Smith were enough to bring it all crashing down. Causing problems was one of the few things Smith could be counted on for, and she didn't need it. She'd had enough to last her a lifetime. It was her wedding day, and they were surrounded by influential, respectable people. Thanks to Oliver, she was one of them now. She wasn't sorry for the turn her life had taken. She finally had everything she had ever wanted, and she wasn't about to let Smith ruin it all.

'You mean like you apologised for all the stuff you did? It's funny, because I don't remember you ever saying sorry for shagging around behind my back.'

'Come on, Eff – it wasn't as simple as that.'

'Do you know what, Smith? I don't care anymore. Really, I don't. And if you're seriously waiting to hear me say sorry for moving on, then I suggest you go and hold your breath.'

She bent down to pick her shoes up and stalked away from him. Why was he here, ruining everything? Her life was so much simpler now. It was easy, stable and reliable, and she could trust Oliver in a way she never could Smith. She never had to analyse with Oliver. She always knew where she stood, without question. Smith, on the other hand, was a walking enigma, and she'd failed to solve it.

'I hope it's worth it,' he called after her.

'It is,' Effie replied without turning back. '*He* is.'

'Well then, I wish you nothing but happiness.' His voice dripped with sarcasm, and she stopped, gripping the shoes in her hand. She turned and walked back over to him.

'Why did you really come back?'

His excuse about money was balls. Travelling was one of the things he always used to talk about, and a year around the world was his dream come true. It had come about after a dire chain of events, but even still, he'd used the money left to him by his grandpa, and there was no way he could've spent twenty grand already.

He stared back at her with his grey eyes. 'I had to see if it was true.'

'If what was true?'

'You. Getting married to someone you barely even know, for no good reason.'

Behind him, Lou came through the doors, holding two glasses of champagne, and her jaw dropped, her mouth forming a perfect O when she saw the two of them standing inches apart. Effie looked over Smith's shoulder at her as Lou discreetly jerked her head to one side, and Oliver followed her through the doors.

Oliver smiled when he saw her. 'There you are.'

Effie froze with panic at the sound of Oliver's voice, and Lou scarpered, closing the door behind her in a vain attempt to protect the wedding guests from the impending drama about to be unleashed outside.

'I thought you might need this – it's cold out here,' Oliver said, holding the faux fur shrug to match her dress. He looked at Smith, and Effie opened her mouth. Why weren't the words coming out to explain who Smith was?

'I'm Smith.' He outstretched a hand, breaking the silence. 'I take it you're the husband.'

'Guilty as charged. Oliver Barton-Cole.' Oliver laughed, his perfectly pronounced words sounding woefully out of place as he shook Smith's hand.

She looked at the two of them. Oliver stood a couple of inches taller than Smith, and in his smart tux, he looked devastatingly handsome and every bit the charming, thirty-year-old man with the world at his feet. Smith's naturally rugged edge stripped away any kind of respectability the suit should have given him and left him looking like the brooding, dangerous kind of guy that any woman in her right mind would do her best to avoid. Effie couldn't take her eyes off him.

Smith looked from Effie to Oliver and back again. 'I'd better leave you to it.'

'You're not staying?' Oliver asked, and Smith shook his head.

'Nah, I've got places to be. I just wanted to give my congrats.' He looked at Effie and nodded. 'Nice seeing you again, Eff.'

She looked away from him as he left. It hadn't been nice seeing him – it was the complete opposite in fact. It had made her head fight for control over the natural impulses of her body, the impulses that Smith had always elicited in her.

Oliver put the shrug around her shoulders, and her body sighed under its warmth. After Smith's unexpected appearance, the shrug was almost as comforting as Oliver's reassuring presence.

'Who was that?' Oliver asked, stroking the back of her neck as he watched Smith leave.

'Smith. He used to hang out with us.'

'Did we invite him?'

She shook her head, trembling. 'Definitely not. He's nothing but trouble.'

'Speaking of trouble, if I don't get you out of this dress soon, I'm going to end up getting arrested for harassment.'

He nuzzled her neck, but all Effie could think about were the grey eyes that had stared back at her and rocked her world.

2.

Turquoise water stretched for as far as Effie could see, punctuated by brightly coloured fishing boats and a few huge slabs of rock, poking out from the seabed like pillars. The last ten days had been bliss: snorkelling with tropical fish in the crystal-clear, coral-lined waters, sleeping in and sunbathing.

Lifting the brim of her enormous sun hat, she watched Oliver as he emerged from the sea. His skin had bronzed in the sun, and water ran in streaks down his chest, clinging to his abs. He jogged across the sand and kissed her, sending tiny drops of water onto her chest.

'Morning, sleepyhead. Have you had breakfast yet?'

Effie shook her head. She'd gorged herself from the moment they'd arrived on Koh Tao, with enormous, juicy tiger prawns drenched in lemon and garlic sauce, mouth-watering curries and the best pad thai she'd ever tasted, not to mention a frankly overindulgent amount of mangos.

'How was the swim?'

'Amazing,' Oliver replied, grabbing the towel from the back of the lounger next to her. 'You should go in.'

'Maybe later.'

As beautiful as the sea was, she could do without the disastrous effect it would have on her hair today, but nothing could stop him.

He'd headed out for a swim every morning and usually followed it up with a run.

'Later might be tricky. We've got plans today.'

She raised an eyebrow. 'We do?'

Aside from finishing her book and topping up her tan, she hadn't planned on doing anything else. The sun was doing a great job of enhancing her already brown skin, and they only had two days left before returning to the depressingly bleak London winter.

She took her hat off and shook out her frizzy curls. 'Where are we going?'

'It's a surprise,' Oliver replied, throwing the towel down on the ground. 'Christ, you look good.'

She grinned as he climbed astride her on the sunlounger, his blonde hair glistening in the sunlight.

'Do you have any idea how much I want you right now?'

Effie raised an eyebrow and lifted her thigh between his legs. 'I think the whole of Thailand does.'

He leaned down to kiss her, and for what felt like the millionth time over the last ten days, she thanked god for Lou and her skills of persuasion. If she hadn't dragged a heartbroken Effie out of her bed for that night out back in July, she would never have met Oliver, and she wouldn't be on this paradise island now.

She broke away from his kiss, and he looked down at her with a frown. 'What?'

'We can't.' Effie glanced around at the beach.

'Can't what?' he mumbled into the hollow in her throat as he stroked his hand down over her bikini top, pushing a triangular strip of material to one side.

'You know what.'

'Nobody's around – it's fine.'

The beach stretched for miles on either side, and there was nobody else around, but still, she didn't feel comfortable with the idea of getting frisky on a public beach, whether they were alone or not. Oliver's blue eyes twinkled, and he grinned at her before leaning in for another kiss. Maybe she was being too prim. Effie lay back on her lounger and ran her hands over her husband's shoulders. Husband. Could she ever get tired of the word?

❧

I'm going to die.

Effie's stomach churned as her heart raced under her light cotton shirt. After their risqué sex on the beach, Oliver revealed her surprise – a bike ride to Mango Lookout Point, apparently an absolute must for sunset views across the tiny island of Koh Tao. It wasn't exactly the kind of surprise she'd had in mind, *amazing views* translating as *heights* in her head.

'The view will be fantastic,' Oliver had said, oblivious to the reluctance on Effie's face as he mounted the scooter.

She was no Girl Guide, but she was willing to bet it would involve driving off road, and she'd seen enough of the island to know it would be a bumpy ride. He'd given her the camera and waited for her to get on behind him. As they made their way up the insanely steep road surrounded by lush forest, she clung to Oliver as tightly as she could, only letting go when he stopped to admire the view. Each time, he'd asked how she was, and each time she'd replied that she was fine, despite being anything but. She was utterly terrified. Smith drove a motorbike, and she'd been on the back of it countless times before, but she'd never felt this vulnerable, and Oliver's speed as they took the bends didn't help.

'Can you slow down?' she shouted so he'd hear her through his helmet. They sped up the slope, and try as she might, she couldn't stop herself from looking over her shoulder. She tightened her arms around him. 'Olly, slow down.'

'It's fine – stop fussing.'

He sounded so sure of himself, but she gulped as they turned yet another hairpin bend. She didn't want to end up hurtling forty feet to a grisly death, and if it wasn't caused by their speed, it would likely be caused by the other cars on the road. Everyone they'd passed had sped by, confidently familiar with the road lay-out, and they were as vulnerable on their tiny 125cc scooter as a fly in a spider's web. She swallowed against the nausea hitting her like tidal swells and kept her head down, pressed against Oliver's back, but as they approached an S-bend, they skirted way too close to the edge.

'Olly, what the hell are you doing? Slow down.'

'Relax.'

'You can't go any closer – we'll fall off.'

'God, Effie, just let me drive, will you?'

Her sense of balance disappeared, leaving her with only dizziness for company. They were going to lurch to the side and fall off the bike at any minute.

'Stop and let me off.'

'Calm down, Effie, for god's sake,' he shouted, twisting his head round to face her.

He wasn't going to stop. She had no choice but to stay on the death-trap bike until they reached the top. She squeezed her eyes shut. What if they lost traction and spun out of control? They would go head first down the ravine and end up in a crumpled heap below. Nobody knew where they were; they'd be hidden under a thick layer of trees and wouldn't be found for days. She'd seen tens of backpackers hobbling around with iodine-stained bandages from scooter mishaps, and every story she'd ever heard about travellers meeting untimely deaths on foreign roads rolled around her head.

We're riding up a mountain on a dodgy bike with crap, badly fitted helmets. We're going to die.

Her head swam with morbid images and headlines. She couldn't breathe. Her lungs were aching for air, her helmet seemed to be getting smaller, and she felt like she was about to throw up. She tried shouting again to ask him to stop the bike, but it was too late, and she heaved over the side.

The bike skidded to a halt, and Effie clambered off to run to the side of the road. She stood, retching, as she held on to the craggy rock face.

'Jesus, Effie, what's wrong with you?' he shouted.

She spat on the ground, her legs shaking so much it was a miracle they were still managing to hold her up.

'What do you think? I asked you to slow down.'

'If we'd been going any slower, we'd have lost balance.'

She looked up at him as he stormed off back to the bike and lifted the seat to get a bottle of water. It didn't take a rocket scientist to see that he was angry as he slammed the seat back down and marched towards her, holding the bottle out, with a face like thunder. She looked past him at the bike. He hadn't even asked if she was feeling better, and she fought to keep the tears inside. She'd never seen him lose his temper like that. He was usually so cool and collected, but she had to remind herself that he was only human. He'd have to get angry at some point; it was inevitable. It was just a shame it had to happen on their honeymoon. The last thing she wanted was to argue, especially when the day had got off to such a great start.

'I knew what I was doing, Effie. You didn't have to freak out.'

'Well *you* didn't have to go so close to the edge,' she muttered, snatching the bottle.

'It was either that or drive over those potholes, which would've been a lot worse.'

She looked away and took a sip of the lukewarm water. There was no denying there were a lot of potholes, but to her mind that should have meant driving slower, not trying to become the next Valentino Rossi.

'I was in control. There was no need to second-guess me. You either trust me or you don't.'

She'd asked a billion times for him to slow down, to stay away from the edge and not to brake too hard, but he hadn't listened. She looked up at him as he stood with his hands on his hips. His eyebrows were pulled tightly together, and his mouth was set into a furious scowl.

'You know I do.'

'Good.' His face softened, and he held out a hand to help her up. 'We've not got long to go now anyway.'

She took his hand and slowly walked back to the bike. Maybe he was right. Maybe she had overreacted. When he sat back down on the bike and looked up at her, she took a deep breath.

'I'm sorry,' she mumbled, passing the bottle of water from one hand to the other.

He shook his head. 'It's fine. Just try to relax, okay?'

Effie nodded and climbed on behind him, willing her nerves to stay calm. Twenty minutes later, Oliver parked up and took her hand, leading her to the lookout point. She held on to him as tightly as she could and breathed a sigh of relief when they stopped a few feet from the edge. Thanks to her being sick, they'd missed the sunset, but the sky was still cast with a warm, orange glow. Oliver sat on the ground and pulled her down with him before kissing her shoulder.

'Are you feeling better?'

Effie nodded and blushed. 'I'm sorry about earlier. I totally overreacted.'

'What happened back there?'

'I just hate heights. Always have.' She sighed, replaying the way she'd leapt from the bike in her head.

18

'But you sat on a plane for twelve hours at thirty-five thousand feet.'

'Yeah, and I also drank enough wine to send me to sleep for most of it.' She gave him a wry smile, and a frown flickered across his face,

'I'm sorry.' He kissed her knuckles. 'I had no idea. I didn't even think I was going that fast – I just wanted to get here for the sunset. I wanted everything to be perfect.'

Effie looked at the rueful smile on his lips. He'd tried to give her the perfect day, and she'd ruined it. She shook her head and kissed his cheek.

'It has been. I'm sorry we missed the sunset.'

He turned her head to face him and kissed her tenderly, as if she were made of something precious, and she let herself relax. What had happened earlier was just a small blip. He hadn't known that she hated heights, and she trusted him to the ends of the earth and back. It was a trust that was warranted when he drove with extra care as they descended the mountain, and Effie couldn't help but smile as he stuck to the middle of the road.

3.

The following Monday afternoon, Effie sat behind her office desk and yawned. 'Is it home time yet?'

Their flight had arrived back in London on Saturday afternoon, but her body clock seemed to have been left behind in Thailand.

Her workmate Nikki shook her head. 'Nope. A hottie turned up for an interview while you were on lunch, though. I think Doug said something about him being a temp.'

'But we don't have any vacancies.'

'Who knows? Doug's the boss.' Nikki shrugged. 'I hope they make him permanent. Seriously, he was fit as.'

'Makes no difference to me; I'm married now,' Effie replied, throwing her a smug smile.

'Married, not blind. You can still look. I'm with Jake, and I can still appreciate a good-looking guy when I see one.'

'You've seen Olly. What's the point in looking when it'll never be better than that?'

Nikki mimed throwing up. 'Honestly, you're mental, coming back. If I were married to a rich barrister, I'd be a stay-at-home wife and spend my days shopping.'

'No way,' Effie replied. 'I'd be bored stiff.'

Oliver had suggested the same thing on their honeymoon, but what else would she do all day? True, he earned enough money to provide for them both, but she loved her job. Archive was only a tiny record label, a goldfish in an ocean, but while the pay wasn't fantastic, and she could do the admin work with her hands tied behind her back, the six-strong team operated like a family.

Nikki handed her a stack of CDs that were waiting to be mailed out. 'Seriously. You have no idea how lucky you are. You've got everything.'

∾

Later that evening, Lou plonked herself into the chair opposite Effie in a bar close to her office, and waved to one of the waiters.

'Okay, spill it,' Lou said. 'I've been dying to catch up properly. The thing at the wedding with Smith? Omigod.'

'Hello. I'm fine, thank you. Thailand was awesome,' Effie replied, deadpan.

'FYI, I know Thailand was good because you kept posting nausea-inducing photos on Facebook. You do look great, though.' Lou turned to the young waiter who'd appeared by their table. 'Chablis, please.'

Effie nodded at the waiter. 'Same.'

'So, Smith. Have you heard anything more from him? I can't believe he actually turned up.' Lou's eyes were wide as she shook her head, and the mere mention of Smith's name made Effie's hair stand on end. 'And I'm sorry to say this, but he looked good.'

'You only saw him from the back,' Effie replied, 'and it was dark.'

'It was light enough for me to see, and he looked fit as.'

'Not helping, Lou.'

'Sorry,' she replied, looking contrite.

Effie sighed. 'As annoying as it is to admit it, he *did* look good. Travelling seems to have agreed with him. Wherever he was.'

His skin was beautifully tanned, and while he'd always had a great physique, lugging a backpack around had only added to it. He seemed to have come back with an air of quiet confidence that clung to him like a second skin.

'Vietnam, Cambodia and Thailand,' Lou said as the waiter came back and filled their glasses. She looked up at him and smiled. 'I think we need the bottle.'

Had he made it to Koh Tao? Effie hoped not. She didn't want to have seen the same things he had on her honeymoon.

'Hang on a minute,' Effie said, frowning. 'You said you couldn't believe he'd *actually* turned up. Did you know he was coming back?'

'Okay, so here's the thing.'

'Lou!' Effie put her head in her hands. 'What the hell?'

'He turned up at ours the night before at stupid o'clock in the morning, but I didn't know until I woke up. By the time Mickey told me, he'd already gone. The last I'd seen, he was posting pictures of himself rock climbing in Thailand. I had no idea he was going to come, not until the last minute. That's why I tried to get you outside.'

Of course. Effie remembered the look Lou had exchanged with Mickey when his phone had beeped just before they'd gone for a cigarette. She looked up at Lou, her best friend, and shook her head with a scowl.

'And you didn't think to tell me?'

'It was your wedding day. I didn't want it to be ruined. The plan was that Mickey would intercept and get rid of him. I promise you, I had no idea he was planning on gatecrashing until he messaged Mickey, and by that time it was too late to say anything.'

Effie sighed. 'God, what a mess. I don't know why he came back at all, other than to piss me off.'

'I really am sorry. I just couldn't tell you in time.'

'It's fine. It will *be* fine. He's just messing with my head like he always did.'

'What did you talk about anyway?'

'Nothing. Apparently, he wanted to see what was so great about *whoever it was* that – and I quote – had me skipping up the aisle so quickly. He called Olly a Hoorah Henry.'

Lou winced. 'Ouch.'

'He was just trying to cause trouble, doing what he does best.'

'He went to a lot of effort to do it. I don't think I've ever seen him suited and booted before.'

Neither had Effie, but, bloody hell, did suited and booted look good on him. She had to grudgingly admit that, despite what he may have thought, he would've blended in with the rest of the guests. Not that she'd have ever allowed that to happen. Hell would've had to be frozen over first.

'You didn't . . . you know . . . feel anything for him when you saw him, did you?'

Effie rolled her eyes. 'Get real.'

'It's just that you've always had a bit of a blind spot with him. I'm not saying you don't love Olly. Who wouldn't love him? He's fab. But this is Smith we're talking about.'

'Exactly,' Effie replied. 'Smith. The guy who strung me along for months on end and shagged around without a second thought.'

'Good. I'm glad you remember that part. I was worried he'd wormed his way back into your head. I mean, he's a great friend and an ace guy, but as a boyfriend?' Lou shook her head.

'I know,' Effie replied, 'and I'm not about to fall back into that, trust me.'

'Olly is so much better for you. It's just that you only had a month apart from Smith before meeting him. It wouldn't be unnatural for you to be confused.'

It wasn't the first time Effie had heard comments about how quickly her relationship with Oliver had moved. It was nothing new,

23

but now Smith and his bloody chiselled cheekbones had shown up, it made it seem less romantic and more foolish.

Effie poured out more wine. 'There's no confusion. Things moved fast with Olly because they were right. I haven't thought about Smith for months, and I refuse to get sucked back into his crap.'

'You know you won't be able to avoid him forever,' Lou said, pointing out the obvious. Effie might have cut him out of her life, but Lou's relationship with Mickey, one of Smith's best friends, guaranteed that Smith would always be around.

'He's not coming on Saturday, is he?' Effie asked. The idea of Smith and Oliver being in the same space again made her feel sick.

Lou shook her head. Thank god. After years of talking about going to the ice rink at Somerset House, they'd finally bought tickets, and the last thing she wanted was to have Smith there.

'I can't believe he's come back now,' Effie said, sighing. 'His timing couldn't be worse. Mum emailed a few days ago. She's passing through and wants to meet Olly.'

She sighed again and drained her glass. Having her mum out of the picture had been convenient, but now Oliver would be confronted with the mess that was Penny Abbott, and she'd probably be a divorcée before she knew it.

'It had to happen some time,' Lou said.

'Did it, though? I mean, how many times have I seen her in the last ten years?' Effie held her hand up, stretching all of her fingers and her thumb out wide. 'Five. Five times in ten years. She couldn't even be arsed to make it to the wedding, so what's the point in her showing up now?'

'I must admit, I thought she'd come for that,' Lou replied with a sad frown on her face. 'What's Olly said about it?'

'I haven't told him yet.' Effie groaned. 'I mean, this is the woman who upped and left when I was fifteen to go live in some hippy-dippy commune and get high all day. It's hardly normal.'

'There's no such thing as *normal*.'

'Oliver grew up in the countryside with his sister, two dogs and a herd of chickens. His childhood was about as normal as you can get.'

'He grew up in a mini mansion, went to private school and holidayed in Courcheval. That's definitely not normal.'

Effie's mum might have left a wad of money behind and called every now and again, but it didn't make up for being abandoned. It was hardly the kind of thing Effie wanted to broadcast.

'You're not happy to see her at all?'

Effie shrugged. 'I've learned not to expect anything when it comes to her. That way I'm never disappointed.'

Lou squeezed her hand, and Effie threw her a small smile. When it rained, it poured.

'Anyway, what's new with you? I feel like all we ever do is talk about me these days.'

'That's because your life is so much more thrilling than mine.' Lou grinned. 'Let's see, what's new with me? Apart from basically wishing Mickey had been born into money too, so I could leave my job and do something I actually *want* to do for a living, not much. Rat-faced Rachel's getting worse every day.'

Effie laughed at the nickname Lou had given to her new boss. 'You shouldn't let her get to you, and it's only for a couple of months.'

'I know, but it's supposed to be a development secondment. How can I learn anything when I'm being micro-managed every second of every day? I can't even breathe without her permission.'

A project management secondment had opened up in Lou's department, and she'd signed up for it, hoping it would stand her in good stead for the next step of her career.

'What's happening with the cottage?' Effie asked. Mickey's aunt owned a property in West Ireland, and they were planning to rent it out for a few days over the Christmas break.

'It's fully booked until the New Year, so it'll probably have to be in January.'

'January works for us. It's been ages since we've been away together, it'll be fun. Focus on that.' Effie smiled. Plus, you'll be all nice and relaxed after Christmas.'

'Ah.' Lou sighed with a smile. 'Christmas. Excessive food, crap telly and time off work. I can't wait.'

As Effie grinned back, her mobile rang, and Oliver's name flashed up at her. She answered it as Lou opened her menu.

'Hey, baby. Where are you?' Oliver asked.

'I'm still with Lou. Are you finished already?'

'Yep. The post-holiday blues have hit me. I'm done for the day. Do you need a lift home?'

Effie looked down at her menu lying on the table. 'I was going to grab some food first.'

'Sounds nice, but you know what could be even nicer? If I come by and pick you up, we can stop in at the supermarket on the way home, and I could make you a nice home-cooked meal. What do you think?'

After two weeks of constantly eating out, the appeal of some comfort food was strong. Effie looked over at Lou. It was clear she'd guessed what Oliver had offered when she shook her head and rolled her eyes with a smile.

'It's fine,' Lou said. 'The food's way too expensive here anyway.'

Effie grinned. 'Okay. I'm in Zaza's, around the corner from the office.'

'Great. I'll be there in no time,' Oliver replied and hung up.

'Are you sure you don't mind?' Effie asked Lou, putting her phone back in her bag.

'Not at all,' Lou replied. 'You're a newly-wed – these things are to be expected. And that was exactly what I meant earlier. Olly's so considerate.'

'He is.' Effie smiled. 'I have to admit, getting a lift home is way more appealing than facing the Tube.'

'If only *my* boyfriend would take a leaf out of his book.' Lou sighed. 'I'd love to be picked up once in a while.'

'We'll take you home too. Olly won't mind.'

'If I didn't love you so much, I'd be racked with jealousy. I'm glad you haven't let Smith mess with your head.'

With a husband like Oliver, she didn't need guys like Smith trying to mess things up. She'd had the best five months of her life, and Christmas was only six weeks away. It would be her first with Oliver, and she couldn't wait. All she had to do was get through an evening with her mum and avoid Smith first. Easy.

4.

But just three days into those six weeks, Effie walked out of
the small hut serving as a cloakroom at Somerset House
to see Smith standing with Mickey. She turned and
scowled at Lou.

'What the hell is he doing here?'

'I had no idea, I swear,' Lou replied.

'You're the one who bought the tickets.'

Lou shrugged. 'He must've bought his own – they're not exclu-
sive, you know. But he's here now, and it's not like we can tell him
to leave.'

Effie sighed as they walked over to the boys, keeping her eyes
well away from Smith's.

'All set?' Mickey asked, taking Lou's hand.

Smith nodded and looked at Effie. 'Hope you don't mind me
crashing the party?'

She looked right back at him, ignoring the intensity of his eyes,
and shrugged. 'Seems like it's becoming quite the habit for you
these days.'

'Now, now. Play nice, you two.' Mickey laughed.

They joined the queue to change their shoes for skates, and
Effie ignored Smith, standing by her side. Didn't he have anything
better to do than tag along with them and fill her nose with his

scent? He didn't even wear aftershave; it was just *his* smell, and it was intoxicating. Effie buried her nose into her scarf, and once they'd got their skates, she made sure not to end up sitting next to him on the bench. Unfortunately for her, he sat right opposite.

'So where's lover-boy Henry?' he asked.

Effie looked at his legs as he stretched them out, trying to ignore the way his raw denim jeans fitted him so snugly, but it was hard when he was sitting there, right in front of her. He wore them so effortlessly, like a second skin, and for a split second she allowed her gaze to linger on his thighs before mentally slapping herself. God, she was pathetic. He flexed his feet, and she looked up at him.

'His name's Oliver, and he's coming later on. He's got a rugby do first.'

'Figures.'

Effie glared at him, and Lou clapped her hands together loudly. 'Well, I don't know about you lot, but I'm beyond excited.'

Mickey laughed. 'I'm looking forward to watching you fall flat on your arse.'

'If I fall, you're coming with me, so I'd be careful what I wished for if I were you.'

'Man, I'd forgotten what you two were like together.' Smith grinned, shaking his head. 'You watch – I bet you'll end up like Torvill and Dean out there.'

'Hardly,' Mickey snorted. 'She can barely walk on a normal pavement, let alone on ice. She trips over about ten times a day.'

'*Slight* exaggeration,' Lou replied, rolling her eyes.

Effie grabbed the bobbles on the ends of the long strings dangling from the sides of her hat and yanked them down. Lou and Mickey were too cute together, and even though they'd always acted like that, it was different now that Smith was back. Effie and Smith had been the same way when they were together, and she knew by the way he was staring at her that he was being reminded of it too.

She flicked her eyes up to the clock on the wall and hoped Oliver would turn up sooner rather than later.

As they stood up, Effie wobbled on her skates, and Smith steadied her, holding her elbow. 'Careful. We're not even on the ice yet.'

Since when did someone touching her elbow make her body flood with heat? She yanked it away and turned her back to him.

'I'm fine.'

She wasn't. It was the first time he'd touched her in months, and her skin was buzzing with electricity. She shook her head a little, feeling foolish for reacting so strongly, because even with her back to him, she knew his know-it-all grin would be plastered all over his face.

When the rink was finally opened up, Mickey and Lou shot out, laughing as they held hands, and Effie gingerly stepped off the rubber mats. She grabbed the barrier and slowly started making her way around the edge. Mickey and Lou were long gone, and so was Smith. He'd skilfully skated past her, annoyingly efficient on his blades. Effie didn't care. She'd rather shuffle her way around than end up on the ground with her fingers splayed out for some over-zealous show-off to run over. The last time she'd been ice skating was when she was fourteen, and she'd spent more time on her arse than her feet. She'd hated every minute of it, but Somerset House was different.

It wasn't just about the skating; otherwise, she'd never have wanted to come. It was more to do with the beauty of it all. It was frequently named as the most glamorous ice rink in London, and it was only open for a few weeks each year. She'd seen it in films and TV shows, and now she was here, on the blue-lit ice, being bathed in the yellow lights from the buildings lining the courtyard.

After ten minutes, she'd made her first lap and still had all her fingers intact. Spotting Lou up ahead, resting against the barrier with Mickey, she gestured to them to wait for her. Laughter, shrieks and pop music filled the air, and it felt like she really was in the middle of a winter wonderland. It was cold and windy, but everyone was having fun, including, surprisingly, her.

Courage bolstered her, and as she approached a boy shuffling along ahead of her, she decided to overtake. She let go of the barrier just as someone whizzed past and knocked her shoulder. She squealed as her feet slid underneath her while she tried to regain her balance, but with nothing to hold on to, all she could do was close her eyes and remind herself to ball her hands into fists.

She landed with a small thud and gasped as the coldness seeped through her skinny jeans. A pair of skates skidded to a halt next to her, and she looked up at Smith extending his arm, and sighed. Of course it just *had* to be him coming to her rescue. Frustration rose inside her like a wave, and she scowled as she took his hand, scrambling to get back onto her feet.

'Thanks,' she mumbled, fighting to keep the blush from her cheeks as a group of teenage girls passed them and laughed.

He smiled back and squeezed her hand. 'Any time.'

Effie dropped her hand from his and shoved it in her pocket. She'd expected to see Lou and Mickey making their way over, but instead they were doubled over laughing. What great friends she had.

'You okay?' Smith asked.

'Fine.'

'You know, the problem is that you're trying to walk,' he explained. 'It doesn't work that way on ice. If you do it like that, you can't balance properly. You need to push your feet outwards, like this.' He skated a few feet ahead of her, demonstrating how perfect he was at it before coming back. 'Try it.'

Was he seriously trying to teach her how to skate? She shook her head, but he laughed and held out his hand.

'Come on. You can't just stand there forever. You'll get knocked over again.'

She looked at the barrier, but it was four feet away. Swearing, she stuck her hand in his, ignoring the way his fingers curled around hers. Taking his advice, she pushed her feet out and tightened her grip on his hand.

He held her hand close to his chest. 'Don't worry, I've got you.'

Effie opened her mouth to retort, but instead she smiled. He'd been right – it was no wonder she'd fallen over before. She'd barely taken two glides, but already she felt centred and balanced, and as they approached Lou and Mickey, she couldn't help but grin as they cheered her on.

∽

'Now that I wasn't expecting,' Mickey said as they sat in a chain cafe around the corner an hour and a half later. 'Seems the Torvill and Dean award should go to you two.'

Smith took a gulp of his hot chocolate. 'Hardly. She left me way behind.'

Effie grinned. After five minutes skating hand in hand with Smith, she'd let go and glided around the rink on her own. She'd wanted to see if she'd really got to grips with it, and if she was being honest, she needed to get away from him. Holding his hand had felt better than it should have, so much so that she hadn't wanted to let go. From the moment he'd turned up at her wedding, she'd been abrasive towards him, but as they'd skated together, she found herself laughing at his jokes. It was all too familiar, and she didn't want any part in it. And, she didn't want Oliver to arrive and see them together. It turned out she needn't have worried, because he'd decided to stay out with his friends and head into the West End. She couldn't begrudge him a night out; he worked hard and rarely went out, but still. Somerset House was the perfect place for romance.

'I'm just glad it wasn't *me* on my arse. Some of those people were maniacs,' Lou said.

As more people piled into the cafe, the smell of cigarette smoke breezed in through the door, and Effie sighed with longing. 'God, I'd kill for a smoke right now.'

True to her word, she'd quit the day after the wedding, but the urge was overwhelming, and it wasn't helped when Lou chucked a packet across the table.

'I can't,' Effie said. 'I've quit.'

'Whatever,' Lou replied and rolled her eyes.

Oliver would be so disappointed in her, but after a few seconds of internal debate, Effie shook a cigarette from the box and grimaced. 'Not a word to Olly.'

Lou shrugged her shoulders and wrapped her hands around her mug. 'A word about what? I'll come for the next one. I'm still frozen to the bone.'

Effie shrugged her jacket on and ducked outside. As she leaned against the wall, she lit the cigarette and took a long, deep drag. She hadn't realised how much she'd missed it until then. She knew it was bad for her, and she'd promised Oliver, but sometimes it was nice to just take a few minutes of time out. The nicotine rushed to her head as she blew out her second plume of smoke, and when she blew the third, Smith joined her.

'You got a light?' He held up his cigarette and Effie threw the lighter, aiming for his head. His hand shot up as he caught it effortlessly with a grin. She threw him an unimpressed look. Why did he have to be so annoyingly good at everything?

'Did you have fun?' he asked as he lit the tip of his cigarette.

She shrugged. 'It was alright.'

'What?' He raised an eyebrow and blew his smoke out of the side of his mouth. 'Ice skating too lowbrow in your world now, is it?'

Effie shook her head. 'Don't be stupid.'

He leaned against the wall and looked down at her. 'So, lover boy Henry didn't show. What a shame.'

'Did you come out here just to piss me off?' She glowered at him, wishing he'd disappear as quickly as the smoke trailing off the end of her cigarette.

'You know, I've been trying to figure it out. I mean, nobody gets married that quickly after meeting someone.'

'Let me save you the trouble: I love him.'

'You said the same thing to me once. I'm not convinced you mean it this time round.'

'Whatever.' Effie flicked her cigarette into the road. 'You have no idea how arrogant you sound.'

'Oh, I dunno. I don't think you'd react to me like you do if you didn't still feel something for me. The way you yanked your elbow away from me earlier was like I'd just tried to kill you rather than help you.'

'And you think that's a sign that I've got feelings for you? Sounds like you're a bit deluded to me,' Effie replied.

'No. It was the way you were holding on to me while we were skating that did it.'

How did he do that? How did he always manage to seem like he knew what was going on in her head? She looked up at him, expecting to see the know-it-all smirk, but instead all she saw were his eyes searching hers. She sighed and leaned back against the wall.

'This conversation is irrelevant. We were never a real couple – you were pretty clear about that. And you left. You made your decision, and I made mine.'

'It wasn't like I had a choice.'

She pushed herself off the wall. 'That's exactly what I mean. You're always surrounded by drama. You left, and you know what? It was the best thing you could've done, because I'm happy. I've got everything I've ever wanted. Love, happiness – stability.'

'Stability? You're twenty-five, not forty-five. Is that why you got a ring on your finger? Did he promise you a house and two-point-five kids? Yearly holidays to the Bahamas?'

A house, kids and holidays. Yes, it was what she wanted. She wanted stability. She *needed* it, and Smith leaving had made her realise that he could never have been the one to give it to her. Like fate, she'd met Oliver a month later, and he'd offered to give her everything she'd ever wanted. At the time it had felt like pure romance, but now Smith was back, gazing at her with that look of his, the one that always made her feel like he was undressing her with his eyes, Oliver's romancing suddenly felt like the dullest thing in the world.

'I would have given you all that. You know I would. Screw the Bahamas, I'd have given you the world.'

'I'd like to know how, exactly, when you couldn't even bring yourself to call me your girlfriend?'

'Don't do that, Eff.' He shook his head. 'Don't make out that what we had didn't mean anything. I *know* you, and I know you don't belong in some rich boy's la-la land. I know he can't make you happy.'

'And why is that?' she replied with her hands on her hips.

'Because, Effie, he's not me.'

The way he said her name made her flinch. It had fallen from his mouth like molten gold, and she wished she hadn't noticed, just like she wished she could pretend her skin wasn't burning as he ran a thumb across her cheekbone and down to her lower lip. Why was she letting him do this? Her heart was beating so hard, it almost tripped itself up, but she jerked her head away. She was over him. She didn't want him. And she was married – he was stepping way over the line.

'Stop it, Smith. I mean it. You can't just come back and derail my life.'

'I'm not derailing anything; you've done that yourself. We might not have been conventional, but we worked, and you know it.'

'No, we didn't. You're right about one thing, though. Oliver isn't you and that's why we *work* better than you and I ever did.' She barged past him and stopped by the door, looking at him with as much bravado as she could muster. 'Stay away from me, Smith. I don't need your shit in my life anymore.'

5.

A few days later, Effie swore as she untangled the set of fairy lights at her feet. Last year, she'd put up her artificial tree and hung pound shop ornaments on it. This year, things were different and altogether classier. At least, she hoped it would be. She'd spent an hour in John Lewis, trying to decide which decorations to buy, staying as far away as possible from anything with even a hint of gaudiness about it.

After untangling the lights, she strung them up around the windows and looked outside, watching a plastic bag being pushed along the pavement by the wind. The sky was a depressing shade of grey, and their honeymoon in sunny Thailand felt like a million years ago. Oliver had worked late almost every night since, and she tried to shake the feeling of loneliness that had settled over her for the past few days.

She hung the silver and blue baubles on the eight-foot Norwegian spruce standing in the corner of the living room, before looking at the small, wooden nutcracker princes next to the white candles on top of the fireplace. Would Oliver like it? She'd gone for the most tasteful decorations she could find, knowing that he hated anything that could ever be described as remotely tacky. Effie looked around the living room again. She'd done her best, and that was all she could do, so when she heard his key in the lock earlier than usual, she pushed her doubts out of her mind and went to greet him at the door.

She threw her arms around his neck. 'What are you doing back so early?'

He grinned, his trademark cheeky grin that had beamed at her from across a packed-out bar and changed her life forever.

'I was let off early for good behaviour.'

She melted as his lips met hers.

'Now that,' she replied between kisses, 'I find hard to believe.'

He grinned. 'Court was adjourned early, so I thought I'd come back and keep my wife company.'

It was music to her ears, and Effie smiled before leading him into the living room. 'Dinner's already cooked and . . . it's beginning to look a lot like Christmas.'

'Well, aren't you the perfect little housewife?'

If it had come from anyone else, it would have sounded condescending, but she knew it was a compliment. Since their wedding, she'd tried her best to keep the house perfect and dinner ready for when he returned from a hard day at work. She *wanted* to be the perfect little housewife, and she hoped the decorations would do her efforts justice. She pulled at her little finger and held her breath as he shook off his long black overcoat.

'It looks great.'

A satisfied smile pulled at her mouth, and she silently sighed with relief. She'd been right to go with the blue and silver colour scheme. The white fairy lights gave a warm glow to the room, contrasting with the darkness outside, and the scent of cinnamon-scented candles on the windowsill wafted through the air. A bottle of wine with two sparkling glasses sat on the coffee table, and she'd draped the freshly washed woollen blanket over the impossibly large mocha-brown sofa.

'Not sure about the lights on the window, though,' he said, throwing his coat on the sofa. 'Looks a bit . . .' – he scrunched his nose up – 'tacky, don't you think?'

Effie looked at the window, and her body sagged. Tacky. It was the one word she'd been trying to avoid hearing him say. She thought it looked nice and homey, but she had noticed that only two other houses on the street had done the same.

'I wasn't really sure,' she said, 'but I think you're right. I'll take them down.'

'You can do it later.' He kissed the side of her head and pulled at his tie as he walked into the kitchen. 'What time's your mum coming tomorrow?'

'About seven,' Effie replied, following him.

'I'll make sure I'm back in time. I'm looking forward to it.'

She took two plates from the cupboard and laughed. 'Why can't you despise your mother-in-law like a normal husband?'

'Because, firstly, it'd be hard to despise someone I've never even met, and secondly, she can't be any worse than the mother-in-law you've been landed with courtesy of me.'

'But your mum's lovely.'

'Okay, she can't be any worse than your *step*mother-in-law then. Now, enough about your mother. What do you say to us eating this dinner, and then I'll run you a bubble bath?'

Effie grinned and lifted the lid from the saucepan. Just when she thought he couldn't get any more perfect.

❧

'Hello, Sweetpea,' Penny said, pulling Effie into a hug as soon as she opened the door.

Effie stiffly hugged her back. 'Hi, Mum. Did you find the house alright?'

'No problem at all.' Penny unwound the chunky scarf around her neck as she stepped inside, and Effie tried not to sigh when she took her coat off.

Of course it was silly to have expected her mum to make an effort for dinner, but she was wearing dark green Aladdin pants and a long-sleeved hemp sweater that looked like it had been picked up in a flea market somewhere. In fact, it probably had.

'Couldn't you have at least put a bra on?' Effie asked, screwing up her face.

'Why? You know I don't like them. Anyway, I had my nipple pierced, and I don't like the way it rubs.'

Effie's jaw fell open. Could her mum get any more embarrassing?

'Oh, Sweetpea. Close your mouth. You know your face will stay like that if the wind changes.'

Effie shook her head at Penny's girlish grin and looked up at the ceiling. This was the woman Oliver would walk through the door to be greeted by for the first time. God help him.

'Just don't go mentioning that to Olly. He'll be home soon.'

Penny shrugged. 'I don't know why you'd think I would. I wouldn't even have told you if you hadn't commented about my lack of a bra. I know how prudish you can get.'

'I'm not a prude. I just don't need to know about your intimate piercings.'

Couldn't her mum act like a normal forty-five-year-old?

'Oh, stop.' Penny tutted and linked her arm through Effie's as if it hadn't been years since they'd last seen each other and months since they'd spoken. 'Come on – I'm sure you're dying to show me around.'

Thankful to get away from the impossibly embarrassing thought of her mum's piercings, Effie showed her mum around the beautifully decorated three-storey house, proudly pointing everything out. She'd devoured decorating magazines for ideas and gone to great pains to make sure the coffee table was the right shade of oak to match the floors, and she'd spent two hours deliberating over which colour to paint the bathroom. It was duck-egg blue. Oliver had said it looked elegant and fresh, and she completely agreed with him. Everything had been thought through, right down to the last little detail.

'Do you really need this much space?' Penny asked as they stood in the kitchen.

'It's not that big.'

True, it was larger than average, and at a cost of over half a million pounds, it was more expensive than average, but Clapham wasn't a cheap place to live, and the whitewashed Georgian houses on their street were highly sought after. Oliver had only been able to afford the deposit himself thanks to the trust fund his parents had set up.

'Rented?'

Effie shook her head. 'I emailed you, remember? Olly bought it. We moved in a few weeks before the wedding.'

She searched her mum's face for any ounce of recognition. Despite their irregular relationship, Effie had sent her a long email, offloading her excitement at moving into the physical embodiment of her dream home, but clearly Penny couldn't remember reading it, if she'd read it at all. She'd probably been too engrossed in her downward-facing dog or saluting the sun, or whatever it was she did in the ashrams she visited.

'For how much?'

'Four hundred,' Effie replied, picking up the knife from the side to make a start on the salad.

'*Thousand*?' Penny's voice rose an octave. 'Euphemia Willow Abbott, that's ridiculous. Vulgar, even.'

'It's London.' Effie shrugged, ignoring the way her mum used her full name to get her point across. 'And I'm not an Abbott anymore, remember?'

She was glad she'd shaved a hundred grand off the real figure. Otherwise, her mum's voice would've shattered the windows. Half a million pounds was a lot of money, but the house was worth every penny.

Their clean, quiet street was surrounded by delicatessens and Parisian-style coffee shops serving delicate patisseries. When her mum had left, Effie had stayed in hostels until getting her own council flat in Kennington, and though it wasn't far away, it might as well have been another world. Communal metal bins and gangs of kids with hoodies and dogs had been replaced by recycling boxes and kids on skateboards, wearing skinny jeans. For as long as she could remember, she'd wanted a house of her own, and now she had it. It wasn't a caravan with random waifs and strays camping outside, and it wasn't a shared house with backpackers and hippies.

'I love this house,' she said, more to herself than her mum.

'I never would have thought you'd want something so conventional.'

Effie gripped the knife in her hand as she cut up the lettuce. *Conventional* wasn't even worthy of a dignified definition in her mum's world, and Effie had been brought up without a shred of it. Sure, there were times when it had been great. There'd be parties and late-night music sessions, and none of her school friends came back from the summer holidays with stories of listening to a live folk band playing under the stars in Tuscany, or cooking a fish they'd caught that day over an open fire in Greece, like she did. But then again, they didn't come back with stories of having their phone stolen by a shifty traveller or waking up to see a different man emerging from their mum's bedroom on a frighteningly regular basis either.

Penny ran her finger across the worktop. 'I suppose it's pretty in its own way, but it's not really yours, is it?'

Effie frowned. 'Of course it is. I live here.'

'You might *live* here, but it's not *yours*.'

True, it was Oliver's name on the mortgage and not hers, but she was the one who had made it a home. If it had been left up to him, there would be barely any furniture, no pictures on the walls and only the absolute basics in the fridge.

'Are you paying for the mortgage too?'

'Of course,' Effie replied.

'Can you even afford it? Being a receptionist doesn't pay enough to live in a house like this. Or at least it didn't in my day.'

'Well, that was, like, a hundred years ago.' Effie flicked her eyes up to the ceiling. What was it about her mum that made her revert to a petulant teenager? 'And I'm not a receptionist.'

'Admin, receptionist – same, same.' Penny waved her hand. 'What did you say Oliver does again?'

'He's a barrister – high profile too. He earns well. We can manage.'

'I don't doubt that you can. You've always been resourceful.'

'That's because I've had to be.'

Penny looked away and flicked through the copy of *Grazia* that Effie had left out, with her lips pursed. Effie tutted. She was the one who'd been left on her own. Her mum had no right to sulk, but somehow she'd made Effie feel like the bad one.

'What's for dinner?'

'Beef.'

Penny wrinkled her nose, and Effie put the knife down.

'What's wrong with beef? Have you gone veggie?'

'No, but I don't think my stomach is quite up to it. Did you know that cows are considered holy in India?'

'Yes, I do, but newsflash: you're not there anymore.'

'Try telling my stomach that,' Penny replied and looked around at the kitchen.

Effie grabbed a perfectly ripened tomato and sliced it in half on the wooden chopping board. She'd already been told about her mum's pierced nipple – she definitely didn't need to hear about her Delhi belly too, especially not when preparing dinner.

'So,' she said, slicing the tomato halves into quarters, 'tell me about India.'

※

With her chin in the palm of her hand, Effie looked at her mum. She wanted to be objective, but all she could see was a wafer-thin, bra-less hippy with green feathers braided into her wiry, greying hair. Why couldn't her mum just be normal? Still, Oliver was charm personified and didn't seem to mind, or even notice, her mum's wacky appearance at all.

'It was a great day, wasn't it?' Oliver grinned, squeezing Effie's hand as Penny flicked through the wedding photos on his iPad.

'Yeah.' Effie smiled. 'It was.' Or at least it had been until Smith had shown up.

'It's a shame you missed it,' he continued, topping up Penny's glass with a full-bodied Rioja.

'You didn't leave much time. Only my daughter could marry someone she's only known for two minutes.'

It wasn't two minutes; it was a month, but Effie refused to argue back.

'Besides, I was in the middle of my course, and it was monsoon season. It makes it almost impossible to leave.'

'Most people go away to get some sun. I don't understand how you can like being stuck in the heat and rain all day.' Effie wrinkled her nose.

'It's a very enlightening experience being able to dedicate time to meditating and cleansing. It sets me up for the cold winter months.'

'If you can call the Spanish sun cold,' Effie replied. When was the last time her mum had been in England for Christmas? Ten years ago, just before she'd left for good, probably.

'You should try it sometime. Nobody is forcing you to stay in this depressing place.'

Effie sighed. What else was she supposed to do? Run around naked in communes, like her mum? No, thank you.

'It's amazing you managed to get everything organised so quickly. It all looks very grand,' Penny said, looking back at the iPad and swiping her finger across the screen. 'Are these your parents?'

Oliver leaned over and nodded, pointing his finger. 'My dad, Giles, and my mum, Celeste. That's Isobel, or Izzy, my older sister.'

'Very nice.'

The tone of her voice suggested otherwise, and Effie knew what she was thinking. The Barton-Coles represented everything her mum hated: wealth and power. She looked down at the photo of herself and Oliver sandwiched between his parents, with Izzy on the end. Everyone was smiling, but the atmosphere between his parents had been as frosty as the air around them, and Oliver had refused to have his stepbrother and sister in the photo.

'And what do they do?' Penny asked.

'Mummy and Daddy are both retired now. She used to be an editor for a lifestyle magazine and he was a top Queen's Counsel. Being a barrister is kind of a tradition in our family; my grandfather was one too. Izzy owns an ethical beauty company.'

'Well, isn't that lovely.'

Effie scowled at her mum's rudeness. Oliver had been nothing but unwaveringly polite and even interested when she'd talked for an hour about yoga and the meaning of chakras, but she couldn't seem to return the favour.

Oliver's eyes flicked down to Effie's plate. She'd eaten everything except the beef.

'Are you not hungry?' he asked, tipping his head to one side.

'It was a little too rare for me.'

Effie had stuck to the cooking time in the recipe rigidly and thought it would come out medium to well done at the edges at least, but when she'd carved into it, it was still too pink for her tastes. It was a fine balance cooking for Oliver, who liked it almost blue, and herself. At least her mum was the type to eat whatever was put in front of her without complaining.

'It loses all the flavour if it's cooked too much,' Oliver replied.

Effie looked at his plate, wiped clean. She was the type to cremate her meat, but he ate out at top-end restaurants all the time, and his palate was a thousand times better than hers. She picked up a tiny piece of beef and ate it, holding back the gag at the thought of eating near raw flesh. He smiled a little and stood up from the table.

'Here, I'll make you a sandwich or something.'

Penny's forehead creased as she pulled her eyebrows together, frowning at him as he walked towards the sink. She was a firm feminist and probably thought Effie was a pampered lady of luxury, simply because Oliver had offered to make her a sandwich.

'I should get going. I didn't realise it was so late, and I need to be at the airport early in the morning.'

'You only just got here,' Effie replied. She'd only been back for two days, and already she was jetting off again.

'You know I don't like it here. I just wanted to see you and make sure you were okay. And meet Oliver, of course.'

Her mum wanted to make sure she was okay? That was a first, and probably a last.

After waving goodbye to Oliver, Penny zipped up her coat as they stood by the front door. 'Are you sure you're happy, Sweetpea?'

'Of course I am,' Effie replied. Happiness was calling her in the form of chilling on the sofa with Oliver and a DVD.

'You're just so different now. Do you really want to spend the rest of your life with him?'

Effie held down a sigh. Couldn't she give the psychoanalysing a rest, just for one evening? 'Obviously. He's my husband.'

Penny leaned in close. 'I'm sorry to say this, Sweetpea, but he just seems so . . . superficial. All that posturing about his work.' She pulled a face. 'I'm sorry, but I don't trust him.'

Effie pulled the front door closed and stepped outside. 'You don't even know him, and it's a bit rich, coming from you. You're hardly in a position to give me relationship advice.'

Throughout Effie's childhood, Penny had flitted from man to man in a haze of drugs and free love, so free that even her own dad had disappeared before she was born. She couldn't remember a man ever being around for more than six months.

'And okay,' Effie continued, 'he boasts a bit, but he's worked hard to get to where he is. He's allowed to be proud.'

'Pride isn't a positive quality, Effie. You shouldn't simply assume that just because he has a good job and is well brought up that he's perfect. I just want you to be careful, that's all.'

'Thanks for your concern,' Effie replied with a sarcasm-laden voice, 'but I think I can manage.'

Penny's eyes scanned her face before she sighed. 'I know we haven't always seen eye to eye, but—'

'But what?' Effie folded her arms.

'Nothing.' Penny sighed. 'But you know where I am if you need me, for anything at all. At any time.'

Actually, I don't.

It was always the same. Her mum was always just out of reach.

Penny pulled her in for a hug and kissed her cheek. 'I do love you, Sweetpea.'

She squeezed Effie's shoulders before disappearing down the street, leaving a trail of sandalwood scent in her wake. After months of hardly any communication at all, Penny had floated back into her life with her namby-pamby hippy talk and left with a sting in her tail. Effie shook her head. If that was her way of expressing love, she'd rather not have it at all. She walked back into the house, slamming the door behind her.

'What did the door ever do to you?' Oliver asked, leaning against the hallway wall with a tea towel in his hands.

'She makes me so mad sometimes.'

He pulled her into a hug. 'I thought she was nice.'

'Everyone does.'

Effie buried her head into his chest, wrapping her arms around his waist. Everyone loved Penny. She was the cool mum who used to let her have parties all the time and gave everyone advice. After meeting at school, Lou, Smith and Mickey were permanent fixtures in her house, and whenever any of them had problems, Penny would be there with a cup of tea and an ear to listen. And it extended past Effie's friends. She'd often come home to find people she recognised from school, sitting around the table, chatting away with Penny as if she were a counsellor. Penny seemed to have an infinite supply of love and compassion, and she treated Effie's friends and fellow students as if they were all her friends, and not kids. Effie was the envy of them all, but all she wanted was to be loved as a daughter instead of a friend.

'I guess none of our parents are perfect,' Oliver said.

'At least yours showed up to the wedding,' Effie muttered. As much as she was pleased to have been spared the embarrassment of her mum mixing with the Barton-Coles, her lack of presence had still stung.

'Baby, nobody noticed.'

'Of course they did, and it didn't help having to walk down the aisle with Mickey.'

Oliver squeezed her tighter. 'Not everyone has a dad to do that.'

No, but at least most people know who their dad is.

Thanks to Penny's inability to settle with one person, Effie'd had to be given away by her best friend. The day that Penny would tell her about her dad had never arrived, despite the constant promises to do so when she was old enough to understand. Effie sighed. She understood, alright. She understood that her mum probably couldn't even remember who he was.

Oliver kissed the top of her head and held her close. It didn't matter now anyway. She had him. She didn't need, or want, anyone else.

6.

Effie sighed and put the phone down. She'd only been in the office for a little over an hour, but already she could tell that today would be a battle she wouldn't win.

'Everything okay?' Doug asked, perching on the end of her desk.

'I'm just having a nightmare, trying to get through to the photographer for that album cover,' Effie replied, leaning back in her swivel chair and looking back at her boss. 'Don't worry, though; it's nothing I can't handle.'

'Good. So, James starts today. We'll do an introduction at the team meeting, and if you could do a familiarisation with him afterwards, that'd be great.'

'No problem. Where is he?' She looked down at her watch. It was already 10.15, and this James was hardly making a good impression being late on his first day.

'He's over at the studio with Sketch.'

Effie raised an eyebrow. Sketch was Archive's newest signing, an indie trio from Brighton, and Doug had high hopes for them. It looked like the new boy was hitting the ground running.

'He should be back around two,' Doug said, standing up.

'Sure. I'll take care of it.'

She watched as he went back to his desk. Had he seriously sent this James out already? He hadn't even met the rest of the team yet, or had a proper induction. Doug picked up the phone and ran a hand through his grey hair. Archive was his baby. He'd started it in his bedroom years ago and involved himself with every step of every process. He knew what he was doing, but even so, Effie couldn't help the uneasy feeling in the pit of her stomach.

❦

At two thirty, she sat around the glass table with the rest of the team. Two minutes later, the door to the meeting room opened.

'See?' Nikki nudged her. 'I told you. Fit or what?'

Effie's breath caught in her throat, and her eyes widened as she looked at the man walking through the door.

Oh, you have got *to be joking.*

'Everyone, this is James,' Doug said. 'He'll be helping us out with Artists and Repertoire for a while.'

Smith, or was it *James*, shook hands with everyone around the table, leaving her until last. Effie scowled as he gripped her hand and squeezed it with a brief, satisfied smile on his face before sitting in a chair at the end of the table. What the hell was he doing? Why was he sitting in their meeting room, filling the space with his . . . with his . . . ?

Ugh.

She chewed the end of her pen and turned to Doug, listening as intently as she could, which was no easy feat.

Because, Effie, he's not me.

Her skin burned. Was he looking at her? Because it felt like it. It felt like he was scanning every inch of her body from across the table, but she refused to look at him. She pulled her eyebrows together, trying to focus on what Doug was saying, but it was as if someone had pressed the mute button on a remote control. All she was aware of was *him*. After five minutes, she gave in, sneaking a glance at him. He was focusing on Doug as if she weren't even in the room. Irrationally, it only made her even angrier.

'Effie, did you get that?'

She looked up at Doug. Crap. What had he been talking about?

'Can you set up a meeting with Kingsley for this week to look at the new website?'

Effie nodded, scribbling in her notepad, trying to stop her cheeks from burning. Bloody Smith had only been here five minutes, and already he was distracting her. He wasn't happy just ruining her wedding; he now wanted to move in on her job too.

'And can you make sure James gets his familiarisation today as well, please.'

'Yep, sure.'

After I've wrung his bloody neck.

When everyone filed out of the room twenty minutes later, she hung back, glaring at Smith to do the same. Behind his back, Nikki mock-swooned and closed the door behind her, leaving the two of them alone. Suddenly, the room felt a whole lot smaller.

He looked at her with his know-it-all grin. 'Fancy seeing you here.'

The anger inside her spilled out as she slammed her hands on the table and leaned forward in her chair. 'Are you insane? What the hell is this?'

He calmly looked around at the posters and discs on the walls. 'I believe this is called work.'

Effie screwed her eyes shut and gripped her pen, taking a deep breath before opening her eyes again. 'You know what I mean. Why are you *here*?'

'Like I said, I'm here to work.'

'You don't even know anything about A&R.'

'Really?' He folded his arms and leaned back in his chair. 'Doug thinks differently; otherwise, he wouldn't have asked me to help out.'

'What do you mean, he asked you?'

He put his hands behind his head, and Effie's eyes flicked down to the tiny strip of tanned skin peeking out from under the hem of his T-shirt. She quickly looked away.

'He knows I know my stuff. Sean told him I was back, and he called me.'

'But that's not possible.' Effie shook her head.

'And yet, here we are.'

His eyes twinkled at her from across the table. He was obviously finding all this thoroughly entertaining. She pressed her fingers against the edge of the table, battling with the idea of scrambling over it and lunging at him. He made her so unbelievably angry that she didn't trust herself not to gouge his eyes out of his head.

'Oh, wait a minute,' Smith said, slowly leaning forward and resting his arms on the table. 'You thought I was here because of you, didn't you? Do you know how arrogant that sounds?'

Oh, he was good. He was throwing her words from Somerset House right back at her.

She snorted. 'Do me a favour. I don't go around thinking the world revolves around me, unlike some people.'

Effie looked away, not wanting Smith to see her face because the truth was, for a fleeting moment, she had thought he *was* there for her, and even with the shock of seeing him walk into the meeting room, she couldn't deny the way butterflies had flitted around her stomach.

'Then why is it written all over your face?'

'It isn't,' she replied, crossing her arms.

'I mean, I wouldn't want you to get the wrong idea since you were pretty clear the last time we spoke. What was it you said again?' He looked up at the ceiling, frowned and looked back at her. 'Oh, yeah. You didn't need my shit in your life anymore — that was it.'

He leaned back in his chair again, his long, jeans-clad legs spread out wide.

'And yet, here we are,' Effie replied, mimicking his words as she threw him a look of disgust. 'Does Doug actually know who you are? Does he know that *James* used to make a living shifting pills around in clubs?'

'Man, I've missed the mouth you have on you.' Smith laughed, sending tingling vibrations straight to the pit of her belly, but she willed the feeling away. 'But let's not get carried away. I was never a dealer and you know it. Doug knows everything about me; he's one of Sean's best mates, remember? Don't forget who got you this job.'

She wanted to retort, but she couldn't. Instead, she slumped back in her chair and sighed. Doug was an old-time friend of Smith's older brother, Sean, and it was thanks to her friendship with Smith that she'd ended up at Archive in the first place. Doug must've assumed she knew it was Smith when he'd referred to him as James.

'You can run along and tell tales if you want, but it won't make a blind bit of difference. Or we could try to be civil. I mean, we're going to have to see each other every day now.'

That wasn't a good thing, so why was the swirling in her stomach bordering on being pleasurable?

'Fine,' she said, standing up. 'We can be civil, but that's it. I meant what I said at Somerset House.'

'I know.' He stood up and stuffed his hands into his pockets as he looked at her. 'Like I said, message received loud and clear.'

His voice sounded monotone and matter-of-fact, but instead of feeling relieved at his apparent acceptance, Effie felt a flash of disappointment. She looked back at him and told herself to get a grip. This was exactly what she'd wanted from the moment he'd got back, and he was finally playing along.

She nodded. 'Good.'

'Good.' He nodded back.

She stalked past him, swinging the door open and not even caring that it nearly hit him in the face. Bloody Smith.

∽

After her disastrous day at work, she took herself off to get her Christmas shopping done. It was a bad idea. Thanks to Smith, she was in a foul mood. He'd shocked her out of her skin, showing up in the office like that.

'So, I heard you've got a new colleague. Mickey just told me,' Lou said.

Effie held the phone in her hand as she toyed with the price tag on the Ted Baker jumper. Oliver would look amazing in it, which wouldn't be difficult. He looked amazing in pretty much everything.

'Apparently, Doug asked him in to help out with A&R. He's like a bad smell that won't go away.'

'It's hardly surprising, though. He did used to be a DJ, and he's massively into music. He knows a heap of people.'

Effie rolled her eyes. 'Well, yes, of course he does. He spent every weekend getting high with them, remember?'

'So, I guess now's a good time to tell you he's coming to Ireland.'

A frustrated sigh left Effie's mouth, and she dropped the price tag on the sweater. 'You have got to be having a laugh.'

'Well, it would've been hard to leave him out, not to mention unfair,' Lou pointed out. 'What difference does it make anyway? You'll be with Olly, and you've told Smith to stay away. It's not like he's going to pounce on you.'

Effie moved out of the way as someone else picked up one of the sweaters and took it straight to the till. It did make a difference. It made all the difference in the world.

'I've got to go and get dinner on,' Lou said. 'Good luck with your shopping. We'll catch up soon.'

Lou blew a kiss down the phone and hung up, and Effie left the shop feeling deflated. So far, she hadn't seen anything she even remotely liked that came within her measly budget. Oliver had offered to set her up with an allowance, but she'd turned it down. Having an allowance from your husband seemed to be like travelling back sixty years, and she didn't like the idea of him effectively paying for his own Christmas present. She had her own income, as meagre as it felt.

She meandered through the crowds of shoppers, scrolling through her phone to check her bank balance, just in case some money had magically appeared. It hadn't. Sliding into an empty chair in the rest area, she sighed. The mere fact that a shopping centre had to have rest areas depressed her. She'd never needed a rest from shopping in her life. Everyone else seemed to have a minimum of five bags each, and she could only begin to imagine the cumulative cost of them all. She'd wanted this year to be different. She'd wanted to shower Oliver with gifts.

How would Smith be spending Christmas?

She scowled at the unwelcome way Smith had popped into her head. It was bad enough, him turning up unannounced at her wedding and Somerset House, but at work? It was such a small team, she wouldn't be able to avoid him, and even though he'd apparently accepted that she wanted him to stay away, it wasn't him she was worried about. It was herself. Smith had been perfectly professional after they'd left the meeting room, following her around as she familiarised him with the building, policies and processes, all while she'd tried not to re-familiarise herself with his smell, the way he ran his fingers through his hair, or the way the skin around his eyes crinkled when he smiled.

She'd been getting on with her life until he'd come back, and now it felt like it was spiralling out of control. As far as she was concerned, her anger at him was wholly justified. What she didn't understand was why the idea of him being in Ireland made her skin ripple in a way that was disturbingly on the border of being pleasurable.

From the day she'd met Oliver, she'd never looked back. He'd showered her with flowers and gifts and taken her on thoughtful dates. And when he'd knelt on the scuffed lino floor of her kitchen, offering her a ring a month later, she hadn't hesitated in saying yes. So why was she looking back now?

She shook her head again. She wasn't looking back – that was wrong. She was being pulled back, and she didn't want to be. She had a good life with Oliver, and everything had been moving along quite nicely until Smith had shown up with that bloody face of his.

The lead-up to Christmas was turning out to be much more fraught than she wanted it to be. Her mum's parting words hadn't helped either, and, as predicted, she hadn't heard a peep from her since. It was probably for the best anyway. Her mum and Smith were too negative, and she didn't want that around her – not now that she had Oliver. He was everything her mum and Smith weren't. He considered her all the time, picking her up and dropping her off and cooking her dinner whenever he got home from work early enough. Even his offer of an allowance seemed to come from a good place, however uncomfortable it made her feel. Being with him made her feel secure and calm. It made her feel like an adult, whereas being around her mum and Smith made her regress to a sulky teenager who knew nothing about the world or what relationships meant. With Oliver, she was learning all the time, and regardless of what Penny and Smith thought, she was one hundred per cent sure she'd made the right decision to marry him.

'One hundred and *ten* per cent,' Effie said aloud.

The woman sitting next to her turned and looked at her. 'I'm sorry?'

Effie blushed. 'Oh, nothing. Just thinking out loud.'

The woman smiled tightly and turned herself away a fraction, moving the Gucci and Karen Millen bags sat next to her legs with her. Effie twisted the platinum wedding ring on her finger. Oliver was her husband. He didn't deserve to be doubted by the mother-in-law who barely even knew him, and he didn't deserve to have his wife thinking about someone else, especially when that someone was Smith. She stood up and walked quickly back to Ted Baker.

7.

'Thanks, baby, I love it.' Oliver smiled and kissed her on the mouth. She'd been right to go back to Ted Baker after all. 'Happy Christmas.'

Effie smiled as she took the small box from him and unwrapped it. The smile gave way to a grin when she saw the duck-egg blue Tiffany box. The man had taste.

She picked up the sterling silver bracelet. It would look perfect with her platinum drop earrings, the ones Oliver had bought her when she agreed to move in with him.

'It's beautiful.'

'Here, let's put it on.' He went to undo the clasp of her charm bracelet and Effie frowned.

'I don't need to take that one off.' She held her other wrist out towards him. 'Put it on this one.'

'Baby,' Oliver said with a lopsided smile. 'No offence, but you can't wear a Tiffany bracelet on one hand and that thing on the other.'

'What's wrong with it?' She frowned again, looking at the charm bracelet. Okay, so it wasn't expensive, but she'd had it for years.

'It's tacky. And the jangling noise it always makes is a little annoying.'

Effie touched the tiny butterfly charm Smith had bought for her the Christmas before. It sat nicely with the heart from Lou, the feather from her mum and the angel from Mickey. She'd never taken it off before, but when she looked at Oliver, holding the shiny Tiffany bracelet, she could see how it would look mismatched to wear them both.

'This,' Oliver said, taking her wrist and working the clasp of her charm bracelet, 'will look so much better.'

Effie didn't say anything as she watched the charm bracelet fall from her wrist and onto the floor. It was only a bracelet, and it wasn't like she was throwing it away. It was simply making way for something else. Besides, she was a married twenty-five-year-old, not a teenager. She was finally growing up into the life she'd always wanted. What was the point in hanging on to things from the past? Oliver fastened the new one around her wrist, and she picked up her charm bracelet off the floor and put it on the coffee table. She'd put it away somewhere safe later.

'Thanks,' she said, remembering to smile. It really *was* beautiful, and while it didn't have the sentimental value of her old one, it held the promise of so much more.

'You're welcome. You know I only want the very best for you, baby.'

He kissed her lips again before giving her a glass of champagne. The bracelet felt heavy on her wrist, surely a sign of its worth and hopefully a sign that the thunderous mood Oliver had been in for the last few days was finally gone. He'd got a new client who was up for fraud to the tune of hundreds of thousands of pounds, and she'd been worried that his short, snappy temper would carry on through the Christmas break, but he'd practically bounced out of bed that morning to shower her with gifts: perfume, jewellery, an e-book reader and a new pair of Uggs to replace her old ones. Add that to the presents from his family, and she'd been totally overwhelmed.

'Who's this one from?' Oliver asked, stretching behind the tree to pick up the last of the presents. 'There's no label on it. Must be yours.'

He didn't need to say why; it was obvious. The newspaper it had been wrapped in was written in Hindi. It was obviously from her mum. She must've hidden it there before she'd left.

Effie frowned, but after opening the parcel, her throat choked. Inside the box was a long gold necklace with five peacock feathers hanging from the end. She'd seen one like it once when her mum had taken her to France for the summer holidays and had pointed it out. She'd remembered all these years later.

'Who's it from?' Oliver asked.

'Mum.'

'Bit OTT, isn't it? Sweet of her, though.'

Effie shrugged and put it back in the box. It was lovely, but really, when would she ever be able to wear it? Halloween, maybe.

'I'll call her later and say thanks,' she said and sipped her champagne. 'Have you called your mum yet?'

'I'll do it later on,' he said and leaned over, his mouth inches away from hers. 'For now, I want to get my last present.'

Effie looked under the tree. It was empty, but when she saw the twinkle in his eye, she grinned. She loved Christmas.

༄

'I'll just call Izzy,' Oliver said, hitting 'Pause' on the remote. 'She'll go mad if I don't.'

Effie nodded and uncorked yet more wine, as if they hadn't had enough already. She hadn't anticipated that they'd spend Christmas day alone, but Izzy had taken her husband, Tom, to spend the day with their dad, and when Effie had suggested that they do the same, Oliver wasn't having any of it. Still, it had worked out nicely. They'd had a quiet but romantic morning, and being at home meant they could settle down and watch *It's A Wonderful Life*. Clichéd maybe, but it was something Effie had always wanted to do, and Oliver seemed happy to indulge her.

She looked over at him as he leaned against the kitchen island while he spoke with his sister on the phone. He looked back and shook his head, holding his hand up and tapping his thumb against his fingers. She didn't need him to point out that Izzy was nattering away; Effie could hear it from the other end of the room. He really needed to turn the volume down on his phone.

'It's lovely, Izzy. Thank you,' he said, looking down at the TAG Heuer watch on his wrist. 'Yep, I spoke to her earlier. At least she's got Stepdad to spend the day with.'

Effie poured the wine and thought about her own mum. She always used to celebrate Christmas, but Effie wasn't so sure now. Did hippies celebrate it, or had she moved on to wor-shipping trees?

'Yes, we got them.' Oliver sighed and rubbed his forehead. 'No . . . he can't just buy his way out of things . . . No, I don't want to speak to him.'

Effie grimaced and took a sip of her wine. There were no prizes for guessing who he was talking about, but it was Christmas. What-ever happened to goodwill to all men? She might not get on with her mum, but at least she'd called to thank her for the present. Okay, so she hadn't been able to get through, but at least she'd tried.

'Izzy wants you,' Oliver said, handing her the phone before flopping next to her on the sofa.

'Happy Christmas,' Effie said, smiling into the phone as Oliver draped her legs over his.

'Happy Christmas, sweetie.' Izzy's slurred voice came through on the other end. Effie frowned as Oliver took the glass from her hand and downed it in one go.

He looked at her and mouthed, 'She's pissed as a fart.' Effie stifled a giggle. He wasn't wrong.

'I adore Christmas, don't you? I've had a litre of champagne and eaten enough to feed an army,' Izzy continued, and Effie laughed. She'd yet to see Izzy eat more than three mouthfuls of food. 'How's yours been?'

'Lovely. We're just about to watch a film. Thanks for the scarf, by the way – it's beautiful.'

'Don't mention it. Oh, I do wish you two were here. The twins are nice, but I feel positively ancient.'

Effie could imagine that thirty-three-year-old Izzy probably wouldn't have much in common with a pair of nineteen-year-olds, whether they were family or not.

'Are you coming to our New Year's party?' Izzy asked. 'Please say yes. It's going to be extra special.'

Effie looked over at Oliver, and he nodded back. 'Of course – we wouldn't miss it for the world.'

'And please try to drag my little brother out of that bad mood he's in. Honestly, it's intolerable.' Izzy sighed with a heap of drama.

'I hadn't noticed,' Effie lied, all too aware that he could hear everything Izzy said down the phone.

'If only he'd try and make a bit more effort with Daddy, I'm sure he wouldn't feel half as angry. It wouldn't kill him to spend a day up here; it's only once a year after all.'

Effie pressed the phone against her ear to protect Oliver from his sister's words, but it was pointless. He had an almighty scowl on his face.

'Anyway, sweetie, must dash. I'll see you at the party.'

'Never could handle her alcohol,' Oliver said after Effie hung up and propped her feet up on his legs. 'She turns into one of those "let's put the world to rights" types after she's had a few. It's intensely annoying.'

He picked up the remote and pressed 'Play', signalling the end of the discussion, and they settled down to watch the film, but the images on the screen barely registered in Effie's mind. His parents had divorced years ago, and while it must have been horrific to find out that their dad had not only cheated on their mum but had also fathered the twins, surely the grudge couldn't go on forever. Effie's mum had upped and left with barely a backward glance, and although it burned her inside, they still maintained some kind of relationship, however messed up it was. Couldn't Oliver do the same, just like Izzy did? He was so self-assured, grown up and forgiving in seemingly every other part of his life, why couldn't he be the same with his dad? Oliver sighed and sipped his wine. Apparently, he wasn't focusing on the film either.

'Are you okay?' Effie asked.

'Fine.'

He sighed again, and she looked at him as he absent-mindedly rubbed one of her feet.

'Have you ever spoken to your dad about what he did?'

'Why would I do that?' he replied without looking at her.

'Because it clearly affects you. It happened such a long time ago, I just wondered if maybe it's time to try and put what happened behind you.'

He looked at her and scowled. 'What do you mean?'

'It clearly makes you miserable. I know I'm not one to talk given my relationship with Mum, but it's Christmas.'

Oliver sighed and looked back at the television. 'You have no idea what you're talking about.'

Effie bit down on her lip. 'But—'

Just as James Stewart's car ploughed into a tree on the screen, Oliver pressed 'Pause' and looked at her.

'Effie?'

She turned to face him, and a flicker of apprehension passed across her face at his monotone voice.

'Please, drop it. It's Christmas and we've had a great day. Don't ruin it. Okay?'

Effie slowly nodded, and he squeezed a hand around her foot. She didn't want to ruin Christmas, not when he'd gone so out of his way to make it perfect. It would be like their honeymoon all over again, and she wanted to play her part in making it perfect. Maybe she was being childish, expecting him to be able to open up about his dad. After all, she was pretty closed off herself when it came to her relationship with her mum sometimes.

'Shall we carry on watching the film?' he asked. 'No more talk about messed-up families.'

'Sure.' Effie smiled and he returned it before turning back to the television and pressing 'Play'.

'Come here.' Oliver stretched his arm out, inviting her to curl up next to him, and she folded herself into him. Being like this was exactly what she'd been looking forward to all day.

'I'm sorry if I sounded short,' he said and dropped a kiss onto the top of her head. 'It's just annoying when Izzy starts banging on about making up with Dad. I really don't want you to start doing the same.'

'I won't. I get what it's like to have a parent who screws things up for you.'

'Good. I don't want their crap to start spoiling what we have.'

He kissed her again, and she snuggled deeper into him. She couldn't have said it better herself.

8.

'You look stunning,' Oliver said, standing behind Effie with his arms wrapped around her waist. 'I say we stay here instead.'

'Stop it.' She laughed and wriggled out of his arms as she put her earring in.

He ran a hand through his hair before straightening his tie. 'You can hardly blame me. You look good enough to eat. In fact, I may well do that later.'

Effie smiled and checked her reflection. She was dressed to the nines for Izzy's New Year's Eve party. Oliver had insisted they buy new outfits and treated her to a day out on King's Road. They'd wandered in and out of shops, and she'd been overwhelmed by the expense of it all. She'd actually seen a pair of socks for seventy pounds. *Socks.* It was mental. She loved beautiful clothes as much as the next girl, but she'd never dream of dropping seventy quid on a pair of socks. She'd eventually settled on a black Biba shift dress. She'd wanted the one with the embellished collar, but Oliver had told her it might look too over the top.

'If you're going to insist we go, we need to go now – otherwise, we'll be late,' Oliver said, and she gave herself a quick squirt of Christian Dior.

'I'm ready.'

He hooked an arm around her waist and dropped a kiss onto her shoulder. 'Have I told you how much I love you lately?'

She smiled. He had. Over and over again. And she could never get tired of hearing it.

∾

A couple of hours later, Effie and Oliver sat in their new BMW, crawling down the private country lane to Izzy and Tom's house. Or was it a mansion? Nestled in the Surrey countryside, their detached, five-bedroom house sat in ten acres of ancient woodland. The smell of damp leaves wafted through the open window of the car, mixing with the comforting smell of new leather. Oliver had pushed the new BMW's engine as hard as he could legally get away with, and sometimes more. Effie had settled back into the heated seats and had to mentally congratulate him on his need for impeccability. The car suited him. It was sophisticated, understated, sleek and expensive.

As they passed the trees strung up with lanterns and the elegant copper torches lining both sides of the lane, she glanced over at Oliver. He looked handsome in a crisp white shirt and blue chinos, and a rush of love hit her.

'What?' he asked warily, looking back at her. 'Are you okay?'

She nodded and beamed a smile. 'Yep. Better than okay.'

Things were perfect. She was sitting in a fabulous car, next to her handsome husband, on their way to a glamorous party. This was living. This was her life. She thought back to life with Smith, so full of uncertainty and doubt, never quite knowing where she stood. When he said that their 'relationship' had worked, he'd been so wrong it was laughable, and Effie couldn't do anything other *than* laugh at the way she'd reacted to seeing him again. Thank god, her mind was stronger than her body. Now that she had Oliver, she never needed to have an uncertain day again. He loved her, plain and simple.

Effie looked at the house coming into view around the gentle curve of the lane, until Oliver killed the purring engine and parked up among the Mercedes, Audis and a couple of Aston Martins. They stepped out of the car, and Effie looked up at Sky House, the three-storey, forty-eight-hundred-square-foot property that Izzy and Tom called home. On the ground level, the floor-to-ceiling glass doors were folded all the way open, allowing the chilled house music, tinkles of laughter and buzz of conversation to float outside. Its sleek lines, timber exterior walls and two floors of wrap-around windows were wedged into a slope, and it sat under a canopy of oak and birch trees. The lights from the house spilled out, dappling the woodland floor in an orange glow.

'I don't think I'll ever get used to seeing this place. It's beautiful,' Effie said.

'I know. I'd have loved to design something like this.'

She looked at him. 'You still regret not being an architect, don't you?'

'Sometimes.' He shrugged. 'But law is the family business. Sometimes, life means making compromises.' He took her hand, and they ascended the huge slabs of slate serving as stairs. Effie could only nod. She didn't feel like she'd had to compromise anything being with him.

'Anyway,' he continued, 'it's nice, but there's no point having a place like this in the city. A house like this needs to breathe.'

'Do houses breathe?'

'This one does.' He grinned, and as if to prove his point, a gust of wind blew behind them, almost ushering them into the house.

How many people had turned up? A hundred, maybe? On the ground floor alone, the entire open space was packed with people lounging on oversized, charcoal-grey sofas, sitting on the stairs or talking in groups. An impeccably dressed waiter offered champagne from a silver tray, and Effie took one, grateful for something to hold. She never knew what to do with her hands in situations like this and usually reverted to picking at her nails. As lovely as Izzy and Tom were, they could be intimidating, and from what she'd seen so far, the same could be said for their friends. She could have sworn that was Jude Law over by the kitchen, but she couldn't see past the redhead in front of him, and she refused to gawp like a fangirl.

'I fancy a Scotch,' Oliver said. 'I'll be back in a tick.'

Effie frowned as he left her standing in the middle of the living room, looking for a familiar face and failing to find one. She watched the waiters offering delicious-looking canapés, before taking one and almost melting as the smooth goat's cheese blended with roasted peppers in her mouth. Izzy and Tom really knew how to throw a party – good music, tasty nibbles and a seemingly endless supply of alcohol. Not to mention a perfect house. Everything about it oozed money and class, from the undoubtedly original paintings and hand-woven Tibetan rugs hanging on the walls to the shiny black Steinway in the corner of the living room.

She looked around again, waiting for Oliver to come back, but it was pointless. He'd probably got talking to someone somewhere, and his mind would only be on one thing: work. She sipped at her champagne, resisting the urge to wilt away into the background, and slowly walked through the living room towards the terrace, then stepped outside.

'Effie, darling. I'm so glad you're here.' Izzy's voice floated down from the terrace above, and Effie looked up to see her leaning over the rail, her blonde hair fanning around her face like a golden halo. 'Don't move – I'll be there in a flash.'

Izzy made her way down the stairs at the side of the house, her long purple dress swishing around her legs and her hair scooped around one bare shoulder. With a large, gold statement necklace and armband, she wouldn't have looked out of place on a red carpet somewhere. Izzy hugged her, releasing her floral perfume.

'Thank god you're here. I was beginning to think I'd have to spend all night with Tom's one-dimensional friends. Complete and utter bores. Drink?'

'Got one,' Effie replied, holding up her champagne. 'Where is he?'

'Upstairs, talking shop, as usual. Honestly, you'd think he could give it a rest for just one night.'

Tom did something inexplicable in The City, something that Effie understood involved moving lots of money around for lots of obscenely wealthy people.

'When did you get back from your dad's?'

'Boxing Day.' Izzy hooked her arm through Effie's and led her through the crowd. 'It was intolerable. Daddy was positively morose because you and Olly didn't come, and Anna was – well, Anna.'

Izzy shuddered, and Effie frowned as they sat in two chairs, tucked away in the corner of the terrace. 'But I thought you liked her?'

'I can't stand her,' Izzy said with a giggle.

'You seemed really friendly at the wedding.'

'Well, of course. It was your wedding, and I suppose I try to be civil for Daddy's sake. I might not like her, but for some inexplicable reason, she genuinely seems to make him happy. And that makes me happy.'

'Except he wasn't happy at Christmas?' Effie asked. 'Why did he think Olly would want to go round? I mean, this has been going on for ages, right?'

Izzy sighed, lounging back in her chair and hanging her arm over the back. 'Since forever. They used to be super close but when Mum caught him with Anna, Olly refused to speak to him, and he barely has ever since.'

'Your mum *caught* them?'

'In flagrante, no less. There'd been rumours, of course. Daddy worked in London five days a week and came home at the weekends. He'd had Anna shacked up in a town house for five years.'

Effie tried not to let her jaw hang open. She knew about Giles's affair, but *five years*? Oliver hadn't told her that.

'And Rosie and Henry?'

'They were three when it all came out. Olly was fifteen, and I'd just left for uni. He went off the rails for a while, and in the end he started boarding at weekends. Can you imagine rather being at school than at home?'

'He never told me,' Effie said, feeling a twinge of guilt in her chest for trying to push him to talk about it. If she'd known, she'd have kept quiet. Poor Oliver.

'Do you think it'll ever go back to how it was with your dad?'

'I don't know. I hope so.' Izzy crossed her legs. 'Maybe Olly will change his perspective on things. He seems a lot less highly-strung since you two got together. Admittedly, there were a few raised eyebrows about you at first. You're so very different from the girls Olly used to date.'

Effie's cheeks burned, and she drained her champagne, frowning into the glass.

'I had a feeling I wasn't exactly Barton-Cole standard,' she muttered.

'Don't be silly – of *course* you are. I didn't mean for it to sound bad. If anything, it's a compliment. The girls Olly used to date were all airheads, each one more vacant than the last. He'd say "Jump", and they'd practically pole vault. You're different. And you're good for him.'

Was she? Judging by his mood in the lead-up to Christmas and his reaction to Effie's suggestion that he patch things up with his dad, it didn't seem like it. And Izzy's endorsement didn't sound like much of a compliment either.

'Honestly, Effie, I didn't mean anything bad by it. Who cares what other people think anyway? We all think you're fabulous.'

'Well, of course she is, that's why I married her,' Oliver said, slipping into the chair next to Effie. 'What's going on?'

'Nothing. We're just catching up,' Izzy said. 'Where have you been? Charming bees?'

'As always,' he replied and quickly rubbed the end of his nose.

'Liar, liar,' Izzy said. 'You've done a line.'

Oliver shrugged. 'It's a party. You not doing any?'

'Of course not.'

'Izzy's the sensible one,' Oliver said, and Izzy tinkled a laugh.

Effie looked at them both as they caught up. She was suddenly disturbed. Just how well did she really know her husband? He'd never told her he did coke, and given his job, she'd have thought he'd be diametrically opposed to it. He'd pressed her to quit smoking, yet here he was, getting high on coke, with his jaw twitching away as if it were the most normal thing in the world.

When Izzy got up, she kissed Effie on the cheek and left, leaving Effie and Oliver alone.

'How are you, baby? Are you having a nice time?' Oliver asked.

Effie hesitated. 'I didn't realise you did coke.'

'It's New Year's Eve, baby. It only happens once a year.' He dropped a kiss on her shoulder. 'Don't make a big deal out of it.'

It might only be once a year, but she'd thought she'd never see a drug stronger than paracetamol in her life again after Smith left. Oliver was so *together*. Not being involved in drugs was part of his appeal.

'No, I wasn't. I just . . .' She shook her head, fighting the disappointment settling over her. 'Never mind.'

She didn't want to push the issue. He was a responsible adult, and really, it was only once a year, like he said. She leaned back in her chair and looked around at the other guests. If Oliver had taken some cocaine, it was fairly likely that others had too. The guests were all professionals, with high-powered jobs. It wasn't like it had been with Smith, surrounded by DJs and PR people. Maybe this was how things worked in the Barton-Cole world.

He leaned over and kissed her cheek, and Effie smiled back, ignoring his dilated pupils. Drugs weren't a part of Oliver's life the way they had been a part of Smith's. It was a compromise she was willing to make.

୶

'I need to take my shoes off,' Effie said, holding on to the wall of their neighbour's front garden to steady herself as the rising sun peeked over the roofs of their terraced street. Her head was throbbing after too much champagne, and her shoes had inexplicably morphed into instruments of torture.

'No pain, no gain.' Oliver laughed and grabbed her hand, but she wasn't budging.

'I'm serious. My feet feel like they're going to fall off.'

He shook his head as if she was being a melodramatic diva, hooked an arm under her legs and picked her up. After the champagne and Oliver's admittedly coke-tinted attentiveness, she'd put Izzy's comments out of her head. She might not be Barton-Cole standard, but the facts were, she had the ring on her finger and she had their name.

After negotiating their way through the front gate, Oliver kicked it closed behind him, and Effie released an arm from around his neck to root around her tiny bag for the keys.

'I think we should try for a baby.'

Say what?

Effie's eyes almost popped out of her head, and she very nearly dropped the keys in her hand. She stood up and smoothed down the front of her dress. 'Are you serious?'

'I'm thirty. I don't want to leave it much longer. Besides, we're pretty much set up now.'

They *were* pretty much set up. They both had stable jobs, his business was doing well, they had a house, they were married. It all looked great on paper. It wasn't like they'd never spoken about having a family before; it was just that she hadn't thought he'd want to start so soon. None of her friends were at that stage yet. If anything, she was already leading the way by getting married, and she didn't know if she was ready to take the next step so soon.

He held her face in his hands. 'I love you. I want a family with you. We don't have to start trying right now, but I want to be a dad.'

'You sure know how to knock a girl for six,' Effie replied with a nervous laugh as she unlocked the door.

'I really want to be a dad. I want to be what mine wasn't.'

Effie looked into his eyes. She'd had no idea how much the rift in their family had affected him until she'd spoken to Izzy, and she couldn't blame him for wanting to prove he was different from Giles. Not that he'd have to do much. He was a pretty much perfect husband, and she had no doubts that he'd be an even better dad.

'Okay.'

'Really?' he replied, raising his eyebrows.

'Yeah.' She nodded. 'Really.'

It wasn't like he was the only one with parental issues. Effie had always said when she had kids, she wanted it to be with a man she loved, and she would never, ever run out on them. Marriage was for life, and even though kids were too, it felt like a much bigger commitment. Effie had always told herself that when she had kids, she'd do a much better job than her mum had done, but after her own upbringing, she wasn't entirely sure she was up to the job.

Oliver swooped her up into his arms again and carried her through the front door. They might not have to start trying straight away, but there was nothing like a bit of practice.

9.

Effie pulled the collar of her coat up around her neck as she climbed out of the car. With the wind buffeting her hair around her head and the drizzly rain whipping her face, there were only two words to describe the Irish weather: *thoroughly* and *miserable*.

'Blimey, it's cold,' Oliver said, closing the car door behind him just as the second hired VW Golf carrying Lou, Mickey and Smith pulled up behind them in the driveway.

Effie looked out at the sea with its foaming, white-tipped waves. It was almost the same shade of grey as the sky, so much so that she could barely see the horizon, and it was much safer than looking at Smith. Despite his supposed acceptance of her wanting to keep him at arm's length, she still didn't trust him.

'Isn't she beautiful?' Mickey said, looking up at the bungalow and jangling the keys in his hand.

Lou rubbed her hands together. 'And frigging cold – can we get inside?'

It was the best idea Effie had heard all day. Since they'd left London, she'd been jumpy. Jumpy about the flight, jumpy about Smith being there, jumpy about him being in the same space as Oliver for an entire weekend. It was exhausting, and the idea of having a nap before dinner was the only thing keeping her from having a breakdown altogether.

'This place is great,' Smith said as they dumped their bags into the cosy living room. 'I'm glad I tagged along.'

'My aunt Oona rents it out. Three double rooms, two bathrooms and the best bit.' Mickey walked over to the window and pushed the curtain aside to look out at the sea. 'Look at that. It's the best view in all of Ireland.'

Lou went to join him by the window and tutted. 'You can't even see anything.'

'Wait till the sky clears,' Mickey replied. 'You can even see Croagh Phadraig from here, our highest mountain. That's why I suggested the hiking boots.'

Effie shook her head. 'I don't think so. The only reason I'm wearing these things is because of the rain. I don't do mountains.'

'Shame,' Mickey replied. 'It really is a beaut.'

He led the way through the open plan kitchen and down the corridor. Couple by couple, they disappeared into their rooms, and Effie was relieved when Smith continued walking down to the room at the far end of the hallway.

She closed the door to their room behind her and looked at the lilac walls. 'It's cute, isn't it?'

'I guess, if you're into this sort of thing,' Oliver replied, looking doubtfully at the lace-trimmed duvet cover.

She looked at him as he started unpacking his precisely packed bag. Okay, so it wasn't the Hilton, but she liked it. Mickey had basically offered them a free weekend away, and it was hardly slumming it.

Effie shrugged and unzipped her bag. It might not have been the luxury he was used to, but surely he could do it for one weekend.

❧

Later that evening, she sat at the kitchen table and wiped a finger across her plate, soaking up the last of the heavenly cream sauce.

'Enjoy it, did you?' Smith grinned.

'Divine.'

Effie sucked the tip of her finger and pushed the plate away, wishing she could do the same to Smith. How had they ended up sitting next to each other anyway? He was so close she could see the tiny hairs on the backs of his arms and almost feel his heat. It was some kind of sick, twisted torture being so close to him, doused with his eau de arrogance.

'Since when did you start liking mussels anyway? You always said you hated them.'

Effie shrugged. 'Olly convinced me to try them again, and he was right.'

'Do you remember the time I made that crab pasta thing?' He laughed and put his elbows on the table. She looked at the hairs on his arm and picked up her glass.

'I remember you making me sick.'

Some things never change.

'Oh yeah. I forgot about that,' he replied, laughing behind a hand.

She put her glass to her lips. 'Well, you always did have a selective memory.'

She drank her water and looked away, but she had a selective memory too. He might have poisoned her with his dodgy cooking, but he'd looked after her too, almost taking her to A&E when he got concerned about her inability to even hold down a sip of water. She sighed. That was the problem with Smith. He'd do something, screw it up and then somehow manage to win her over by making it up to her.

'So, Smith. Apparently you were away travelling?' Oliver said, leaning back in his chair.

Smith nodded. 'For five months.'

'Where did you go?'

77

'Vietnam, Cambodia and Thailand. I was meant to make my way to Australia but came back early.'

'We were in Thailand for our honeymoon. Koh Tao, beautiful place. Did you make it there?'

Smith took a swig of beer. 'Yeah, but only for a few days.'

Great. Not only had he gatecrashed her wedding, invaded her workplace and tagged along on their weekend away, he'd also stayed on the same island she'd honeymooned on. What next?

'The views from the lookout point were fantastic,' Oliver said.

'Yeah, it was decent.'

Oh, for god's sake.

'Maybe we could go to Thailand for our honeymoon,' Lou said. 'Or Japan. I've always wanted to go there.'

Mickey pulled a face. 'What honeymoon? Who said anything about getting married?'

'Well not now, obviously.' Lou looked at him. 'I meant in the future.'

'I thought you weren't into the whole marriage thing?'

An air of awkwardness settled across the table, and Effie watched the both of them. Mickey looked downright uncomfortable as he avoided eye contact with Lou, and Lou's face was creeping red. Effie glanced sideways at Smith. He was watching them too, and just when the silence started to reach uncomfortable status, he laughed.

'Nah, you don't want to go there. Thailand's overrated, and as for Koh Tao, it was way too highbrow. Everything was at least twice the price it was anywhere else.'

Smith had broken through the tension, and Lou sulkily looked away, turning her body away from Mickey.

Oliver popped open another bottle of beer. 'I guess when you're backpacking, every penny counts.'

'It makes you rethink your views on money, if that's what you mean. Have you ever done it?'

'Christ, no.' Oliver scrunched up his nose. 'Sweaty hostels aren't for me. I prefer to stay in a nice hotel, especially somewhere tropical.'

'Yeah, I thought so. Nothing less than five star, right?'

Effie kicked his leg under the table. He looked down at her, and she widened her eyes at him. There was no way Oliver could've missed the sneer in Smith's voice.

'Oh, I don't know. I love how vintage this place is,' he said, looking around the room.

Effie looked at him with a raised eyebrow. He was singing a very different tune than he had earlier, and while his face was smiling, she couldn't help interpreting what he'd said to be a bit of an insult, knowing that what he really meant by *vintage* was that it was old and a bit shabby around the edges. She looked around the table but her friends hadn't seemed to pick up anything behind what he'd said. Maybe she was imagining it.

'So, what's your story anyway?' Oliver asked. 'I never heard much about you before the wedding.'

Smith shrugged and looked down at his bottle. 'Hardly surprising. I used to be a bit of a dick. I did a lot of things I'm not proud of.'

'Well, we've all done that,' Oliver replied. 'Making mistakes is part and parcel of life.'

'It *was* his life, not part and parcel of it,' Effie said. 'He used to be well into the drugs scene, handing out pills like they were Smarties at the raves he DJ'd at. Isn't that right, Smith?'

'Not exactly.' He turned in his chair to look at her. 'And thanks for blurting that out to a barrister, Eff.' Smith turned back to Oliver. 'I hung around with some shady people for a while and got way too heavily into the scene, but I never sold anything to anyone.'

'And then he shagged the wrong person's girlfriend, ended up half dead on a roadside somewhere and had to go to the other side of the world to get himself out of trouble,' Effie added.

She shook her head. Why had she blurted that out? Yes, it was all true, but she hadn't thought she cared anymore, not really. Smith squirmed a little in his chair next to her, and she had to admit that outing him like she had gave her a small sense of satisfaction. It was nowhere near the humiliation she'd felt when she'd found out about his cheating, but it was close enough.

'I know, I'm a fuck-up,' he said in a tone that made it clear he'd heard it all before.

'Mate, you're not fucked up,' Mickey replied. 'You *fucked up*, there's a difference.'

Oliver shrugged, apparently not shocked. 'Like I said, everyone screws up now and again.'

'It was dumb,' Smith said, 'but I'm not that person anymore.'

Effie flicked her eyes up at the ceiling. Smith was talking like it had all happened years ago, but it had only been a matter of months.

'Like Effie said, I nearly died and it kind of put things into perspective. She sat there every day in the hospital with me.' Smith looked around the table. 'They all did. I had to leave, but now I'm back and I'm on the straight and narrow.'

'We're proud of you, man,' Mickey said, clinking his bottle against Smith's.

'What are you doing with yourself now?' Oliver asked.

'I'm working for a family friend at his record label.'

'Ah, you and Effie have something in common.'

Effie looked at Smith as he just about managed to contain the smirk on his face. They had more in common than just a job.

'Yeah,' Smith replied. 'I'm at the same place. A friend of the family owns it.'

'Oh, yes, that's right. She did mention it.'

She looked up at Oliver as he swigged his beer. They both knew she'd done no such thing. She hadn't told him about Smith joining

Archive because it seemed like a pointless thing to do. Why bring attention to it?

He put his bottle back down on the table. 'I must've forgotten.'

∾

'Why don't you like the cottage?' Effie said as she lay in bed, watching Oliver as he undressed for bed. He threw his jeans across the arm of the chair standing in the corner and looked back at her.

'I do.'

She propped herself up on her elbow. 'But you said it was vintage.'

'That's because it is.'

'Yeah, but the way you said it, it sounded as if you didn't like it.'

Oliver looked at her with a raised eyebrow. 'Did it? I didn't mean it that way.'

He laughed and shook his head as if she was being silly, and Effie shrugged. Maybe she'd taken what he'd said the wrong way after all.

'Smith's an interesting one,' he said, and for a second Effie stopped breathing.

'What do you mean?'

He climbed into the bed next to her and lay on his back, folding his arms behind his head. '"Thailand is overrated. Koh Tao is too highbrow." He seems a bit of a twat.'

Effie looked at him, stunned. By the way he'd childishly mimicked Smith, if she didn't know any better, she'd have thought he was jealous. 'But you were so nice to him.'

'Well, obviously. I didn't want to be the guy who acts like a prat around their partner's ex.'

The stunned look on her face deepened. She hadn't said anything about her relationship with Smith, and she was more than certain that neither Mickey nor Lou had either.

'Come on, Effie. It's obvious, especially when you still have photos of the two of you on Facebook.' He looked at her and pulled his eyebrows together. 'I just don't get what you saw in him. I can't picture you two together at all.'

Effie lay back down on her side. He might not be able to see it, but she could, and it played out like a montage from a film. The amazing highs, feeling like she was walking on air when they first got together, to the crashing low when Smith left.

'Why didn't you tell me you worked together?'

She heaved a silent sigh. She'd known from his reaction at the dinner table that he'd bring it up sooner or later.

'Well,' she said, keeping her eyes closed, 'you heard what he was like. I didn't want you to think badly of me for having friends who were mixed up in that stuff.'

'Fair enough. Besides, maybe it's time to find new friends. Ones who aren't so caught up in drugs. It's a bit juvenile.'

She fought to keep the frown from her face at his apparently short-term memory. It was only just on New Year's Eve that he'd been shovelling cocaine up his nose.

'But from now on, no secrets, okay?' Oliver continued.

Effie nodded. Her stomach turned. Smith's past wasn't the only reason she'd kept the truth about them working together to herself, but the fact that Smith still somehow seemed to be able to provoke an emotional reaction from her was something she couldn't bring herself to say. For the first time, she was keeping a secret from Oliver, but something told her that in this case, honesty probably wasn't the best policy. Still, he'd asked for no secrets, and she promised herself that from that moment on, she wouldn't hide anything from him.

'Hopefully, we won't have to see him so much when we meet up with Lou and Mickey. I mean, it's a bit uncomfortable for me to have your ex constantly hanging around,' Oliver said, turning to face her and draping an arm across her waist. 'Besides, it's probably a bit weird for him too.'

'How do you mean?'

'Well, you're not with him now.'

'Nope.' Effie sighed and closed her eyes. Even knowing that he was a little jealous of Smith, he was still being considerate, and she loved him for it. 'I have you.'

❧

The next evening, Effie stood in Lou's bedroom, with Rihanna belting out a song from the tiny stereo.

'Why don't you leave your hair out?' Lou asked.

'Because it's blowing a gale outside and I'll end up with an Afro,' Effie replied, standing in front of the mirror as she fixed a hairpin into her quiff.

Lou nudged her out of the way to apply some mascara. 'Okay, but you look like you've just stepped off a catwalk, and I look like I'm showcasing the best of Peckham Market. What are you wearing anyway? Prada?'

'River Island and Zara, actually.' Effie sighed and sat on the bed. 'So, last night was interesting.'

'I'll say,' Lou replied, looking at her through the mirror. 'You bringing up Keisha was a bit of a shock.'

Effie scowled at the name. Keisha. She was the girl who Smith had cheated on her with and ended up in a whole heap of mess over. 'I didn't mean to. It just came out.'

'I know you said you don't have feelings for Smith, but I've got to tell you, the way you're acting says different. The way you were with him last night, putting him down, bringing up Keisha . . .'

'That's because he makes me angry.' Effie wiped her clammy hands on her jeans.

'I'm not saying he doesn't get under your skin, because he obviously does. We can all see that. But Olly's not stupid, and it's not fair on him to see you react like that with Smith. You don't want him to think something's going on.'

Effie shook her head and looked in the mirror, smoothing her already perfect hair. 'He won't think that, because nothing *is* going on.'

'Are you sure? If you promise me that you don't have any feelings for Smith, then I won't mention it again.'

Effie took a moment to think about it all. So she hadn't told Oliver about them working together, and she'd brought up the mess Smith had got himself into last summer, but was it any wonder? She'd been close to Smith, and he'd nearly died out of sheer stupidity, not to mention betraying her. She was allowed to be angry with him for that, and of course she wasn't going to tell her barrister husband that she was working with a friend who was a one-time criminal. Maybe she did have some feelings for Smith, even if they were mostly bad, but that was natural. She'd been in love with him, and it was impossible to completely switch herself off, but she was sure that eventually she'd be able to look at him and not feel anything at all.

'I don't have feelings for Smith.'

Why would she still be in love with Smith when she had everything she ever wanted with Oliver? Oliver had said he couldn't see what she'd seen in Smith the night before, and the more she thought about it, the more she wondered if he'd been right. He might not have liked Smith, but he'd still been perfectly polite and friendly, whereas Smith had taken digs at Oliver whenever he could. Knowing that he was slightly jealous only made her love Oliver more. Smith had never displayed jealousy when other guys had shown an interest in her. But then again, why would he have? They'd never really been together in the first place.

'If you say so. I just needed to check. I was worried you were on a road you wouldn't be able to come back from after last night, but now I'm relieved. That's one guy that'll never change, and I'd hate for you to do something stupid.'

'There's no danger of that happening,' Effie replied. 'I'm happy with Olly. Really happy.'

'Good. One of us has to be.' Lou sighed.

Effie frowned. 'What do you mean?'

'Oh, come on. You saw what happened with Mickey last night. Talk about embarrassing.'

'I wouldn't say it was embarrassing exactly,' Effie replied. It wasn't really a lie. The situation itself wasn't embarrassing, but she felt it on Lou's behalf.

Lou sniffed and turned back to the mirror.

'Are you crying? You never cry.'

'I'm not crying.' She sniffed again and dragged a brush through her hair for a few seconds before swearing and throwing it on the bed. 'What he said last night . . . I felt so stupid.'

'Why?'

'Because everything's changing apart from me. You're married, Smith's found himself a good job and a nice flat, and me . . .'

Lou sat next to her and Effie shook her head as she rubbed her best friend's back. 'And you?'

'I'm going nowhere,' she replied, dropping her hands. 'I'm in exactly the same place I was in a year ago.'

'That's not true.' Effie shook her head. 'You've got a great job, you've got Mickey.'

Lou scoffed. 'I hate my job, and as for Mickey? You heard what he said.'

'He said he didn't think you were into marriage, which is true. Isn't it?'

'It used to be. After Mum and Dad divorced, I swore I wouldn't go through that, but seeing you and Olly on your wedding day made me think differently.'

'So maybe he just needs time to catch up,' Effie reasoned.

'No, he doesn't.' A tear rolled down Lou's cheek. 'That's what he likes about me, that I don't go gaga over wedding dresses and diamond rings. I've always insisted I wasn't bothered about the whole marriage and kids thing because I'm all about fun, fun, fun.' She waved her hands around her head. 'I didn't even mean to say anything about our hypothetical honeymoon – it just slipped out. But now it feels like he's looking at me as if I've duped him, like I'm trying to trap him into something he doesn't want.'

Effie opened her mouth to reply, but what could she say?

'I feel like I'm being left behind,' Lou said in a tiny voice, and her shoulders drooped. 'I mean, there you are with a guy who bends over backwards to do nice things for you, and here I am with a guy who has to be poked and prodded just to make a cup of tea. I don't want to simply coast along, but what's killing me is that I think he does. I don't think we want the same things anymore.'

Effie sighed and kissed the side of Lou's head. 'I don't know what to say.'

She'd never seen Lou look so lost before. It was horrible seeing her so upset, and Effie had to swallow against the sympathy tears clogging up her throat.

'I'm sorry,' Effie said. 'I've been going on about my house, the wedding and honeymoon. I didn't realise.'

She didn't doubt that Lou was happy for her, but it must have been hard watching Effie get everything Lou wanted when she was feeling so low.

'It's not your fault. I'm super happy that you've got everything you've ever wanted; it's just making me think about what it is that *I* want,' Lou replied, wiping her eyes with the tips of her little fingers. She blew out a long breath and shook her head. 'I don't want to ruin the holiday.'

'You're not ruining anything,' Effie said, squeezing Lou's shoulder. 'I just wish you'd said something sooner.'

'Whatever.' Lou flashed her a quick, unconvincing smile. It was rare for her to really open up about her feelings, and seemingly she was keen to push them back into their box. 'We're in Ireland, and we're together. I'm sure all this will still be here in the morning, so let's just go out, have fun and forget about it for one night.'

Effie nodded and hugged her. 'If that's what you want.'

'It is. But I have to warn you: I'm probably going to get smashed with this mood I'm in.'

∽

Early the next morning, sunlight streamed through a tiny slit between the curtains directly onto Effie's face, and she squinted as she slowly prised her eyes open. Her mobile lay next to her head and she looked at it, her face scrunching in disgust. Why was she awake at seven in the morning, especially when she'd only gone to bed three hours ago? And why, oh why, had she taken that last shot of tequila? Just thinking about it made her stomach roll over. Lou wasn't the only one who'd got wasted.

Oliver snored with his back to her. He'd been on top form, making everyone laugh and generally being the most charming man in the room, even with Smith. She smiled and turned to cuddle him, grateful for his presence in her hung-over state. She needed to go back to sleep. The last thing she wanted was to be awake for the onslaught of the hangover that was already brewing, but as she buried her head into his back, she almost gagged at the whisky fumes seeping from his skin.

She turned away and lay on her back, trying desperately to fall asleep again, but the smell of whisky was overpowering. She sighed, threw back the covers and pulled on a pair of leggings before padding into the kitchen. As she stood in front of the kettle, waiting for it to boil, she massaged her temples, pressing her fingers into her skin as hard as she could.

'You look about as rough as I feel,' Smith croaked.

She turned around to see him looking at her over the back of the sofa. 'And you look like death. What are you doing there?'

'Haven't got a clue. I must've decided my room was too far. You making a brew?'

'Yep. Want one?'

He nodded. 'Three sugars, please.'

She remembered perfectly well how he took his tea, but as he flopped back down on the sofa, she realised that, for the first time since he'd come back, the sight of him hadn't filled her with nervous, angry energy. Maybe it was the hangover, or maybe his coming to Ireland with them had actually been a good idea. She poured the steaming water into the mugs. That was it – she must be starting to get used to having him around again. Maybe he wasn't a threat to her at all. Ever since Oliver had told her he'd guessed about her history with Smith, she'd been on tenterhooks about every move Smith made. She didn't want Oliver to be jealous, because as far as she was concerned, there was nothing for him to be jealous of. It turned out she needn't have worried. So far, Smith was sticking to his word and accepting what she'd said.

She put the milk back in the fridge as Smith stood up.

Oh, dear god.

The tattoos on his arms had been added to since he'd left, and now wound around his ribcage. The slightly raised, pale scar from the operation to repair his punctured lung after his attack was worked into the cranium of a skull composed entirely of small dots. As he yawned, stretching his arms out wide behind him and arching his back, his taut abs rippled, and before she even realised what she was doing, she followed the trail of brown hair sneaking from his belly button into his boxers with her eyes.

Pull yourself together, Effie. Get. A. Flipping. Grip.

Her body's reaction shook her, and she had to firmly tell herself to stop. Of course Smith was attractive; anyone with eyes could see that, but up until that moment, all she'd felt since he'd come back was a confusing mix of simmering attraction that somehow led to anger. This was something else. And she had to admit to herself that her reaction was probably exactly the kind of thing that Oliver would be jealous about.

'Here,' she said, averting her eyes as she held the mug out to him.

He took it from her and the merest flicker of a smile twitched at his lips. 'So on a scale of one to kill me now, how bad are you feeling?'

'I dunno. Somewhere in the middle.'

'Lies.' He grinned and leaned against the counter, crossing his long legs at the ankle. Couldn't he at least put some clothes on? 'It was a good night, though.'

'Yeah, it was.'

Westport only had two main streets, but they were lined with pubs, and they'd ended up going into every single one, having different drinks in each before going to the only club in town. It was no wonder they'd all got so wasted.

'Am I the first one up?' Effie asked.

'Yeah. Everyone else is doing the smart thing and trying to sleep through their hangovers, I guess.'

Effie raised an eyebrow and took a sip of her tea. 'Now, why didn't *I* think of that? What are you doing up so early anyway?'

Smith shrugged. 'I rarely sleep in past seven nowadays.'

Well that was new. Before, he wouldn't get up before midday, a consequence of being such a night owl. Effie winced at the throbbing in her head and took another sip of tea.

'God, I don't think I can drink this.' She'd put way too much milk in it, and just the smell had her stomach contracting.

'Me neither. I forgot how bad your tea making is.' Smith grinned and she put her cup on the side.

Despite the hangover, his eyes shone, and for the first time since he'd come back, she felt able to relax in his company. Until her stomach rolled over again.

'I'm heading back to bed. I really need to sleep this off, or I'll feel like death for the flight back.'

Smith nodded. 'Good idea.'

She turned to walk to her room, but knowing that he was following only inches behind her was making her feel self-conscious. Was he watching her? For the first time since he'd got back, they'd had a conversation without him winding her up or her sniping back at him. Effie looked back and threw him a small smile before slipping into her room. She was sure their progression into something less hostile was a good thing, but she felt too rough to analyse it. Oliver had barely moved since she'd recoiled away from him after waking, and even standing by the door, she could detect the sickly sweet undertones of whisky in the room. She heard Smith's bedroom door close down the hallway, and sighed as she cracked the window open before climbing back into bed.

∾

After what felt like hours, Effie woke again and looked at her phone. She'd slept for forty minutes, and although her skin was clammy under the covers, her headache had eased considerably. She peeled the cover back and sat up, her body cutting through the thick, hot air. Mickey had preset the central heating, and even with the bedroom window open, it was overwhelmingly warm.

She looked back at Oliver, knowing he'd probably stay in his alcohol-induced coma until she woke him, but what would she do until then? There was no television in the cottage, and she couldn't go back to sleep – not in this heat. She looked at her hiking boots in the corner of the room. Hiking wasn't her thing, but she could go for a walk down to the sea front. It wasn't that far away, and the prospect of tangy, salty air was a welcome contrast to the stifling interior of the cottage. She quickly pulled a pair of jeans over her leggings, threw on a jumper and bundled herself up into her coat before leaving the cottage.

The fresh air cleared the fuzziness in her head, and the sky was a curious shade of mauve and pink as dawn beckoned. The gravelly footpath at the side of the narrow road crunched underfoot, and she burrowed her gloved hands into her pockets. A gust of wind buffeted against her, and she shivered. What she'd intended to be a relaxing way to pass the time became a brisk walk, and soon her breath became shallow as she marched along the road. Why hadn't she brought her headphones? The air had swept away her pounding headache, and the only thing she could hear was the squawk of gulls overhead.

The Irish weather had been unforgiving from the moment they'd arrived, but at least it had stopped raining. She stopped to look at the view ahead of her, the surface of the sea shimmering, and sat on the gritty shore facing the horizon. There was nobody around for as far as she could see, and she thought back to the last time she'd been on a deserted beach. Admittedly, the one in Koh Tao had had beautiful golden sand, a cloudless sky and crystal-clear water, but even still, Tintern Bay held its own charm.

Effie made an effort to sit still and pointedly did her best not to think about Oliver or Smith. She was alone, in her own company, and she wanted to enjoy it without thinking of either of the men who had occupied her thoughts for weeks on end. The way Oliver and Smith had talked over dinner on their first night was like a pissing contest. Backpacking was something Oliver would never do, whereas Smith would always choose a basic hostel over a swanky five-star resort. The underlying jibes they'd thrown at each other would have been amusing if she wasn't caught in the middle. As much as she hated it, she felt torn between the two. As amazing as her honeymoon had been, she let herself wonder what it might have been like if she'd been there with Smith, seeing it from a completely different viewpoint. In her head, she'd have enjoyed the adventure, sleeping in a hostel or a beach shack, spending time with the locals and partying with other backpackers, but in reality she'd become so quickly accustomed to Oliver's way of living. It was classy and glamorous, just like he was. She smiled and shook her head. She'd changed. She wasn't the same girl Smith had left behind. He could keep his beach shacks and backpacks, and all the chaos and uncertainty that went with them.

After a while, she heard the crunch of boots on the gritty sand behind her. Effie turned to look, expecting to see a dog-walker, but instead saw the dark blue of Smith's jacket. She swallowed as she turned back to face the sea. She'd been enjoying her moment of solitude, and the realisation that she'd evolved into the version of herself she'd always wanted to be, but instead of feeling annoyed that Smith was about to intrude, yet again, she had to bury the excitement fluttering in her stomach.

'Fancy seeing you here,' he said when he reached her.

'Out of all the beaches in Ireland you just happened to show up on this one, huh?' Effie looked up at him, shielding her eyes with her hand, even though there was no reason to. Morning had broken, but the sun was staying put behind the clouds.

'Well, obviously I heard you leave the cottage and followed you down here.' He sat next to her, and Effie noted the sarcasm in his voice. She wondered if what he was saying was true.

She looked at him with mock horror. 'Stalker alert.'

'Yeah.' He nodded. 'You should be careful, hanging around on a deserted beach with the likes of me. Now's your chance to make a quick getaway.'

Effie laughed and turned to look out at the sea again.

'How's the hangover?' he asked.

She nodded and looked back at him. 'Better, actually. The walk helped. It's been ages since I've walked somewhere just for the hell of it.'

'I'm not surprised. Olly doesn't seem the type to don a pair of hiking boots.'

'You know, Mum used to take me walking all the time,' she replied, ignoring his comment and refusing to take the bait. 'I forgot how nice it could be.'

'How is she?'

Effie shrugged. 'The same as always. That's one person who'll never change.'

'She might have been a crap mum, but as a person, she doesn't need to,' Smith said, leaning back to rest on his hands. He was definitely one of the 'We love Penny' brigade. 'What did she think of Olly?'

'Not much. They only met for a few hours.'

Smith nodded, and Effie wondered whether he was reading between the lines. He'd always had a good sense for detecting the hidden truth in things, but if he suspected that Penny hadn't taken to her new son-in-law, he didn't let on.

'I'm sorry I called him a Hoorah Henry. That was probably a bit out of order. To give him credit, he seems like an alright guy.'

Effie blinked. She definitely hadn't expected that. Smith never apologised for anything, ever. Who was this new Smith? It was as if he'd woken up that morning and morphed into someone else – someone who apologised for things and didn't make her angry from the outset.

'It's fine,' she replied, remembering the way he'd said it at the wedding. With everything that had happened since, it felt like a lifetime ago, and an involuntary laugh fell from her mouth.

Smith looked at her with a confused smile. 'What?'

'It's bad.' She shook her head. 'I shouldn't be saying this, but it was actually pretty funny.'

'Yes!' Smith grinned. 'I knew you were still in there somewhere.'

'Of course I'm still in here.'

'I'm not going to lie, Eff – I did wonder for a while.' He reached over and gently poked her arm. 'All this Stepford Wife stuff you've got going on . . . I wasn't sure you were still *you*.'

He was teasing her, just like he always had done. Something had shifted since they'd come to Ireland. It was like they'd gone back to being friends – real friends. The kind of friends they used to be.

Before I started shagging him.

Effie shook her head a fraction and buried her face into the collar of her North Face jacket, thinking about what he'd said in an effort to distract herself from the thought that their sleeping together had ever been a bad thing.

'I haven't changed that much, have I?'

Smith leaned forward and drew lines in the sand with his finger. 'Honestly?'

Effie nodded.

'When I saw you at the wedding, I was like, *wow*. Who *is* this girl? I mean you looked . . . different. And I'm not talking about your hairstyle or whatever, but just in general. I thought the same at Somerset House, but when I started at Archive . . .' Smith tailed off and laughed a little, shaking his head.

'What?' Effie asked, immediately on the defensive.

'The way you reacted when you shot me down after the team meeting.' He shook his head again. 'That's when I knew you hadn't changed, not really. The hair, the makeup, the clothes, the husband – they're irrelevant. You're still the same Effie who used to give me shit all the time and pull me back into line.'

Effie thought back to that day in the meeting room. She'd been angry with him for showing up at her office, angry at the way he swaggered into the room like he belonged there and angry with herself for reacting so strongly.

'You always did like to overstep the mark.' She shrugged, hiding her smile.

'Yeah, I did.' He nodded. 'But it paid off, didn't it?'

His eyes bored into her, and she blushed. She knew full well what he was talking about. Time and time again, they used to find themselves face-to-face with the air crackling between them, millimetres away from kissing, and it was always her who pulled away. They were practically best friends, and she knew way too much about him. His bedroom might as well have had a revolving door, and she was way too cautious to let herself step through it herself. But then, one night after going to the Notting Hill Carnival, she'd been the one to close the gap and give in. They'd woken up together, and it was true: sex changed everything. They weren't the friends they used to be; they became something else, something better. Until he screwed it up, and things fell apart. The thought of it, combined with a strong gust of wind blowing around them, made her shiver.

'Cold?' he asked, clearly as observant as ever.

Effie nodded. 'I should have stuck another layer on.'

He looked at her for a second and then brushed the sand from his hands. 'Turn around.'

'Why?' She frowned, warily.

'Do you want to get warm or not?'

She turned her back to him, the frown still on her face, and behind her, Smith pushed aside her ponytail and turned down the collar of her jacket. The cold air licked the nape of her neck, and her skin bloomed with goosebumps.

'What are you doing? It's freezing.'

She turned her head a fraction but stopped as she felt his cupped hands on the back of her neck, followed by the warmth of his breath. When he exhaled again, the heat spread farther down across her back. Effie shivered, despite the heat. Every exhalation he made carried signals along her nerves, down her spine, into the tops of her thighs and into the pit of her stomach. Every inch of her body tingled in a way it hadn't done for a long time. She waited for the next one, but instead he turned her collar back up and patted her back.

'Better?' He looked down at her, and her cheeks flushed.

'Yeah. Thanks,' she mumbled.

What was that about? Why did he stop?

'Eff . . .'

She turned towards him, her body buzzing from the warmth of his breath. She could still feel it on her back, through her jacket and under her clothes. Everything about him seemed to be pulling her in like a magnet. She looked at him and realised how close together they were – so close that moving a few mere inches would put their lips together.

No, no, no, no. This is Smith.

She was confused and hung-over, but she didn't want to kiss him. No way. And Smith was out of order for trying to make a move on her, especially when she was in such a fragile state.

'I just wanted to apologise,' he said.

Oh. An apology wasn't the best way to make a move on someone.

'What for?'

There were so many things he could be apologising for. For sleeping with another girl, for not wanting to commit, for getting himself hospitalised and having to leave.

'I should never have turned up at your wedding like that.' He shook his head. 'It was an immensely stupid thing to do. And what happened after Somerset House . . .'

Effie's heart tripped in her chest as she remembered how he'd run his thumb across her cheek, grazing her lower lip. How he'd been inches away from kissing her.

'It was way, way out of order. I shouldn't have done it.'

'No. You shouldn't,' she replied, even though every cell in her body screamed to the contrary.

'You were right.'

'About what?'

'A lot of things. Keisha, especially.'

Effie shrugged and played with the Velcro on the cuff of her coat sleeve. Smith had always been reluctant to label their relationship, but she'd seen the two of them as being more than just friends with benefits. Making the assumption that he felt the same had been a huge mistake. It had led to her being heartbroken when he'd slept with someone else.

He looked back at her and ran a hand over his stubble. 'I'm sorry.'

She looked down at the sand. At least he'd apologised, the second time in one day, surely some kind of record. But instead of feeling happy and relieved, she felt worse than she had when she'd woken up.

'I'm glad you didn't let me kiss you outside the cafe, because I don't want that.'

Her shoulders dropped, and she burrowed down into her jacket, trying to hide her blushing cheeks. Why was her stomach sinking with disappointment? This was what she'd wanted ever since he'd stepped out of the darkness at her wedding reception, but she wished he'd stop talking. Every word hurt in a way she knew it shouldn't. Every syllable twisted and pulled in her chest. He didn't want her. He might have been jealous that she'd moved on after such a short time, but he'd obviously done the same, and she'd made a big deal about his return for nothing.

'I won't ever really get what it is about Oliver that makes you so happy, but you say he does. And you being happy makes me happy.' He threw her a small smile. 'I just don't want to fight with you anymore. I want us to be mates again.'

Thank god for the wind making her eyes water, because it meant she could let the tears spill down her face with no shame. She didn't even know why she was crying in the first place, whether it was because what he'd said was what she'd been waiting for or because it was what she'd never wanted to hear.

'Mates?' He stuck his hand out.

His fingers curled around her hand, cradling it in warmth. Her head told her it was for the best this way, but something in her seemed to need more convincing.

'Mates.'

10.

'You know there's no need for you to work,' Oliver said, watching Effie as she dawdled while getting ready.

If only. Outside, the ground was covered in a thin but slick film of ice as London finally succumbed to the depths of winter, and she wanted nothing more than to hibernate until spring came around.

'You could just resign and become a little housewife.'

Effie pulled a face. 'And do what?'

'Oh, I don't know,' he replied, rubbing her shoulders as she brushed her hair in front of the mirror. 'Look after the kids.'

'We don't have any.'

'Exactly. Babies don't make themselves, you know.'

Effie held down a sigh. Since returning from Ireland, he'd raised the subject of having children more and more, and despite her initially agreeing to it, she'd started to feel increasingly under pressure.

'Aren't you going to eat your toast?' he asked, looking down at the plate he'd brought in while she was in the shower.

'I haven't got time for breakfast. I'm seriously late.'

He put a hand on her shoulder and frowned. 'You need to eat. If you hadn't slept in, you'd have time.' He gave her shoulders another squeeze. 'Oh, I almost forgot.'

'Forgot what?' She turned as he walked over to the bedside table and shook a bottle of pills.

'Iron tablets.'

'What do I need those for?'

'It's supposed to help when you're considering getting pregnant. And I've made an appointment with the bank for Saturday morning about the joint bank account.'

'What joint bank account?'

'The one we spoke about a few days ago, remember?' he replied slowly, as if he were talking to a child. 'We talked about combining our salaries into one account since it doesn't make sense for you to worry about the bills when you earn so much less than I do. And this way, we can save for the baby.'

Effie frowned. Had she missed something? Not only were they now trying for a baby, they were saving money for it too?

'You do remember, don't you, Effie?'

'I don't know.' She hesitated. 'I guess so.'

'Good.' He laughed. 'I was worried you were going to say you'd forgotten about it. You have the memory of a goldfish.'

She was one hundred per cent sure they hadn't spoken about it, but why would he make it up? She thought back to what Lou had said about him being considerate. She guessed it was kind of romantic that he wanted to take care of her. Maybe her reluctance about being a kept woman was misplaced. Maybe this was what being married was about. Compromise.

'So. Toast?'

She looked down at the plate in his hand and repeated the word in her head. *Compromise.*

'Don't forget the iron tablets.'

He watched as she swallowed them and washed them down with the glass of water on her bedside table. She pecked him on the cheek and ran down the stairs, holding the toast in her teeth as she went. She felt like a kid, being sent off to school with a full stomach. If this was what he was like now, how would he be when she actually got pregnant? She wouldn't put it past him to come home tonight armed with a bookshop's worth of pregnancy books.

She walked to the Tube station, her feet occasionally sliding in the layer of slush being washed away by the rain. When had she become so ungrateful? Why was she complaining about her husband taking care of her? What was so wrong with her that she had to question these things? Maybe it was because she didn't have a barometer for what a normal, healthy relationship looked like. She could hardly use her mum as a role model, but when she thought about the guys Penny had been with over the years, she could see that they were nothing like Oliver. She never had to ask for anything with him, and he treated her so much better than the random men had ever treated her mum. Him being so keen on them having a baby probably wasn't something she should be worrying about. Besides, they'd have to have kids sometime.

Just not yet.

She pushed the thought away, and as the Tube carried her to work, she tried to imagine a life with children. A boy and a girl, maybe, with names like Tilly and Alfie. They'd have holidays by the beach, and she and Oliver would watch them play in the sand for the first time. The scenes played out in her head in full Technicolor glory, but they left her feeling empty. Having kids was huge, and despite Oliver being nothing but perfect, she still wasn't sure that she was ready to take that next step.

❧

'No. Freaking. Way,' Nikki said, looking down at her mobile.

'What?' Effie looked away from her screen and rubbed her eyes. She hated spreadsheets with a passion.

'Look who's on Tinder.' Nikki handed her the phone, and Effie looked down at the screen.

Her stomach lurched as she looked at a picture of Smith, leaning against a wall, wearing a vest, with his hands stuffed into his jeans. She knew exactly when it had been taken. She thought back to that day, when the air had been filled with blending bass lines and the smell of barbecued food as Ladbroke Grove throbbed with the pulse of the Notting Hill Carnival. She'd taken the picture, and he'd used it as his Facebook profile picture ever since. It was that night, after the carnival, that they'd got together, and now he was using the picture she'd loved to pull girls on bloody Tinder. She handed the phone back to Nikki.

'"Smith, twenty-five",' Nikki read from his profile. '"Six feet tall, tattooed. Swipe right and say hello".'

'Did you hear back about the contract for Peter Oriel yet?' Effie asked, ignoring Nikki. She had work to do.

'"Interests: Arcade Fire, I Fucking Love Science and *Top Gear*",' Nikki continued.

Effie clicked on her mouse and squinted at her screen. 'This formula isn't working.'

'What should I do? Should I tell him?'

Effie deleted the formula in the cell and tried again.

'Hello? Earth to Effie?'

'Hmm?' she replied without taking her eyes from the screen.

'Smith. Tinder. What should I do?'

'I don't know.' Effie shrugged. 'Why are you on there anyway? You're still seeing Jake.'

'He knows about it. It's research for my blog.'

Nikki hosted a blog about London life, but from what Effie could gather, it wasn't particularly big, with a following of about twenty people.

'Should I swipe right to like him and see what happens? It could be a laugh, and I bet it'd freak him out.'

No, you bloody well shouldn't.

'I thought people only used Tinder for hooking up?'

'Yeah, some do. Some of the profile photos I've seen are ridiculous. One guy even used a picture of his boner.'

'Nice.' Effie grimaced.

'You wouldn't believe some of the messages I've got since I joined. The best opening line I've had so far said, "Show me your tits".'

'How old were they? Twelve?'

'Obviously, I didn't reply. Jake and I spend most nights laughing at them.'

'Doesn't he care that you're using a dating app?'

Nikki shook her head. 'Not at all. We trust each other completely, and he's doing it too, to give me the male perspective.'

Effie raised her eyebrows. 'Each to their own, I guess.'

'So, what do we think? Should I swipe right or left?'

Effie stopped and swallowed against the irrational jealousy pulling at her. Nikki was in a relationship, and this was all for research, but what if Smith thought differently?

'Maybe you're right,' Nikki said, even though Effie hadn't said anything. 'He wouldn't know I've liked him unless he likes me too, but what if he did swipe right? I don't want things to get awkward.'

'Yeah.' Effie nodded with relief. 'It's probably best not to.'

'I'll bet he's racking them up anyway. It's a hot photo.'

Effie looked down at her keyboard as she typed. It *was* a good photo, but she was the one who'd seen it live. She remembered the way he'd held her hand the whole day to make sure they weren't separated in the crowd, and how he'd danced right behind her, his hands on her hips. She'd spent most of the day hoping he'd try to kiss her again, telling herself that she wouldn't turn him down like she always had done before. And when he finally did, she'd sworn she'd never kiss anyone else again. She looked at her wedding ring as her fingers hit the keyboard.

Smith might have made her body flutter back in Ireland, but it was understandable, really. She'd been hung-over and cold. It was a purely biological response, and regardless, they'd made a pact. She was married – happily married – and Smith and she were just *mates*.

∽

A few days later, Effie woke up to see Oliver sitting next to her. She pulled herself up on her elbow, and he handed her a Valentine's card.

'Happy Valentine's Day, baby.' He kissed her softly on the lips and smiled. 'I haven't had time to get your present yet.'

'Thank you. And it's fine – you really don't have to get me anything,' she replied. He already showered her with gifts; having one just for Valentine's Day wasn't such a huge deal. She opened the card and read the simple message *I love you* in Oliver's sloped handwriting. 'Here's yours.'

She reached into her bedside drawer and gave him his card and a small box. He opened it and looked at the cufflinks inside. He picked one up and held it between his finger and thumb, and Effie held her breath. She'd spent ages in Selfridges, trying to find something he'd like. His cufflink collection was huge, and she didn't want to get him a pair he'd hate.

'They're really nice,' he said, and Effie smiled with relief. 'I'll wear them today. First, though, it's time for breakfast.'

He kissed her forehead and disappeared for a few minutes, returning with a tray of pancakes, orange juice and, as had become standard, two iron tablets.

'Breakfast fit for a queen.' He handed her the glass of juice before dropping the tablets into her open hand.

At the very least, they were good for her health. Oliver dressed as she ate her breakfast, and when she'd finished, she leaned over and picked up the strip of foil containing her contraceptive pill.

'You know,' Oliver said, looking at her through the mirror, 'I was thinking. We're never going to get anywhere unless you stop taking your pill.'

Effie looked at the pale blue tablet in her hand and frowned. 'But I thought we weren't really trying yet. Not properly.'

'No, but I think we should. We're just wasting time, and it'll probably take ages for anything to happen anyway.'

What if it didn't? What if she stopped taking it and got pregnant straight away? Was she really ready to give up her life for a baby? She looked at the pill again, knowing that the answer to her question was a resounding *no*.

She looked up at his reflection as he stared back at her, knotting his tie, remembering what he'd said on New Year's Eve. He'd been so sincere, and she'd seen how much he really wanted it. What was holding her back?

'Can we talk about it once this pack's finished?' she asked. It was a fair compromise and neither a yes nor a no. At the very least it would buy her some time.

Oliver looked away and shrugged. 'Okay. Whatever you want.'

She heard the disappointment in his voice and watched as he took off the cufflinks she'd bought him, replacing them with an older pair. Maybe the old pair matched his suit better, but she couldn't shake the feeling that he was making a show of throwing the gift back in her face. It was so out of character that she didn't know whether she was imagining it and whether the hurt was warranted or not.

'So, I've reserved the table for eight,' she said. She was being silly; of course he wasn't throwing it back at her. He wasn't like that. He leaned forward and looked in the mirror, preening his hair. 'Olly?'

'What?' he replied without looking at her.

'I said, the table's booked for eight tonight.'

'Yeah, sure. I'd better be off.'

He left the room without a goodbye or a kiss. Why had he got his hopes up so much? He'd made her feel pressured, and now he was making no secret of the fact that she'd disappointed him. Effie looked at the small pill again and sighed, feeling like her insides had fallen to the floor.

∾

'Oh, for god's sake,' Effie said, repeatedly clicking her mouse.

'What's up?'

Smith stood next to her, resting one hand on the back of her chair and the other on her desk. Effie sighed. Even if her computer were working normally, she'd still be in a bad mood. Oliver's attitude that morning had thrown her off.

'I can't get into this bloody calendar. It keeps booting me out.'

Smith laughed, and for a moment, the black cloud over Effie's head disappeared.

'Yeah, I had the same problem yesterday. Here, let me.' He moved the keyboard towards him and leaned across her.

His Hugo Boss aftershave attacked her senses. It reminded her of the way he used to scoop her up in his arms to say hello, and filled her head with memories of waking up in his bed on a sunny morning. She looked at the swirls of clouds and demons tattooed on the side of his upper arm. He had a twin version with angels on the other. How many times had she run her fingers over them? She shook her head. She should not be thinking like this. There was no room for nostalgia in her life where Smith was concerned, especially not when her husband was moody with her for not wanting to reproduce right away.

'There you go – all done.' He slid the keyboard back over to her and straightened up. 'So, what are you up to tonight? Hubby taking you out?'

Hubby? It sounded so wrong coming from Smith's mouth.

'We're going for dinner. You? TV dinner for one?'

He perched himself on the edge of her desk. 'Actually, I've got a date.'

'On Valentine's Day?' Effie pulled a tight smile. 'How romantic.'

He shrugged. 'It's only a drink. I figured, why not.'

Smith didn't *do* Valentine's Day. Or at least, he didn't used to. She didn't mention that when she'd suggested they do something last year, he'd almost broken out in hives at the thought.

'Where did you meet her?'

'Tinder.'

Ugh. Tinder. Also known as hook-up-ville. What was the betting he'd be getting laid tonight? Effie pushed the thought from her mind.

'Nikki's on Tinder too.'

'I know. I've seen her profile already.'

'Did you swipe right?'

Smith chuckled. 'No. For one thing, I've learned not to shit where I sleep.'

'You mean you don't want to have to work with someone you've screwed over.'

'She's a nice girl.' He shrugged. 'Too nice.'

'So you just want a shag then?'

'Well, it has been a while. Know anyone who can help?' He grinned and raised an eyebrow.

It was just chat. Banter. That was all. Except, coming from him, it didn't sound as innocent as that, and the way her skin flushed wasn't an innocent way of reacting. Effie rolled her eyes. 'Mates, remember?'

'Can't blame a guy for trying.' He laughed. 'No, I'm not just looking for a shag. But if it happens, then . . .'

'And this girl you're meeting, what does she want?'

'I don't know yet.'

'Let's see her.'

'Really?'

'Yeah, why not? We're mates after all, right?'

'Yeah.' He nodded with a frown and flicked through his phone. 'I guess.'

Effie took it from him as nonchalantly as she could. It was an awkward situation, but she'd have to get used to the idea of him dating sooner or later, whether she liked it or not. She looked at the screen.

'She's pretty.'

And she was. She had honey-coloured hair and light brown skin, and her eyes were a curious shade of amber. Effie read her profile.

'"Claire. Thirty-one"? Bit old for you, isn't it?'

Smith shrugged. 'Nothing wrong with an older woman. They're much less complicated.'

'"Cabin crew, always mile high",' Effie continued, reading the words under Claire's Hollywood smile photo. 'Classy.'

'Don't.' Smith frowned.

'What? I didn't say anything.'

'Give it.' He held his hand out, and she gave him back the phone.

'I'm sure she's lovely.' Always mile high . . . of course they were going to end up in bed. 'Where are you taking her?'

'The Social Experiment, some cocktail place in Chinatown.'

'I know it. It's a nice place.'

'Hope so. I'd hate to be a disappointment.'

Smith's phone rang, and he went back to his desk to answer it. Effie watched him as he reclined in his swivel chair. He was a bad boy; disappointment was to be expected.

∼

Later that evening, she sat with a glass of wine and looked again at her watch. Oliver was late. The door opened, and she turned to look, but instead of her husband, a couple walked in, arm in arm.

A blend of spices trailed their scent behind a waitress walking past with plates of food. Effie picked up the menu and scanned the pages: filo pastry stuffed with chicken and almonds, tiger prawns with pimento, okra with tomatoes and coriander. Everything sounded so good. She took another sip of wine to try to keep the hunger at bay. Hopefully, he wouldn't be much longer.

She looked up at the ceiling, draped with material to create a canopy of dark oranges and olive greens. It was a cosy place, with circular booths housing round tables and low seating wrapped in dark steel to create a nest-like effect. Understated paper hearts hung from the ceiling, the only concession to Valentine's Day, which was just fine. It hadn't gotten off to the most romantic of starts, but they could talk it through. She wanted Oliver to be happy, just as he wished for her.

To Effie's left, a couple sat close together, smiling and whispering into each other's ears. She looked at the menu again, wishing he'd hurry up. Was there anything worse than sitting in a restaurant alone? Sitting alone in a bar, maybe. She hated feeling like people were looking at her, wondering if she'd been stood up.

'Can I get you anything, madam?'

Effie looked up and nodded at the young waitress. 'I'll have another wine, please.'

One more wouldn't hurt.

♁

An hour later, Effie picked up her mobile and pressed redial. Oliver's voicemail came through, again. Where the hell was he? It wasn't like him to just not show up, and she started to wonder if something had happened to him. She tried calling again and disconnected as soon as the first few words of his recorded message played out. Maybe he'd lost his phone. She was beyond hungry but hadn't ordered anything, and the complimentary bowl of olives was long gone. She picked up the phone again.

'Hello?' Amid a cacophony of noise, Oliver's voice filtered through the earpiece.

'Where the hell are you?'

Judging by the sound of laughter and clinking glasses in the background, she had a fair idea. She looked up at the ceiling, blinking back tears. There was no way he'd deliberately stand her up, especially not on Valentine's Day.

'I'm out.'

'I've been waiting for you for over an hour.'

'Some of the guys from work wanted to go for a drink. It's been a long day. We'll do dinner some other time.'

Effie could almost picture the nonchalant shrug that would have accompanied his strangely emotionless tone, and when he hung up, her face burned. She stared at the phone. Had she really heard that correctly? Had her husband really decided it was perfectly acceptable to just not turn up to a dinner date? She swallowed back the tears as she signalled for the bill, and the waitress didn't even blink when she handed her the card machine. She probably saw people

110

being stood up all the time, but Effie wanted to tell her she was different. She was married. She wasn't sat there waiting for a faceless first date.

She thought about Claire, Smith's Tinder date. It was highly unlikely she'd be stood up. Smith was a lot of things, but he wasn't the type to do that. Despite his rough edges, he could be the perfect gent when the time called for it. How did any of this make sense? How could Smith be out on a date while she'd been stood up by her husband?

She walked out of the restaurant with the feeling that everyone was looking at her, pitying the woman who'd been stood up on Valentine's Day, and made her way home.

∞

At two in the morning, the front door opened and closed, and Effie lay in bed, listening to Oliver staggering up the stairs. He'd made no attempt to call or text to apologise, and she'd spent all evening alone, trying to avoid the multitude of romantic comedies on TV.

'Where have you been?' she asked, looking at his silhouette in the doorway.

He tried to lean a hand against the doorjamb but slipped and stumbled a few feet forward. Effie shook her head and turned on her side, lying with her back to him. A few seconds later, he blew a raspberry and collapsed on the bed next to her. Within seconds, the stench of alcohol seeped through his clothes, and she sighed as she threw back the duvet. He didn't even stir as she slammed the bedroom door and made her way to the spare room.

The next morning, she sat at the kitchen island when Oliver shuffled in, looking like death, with ruffled hair and grey, waxy skin.

'Any coffee going?' he croaked. Effie silently slid the percolator towards him as he sat on a stool and laid his head on the cold surface. 'Christ, I feel awful.'

'I'm not surprised.'

He reached for the percolator but didn't reply.

'Where were you last night?'

'I told you.' He sighed. 'It was a long day, and I went for a drink to unwind.'

Effie shook her head. 'But we had dinner plans. Do you have any idea how embarrassed I was being stood up?'

'Please, not now. I can't handle a conversation like this.'

'I was waiting for over an hour.'

'Come on, Effie, it wasn't that big a deal. I didn't realise the plans were concrete.'

She pushed her cereal bowl away. 'It was Valentine's Day. Of course it was a big deal. You made me look like an idiot. You knew it was booked – I reminded you yesterday morning.'

'Yesterday morning.' He sighed again and shook his head. 'Did you really think I'd want to go out for some romantic dinner after yesterday morning?'

Effie opened her mouth and closed it again as she realised what was happening.

'You did it to punish me for taking the pill?' She stared at him, but he stayed silent. 'If you must know, I was planning on telling you last night that I'd stop taking it because it was what you wanted.'

'And now you've changed your mind?' he asked, his voice laden with sarcasm.

'Can you blame me?'

Oliver shook his head and got off his stool. 'You can't play about with things like this, Effie. You know how much I want kids.'

'And you can't just play about with my feelings,' she replied, getting off her stool and standing in front of him.

He looked at her, and his grey face was etched with disappointment. 'You know, if you're going to play about with things like this then maybe it's better that we don't have kids. A mother has to be responsible for them, stick around for them through thick and thin. I'd hate to think you'd just change your mind about them once it's too late.'

Oliver turned to leave the kitchen, and tears stung Effie's eyes. What was he implying? That she'd simply decide she couldn't take any more and run out on her family? That she was like Penny?

'How could you say that?' She strode after him. He knew that her mum had left her, and he knew how much it had messed her up. To throw that in her face was a low blow.

'Just leave it, Effie,' he replied without turning around.

'No, I won't just leave it.'

She reached out and grabbed his arm to make him face her, and as he turned, his hand flew, hitting her right across the cheek. The sharp slap stung, and Effie's hand flew straight to her cheek. Tears filled her unblinking eyes as she stared at him with her mouth hanging open.

'Effie . . .' He shook his head and reached out to touch her, but she took a step back. 'Effie, I'm sorry.'

'You slapped me.'

Her chest heaved with shallow breaths as shock settled over her. He'd slapped her. If it weren't for the stinging in her cheek, she'd never have believed it were real.

'How could you say that? It was an accident.'

She looked at the uncertainty in his eyes, wishing she could believe it, but she couldn't understand how something like that could ever be an accident. Apart from the bike ride in Thailand, this was the only other time they'd argued, and it had ended with her getting slapped. She hadn't even thought he was that angry.

Oliver stepped forward again and put his hands on her shoulders, trying to pull her in for a hug. 'Come on, Effie, I'm sorry.

You know I didn't mean it. You know I'd never do something like that on purpose. I didn't realise you were standing so close to me. I just spun round, and you were right there. My hand flew out of reflex.'

Effie tried to replay what had happened in her head. She'd grabbed his arm and he'd spun around to do what? To slap her, or to turn and face her like she'd wanted? He stepped forward and hugged her, stroking the back of her head. She felt his arms wrap around her and wondered if the same man who usually made her feel safe could really be the same man who'd just struck her.

She'd thought she knew him, but now she wasn't so sure. He'd stood her up to teach her a lesson and then hinted that she'd be no better a mother than her own, things she thought he'd never do and say.

Maybe she didn't really know him at all.

11.

'So, birthday girl, what are the plans?' Lou asked.

Effie shrugged as she splayed her fingers out wide for the nail technician to get to work. 'I have no idea. I've barely thought about it.'

'I reckon we should go clubbing. Make a proper night of it.'

'I don't know. I'm not really in the mood for that. Maybe we'll just get the gang together and go for a meal or something.'

A week later, things still weren't back to normal with Oliver, and it wasn't helped by him constantly working late. She ate by herself and went to bed by herself. They hadn't spent any time together and had somehow entered into a warped stalemate. She didn't want to be the one to reach out first. It might have been immature, but she wanted him to do something to make up for the whole Valentine's Day fiasco. She had no choice but to forgive him because, on balance, she didn't know him to be a violent or vindictive guy. It made more sense that what happened had been a genuine accident, and the more time went on, the more she started to wonder if, in some twisted way, he'd been right to be angry with her. Standing her up was an awful thing to do, but was she really any better, dangling her acceptance to start a family in front of him and then taking it away again?

Lou shook her head. 'Push the boat out, why don't you. It's only your birthday.'

Effie shrugged as the nail technician expertly applied a coat of pale pink varnish. 'I'll look at sorting something out. I just don't want it to be a big deal. How are you anyway? It feels like ages since we've caught up.'

She didn't really need an answer. Lou's usual sparkle had dimmed since Ireland, and she hadn't seen it since. On the occasions when they had met up, Lou was usually distracted and distant.

'Worse than before.' Lou sighed. 'We've kind of reached a standoff. We were fighting last night, and he told me he didn't want to settle down. As in *ever*, and if that's what I wanted, then I might as well leave.'

'Really?' Effie raised her eyebrows. It sounded so uncharacteristically harsh that she couldn't imagine Mickey saying it. Then again, what did she know? She could never have imagined Oliver slapping her, but it had still happened.

'He tried to take it back after, but now I feel like I can't be around him if that's really how he feels.'

'So what are you doing to do? Wait for him to change his mind?' Effie asked with a frown as her technician buffed her nails.

'I have no idea. I mean, call me crazy, but aren't we kind of settled already? It's not as if we're in an open relationship.' Lou shrugged. 'I don't know. Maybe one of us just needs to admit the truth.'

'Which is?'

'That maybe we should just call it a day. He's basically put the skids on any kind of future vision for the two of us, so what's the point?'

Effie gawped and shook her head. Lou and Mickey splitting up? They were the golden couple – they couldn't.

'But you love him. Don't you?'

'Of course I do, but love isn't always enough. You loved Smith and look what happened there.'

Effie scowled. 'It's hardly the same thing.'

'What I mean is, there's no point loving someone who doesn't love you back the same way.'

She couldn't argue with that.

'Would you want to split up if you'd never mentioned the honeymoon thing?' Effie asked. 'Because if the answer is no, my advice would be to really think about this. Guys like Mickey don't come along every day.'

Lou looked down at her hands and swallowed. 'I know. But I'm trying to be sensible here. You've sorted your life out and got everything you wanted. I need to do the same.'

'It's not a competition, Lou.' Effie shook her head. 'Marriage doesn't make everything perfect. If things were good between you two before, then maybe you should think this through a bit more.'

Lou heaved a huge sigh. 'Look. I'm not saying I'm going to split up with him right now – just that it's something I can't ignore.'

Effie looked at the sadness pulling at Lou's lips. Maybe she should do something for her birthday. At the very least, it would be fun, and it might take Lou's mind off things.

'You know,' Effie said, 'you might be right about my birthday. Not about clubbing, but there's that cocktail bar near Baker Street I've been wanting to check out. It'll be fun.'

She smiled and shot a wink at Lou. It was time for her to play Cupid.

❧

Three days later, Oliver finally finished work early enough to walk through their front door as she was busy cooking dinner in the kitchen. He kissed her hello for the first time in what felt like forever, apparently caving and dissolving the stalemate.

'Hey,' he said as Effie stood chopping carrots.

She looked at him, sitting on a stool, with an uncertain smile twitching around his downturned mouth. 'Hey.'

'So, I know I've been the worst husband in the world lately, but will it help if I tell you I've got us a table at Le Gavroche for your birthday?'

A wide smile stretched her mouth. 'Yes. It helps.'

She'd dropped hints about wanting to go there for ages and always thought he'd ignored her. Clearly she was wrong. She remembered what Lou said about him being ultra considerate, and despite what had happened between them since Valentine's Day, happiness tugged at her.

'I really am sorry about Valentine's Day and what happened after.' He got up and wrapped her in a hug. 'I was just disappointed about the pill thing, and I behaved like a spoilt brat. I know it was wrong to do what I did, but I don't deal well with emotional stuff, and I know it must not have felt like it, but it was better that I didn't come to the dinner. I would have just lashed out, and it would have been worse in the end.'

Effie frowned into his chest. Was it still an apology if he justified his behaviour afterwards?

'I promise not to do anything like that again. I really need you to understand that I never meant to slap you. It really was an accident. And as for the baby thing, we can wait, as long as it isn't forever.'

He pulled away and kissed her cheek before pinching a carrot slice from the chopping board. He flashed a grin at her, and she smiled back, relieved not only that they'd cleared the air between them but also that he'd given her some breathing space about having a child. She dismissed the niggle in her mind, pointing out that he hadn't apologised for what he'd said about her being an unsuitable mother.

'Have you *really* booked us a table at Le Gavroche?' Effie asked, turning back to the chopping board. 'I'm going to have to get something proper to wear. I could always wear the black and cream dress, I suppose.'

'Really? It's a bit garish, isn't it? I mean, you'd look beautiful in a black bag, but I want you to get properly dressed up in something nice.'

Effie frowned. Her dress was patterned, but she certainly wouldn't call it garish. 'I like it.'

'Le Gavroche is a top-end restaurant, though, and it'd be nice to see you in something designer. Luxury tends to be understated, remember?'

'Yeah, I remember.' She nodded, recalling the time when he'd said the same thing, nixing the idea to make a feature wall in the living room. He'd been right then too. It would have looked hideous. 'When's it booked for?'

'I pulled in a contact who owed me a favour, and he pulled some strings, so we'll be going on your actual birthday.' He grinned then looked at the frown on her face. 'What is it?'

'I've booked a table at Purl that night. You know, that bar in Baker Street I've been wanting to go to for ages.'

'Can't you go another day?'

She shook her head. 'Everyone's kept that night clear because it's my birthday. They're all busy.'

'You could have told me.'

'Well, you haven't been around. Or that keen on speaking to me.'

Oliver grimaced. 'I hope you don't really think that. I was just busy, that's all.'

Effie nodded. Maybe that was what he was like in times of stress. They were still getting to know each other, after all. Maybe she'd have to get used to him being non-communicative and less attentive when his work got in the way.

'But I can't rearrange dinner,' he said. 'Otherwise, we'll have to wait till June for another booking.'

'Maybe we could do both? What time did you book it for?'

'Seven thirty. We can't go for drinks in Baker Street and then schlep over to Park Lane in time.'

'I can't cancel. Everyone's looking forward to it.'

'I suppose Smith will be there?'

'Yeah. He's part of the group, so . . .' She tailed off and caught the quick pull of a pout on his mouth before he let it go. 'Everyone needs a night out. Especially Lou. She's having a really tough time.'

'Really? With what?'

'Mickey. They're not getting on so well.'

Oliver stood behind her and wrapped his arms around her waist. 'That's unfortunate.'

Unfortunate? Effie sliced through an onion and frowned. It was unfortunate to lose your keys or step in dog mess. Having to question whether you were in the right relationship was much more than that.

'Baby,' he continued, 'I'm sure she'll understand. They all will.'

'But they're my best mates. I always celebrate my birthday with them.'

'Effie, it's not like you don't see them all the time anyway. We're always spending time with your friends.'

'Well, that's because you don't have any,' Effie jokingly replied, but it wasn't far from the truth. Apart from work colleagues and acquaintances, Oliver didn't seem to have a close group of friends like she did.

'You don't need friends; you've got me.' He kissed the side of her neck. 'Besides, this is the first time *I'll* celebrate your birthday with you. Can you honestly tell me you'd rather go to some wanky bar instead of one of the best restaurants in town?'

Purl wasn't wanky – it was one of the most booked cocktail bars in London, and it had cost her eighty pounds to secure a table.

'We'll get properly dressed up and celebrate in style.' He leaned down and kissed the side of her neck. 'You deserve it, and I really want to make it up to you, to say sorry.'

Effie slid the chopped vegetables into a pan. 'Okay. I'll speak to the guys and let them know.'

It wasn't every day she got invited to a Michelin-starred restaurant, and she could always rearrange the booking at Purl. Hopefully, she wouldn't lose her deposit. And there was always Sketch's album launch party, which they were all invited to anyway. She could double that up as a birthday celebration.

Oliver had broken the tension between them. Turning him down now would only inflame a situation that had already gone on for long enough. And he was right. It was her first birthday as his wife, and she had to remember that she wasn't a single girl anymore. Like he'd told her on New Year's Eve, sometimes life meant compromise. Surely marriage was no different? Besides, it might be nice to do something different for her birthday other than spending it in a bar getting drunk. Her friends would understand.

12.

'Nervous?' Effie looked at Smith as he ran a hand through his hair for the hundredth time in ten minutes.

'Not at all.'

Effie laughed and shook her head. He'd never admit it, but he didn't have to; the apprehension was written all over his face. She looked around at The Hub, a small bar sandwiched between a Thai restaurant and a vintage clothes shop on Brick Lane. It was owned by a friend of Doug's, and coincidentally, it was where Doug had watched Sketch play for the first time before almost signing them on the spot.

Chaos reigned as the last-minute preparations took place. The boxes stacked on tables were being unloaded, cables tangled and trailed along the heavily scuffed wooden floor and plywood sheets sprayed with art by a graffiti artist were being tacked along the exposed brick walls. A sound engineer jumped down from the stage to fiddle with his laptop while another man laid a large square of lacquered flooring in front of the stage.

Effie watched as a man wheeling a BMX bike came in, his face breaking into a grin when he looked at Smith.

'Smith.' He grabbed Smith into a hug, almost squeezing the life out of him. 'How's it going, bro?'

Smith laughed as they broke away, and he ran a hand through his hair. 'Mental, as you can see. It's good to see you, man. Effie, this is Ben,' he said, gesturing to his friend. 'He's the one who'll be doing the display.'

Ben Morel, the twenty-four-year-old BMXer who'd already won two world championships and was getting ready to defend his title for the third time, looked remarkably similar to Smith. Both had dark hair and tattoos, but they had a different kind of energy. Smith's was laid back, exuding a quiet air of confidence and nonchalance, whereas Ben looked ready to bounce off the walls with excitement as he shook Effie's hand.

'Ah, so *you're* Effie.' Ben laughed.

Effie looked at Smith, shaking his head with a laugh, clearly trying to look less embarrassed than she was. She smiled at Ben. 'That's me. It's nice to meet you and your bike. Sounds like a pretty cool job you've got.'

'I like it too much to call it a job, but yeah, stuff like this is cool. I've followed Sketch for a while, and when Smith mentioned the launch . . .' He shrugged with a grin. 'It would have been rude not to.' He turned back to Smith. 'So listen, if it's alright with you, I'm just gonna go dump my bag and get a little practice in. We can catch up later?'

Smith nodded as they bumped fists, and Effie watched as he propped his bike up against a table before heading downstairs to the cloakroom.

Effie looked at Ben's bike. 'He seems cool.'

Smith had the most diverse group of friends she'd ever come across.

Smith nodded. 'Yeah, he is. I met him in Vietnam. He's ridiculously talented, and he's doing this for free, just for the fun of it. To be honest, I didn't think he'd be able to make it. He shattered his coccyx a few weeks ago after falling mid-trick.'

'Clearly he likes to live dangerously. No wonder you two are friends.'

Effie grinned at him, and for the billionth time that day, her stomach fluttered. Even though The Hub was only filled with workers, the anticipation was building. Drinks were being stocked behind the bar, the DJ had finished setting up his decks and the Sketch trio were sound-checking with The Starlets, the band booked as the opening act.

'So,' Effie said, 'he knows about me, huh?'

Smith laughed and raked a hand through his hair. 'Don't start.'

Knowing that he talked about her with friends other than Mickey made her feel oddly warm inside. She'd bet he didn't speak about Claire. So far, he'd remained tight-lipped about their date, which was fine by her. She didn't want to hear about it anyway. She looked at him as he opened the flap on one of the boxes on the table.

'What did you tell him exactly?'

'Why do you want to know?' he replied, looking at her.

'Wouldn't you want to know what I tell people about you?'

Smith shrugged. 'I don't really care what people say about me. Unless it's something fuck awful.'

'Exactly. How do I know you haven't said something really mean about me?'

He laughed and went back to poking around in the box.

'So, come on. What did you say?'

She flicked his arm, and he rolled his eyes as he pulled the lid down. 'I told him you're a pain in the arse. Now come on. We've got a ton of stuff to do.'

He slid the box to the other end of the table, and Effie grinned.

❧

Later, Effie pushed her way through the crowd to where Mickey and Lou were stood with their backs pressed against the wall, having found a sliver of space in the packed-out room. Twenty minutes into a half-hour set, Sketch had seemingly won everyone over. At first, the Archive clan had stood together, feverishly watching the music journalists scattered among the fans and industry types. They were all from local papers except for one from *NME* magazine – the one person Doug had never taken his eyes off. From what Effie had seen, he looked suitably impressed, as did the others, but they'd have to wait for the reviews before being able to really celebrate.

'Where's Smith?' Effie asked. She wanted to congratulate him. They'd all pulled together for the launch, but he'd taken on the project as a personal one and put his heart and soul into it.

She'd been sceptical when he'd turned up at the Archive office back in December, but he'd proved his worth ten times over. His contacts had proved invaluable when it came to almost every aspect – hiring speakers, the graffiti artists, Ben and his BMX; it was all because of Smith. He'd done good.

'He popped outside on the phone,' Lou said. 'Good luck finding him when he comes back.'

The Hub was small enough as it was, but with people packed in, it would be a nightmare trying to find anyone. It had been a tough enough job keeping an eye on the journalists, and they'd only managed that because that bunch seemed to be the only ones who didn't dance. Effie looked down at her watch. The live set was due to finish, and Ben would be taking over the floor for a few minutes, making use of the lacquered surface that had been laid down especially for him and his bike. Smith had to be back for that, surely?

'This is off the chain,' Lou said. 'Everyone seems really cool too.'

Lou took her beer from Effie but barely even looked at Mickey. Clearly, things weren't improving between them any time soon, and the look on his face cut into her. No matter what Lou said, she couldn't believe he was serious when he'd told Lou to take their relationship as it was or leave it.

'Yeah, they're a good crowd.' Effie nodded. 'That's what you get when you're around here.'

'Hipsters,' Lou said with a wink. 'I've lost count of the number of beards in here.'

'Slightly judgemental, are we?' Effie laughed, but Lou wasn't wrong. The Hub had bought right into the hipster scene, even serving cocktails in glass jars, and everyone in the bar seemed to epitomise the spirit of the trendsetting East End of London where anything went. Brightly coloured trainers danced with winkle-picker shoes, jeans mixed with vintage suits and trouser braces, and heads of scruffy hair under an assortment of hats bobbed to the music next to Brylcreemed quiffs. Effie loved it.

As Sketch finished up on stage, Ben came through the parting crowd, and the DJ launched into classic nineties hip hop as he started spinning his bike around.

'I can't believe Smith's missing this,' Effie said. 'I hardly even know what BMXing is, but even I know he's good.'

Mickey nodded. 'He is. Smith messaged me after they met. He was stoked. He loves BMX. He used to ride one around all the time when we were kids.'

Of course he did. Smith loved anything that was remotely cool. Rock climbing, surfing, wakeboarding – he did it all.

'I know it's not Purl,' Effie said, 'but this is pretty cool, right?'

'Because we love you, we'll overlook it this once.' Lou grinned. 'Going to Le Gavroche is pretty special, and you might even get to see Michel Roux Jnr. I'm insanely jealous.'

Effie grinned and turned back to the stage just in time to see Oliver picking his way through the crowd, with his eyes on her. What would he make of this? If he thought Purl was *wanky*, he'd probably think The Hub was unbearably 'try hard'.

'You made it,' Effie said when he finally stood next to her; he dropped a kiss on her lips.

'Getting into this place was a nightmare. The queue's outrageous.' He turned to greet Mickey and Lou, giving them his charming megawatt smile.

An outrageous queue was good. Aside from the hundred invites they'd sent, there was capacity for forty fans who'd won tickets on Twitter and a further thirty for the door. She knew all too well the tactic used by clubs and bars to keep people outside to create a buzz for passers-by and publicity.

'Nice place, though,' he said, looking around, and Effie heaved a tiny sigh of relief. She'd have hated him to slate it, especially after all the work that had gone into the launch. 'Do you want a drink?'

She shook her head. 'It's alright. I'll go. You'll take forever to get served. It's quicker if I do it.'

'The perks of being married to an insider.' Oliver winked and handed her a twenty pound note. 'I'll have a beer, and get another round in for you lot too.'

'Thanks.' Effie grinned and pointed towards Ben and his dizzying display. 'Watch this guy – he's amazing. I'll be back in a tick.'

She kissed him on the cheek and left, weaving her way through the crowd towards the bar. The air was hot and clammy, the music sending the heavy thud of bass lines out towards the crowd. There was a sense of danger in the air. Maybe *danger* was the wrong word, but there was a dark undercurrent, giving her the feeling that it was one of those nights when anything might happen. She put her elbows on the bar to carve out a little space, waiting for one of the bar staff to take her order.

'Grab us two beers, Eff?'

She turned her head at the sound of Smith's voice behind her. 'Finally, I wondered where you'd got to.'

'I was outside. Ben invited some people along, and they had a bit of trouble getting in. The queue is nuts.'

'Olly said the same thing.'

Smith outstretched an arm and laid a hand on the bar next to her. 'Oh. When did he get here?'

'Just now.'

Effie twisted her body to look up at him. 'You should be proud of yourself. Tonight's been great.'

Smith shrugged. 'It wasn't just me. We all did it together.'

'I didn't think you'd be able to pull it off.'

He pulled a face of mock disappointment. 'Thanks for the vote of confidence.'

'I mean it. For a while there, I really thought Doug had lost it, handing Sketch over to you, but this?' She looked around the room. 'It's cool. Really cool.'

'You know me. I like to rise to a challenge. And I didn't want to let him down.'

'Remember when Mickey said he was proud of you back in Ireland?' she asked, and Smith nodded his head. 'Well, I am too. It's nice to have you back. You've changed.'

'Man, that's high praise coming from you.' He laughed, and Effie swatted his arm.

'You have, though. You seem much less . . . I dunno. Twattish.'

Smith laughed again. 'Thanks. I think.'

As someone else joined the queue for the bar, Effie was shoved sideways, and Smith's arm instinctively shot around her waist, pulling her into him to stop her from falling. His arm wrapped across the entire width of her back, his fingers pressed firmly against her side. He'd acted on pure instinct, but the movement was as familiar to Effie as the act of breathing. She'd forgotten how it felt.

Being short, she was used to being jostled around in bars and clubs, especially the ones Smith would go to, where everyone was so drunk or high they barely even noticed her. In an instant, she remembered how Smith would never be too far away from her, silently making sure she was safe at all times, that her glass was never empty, that she knew he was there. She looked up at him as he held her close, starkly aware of his thumb pressing into the side of her bra. All he had to do was move it a centimetre or so, and he'd be brushing it against her breast.

And she wanted him to do it.

The DJ changed the music and Alt-J blared all around them, the slow, seductive bass line pulsing as the crowd throbbed to the beat. He didn't move his arm away. Instead, he continued to look at her, scanning her face and drinking in her features as if he were looking at her for the first time. Her pulse quickened as she felt the heat from his body against hers, but she didn't dare move. He'd said he didn't want her. When they'd sat on the beach in Ireland, he'd made it clear and told her exactly what she'd thought she wanted to hear from the moment he came back. He'd moved on, and he wanted her less than she'd wanted him, just like it had always been.

So why does this feel so good?

And that's when she realised the danger, the darkness she'd felt all evening had been because of him. The Hub, with its underground, slightly grubby feel, had transported her back to the clubs Smith loved so much, where they'd dance until sweat formed a film over their skin, and he'd pull her close, moving against her on the dance floor.

She held her breath, not wanting to break the spell.

The feeling of security just from being in his arms was overwhelming. The world could burst into flames, and she'd still feel safe, as long as Smith was there. She looked at his lips and back up into his grey eyes, melting as he slowly moved his thumb. Even through the material of her top and bra, it scorched, as if he'd touched her bare skin. The music buzzed through her like adrenalin. Did he remember that night after the carnival? The night they'd got together for the first time, when this very song played in the background?

He drew a small circle with his thumb, and she inched forward, closing the tiny gap between them until he was pressed right up against her. She pictured the chiselled abs she'd seen in the kitchen that hung-over morning and slowly put a hand on his hip. His grip tightened on her, and she whimpered as her heart pounded, her pulse beating in her ears louder than the music pumping from the speakers.

Kiss me.

She looked at him, willing him to do it. He was only inches away – all he had to do was lower his head a little. The heat of his body radiated from every square inch of him, through his T-shirt and onto her palm, from his face, from his jeans and between his legs. She could feel it, *see* it, as if she were looking at him through a thermal imaging camera.

Something behind him made her shift her gaze, and she looked past him, straight into Lou's eyes. Lou arched her eyebrow, and Effie looked back up at Smith. She'd seen them, and if she'd seen them . . .

Oh, god. Olly.

She dropped her hand from his hip. 'Smith, I . . .'

'Shit. I'm sorry,' he mumbled and stepped back, his cheeks flaring red as he shook his head.

He looked at the floor, behind the bar, anywhere but at her, and suddenly, he didn't look like laddish, bad-boy Smith. He looked like James, the guy who used to stroke her hair as she fell asleep and make her cups of tea in the morning. She looked through the crowd for Oliver, her chest sinking with relief when she saw the tip of his head. He was talking to Mickey, with his back to them. He hadn't seen. Blood pounded in her ears.

'I don't know what that was,' Smith said, finally meeting her eyes as he scrunched his eyebrows together.

'Yeah.' Effie let out a nervous laugh. 'Me neither.'

'I only came over for beer.'

They looked each other in the eye again before bursting into laughter, shaking their heads and repeatedly telling each other how silly they were, and what *were* they thinking? Clearly she had a death wish, being so stupid. She looked over at Lou, who jerked her head towards the toilets as she mouthed *now*.

Balls.

'I should go,' Effie said.

Smith nodded and looked back at her with eyes that said so much more than the awkward, laughing words they'd shared just seconds ago. The look on his face seemed to be saying, 'Don't go.' Was she being delusional?

'Sure.' He nodded again and Effie closed her eyes for a second.

Friends. They were Just Friends. And now she was in for a bollocking from Lou. She braced herself as she walked away from Smith, forcing herself not to look back at him as she headed down the stairs with Lou and into the Ladies toilet.

'You'd better start speaking,' Lou said, crossing her arms as soon as they got into the tiny bathroom.

Effie looked at the stickers covering the walls. What could she say?

'What the hell are you doing? Do you have any idea of the game you're playing? You practically just shagged your ex by the bar in front of your husband.'

Effie scowled. 'I did no such thing.'

'You said you didn't feel anything for Smith.'

'I don't.'

Lou raised her eyebrows.

'I don't,' Effie insisted, but as soon as the words had left her mouth, her body slouched against the wall. She let out a loud sigh and rubbed her hands over her face. 'God. What a mess.'

'What happened?' Lou asked, taking a much softer tone.

'I don't know.' Effie shrugged and let her arms flop with resignation. 'We were just talking at the bar, and someone pushed into me. Smith grabbed me and . . .'

'You were, like, this far away from kissing,' Lou said, pinching her thumb and forefinger together.

'I know. And the worst thing is, I wanted him to.'

'What's going on with you, Eff?' Lou shook her head. 'You're married. To Olly. The sweetest guy in the world. Why are you risking it all for a quick flutter from *Smith*? Remember how he broke your heart, how unreliable he was? Anyone would think you're in love with him instead of your husband.'

Effie looked down at the ground with tears welling in her eyes. 'I don't love Smith. How could I? You said it yourself – he broke my heart. I can't go back to that, I just . . .'

She just, what? Lou was right. Why was she sabotaging what she had with Oliver for Smith?

'I'm not having a go at you,' Lou said, putting her hand on Effie's shoulder. 'I'm just worried. This isn't like you.'

'I know,' Effie replied, shaking her head.

'Eff, if you're still in love with Smith—'

'I'm not.'

'*If* you are,' Lou said, 'you've got to be honest about it.'

Effie shook her head again. 'I can't trust the man as far as I could throw him.'

'Just because you can't trust him doesn't mean you can't love him.'

'No, it doesn't, but I love Olly.'

Loving Olly sounded right. It felt right. She was married to him; she'd made a big public show of how much she loved him and how certain they were about their relationship after only knowing each other for such a short space of time. How many other couples did that? What she had with Oliver meant something. How could she have put that in jeopardy for Smith? Besides, she couldn't love two people at the same time – it didn't work like that.

She wiped her eyes and looked at Lou. 'You don't need to be worried about me. You're right, I came this close to screwing up, and I honestly don't know why, but I won't do it again. I won't risk my marriage for him. I can't. I love Olly, and we have a great life.'

It wasn't exactly true. It wasn't always great. Since Valentine's Day, there'd been times when it felt like her life was happening to someone else, like she was peering through a window at a life being led by someone who *should* be happy. Her marriage with Oliver wasn't anywhere near as stomach-somersaulting exciting as things had been with Smith, but that was normal, wasn't it?

Lou shook her head. 'You're lucky it was me who saw the two of you and not him, because most people would have looked at what happened like cheating. I know if I'd seen Mickey doing that, I'd have killed him.'

The toilet in the middle cubicle flushed, and Effie stood up straight, turning to look in the mirror. She'd caught the tears just in time, but her skin was flushed with heat from the exchange with Smith. A woman stepped out of the cubicle and smiled meekly at them before washing her hands. She was pretty, dressed in skinny jeans and a blouse – hardly exceptional in comparison to the other women upstairs – but anyone could tell they were designer clothes. There was something vaguely familiar about her, but Effie didn't have the mental energy to figure out why. The woman left the bathroom, and Effie turned to Lou.

'We just need to pretend this didn't happen, okay?' She looked at Lou, who remained silent. 'I mean it. Maybe you're right. Maybe I do still have some feelings for Smith, but I definitely don't love him. Like you said, I was only away from him for a month before meeting Olly, and maybe it was all too soon, but this, whatever it is, *will* fade.'

'Really?' Lou raised an eyebrow. 'I'm not condoning what you just did, but you and Smith are like . . .'

'Like what?'

'Fireworks.' Lou set her mouth into a sad smile. 'I hate to say it because he screwed you over so much, but it's true. In those few seconds I saw you with Smith, I realised I've never seen you like that with Olly. Things like that don't just fade.'

'Fireworks have to burn out some time.' Effie shrugged.

'And then what?'

'And then I'll continue my life with Olly.'

Lou groaned. 'Effie, there's nothing wrong with admitting you made a mistake. You know I think Oliver is great, but what you just said sounds like a compromise nobody should have to make, and it's not fair on him to have to just wait until your feelings for Smith are gone – and there's no guarantee they will go. And I've got to say, it's not fair on Smith either. Whichever way you look at it, it's not fair on anyone, and someone's going to end up getting hurt.'

'Then that person will be Smith, because I'm married, and marriage means compromise,' Effie replied and jutted out her chin.

'Yeah, compromise as in watching the odd game of football in return for having dinner cooked or something, not compromising happiness.'

'I am happy. And I don't ever want to speak about tonight again. It was a lapse in judgement, but it didn't mean anything. Promise me?' She glared at Lou. 'I'm serious, Lou.'

Lou sighed. 'Fine.'

'Pinky promise.'

'Nobody pinky-promises past the age of ten,' Lou said but she stuck her little finger out anyway, and they shook on the promise never to speak about her near vow-breaking moment with Smith again. 'I'll never mention it again unless you want me to. And I really didn't mean to sound like I was having a go. I just want you to be happy, that's all. You know I'm always here, whatever you decide.'

'I know, and I love you for it.'

Effie gave her a hug, grateful to have a friend like Lou, someone who hadn't passed judgement for what had been a mistake, one she knew she'd never repeat.

She tried to shake the last fifteen minutes from her head as they headed back upstairs and picked through the crowd, back to their tiny space in the corner of the bar. She caught a glimpse of Smith, and her face fell. Standing next to him was the girl from the toilets, the one who'd smiled at them before she'd left. Effie stood still in the sea of dancing bodies, and Lou stopped behind her.

'What?' Lou asked.

'It's the girl from the toilets. I knew she looked familiar. That's Claire, the girl Smith met up with off Tinder.'

'Fuck,' Lou said slowly.

Panic rose from the depths of Effie's being, bubbling its way up to her throat. 'She heard *everything*. She knows I nearly just copped off with him, she knows I'm married, she . . .'

'Okay, okay, calm down,' Lou said, standing in front of Effie and putting her hands on her shoulders. 'It'll be fine. She's not going to say anything, especially not if she's interested in him. If she's got any sense at all, she'll keep it to herself.'

'What if she doesn't? What if she blurts everything out?'

Lou frowned. 'What's she doing?'

Effie forced herself to look past Lou's shoulder for a few seconds. 'Laughing and drinking a beer.'

'See?' Lou smiled. 'You've got nothing to worry about. I've got to say, though, if ever there were a case in point as to why Smith is not the man for you, this has to be it.'

Effie didn't need to hear Lou say it; she was thinking the exact same thing herself. She looked over at the two of them again and shook her head. It wasn't even that Claire had overheard everything they'd said. It was the fact that she was there at all that made Effie feel sick. James, the nice guy who'd let his guard down only minutes ago, was nowhere to be seen. Now, all she could see was Smith, the man who'd cheated on her and managed to keep her hanging on with the merest hint of a promise. He'd almost kissed her, and now he was parading his new woman around like a trophy, just like he had with Effie. She was willing to bet that he was probably reluctant to label whatever he had with Claire, just as he had with Effie. He had a knack for keeping girls close, so they'd be there when he needed them, and all the while keeping himself free to do whatever he wanted, knowing that he'd never promised anything to anyone. She'd almost fallen for it, but she damned well wouldn't do it again.

'Screw this. I'm going home.'

She didn't need to see Smith with some other girl. Not when she had her supportive, loyal husband in her life. She walked over to Oliver and took his hand, pointedly ignoring Smith and Claire. 'I'm tired. Shall we go?'

Oliver frowned. 'But you've been talking about this launch for weeks. It's still early.'

'It's fine,' Effie said, trying to sound normal. 'Sketch has finished. I don't need to stay.'

'You're not leaving, are you, Eff?' Smith asked, but she refused to look at him. Instead, she looked back at Oliver until he nodded and led her out into the cool air.

13.

'Happy birthday,' Smith said, putting a cupcake on her desk.

Effie looked at its red velvet goodness. It was from The Hummingbird Bakery, her favourite. He always brought her a cupcake from there for her birthday, but she slid it back towards him.

'I'm on a diet.'

Smith frowned. 'Since when?'

'Since the Sketch launch.'

'But I've seen you eating cake since then.'

She looked up at him. 'Well, then I've been on a diet since whenever you last saw me eat cake.'

'So that'd be yesterday, then?' He folded his arms and looked at her. 'You always said diets were stupid fads you refused to ever take part in.'

Effie sighed. 'Smith, I'm busy. Nikki's off sick, and I've got a heap of work to do. Thanks for the gift, but you really shouldn't have bothered.'

She turned back to her keyboard and tapped the keys, hitting them with extra force as her eyes smarted. Since the launch party, she'd barely spoken to him unless it was absolutely necessary for work. The embarrassment she'd felt when she'd seen him with Claire had made her cringe. She'd been monumentally stupid, almost risking her marriage, and for what? Besides, it was her birthday, and tonight she was off to Le Gavroche for her slap-up meal. Smith could keep his pathetic cupcake.

Smith frowned and rubbed his forehead. 'Have I done something to piss you off?'

'Nope.' Effie spat the word out and pushed the box farther towards him. Smith sighed, picking it up, and went back to this desk.

She watched as he sat in his chair with a puzzled look on his face, and when he looked back at her, she swivelled her gaze back to her computer screen. She only had two hours and forty minutes until she could leave and head to the hairdresser's to start the beautifying process for tonight, and she had a heap of things to do.

James: I saw the Dairy Milk sticking out of your bag. Diet my arse.

Effie sighed, reading the instant message flashing in the corner of her screen. She looked over at Smith, but he was staring intently at his monitor, apparently absorbed in work. He'd sent an instant message on purpose. If he'd sent an email, she could've pretended she hadn't had time to read it. She sighed again and typed out a reply.

Effie: Chocolate is allowed. Cake isn't.

She looked over at him as he noisily opened the cupcake box. He scooped a finger-full of speckled frosting and popped it in his mouth. She'd cut her nose off just to spite her face. Red velvet was her favourite, and he knew it. She could almost feel his smugness when he sent her another message.

James: Shame. Tastes good.
Effie: That's nice. I've got stuff to do before I leave.
James: We'll still be at Purl later, if you change your mind.

Effie: Unlikely.

James: You never know . . . Have a nice day, Eff.

Effie rolled her eyes and closed the chat window before setting her status to 'Do not disturb'. She really did have a never-ending amount of work to do, and Smith had distracted her for long enough.

~

Despite Smith's annoying cupcake intrusion, as birthdays went, her twenty-sixth was shaping up to be the best yet. Oliver had pre-booked her an appointment at a top salon in Knightsbridge, and she'd had her curls chemically straightened, layered and sprinkled with caramel highlights. Her tight, corkscrew curls were gone, and now she had a glossy sheet of hair hanging down past her shoulders, and the whole way home, she couldn't stop running her hands through it.

As she stepped through her front door, a grin spread across her face. She dropped her bag on the side table in the hallway and ran a finger across the velvety soft lily petals sitting in a vase. Oliver must have popped back home during the day, because, as she looked down at the floor, she saw hand-drawn arrows on individual slips of paper disappearing into the living room. She gave the lilies one last sniff before following the trail to the coffee table. She blinked at the box sitting on its wooden surface.

Effie knelt in front of it and traced her fingers along the solitary word on the box – 'Dior'. She carefully lifted the lid, peeled back the tissue paper and lifted out a dress. It was feather-light in her hands, and she stood, holding it up against herself. Split into two sections, the top was loose and peach, while the bottom was black, with one side ruched up to the knee. It was exactly the kind of dress Oliver would pick out for her – sexy, but demure, and perfect for Le Gavroche. Her eyes flicked down to the coffee table again. Propped up against a bottle of champagne was a card. She carefully folded the dress and put it back in its box. Then, after popping the champagne open, she sat on the sofa and opened the card.

To the best wife a man could ever wish for, happy birthday. Hope the dress fits, can't wait to tear it off you later. A car will pick you up at 6.45. I'll see you there. Love you, baby. Olly xoxo

She smiled, reading his looped letters. It was easy to forget how romantic he could be when stalemates and arguments got in the way, but he was clearly trying to make it up to her. She took a sip of champagne and sat back on the sofa, looking at the Dior box. She shook her head as she thought about Smith. What had she been thinking? Guilt weighed down on her as she thought back to their near-kiss at the Sketch launch. She couldn't let anything like that happen again. She had too much to lose and nothing to gain.

❧

At 7.28, Effie stepped out of the black Mercedes CLS and smoothed down her dress. She smiled her thanks to the driver as he closed the door behind her, and looked up at the restaurant. Oliver stood by the door, leaning against the wall. He looked sharp in a tailored navy suit and crisp white shirt, and a smile was curling at his lips as she walked towards him.

'Christ, you look good.' He dropped a kiss on her lips and stepped back to look at her again.

She gave a playful twirl and laughed. 'This is possibly the most beautiful thing I've ever worn. Thank you.'

He hooked a hand around the back of her neck and pulled her in for another kiss. 'A beautiful dress for a beautiful woman. Happy birthday, baby.'

Effie grinned as he took her hand and she saw the cufflinks she'd bought him for Valentine's Day. His wearing them meant more to her than the dinner they were about to eat. She looked up at the town house exterior of the restaurant. It looked like every other building around it, and had Oliver not sent her a car to drop her off, chances were she'd have walked right past it. She'd wanted to eat here ever since she'd first seen Michel Roux Jnr on *MasterChef*, but she'd expected something grander. As Oliver had told her, luxury didn't have to be ostentatious.

'This is amazing – it's so comfy,' Effie said, looking around at the cosy interior of the restaurant after they'd been led to their table. Far from being modern and soulless as she might have expected, it reminded her of a Victorian parlour room with its stuffed cushion seating and circular tables. 'Thank you.'

'You're welcome. Like I said, you deserve it. It's your first birthday as my wife; I had to make it special.'

Oliver grinned and looked down into his menu. It was hard to believe this was the same man who'd stood her up on Valentine's Day and slapped her. But then, she had to remind herself that it *had* been an accident. She couldn't fault the effort he'd put into her birthday so far, and if this was a taste of future ones to come, she was more than ready for it.

When the waiter appeared with their first course, he set the plates on the table with a flourish. 'For your first course, madam, marinated Var salmon accompanied by a lemon and vodka jelly. For sir, a lobster mousse with Aquitaine caviar and champagne butter sauce.'

He tipped his head and quietly slipped away, leaving Effie staring at her plate. It looked so beautiful, she wanted to take a photograph. Maybe she'd better not. She had a feeling Oliver would think it crass.

'Do you want to try some caviar?' Oliver asked, and Effie shook her head.

'Fish eggs? No thanks.'

'Come on,' he said, holding his fork out. 'It's really nice.'

Effie looked at the tiny spheres and stopped herself from pulling a face. How many times in her life had she ever been offered caviar? She leaned forward, and he fed her a tiny mouthful. Her nose wrinkled as she chewed.

Oliver laughed. 'It's an acquired taste.'

She grimaced as she swallowed and washed the taste away with a glug of wine. 'I've never understood that concept. Why force yourself to like something over time? Vodka jelly on the other hand . . .'

'I've already got you into mussels. Caviar won't be far behind.' He grinned and Effie shook her head with a playful smile.

'Unlikely.' She looked around again. 'Do you think we'll get to see Michel Roux Jnr? I've heard he sometimes comes round to speak to the diners.'

'I don't know. Surely this is good enough?'

Oliver pouted and Effie quickly shook her head, putting her hand on his. 'It's more than enough.'

She didn't want him to think her ungrateful, and, really, she had nothing to complain about. She watched Oliver as he ate, noting the dark shadows under his eyes.

'You look tired,' she said as he pushed his plate away and dabbed his mouth with his napkin.

'It's been a long day. This case is slipping into all shades of grey areas.' He rubbed the crease between his eyebrows.

'The fraud one?' she asked, and he nodded. 'Is he innocent?'

'It's not as black and white as that,' Oliver replied. 'Only a judge can decide whether he's innocent or not.'

'What do *you* think?'

'I wouldn't represent him if I thought he was guilty.' He leaned back in his chair as the waiter collected their plates.

Effie nodded. 'That's fair enough.'

It must be a nightmare having to defend people labelled as criminals all the time, and she admired Oliver for sticking to his morals.

'It's a complex case, though. I could do with a few days away.' He picked up her hand and kissed it. 'I was thinking that we could go to see Mummy. What do you think?'

'In Corsica?'

Oliver nodded. She'd been aching to go ever since he'd told her his mum had moved out there four years ago. She'd seen pictures of her old brick villa, surrounded by lemon trees, with a panoramic view of azure sea.

'When?'

'In the next month or so. It'd be nice to go before this all kicks off properly.'

'Will it be hot? It'll be nice to see your mum again.'

Even if she's not my biggest fan.

She cringed, remembering the faux pas she'd made at the wedding. Next time round, she'd be on the charm offensive and Celeste Barton-Cole would have no choice but to love her. Any talk of Oliver's dad would be completely off limits.

'Yes, it should be. I'd like to go for longer, but it's looking unlikely I'll be able to take more time off this side of summer.'

'See? Imagine if we'd started trying for a baby, and I'd got pregnant before the summer. It could have been ages before we'd got a proper holiday.' She grinned, trying to make light of the topic that had caused the whole Valentine's Day fiasco.

'I suppose,' he mumbled.

'Thank you. For giving me a bit of time.'

Oliver shrugged as if it was nothing, but she knew better.

'You know,' he said, 'I never even thought about having children before you came along. You've completely turned my life around, Effie, and it's fine if you want to wait, because I plan on keeping you forever.'

Effie smiled and drank her wine. For some inexplicable reason, a sense of unease was spreading through her body. Forever felt like an awfully long time.

14.

'Happy birthday, Sweetpea.'

'Thanks, but it was yesterday,' Effie replied without hiding the disappointment in her voice. Apparently her mum found it easy to forget the day she'd given birth to her only child.

'No, not quite – there was always a dispute about that. The doctor noted your time of birth as eleven fifty-eight, but you took your sweet time in making your presence known. I go with the time you finally screamed your arrival in the world. You should celebrate it over two days – I would.'

Of course she would. Penny always went against authority, and seeing as Effie had never heard this story before, it was obvious she was simply trying to cover up the fact that she'd clean forgotten.

'What did you do? Did you go out with your friends?'

'No, Olly took me for dinner at Le Gavroche. You know, Michel Roux Jnr's place?'

'Gosh. How very civilised.'

Effie sighed. The word *civilised* was just as bad as *conventional* where Penny was concerned. She must be the only mum in the world who'd rather her daughter go out and get completely wasted instead of having a plush, luxury dinner for her birthday.

'You should have come out here. You'd have been able to go out clubbing down in Bora Bora, and then you could have relaxed up here afterwards,' Penny said as Effie flicked on the kettle.

'You're in Ibiza?'

'Of course, Sweetpea. I always come here in the winter; you know that. It's so beautiful.'

Effie knew her mum spent her winters in Spain, but not in Ibiza. She was sure she'd never mentioned it before because Ibiza had always been a firm bucket list destination. Maybe she should have gone. She pictured her mum looking out onto the hills of northern Ibiza with a cup of coffee, strong and black, the way she always used to take it in the mornings. She'd probably already done a round of yoga and meditation to start her off for the day.

She shook her head. As idyllic as it sounded, the reality would've been very different. She knew the kinds of places where her mum stayed – alternative communities where everything was shared, with a heavy emphasis on natural living. Staying there with Effie's friends, who liked the emphasis to be more on boozy nights out, would never have gone down well, and besides, she would've missed out on Le Gavroche. She had Corsica to look forward to instead.

'How's Oliver?'

'Fine,' Effie replied, surprised that her mum had asked after him. She was hardly his biggest fan after all. 'He's a bit stressed with work, but he's okay.'

'And how's the lovely Lou? It's a shame I couldn't get to see her.'

'She's alright. She's kind of going through a rough patch with Mickey, but it'll blow over.'

'She's such a lovely girl.' Penny sighed wistfully. 'I remember the way you two would lock yourselves in your room all afternoon and make the biggest fuss whenever I tried to join in with you.'

Well, duh. Effie shook her head and began making a cup of tea. What did her mum expect? It was beyond embarrassing when she'd try to include herself in their girly chats about makeup and boy-bands. She used to groan and scowl whenever her mum would barge into her bedroom with mugs of hot chocolate and home-made cookies before plopping herself on the floor with them.

'Yeah. Well.' Effie shrugged.

'You watch. When you have children, you'll do the same thing. It all goes by so quickly. Before I knew it, you'd gone from being my little baby who toddled around naked all day long to being a surly teenager. And now it's your birthday. Twenty-six and married.'

Penny sniffed. Jesus, was she crying? Effie pulled a face. What was with her? She'd suddenly shifted from being absent to sending Christmas presents and crying down the phone.

'Are you menopausal or something?'

'Why must you always do that?'

'Do what?'

'That. Deflect away whenever I say something nice. I'll never understand how I've created a daughter who's so out of touch with her feelings.' Penny sighed. 'You're so resistant. I'm just trying to wish you a happy birthday, that's all. You're my daughter, and I love you.'

Unexpected tears stung Effie's eyes. *She loves me.* She remembered the walks they used to take around the fields in Dorset where they'd holiday during half-term. The barley would scrape against her legs as Penny would chase after her before scooping her up and showering her with kisses.

'Thanks,' Effie mumbled.

'You should try and come out, really. The whole gang. There's more than enough space.'

'Yeah, maybe.'

Maybe she could. It would be nice to escape for the weekend, just her and Lou. They could leave the boys at home, and Lou could take time out from whatever was going on between her and Mickey.

'Flights are cheap at this time of year.'

146

'I'm a bit skint at the minute.'

'You're still working, aren't you? Is it that mortgage of yours? It *is* expensive.'

'It's not that. I'm waiting for my new bank card to arrive, and it's taking ages. Some kind of mix-up with the bank.'

Penny laughed. 'You can go into a branch and take money out, you know.'

Effie tutted. 'Of course I do. It's fine – I'll just wait. Olly opened us up a joint account, but until my card arrives, he has to transfer money into my old account. Maybe I'll look at flights after.'

'So he has a bank card and you don't?'

'I'm still using my old account. It's fine.'

Her mum was silent on the other end of the phone for a few seconds.

'But your wages are paid into that account, aren't they?'

'No . . . I switched it over,' Effie replied.

So, you have to ask him for money?' Penny asked.

'It's not like that. It's my salary – I've earned it.'

'But you still have to ask him?'

'Well, yeah, technically, as he has to transfer it to my old account, but only until my debit card arrives.'

'Right.'

Effie frowned. 'What?'

'Oh, nothing. I'm just not sure I approve, that's all. Nobody should ever have control over your finances but you.'

'He doesn't control anything, it's just a workaround.'

'I still don't like it.'

'Mum, don't.' Effie sighed. They'd been having a nice conversation for once. Why did she have to ruin it? 'It's not like I have to go begging.'

'Whatever you say, Sweetpea. But if you ever need money, you know you only have to ask me and it's yours.'

'Mum, you live on a commune, and you don't work.'

'I live in a house, in a community, and I *do* work. I do my reiki and massage – you know all this. I'm really not sure where you've got this idea of me being a layabout, wasted hippy from.'

'Nope, me neither,' Effie replied sarcastically.

Was she kidding? This was the woman who used to smoke a spliff with her coffee first thing in the morning and spent most of her time protesting about something or other. Wasn't that what hippies did?

'Honestly, I think you'd be pleasantly surprised if you came here. We've got a beautiful creek and an organic vegetable plot and . . .' Effie tuned out. She knew what alternative communities were like.

Before they'd finally settled properly in London, they'd lived on one for a while. That had been the place with no doors, where people would wander around freely as if it were the most normal thing in the world. It was little wonder she hadn't developed a complex about privacy, given how little of it they'd had. What kind of mum would bring her daughter up in that kind of environment? Maybe it wasn't a good idea to visit. She didn't want to be exposed to all that again.

'What do you think?' Penny asked, and Effie tuned back in. She had no idea what she'd been talking about, but she sounded excited.

'Yeah. Yeah, sure,' Effie muttered.

It didn't matter what her mum had said. She might have called to wish her a happy, albeit late, birthday, and she might have told Effie she loved her, but it made no difference. Effie couldn't forgive her mum for letting her suffer, for putting the good of the community before her own daughter, for leaving her behind. Ibiza was well and truly off the cards.

∽

'Bad day?' Oliver asked later that evening. He dropped his gym bag on the floor and stood behind Effie, wrapping his arms around her waist.

'No. Why?'

'Because you only ever make soup when you've had a bad day or you're not feeling well.'

She looked down into the pea and mint soup she was stirring on the hob. 'Do I?'

'You do.' He kissed the side of her head. 'So, which one is it? You don't feel hot, so you can't be sick.'

'Mum called.'

'Ah. Did you have an argument?'

'Not really. She called to wish me a happy birthday.'

'Okay,' Oliver said slowly as he let go of her. 'And this was wrong because?'

Effie shrugged. 'Because it's just what she does. She comes along when I'm really happy and kills it.'

Oliver leaned against the worktop. 'What did she say?'

'Just the usual. I'm not living my life the right way, I'm not taking control enough, yada, yada, yada.'

Or, more accurately, you're controlling everything for me.

'Parents.' He rolled his eyes. 'Just ignore her. She's miles away. It's not like you have to see her every day.'

Effie nodded. He was right, but it was too late. She couldn't just pretend the conversation with her mum hadn't happened. What if she were right? Effie couldn't remember ever talking about the joint bank account, but he'd insisted they had and that she'd gone along with it. She might not have to go begging for money, but she did have to ask him to transfer it over to her when she needed it. The freedom to spend what she earned had been removed, but, as she'd told her mum, it was only temporary. She went back to stirring the soup and told herself that whoever said that mums always knew best clearly didn't have a clue.

⁓

By the time Monday rolled around, Effie had pushed Penny's doom and gloom from her mind. She sat at her office desk and looked at her phone before shutting her computer down. She'd been trying to get hold of Lou all weekend, but so far, her calls hadn't been returned. She was eager to hear about Purl, the place she'd wanted to go to for so long and had ducked out of in favour of Le Gavroche.

As her monitor switched off, the door opened and Smith walked in. Effie looked up at the clock. He hadn't been in the office all day, and it was almost six, way past home time.

'Hey,' he said, stopping by her desk. 'You're here late.'

'So are you,' Effie replied.

'Manic day.' He rubbed a hand over his eyes. 'How was your birthday dinner?'

'Great. Absolutely perfect, in fact.' She smiled, trying to show him how happy she was despite his Claire-shaped curveball at Sketch. 'How was Purl? I've been trying to get hold of Lou to find out, but I'm not having any luck.'

'I'm not surprised. When's the last time you spoke to her?'

'Friday morning. She called to wish me a happy birthday. I've called her since, but no answer.' Effie frowned. 'Why?'

He sighed and ran a hand across his chin. 'Mickey moved out.'

'They've split up?' Effie's jaw dropped as Smith nodded. 'When?'

'He came round to mine on Saturday night. Apparently, they had a huge bust-up. He won't talk about it, but I don't think I've ever seen him this angry before.'

'I knew things weren't great between them, but I didn't think it was this bad.'

'You asked how Purl was . . . To be perfectly honest, it was a nightmare. You should have seen them.' Smith grimaced. 'Lou was totally trashed, and they argued all night. Mickey left early, and Lou just disappeared afterwards.'

'I should have been there,' Effie said. Far from being a night out to play Cupid, it seemed like her birthday drinks had descended into a nightmare while she'd been wined and dined.

'You wouldn't have been able to stop it. You know what Lou's like when she's in one of her moods.'

'Maybe I should go to see her.'

'If she's not returning your calls, then she probably doesn't want to talk. It might be better to just give her some space.'

'Yeah. Maybe you're right.' She picked up her bag from the floor and stood up to leave, and a puzzled frown settled on her face. 'So you stayed on your own, after they left?'

'Not exactly.'

He didn't meet her eyes, but then, he didn't have to. She knew him and she knew what he was like. He wouldn't have stayed alone for long.

'Of course not. You always make new friends.'

Especially the female kind.

'It wasn't like that. Claire came.'

'Claire?'

Effie just about managed to stop her jaw from slacking. Every time she thought Smith couldn't possibly do anything else to twist the knife, he always managed to stick it farther into her heart. And here he was, letting on that he'd invited the girl he was shagging to her birthday drinks.

'Yeah. I wasn't going to invite her, but then you said you weren't coming out, so . . .' He shrugged and every inch of her skin began to crawl with jealousy.

He'd tried to make it sound as if he'd been considerate, but she knew that wasn't the case. He hadn't been considerate at the Sketch launch, so why start now? She felt sick as she pictured them together, knowing how it would have played out. He'd have looked after Claire all night, just the way he used to with her. He'd have bought her drinks, danced with her and kissed her with wild abandon before taking her home. Supposing Effie *had* decided to go along? She'd have been confronted with the two of them, again. Just the idea of it made her stomach drop, especially when Claire knew far more about her than Effie was comfortable with, and what if Lou hadn't been right? What if Claire had told him what she'd heard at the Sketch launch?

'Whatever.' Effie pushed her chair out of the way and went to leave the office.

'You said you weren't coming,' he said again.

'It doesn't matter,' she replied, turning to look at him. 'They were my birthday drinks, Smith. What if I *had* turned up?'

'You mean, what if you'd decided to give up the fancy dinner you'd been flaunting in my face?' Smith snorted. 'It was hardly likely. And anyway, why should it bother you, now that you're living happily ever after?'

Effie fought the urge to retort. Why was she wasting her time with him? He'd already proved that he hadn't changed, that he didn't care about how it felt to see him fawning over someone else. She shook her head again and walked out of the door, letting it slam behind her. She ran down the stairs and threw open the door to the street, letting out a long, shaky breath. Parked up by the curb was Smith's pride and joy, his Royal Enfield Thunderbird. She looked at its curves and matt black chassis, picturing him sitting on it with Claire on the back, her hair blowing in the wind and her arms wrapped around his waist.

'Don't even think about it.'

She spun round at the sound of Smith's voice to see him standing there as the door closed behind him.

'Piss off, Smith.'

'I mean it. If you kick her, I'll never forgive you for it.'

'How old do you think I am? Twelve?'

But he was right. She'd been half a second away from kicking her foot out and sending his stupid bike halfway across the street.

'Why should it matter to you that I asked Claire to come? You weren't even there, and we both know that nothing in the world would have made you come over dinner with *him*.'

'It *doesn't* matter, and I don't want to talk about this anymore. I'm going home.'

She was about to turn and leave, but Smith skipped down the three stairs and stepped in front of her, blocking her path.

'You don't like her, do you?'

Effie sighed and briskly rubbed her forehead. 'I don't know her.' *And I don't want to know her.*

'That's not what I asked.'

'Well, that's irrelevant because that's what I've told you.'

People walked past, skirting them as they stood in the middle of the pavement in a stare-down. His grey eyes were fixed right onto hers, and with every second that came and went, her anger turned into something else, something she couldn't describe, even if she'd known every word in every language in the world. The muscles in Smith's jaw twitched over and over again until he finally caved and dragged a hand through his hair.

'Fuck. You can't do this, Effie.'

'Can't do what?'

'This!' Smith shouted before shaking his head and looking around them. He looked at her again and lowered his voice. 'You can't make me feel bad for having other friends.'

Right down in the depths of her belly, the anger returned. She didn't want to feel this mixture of feelings for him, and she didn't want to feel animosity towards a woman she didn't even know, who hadn't done anything wrong except be collateral damage in the Smith vs Effie saga.

'Friends? How do you think it felt for me to see you with her at the launch, minutes after coming on to me? And now you're trying to bring her into our group – worse, you invited her to my *birthday* drinks.'

'Everyone else happens to like her, and so would you if you gave her a chance. You weren't even there, so what's the problem?'

'You know, after you apologised in Ireland, I actually thought you'd changed, but then at the launch . . .' Effie shook her head and spat out a humourless laugh. 'You're just as fucked up and selfish as you always were, playing games and messing with my head.'

Her heart rammed in her chest. She sounded pathetic and ugly. The jealousy she'd tried to keep hidden was leaping from her mouth, and she couldn't do anything to control it.

'Are you having a laugh? Did you care how it felt for me when I had to look at you in a fucking wedding dress?'

Her face flushed red. She hadn't thought he even cared. He'd told her he didn't want her.

'It's not the same thing.' She shook her head, stuttering. It *wasn't* the same. Smith had broken her heart, not the other way around.

'No? You sure about that?'

She looked at him, his eyes blazing, his beautiful face set into an almighty scowl.

'See, here's the thing, Effie.' He took a step towards her and held her gaze with an invisible force that she couldn't break. 'You're the one who's married, not me.'

Her eyes pricked at his words, but she was damned if she was going to let him see her cry. Instead, she swallowed them away.

'*I'm* single. I can do what I want, see who I want and be friends with whoever I want. You don't get to tell me what to do or try to make me feel bad for doing it. If I want to see Claire, or any other woman, I will.'

Effie clenched her jaw and threw him a look of indifference. 'Good. You do that.'

She walked away as the tears spilled from her eyes, and narrowly dodged a man in a suit, pushing a stroller. She angrily wiped the tears away and headed towards the Tube station, refusing to look back.

15.

roken china crunched beneath Effie's shoes as she walked through Lou's front door. Two days after her showdown with Smith, Effie still hadn't heard from her, despite leaving several voicemails and text messages. An intervention was needed, and after five minutes of ringing Lou's door buzzer, she used the emergency spare key and let herself in.

Lou was ridiculously house-proud. Effie couldn't ever remember visiting and seeing anything out of place. This wasn't like her. The living room looked like it had been ransacked. Her cream sofa cushions were slashed open, the stuffing spilling out like fluffy innards. The wooden blinds at the windows were hanging haphazardly, and the pictures that had once hung on the walls were now scattered on the floor, with their frames smashed.

'Jesus.' Effie looked around the living room until she saw Lou, huddled on the floor between the radiator and the sofa.

Her eyes were puffed out and red, and her cheeks streaked with dried tears. As Effie rushed over to her broken friend, Lou let out a huge sob, and Effie had to resist the urge to cry herself.

After ten minutes, Lou sniffed. 'I'm such a fucking idiot.'

'Hey,' Effie said, rubbing her back, 'don't talk like that.' She wiped the tears from Lou's cheek. 'What happened?'

'I slept with someone else. I've broken his heart.' Lou started to cry again. 'I've fucked it all up.'

'It's okay,' Effie whispered, smoothing down her hair. 'It's going to be okay.'

She looked up at the big mirror above the mock fireplace with a crack right in the middle, spreading out like a spider's web. The wall next to it was splattered with a red stain, and going by the broken wine glass on the floor, Effie reckoned Lou had flung it in a rage.

She kissed the top of Lou's head. 'When was the last time you ate?'

'I'm not hungry.'

'You need to eat.' Effie's voice was tender but firm. In the few days they hadn't seen each other, she looked like she'd lost a stone in weight. 'You need a shower too. We'll talk after, okay?'

Lou nodded, and Effie took her to the bathroom, where she stood motionless as Effie switched on the shower, sending swirls of steam into the air. Lou barely even flinched as Effie undressed her and helped her into the shower cubicle. Lou was slim as it was, but now she had nothing on her, Effie could almost see her ribs, and her skin was grey and waxy. The wine fumes seeping from her made it obvious that she'd been on one hell of a bender. Effie left her in the shower and went into the kitchen.

'Christ, this is a mess.' Effie stood in the middle of the kitchen, surveying the scene.

It looked like someone had gone through every cupboard and swept the contents out onto the floor. It was littered with broken cups, plates, glasses and food. She picked her way over to the sink, opened the cupboard underneath it and pulled out a black bin bag. By the time Lou shuffled in, the dishwasher was whirring quietly, a bag had been filled with debris, the floor had been swept and an omelette and pot of tea had been made. Lou slid into a chair at the tiny table tucked into the corner and sighed as Effie handed her the omelette. They didn't speak as she ate, but colour slowly began to return to Lou's cheeks.

'Thanks,' Lou said, putting her fork on the plate and pushing it away once she'd finished.

She'd scrubbed herself clean and tied her hair back. Dressed in an oversized jumper and leggings, she looked more vulnerable than Effie had ever seen her before. Lou looked around the kitchen, and her eyes settled on the fridge door. Stuck to it was a picture of her and Mickey in fancy dress, grinning at the camera. She exhaled loudly and put her head in her hands.

'So,' Effie said softly. 'What happened?'

Lou shook her head but didn't look up. 'I've royally messed things up – that's what's happened.'

Effie reached across the table and stroked her arm until Lou looked up again.

'We had a huge fight on Friday night at Purl. I was drunk and I snapped. We'd been arguing all week anyway.'

'About what he said in Ireland?'

'More than that. The stuff he said in Ireland, what he said about how I should take our relationship as it is or leave it, the fact that he has no ambition at all.' Lou shook her head. 'The alcohol just made me lose control. I was nasty to him. And I mean really nasty.'

Effie didn't doubt it. Lou had a tongue that could spit words like acid when she put her mind to it.

'What did you say?'

'That he was a layabout waste of space who'd never amount to anything, and maybe I should go and find someone who would. I said that maybe I should go and find a real man.' Lou grimaced. 'And that's the polite version.'

'Ouch.' Effie winced. She knew Mickey. He was exactly like Smith, only without the tendency to cheat and lie. Lou taking a dig at his manhood would have stung.

'And what did he say?' Effie asked.

'That I was drunk and I needed to sober up, which only made me even angrier. I remember screaming at him that it was over in front of everyone. He told Smith to make sure I got home alright and left.'

Effie poured tea into their cups from the polka-dotted teapot. 'But you didn't go home?'

Lou shook her head. 'I went to meet up with some of the guys from work. There were leaving drinks in Soho that I'd turned down, but I thought, fuck it, why not? What did I have to go home to? Nothing. Except a guy who basically didn't want to be with me anymore. So, I went and got even more hammered with the work guys, and then it all went wrong.' She tipped her head back and looked up at the ceiling. 'It's not even like I can excuse it by saying I was drunk because I knew what I was doing. It was like I wanted to test myself to see if I could really do it to Mickey. I wanted to get back at him for hurting me. How fucked up is that?'

Effie didn't say anything as she heaped a teaspoon of sugar into Lou's cup.

'I went back to the guy's flat, and even though everything about it felt wrong – his hands, his mouth, his smell – I went ahead and did it anyway. I waited until he fell asleep, and then I left. It was just some random guy. I don't even remember his name.'

Lou leaned forward, put her elbows on the table and looked back at the photo on the fridge. Effie would never judge her, but what made it all worse was that it was so out of character. Lou had a very hard line when it came to infidelity and had dumped previous boyfriends for less than even talking to another woman. It seemed like only a minute ago that Lou was busy giving Effie a stern talking to after her near miss with Smith, yet here she was, having slept with another man.

'So how did Mickey find out?'

'I told him. I had to. It was five thirty in the morning, and I'd just stumbled in, reeking of alcohol and another man. He was still awake, probably to make sure I got home alright. I couldn't lie to him.' Lou swallowed. 'He cried. I'd never seen him cry before.'

Neither had Effie. Mickey was like Smith in that respect. They both thought of themselves as alpha males, and though they could show their sensitive sides, they didn't *do* crying.

'I'm a horrible person. I cheated on the man I love. I feel like the biggest slut on the planet.'

'You are *not* a slut,' Effie said as Lou started to cry again. 'You were upset and drunk, and you messed up, but you are not a slut. And the most important thing is that you know it felt wrong.'

'I do. It was.' Lou hiccupped. 'God, I've been so stupid.'

'Have you spoken to him?'

'He won't answer my calls or texts. When he came back for his stuff on Sunday, I tried to tell him that I don't care about marriage and kids. I don't care about him being happy to work for someone else his whole life instead of setting up on his own. I don't care about any of that stuff if it means losing him, but he wouldn't even look at me, let alone talk to me.'

'Did he wreck everything?' Effie asked, looking around the kitchen.

'No, that was me. After he left, I just fell apart.' Fresh tears ran down Lou's cheeks as her chin wobbled. 'What am I going to do, Eff? He hates me.'

'He doesn't hate you,' Effie said. 'He's just hurt and angry.'

'He won't ever take me back.'

'You don't know that. Couples work their way through things like this all the time. You're just going to have to give him some space to calm down and process everything, so he can decide what he wants to do next. He loves you – you know he does.'

'And I love him, but that didn't stop me.'

Lou laid her head on the table, and Effie smoothed down her hair. She didn't know what else to say, because Lou was right. She loved Mickey, but she'd slept with someone else anyway. And that was the problem. Love on its own wasn't enough.

∽

Even though it was barely ten when Effie got home, Oliver was already fast asleep. She stood in the doorway looking at him and felt a pang of guilt in her stomach. She'd been cheated on herself by Smith, but seeing Lou so distraught had rammed it home. She needed to let Smith go. She didn't want to lose her husband. He might not be perfect, but she didn't want to end up alone, like Lou. She carefully took the book he'd fallen asleep reading from his hand and put it on his bedside table. He looked so peaceful, with his long eyelashes resting on his cheekbones and his mouth pulled into a slight pout. Effie undressed and climbed into bed next to him, snuggling into him as much as she could.

'How was she?' Oliver mumbled sleepily.

'Bad.'

Effie closed her eyes as Oliver fell back asleep, and she tried to take her mind off Smith. She had to accept the facts. She was married, Smith was single and like he'd said, he could do whatever he wanted.

It was the first time he'd ever been clear with her. No ambiguity, no messing around. His words had stung and replayed in her head. Until tonight. Until she'd seen her best friend, heartbroken because she'd been unfaithful and lost the one thing in the world she'd always wanted to keep. Harsh as it sounded, seeing Lou reeling from what she'd done had given Effie the shock she needed.

She didn't want to end up the same way.

∽

A few days later, Effie shut the front door and dropped her keys into the bowl on the sideboard.

'That you, baby?' Oliver's voice carried down the hallway, and Effie followed it to the kitchen. 'You're on time.'

Effie smiled. 'I said I would be.'

'I know, but you've been going over to Lou's every day. I thought you'd change your mind.'

'And miss out on you cooking dinner?' Effie kissed his cheek. 'No way.'

When he'd called her earlier, Oliver had been so pleased that she'd be coming straight home from work, instead of detouring to Lou's, that he'd offered to cook. She hadn't really believed him, since more often than not, he was the one who came home late from work, but there he was, pulling at lettuce leaves and dropping them into a shallow bowl.

'You know, you never said what happened between those two.'

Effie hesitated for a second. She hadn't told him because she knew he wouldn't approve.

'Well,' she said. 'They grew apart, I suppose. Miscommunication, that kind of thing.'

'Miscommunication,' he echoed. 'That's not a reason to split up. It's pretty immature, if you ask me. It's the kind of thing you work through, not throw in the towel over.'

She held back the need to defend her friends. After all, he didn't know the real reason behind their break-up. Instead, she brushed the comment aside and looked over his shoulder.

'How long till dinner's ready?'

'Few minutes,' he replied and kissed her on the lips.

'Sounds good. Let me just get changed out of my work clothes.'

Upstairs, she fought the urge to yawn as she changed out of her clothes. Heartbreak was a heavy business, and Lou was cracking under the strain of it. Effie opened her drawer for a pair of socks and grimaced. She'd been the same when Smith had ended up in hospital, and she'd finally faced up to the truth about their relationship, or the lack of it. She'd walked around for ages feeling like her world had come to an end, especially when he'd told her he'd booked a flight to Cambodia. She'd barely had time to catch her breath before he'd hopped on a plane and flown out of her life.

She dug around her drawer, searching for her woolly socks. It didn't matter what time of year it was, when she needed comfort, she'd encase her feet in a pair of thick socks. Since Penny did the same, it was clearly a trait she'd inherited. She frowned at the thought of having inherited anything from her mum and closed the drawer, unable to find them. Oliver's would have to do.

Socks selected, she went to close the drawer until an envelope caught her eye. She recognised the logo; it was from the bank. Why would he be hiding post in his drawer? They had a box where that kind of stuff was kept – it made it easier for accounting, and Oliver was meticulous about paperwork being filed away properly.

Gingerly, she lifted out the letter, and her hands shook as she saw the card attached to it. She read the name embossed onto the shiny plastic: Mrs E. W. Barton-Cole.

'Dinner's ready,' Oliver shouted from downstairs.

It was her debit card, the one Oliver had told her hadn't turned up yet because of a mix-up with the bank.

'Coming,' she called back and sat on the bed, unease settling on her shoulders like a cloak. The date on the letter was over a week ago.

Nobody should ever have control over your finances but you.

Her mum had told her it wasn't right, but she hadn't wanted to believe it. He wouldn't deliberately withhold her money from her, would he? But why else would he lie about the card?

'Effie, what are you doing up there? Come on.'

She shook her head and slipped the card back, her hands still shaking. She closed the drawer and silently padded downstairs. Oliver had laid the table out with wine glasses and candles, but as she slipped into her chair, she couldn't take her eyes from his back, as if it could tell her why he'd decided to hide her card.

'For you,' he said, turning from the cooker with a plate in his hand.

Effie fixed a small smile onto her face as he put it in front of her, but she couldn't meet his eyes.

'And one for me.' He put his plate down and sat opposite. 'Bon appétit.'

She looked at the steak on his plate, pink and dripping on a bed of green leaves, before looking at her own. It matched his exactly. She picked up her fork and prodded it, her stomach rolling over as the juices oozed from the points where the prongs had cut into it.

'Izzy called earlier,' Oliver said as he sliced into his lump of steak. 'She was wondering if she's done something to upset you?'

Effie put her fork down, repulsed by the prospect of rare meat. He knew she couldn't eat undercooked food.

'Why would she think that?'

'You tell me. Did you not call her after your birthday?'

Effie swore quietly. Izzy had sent her a package of beauty products from the company she owned – a box full of creamy, honey-infused moisturiser, shampoo and conditioner enriched with Moroccan Argan oil, raw coconut body oil and more bath salts than she could shake a stick at. Effie had meant to call and say thank you, but then her mum had called, and she'd argued with Smith, not to mention the fallout from Lou and Mickey's split.

'I forgot,' Effie said quietly. 'I meant to, but –'

'But you were too busy spending time with your friends.'

She looked up at him as he chewed his food. 'I've been with my best friend, who's heartbroken. It's not like I've been out clubbing every night.'

'Well you haven't been here, and that's my point. She's split up with her boyfriend – so what? I don't see why you need to be over there all the time.'

Effie screwed her eyebrows together. 'It's called moral support.'

She sighed and pushed her plate away. It wasn't like she needed his permission to see her friends.

'The thing about moral support is that you have to spend too much of your energy giving it. Lou's nice enough, but she's so dramatic all the time, and it rubs off on you in a bad way. You've always been so grateful whenever I've cooked for you before, but now you're getting all argumentative.'

She shook her head. 'I'm not argumentative. I'm just not hungry.'

'Effie. I've spent ages on this.'

She looked down at the plate again. It was a salad and a steak that couldn't have touched the frying pan for more than two minutes at the most.

'I'm really not hungry.'

Oliver stayed quiet for a moment before putting his knife and fork down. Effie looked at the smooth skin on his hands, his long fingers and perfectly rounded fingernails. He tapped his index finger on the tablecloth as he fixed his stare onto her.

'Your card arrived today.'

She thought back to the letter she'd seen in his drawer and knew it had arrived a lot sooner than today.

'I'll get it for you after you've eaten.'

Effie blinked and looked at him. Was he trying to bribe her? She shook her head again. She wanted to get up from the table, but his stare was keeping her rooted to the chair like a tractor beam.

'You've hardly spent any time at home lately, and I've gone to the trouble of cooking you dinner. Do you know what it's been like to feel like you don't want to spend time with me? To always come second best to your friends? And now you're saying you don't want the dinner I've made.'

Effie shook her head, confused. He was laying on the guilt, making her feel as if she was rejecting him, but that wasn't the case at all. He leaned across the table and nudged her fork towards her.

'You know I don't like it rare.'

'And you know how many times I've told you it tastes better like that. I won't cook something subpar,' he replied. 'Eat it. Please.'

The *please* was perfectly placed to make it sound like a request, but his monotone voice told her it was anything but. She looked down at the steak again.

'Oh, I get it,' she said, making herself smile to try to hide her unease. 'This is you trying to make me a bit more refined, isn't it?'

She'd hoped that the corners of Oliver's mouth would lift into a smile, and he'd tell her he was simply joking, but instead a chill ran through her at the flash of anger behind his eyes. Effie looked down at the steak, glistening in its own juices amid a sea of lettuce. Maybe she'd only have to eat a mouthful. He couldn't force it down her throat, and he wouldn't, not when he knew how much she hated it.

She picked up the knife and fork. They were part of a set they'd received as a wedding gift, and despite using them countless times since, they now felt heavy in her hands as she sawed through the steak. She had to clamp her mouth shut to hold back the gag at the sight of pale, pink flesh on her plate.

She looked up at him again, expecting him to tell her he was just joking, that she didn't have to eat it, but instead he simply nodded. Her throat constricted as she put the chunk of steak in her mouth. As soon as it hit her tongue, her gag reflex almost made her spit it straight back out again. It was almost cold, and its smooth texture, mixed with the flavour of the meat, made her stomach churn. She closed her eyes as she chewed, trying not to think about what she was doing.

Effie swallowed, holding her breath to keep it down. When she opened her eyes, Oliver was staring back at her.

'Good girl. It wasn't so bad, was it?'

She grimaced and drained her glass of wine, swilling it around her mouth to rid it of the taste of steak. It wasn't bad. It was horrific.

'Go on,' he said. 'Finish up.'

He couldn't be serious? She'd managed a mouthful, but she couldn't do any more than that. She shook her head.

'I'm done, Olly. I can't eat it.'

Why was he pressing this? He'd promised her a nice, romantic dinner, but his expression stayed the same. She didn't want to argue. She was tired. All she wanted to do was throw the steak in the bin and go to bed, but Oliver crossed his arms and leaned back in his chair.

She could just get up and leave the table. He wasn't forcing her. He was trying to persuade her. Surely that was different? He'd always insisted that rare was the best way to eat steak, just as he'd insisted that having her hair straightened looked much better than her wild curls. He thought the style suited her more and made her look more sophisticated. He'd grown up around elegance, money, good food. He knew what he was talking about. But she didn't want to eat another mouthful.

Oliver poured himself another glass of wine and rearranged himself on the chair, as if he were settling down for a long wait, and tears pricked at Effie's eyes as she picked up her fork.

Less than five minutes later, she was heaving over the toilet bowl. When she'd finished, she slumped against the side of the bath and wiped the slick of sweat from her upper lip. She'd managed another two mouthfuls under Oliver's watchful stare, with tears streaming down her face. She'd felt like a child being told she couldn't leave the table until her plate was clean, until she'd had no choice but to get up and run to the bathroom.

She looked up as Oliver came into the bathroom and sat on the edge of the bath, holding her debit card in his hand. She looked at it, knowing that he'd withheld it on purpose, like a punishment for spending too much time at Lou's and not enough at home, just like he'd punished her for changing her mind about trying for a baby by standing her up on Valentine's Day. She'd always thought the romance and charm he'd shown her were unwavering, but it was starting to look like it was all on his terms.

Had she really been so wrong to spend time with Lou? It was instinctive to be there for her best friend, but Oliver had made it seem as if she was being overdramatic. Had she really made him feel so rejected that he'd had to resort to this?

She looked at him holding the bank card. Maybe she *hadn't* been considerate of him over the last few days. Maybe he really did feel rejected by her absence. It wasn't an excuse, but she had to believe there was something to make him do what he'd done, something she could fix to make him go back to the Oliver she married – the Oliver who was kind, considerate and loving. Gingerly, she took the card from him.

'Why don't you get yourself cleaned up, and we'll watch a film. You need to learn to try new things, Effie. I just want you to be the best you can be.'

Effie closed her eyes and tried not to shrink away from him as he leaned down to kiss the top of her head.

16.

Effie looked at the bags piled in the corner of Smith's tiny living room, and a pang of sadness hit her chest. Eighteen months of a relationship and a life together, condensed into three sports bags. If Lou had looked heartbroken, she had nothing on Mickey.

Effie sat on the sofa and looked at him. Like Lou, he looked dishevelled and utterly broken. She'd already popped round to Lou's after work and decided to make the small detour on the way home to look in on Mickey. Instead of the hysterics she'd seen at Lou's half an hour earlier, Mickey gave off an air of detachment, and with the hood of his jumper pulled low over his face, it didn't seem like he was ready to give it up any time soon.

'How is she?' Mickey asked.

Effie grimaced and put her bag on the floor – a surprisingly clean floor, she noticed – and shrugged. It looked like they were getting straight down to the nitty-gritty.

'Honestly? She's been better.'

'I take it you know what happened?'

She nodded but didn't say anything. What *could* she say? They both sat in silence, watching Smith make tea in the kitchen on the other side of the room. He must have only just got home because he was still wearing his football kit with his socks pulled down, exposing his muddy calves.

Smith's flat wasn't what she'd expected. She'd only ever seen his room at his parents' house and it had been cluttered with stuff: DJ decks, stacks of vinyl records and CDs, a spare wheel for his pushbike, a spare helmet for his motorbike and clothes bundled into corners. She'd expected his flat to be the same, but she was surprised when she'd walked in and found it tidy and clean. She looked up and saw him staring back at her, but she quickly looked away. She hadn't come here for him, and she didn't have time to get distracted. She'd taken to working through lunch so she could leave an hour early and quickly check in on Lou, so she wouldn't get home late. The only reason she had time to pop in and see Mickey at all was because she knew Oliver would be working late.

'And how are *you* doing?' she asked. 'I'm worried about you.'

Mickey shrugged. 'Don't be. I'm fine.'

From the corner of her vision, she saw Smith shake his head as he deposited a teabag into the bin.

'You don't look it,' Effie replied.

'My girlfriend just cheated on me. Excuse me if I don't go star jumping around the room.'

His tone was bitter, but she could hardly blame him. She nodded. 'I know. I'm sorry.'

'Look,' – Mickey sighed – 'if you're here to try and talk me into taking her back, you're wasting your time. We're over.'

'No, I'm not. Like I said, I'm here to see you. I know she's one of my best friends, but so are you.' She looked up as Smith walked over with the cups, and took one from him. 'Has she contacted you?'

'Every day.' His voice broke, and he cleared his throat before taking a sip of his tea. 'Whatever. It doesn't matter.'

Smith sat on the armchair, propped his feet up and flicked through the TV channels with the remote. Now he was back in the room, she could smell him – the mixture of sweat and grass. His hair was still damp from the rain outside. By rights, it should have smelled horrific, but it didn't. It was intoxicating. Couldn't he go take a shower or something?

She squeezed her fingers around the hot cup and looked at Mickey. 'Have you actually spoken to her?'

He shook his head and took his phone from his pocket to show her his screen. Today alone, he had twenty-two missed calls, all from Lou. 'I don't know what I'm supposed to say. You know the saying that if you have nothing nice to say, then you shouldn't say anything at all? Well, I don't think she wants to hear the words I've got to say to her.'

'It'll pass, mate,' Smith said. 'A broken heart stinks, but you'll come out of it.'

He'd looked at Mickey as he said it, but Effie could tell he'd directed it at her, which was ridiculous considering she'd never broken his heart. She'd wounded his pride, but his heart had remained intact, unlike hers.

'I know it doesn't excuse it, but she was hurt about what you'd said in Ireland. She thought you didn't want to commit,' Effie said.

Mickey sighed. 'I'm twenty-five years old, why would I be thinking about marriage? You don't have to get married to commit to someone. I was with her for a year and a half – surely that was enough?'

'I know.' Effie frowned. 'I think she just wanted more. She was convinced you didn't want a future with her anymore.'

'So she went and ruined any notion of us having one – makes perfect sense.' He put his cup down on the floor. 'Of course we had a future, but there's no way I could've stayed with her after she told me.'

'She messed up, I know. And she knows it too.'

'Yeah, she has. And I don't think I'll ever be able to look at her the same way again. Once you've cheated on someone, there's no going back.'

This time, it was Smith's turn to look embarrassed as Mickey stood and excused himself to go to the bathroom. When did being unfaithful become so common anyway? Smith had cheated on her, Lou had cheated on Mickey, and Effie had come within a whisper of doing the same to Oliver. An awkward silence settled in the living room, punctuated only by the television. It simply wasn't worth it in the end.

She sighed, thumbing the handle of her mug, and looked at Smith. 'How is he really?'

'How do you think? She's completely blindsided him.'

Effie nodded. 'I know. It was the last thing anyone expected.'

'Least of all him. And all because of a stupid misunderstanding.'

'Do you think he means what he said? About there being no going back?'

Smith shrugged. 'I dunno. Nothing's ever black and white, is it? Couples get through that stuff all the time.'

'Yeah, I suppose.' Effie swallowed a gulp of her sweet tea.

'But then again, some don't. And you have to live with the fact that you fucked up the best thing to ever happen to you.'

She slowly took the cup away from her mouth and looked at him, slouched in the armchair with his long legs stretched out as his feet rested on a leather footstool. Why did life have to be so complicated? It didn't seem so long ago that their group was a happy one, but now it was falling apart at the seams.

'Must be hard. Having to live with that,' she said.

He turned the remote over in his hand. 'I'd like to say you have no idea, but we both know that's not true.'

'How's Claire?' She sniffed. 'Still being mile high?'

Smith rolled his eyes and looked back at the TV. 'Let's not go there, yeah?'

'Fine.'

Her cheeks burned as she waited for Mickey to come back from the toilet. She'd say her goodbyes and get out of there. How dare Smith make her feel like that, like she'd overstepped the mark, simply for asking how his girlfriend was? She tried to ignore the way that acknowledging Claire as his girlfriend had almost choked her. When Mickey came back into the living room, she stood up and pulled him into the hallway, brushing straight past Smith and trying her best not to breathe in his sweaty, grassy scent.

'I can't stay here much longer. I'm sorry.' She looked at Mickey and pushed his hood down. His rust-brown hair was scruffy and clearly hadn't seen fingers, let alone a brush for days. His normally bright blue eyes were dull and red-rimmed. She was willing to bet he'd just shed a few tears in the bathroom. 'I just had to see that you were okay.'

He shrugged. 'I'll survive. It fucking hurts, but I'll survive.'

'I know you don't want to hear it, but she does love you. She knows what she did was wrong and she's sorry.'

His Adam's apple bobbed as he clenched his jaw. 'I know she is, but I meant what I said. You can't go back when something like that's happened. Look at you two.' He nodded towards the living room. 'It fucks everything up.'

She wished she could say that it didn't, that Mickey and Lou could put it behind them, but she couldn't lie. The truth was, it did ruin everything, regardless of how great the relationship was beforehand.

'I know you'll tell her what I've said.' He put his hands on her shoulders as she began to protest. 'It's fine. She's your best friend. It'd be weird if you didn't.'

Effie pulled him into a hug and squeezed him as hard as she could. 'I won't say anything if you don't want me to.'

'I still love her, Eff,' he whispered in her ear. 'I don't know how to not love her.'

Just hearing his voice, so small and lost, just as Lou's was, formed a lump in her throat.

'I know.'

She squeezed him again, trying to give him as much love and warmth as possible. It looked like it really was the end of Mickey and Lou, the couple everyone said was the perfect match.

She let him go, pulled his hood back up and left the flat.

❧

'Have you spoken to Lou lately? You haven't been round there for a while.'

Effie looked over at Oliver as he kept his eyes focused on the television. As far as he knew, she hadn't been back to Lou's since the night he'd practically forced Effie to eat that rare steak. Things hadn't been the same between them since, and Effie felt that soon, she wouldn't be able to hide the tension she felt towards him. To make things worse, there was nobody she could speak to about it. She could hardly tell her friends that he'd forced her to eat until she'd thrown up, and even if she could, they all had their own problems. Her usual go-to was Lou, and she was still in the midst of heartbreak.

'I spoke to her earlier. She's still in a mess. I'd really like to see her this weekend.'

Even though he'd said he'd felt rejected, she didn't even feel remotely bad for lying to him, not when it came to being there for Lou.

'Why?' he asked, flicking through the channels on the TV. 'It's not like the world's ended. They've split up. Maybe you shouldn't be getting so involved.'

'They're my best friends.'

'People break up all the time. She was too headstrong for him anyway.'

Effie looked away, keeping her thoughts to herself. Lou was headstrong, but Mickey could match it. And it wasn't for Oliver to cast judgement.

'It's late,' she said. 'I should go to bed.'

She left him on the sofa to go upstairs, and after her shower, she stood in front of the basin. Effie wiped the steam from the mirror, peering into the blurry reflection in front of her. She looked exhausted. The skin under her eyes was thin and dark. Maybe Oliver was right. Maybe involving herself in Mickey and Lou's problems wasn't good for her. And tonight, having seen Mickey like that . . . it had pulled at her heartstrings. She padded back to the bedroom with the towel wrapped tightly around her. She so badly wished she could fix things, even though she knew there was nothing she could do.

'I thought you said you hadn't seen Lou?'

Her eyes flicked to Oliver's face as he stood in the middle of the bedroom, and her heart leapt to her throat. 'I haven't.'

'So why do you have a text from her saying thanks for going round?'

She shook her head and frowned until she looked down and saw her phone in his hand. 'What are you doing with my phone?'

'You lied to me.'

Effie looked around the room, trying to put together a response. Yes, she'd lied, but he couldn't really expect her to just dump her best friend.

'Shall we see what else you've been hiding?'

He looked down at the screen, and Effie swallowed, trying to remember the texts she had stored. She knew she didn't have any from Smith, but she had some from Lou, and since she hadn't told

Oliver the real reason why Lou and Mickey had split, panic started to set in.

'Olly, don't.'

She took a step forward, but he held his hand up to stop her and looked at the screen. 'Let's see: *Why did I do it? He'll never forgive me.*'

A shiver ran through her as she realised he was reading through her text conversation with Lou.

'Never forgive what?' He looked up at her, but Effie stayed silent. There was nothing she could say because she knew what was coming next. His face darkened as he read the rest of her messages. *'Let's face it, I've never forgiven cheaters, so why should he?'*

Effie pulled at her fingers. 'Olly . . .'

'Don't be so hard on yourself. These things happen. He knows you love him.' He looked back up at her with disgust etched onto his face. 'Wow. Nice advice, Effie.'

She flinched. It was one she'd sent when Lou had been in the grip of self-loathing.

'It's not what it sounds like,' she replied, thumbing the edge of her towel.

Oliver looked straight back at her and raised his eyebrows. 'Really? So Lou didn't cheat on Mickey and you didn't say, "These things happen"?'

'No. Well, yes. I mean . . .'

'No? Yes? It can't be both, so which one is it?'

She took a deep breath. 'Yes, Lou cheated, and yes, I said that, but I wasn't condoning it. I was just trying to make her feel better.'

'So the story about them growing apart was a lie?'

Effie looked down at the floor and didn't look up at him as he walked towards her. She looked at his feet, inches away from hers and shook her head. He was making it sound so black and white, but it wasn't. She didn't have anything to hide – she just hadn't wanted him to judge her best friend, and he'd read the texts out of context. He hadn't seen the state Lou was in at the time.

'You lied to me about seeing Lou, and you lied about why they'd split up. Am I right, or am I wrong?'

Effie's shoulders slumped. 'Yes, you're right.'

'What am I supposed to do with this?'

'I don't know. Nothing?' She daren't look up at him. His voice was calm, but she knew by the sharpness of his tone that he was angry, and she couldn't blame him. Regardless of her intentions, she'd lied, and she'd made a promise not to keep any more secrets from him. 'I didn't know how to tell you the truth.'

'I'm not surprised, since your best friend's a whore who goes around fucking guys behind her boyfriend's back.'

Effie's hand struck his face so quickly that it wasn't until she saw the look in his eyes that she really realised what she'd done.

She took a step back as her eyes darted across his face. 'I'm sorry.'

His cheek was bright red, and she looked down at her tingling hand. She'd never hit anyone in her life. She'd never even hit Smith when she'd found out about his cheating, and she'd burned with fury then.

Oliver's face scrunched up, and she knew then that this was bad. Instinctively, she went to take another step back, but before her heel even touched the floor, the knuckles of his fist connected with her right eye socket. The surprise and force of the blow sent her flying backwards until she fell on the floor by the bedroom door. Her hand flew to her eye as she blinked furiously, trying to clear the blurriness away as intense pain racked through her skull. Seeing Oliver walking towards her, she scrambled backwards, shuffling along the hallway floor, feeling the carpet rubbing against her bare legs until her back was pressed against the wall by the stairs.

'Olly, don't.'

In slow motion, she saw herself put out a hand to stop him, but as his leg swung back, she tried to curl herself into a ball instead, bracing herself as she closed her eyes. The air rushed out of her in one breath as his foot connected with her stomach, sending shots of pain right across her belly.

'Please,' she spluttered before stopping herself. He'd winded her. She couldn't speak, much less breathe.

Again, his foot drove into her stomach almost in the same place as before, and this time, she couldn't cry out. Forcing her eyes open, she glanced up to see him, one hand holding the banister of the stairs and the other on the wall, with his face red and a vein she'd never seen before bulging in the middle of his forehead.

'You fucking, filthy, lying bitch . . .'

Kick.

' . . . covering for that cheating whore.'

Kick.

She gagged as tears fell over the bridge of her nose, burning her skin, and she clenched her stomach muscles, trying to minimise the impact on her insides. It felt like they were being smashed to pieces as he kicked her again. He grabbed a bunch of her hair and twisted her head, forcing her to look up at him before he spat right in her face. Effie's eyes closed as the warm fluid hit her cheekbone.

'You stay away from her. Do you hear me? From now on, you'll have nothing more to do with her.'

He shoved her head back to the floor and kicked her one last time.

'Clean yourself up. You're fucking disgusting.' Oliver prodded her with his foot before stomping down the stairs and leaving her in a crumpled heap.

Effie stayed perfectly still as the warm trickle of his spit ran down the side of her face. She daren't even breathe. She wasn't sure she'd be able to cope with the pain, but when her lungs started to ache, she had no choice.

Breathe.

She tried to get the air she desperately needed as her body trembled with shock. Her heart rammed in her chest, and her lungs tightened.

Breathe!

With the pressure in her lungs increasing, reflex kicked in and she gulped down a mouthful of air, expelling it almost straight away. Her stomach heaved and contracted as she pushed her face into the soft carpet of the floor, gagging. Each breath created spasms of pain in her belly and chest, intensifying the throbbing in the side of her head, but as she filled her lungs, the light from the ceiling beamed down on her, and slowly noises began to filter through to her ears. A car driving past. A pair of heels clacking on the pavement outside. Oliver, swearing and knocking things around downstairs in a fit of rage.

As the wheezing calmed, she lay there until her skin rippled with goosebumps and her teeth began to chatter. She curled up even further into a little ball, and her cold legs moved over a damp patch. Slowly, she sat up, using one hand to anchor herself, and looked down at the carpet. She pressed a hand into the floor and shakily brought it back up to her face, staring at it. She'd wet herself. She'd been so terrified of her husband, she'd literally lost control of her most basic functions.

'You're fucking disgusting.'

She wiped the spit from her face and hobbled to the bedroom, holding onto the wall for support and clutching at her belly, almost doubled over with pain. She looked at her phone in the middle of the floor with its cracked screen and cried.

17.

Effie blinked. How long had she been standing there by the window? When had it rained? Outside, the road was slick, its tarmac shining, and puddles speckled the pavement. She looked down at her arms, covered in goosebumps, and tentatively slipped a hand inside her towel. Her stomach flinched when she touched the tender skin on the area where Oliver had kicked her, and she sucked in a breath. Clenching her eyes shut, she swallowed, trying to block out what had happened. She didn't want to relive the impact of Oliver's foot driving into her stomach or his spit hitting her face. Her head throbbed, and the skin under her eye stung. She didn't dare touch it, but she knew it was swelling. She'd have a black eye in the morning. How was she supposed to go to work with a massive bruise on her face?

She slowly opened her eyes and looked outside again as a curtain in the upstairs window of the house opposite twitched. Was someone looking at her? Could they tell that she was standing there like a broken china doll? Had they seen what had happened?

He'd gone through her phone. He'd told her to stay away from Lou – her best friend. How was she supposed to do that? And why should she? She needed her now more than ever. She couldn't just forget Lou existed. She didn't want to. She wouldn't.

'You're fucking disgusting.'

Effie grimaced as his words echoed around in her head, galvanising her. She knew she needed to shower, but there was no time. She dressed as quickly as she could, taking shallow breaths to control the pain, all the while acutely aware that Oliver was still in the house. The sound of his footsteps on the wooden floor echoed through the silent house, and she could picture him pacing the living room. It would only be a matter of time before he came back upstairs to finish what he'd started.

Dressed in jeans and a jumper, she grabbed a small bag from the bottom of her wardrobe and filled it up, not even looking at what she was packing. It didn't matter. All that mattered was that she leave, but with her bag packed, she sat on the bed and quietly cried, holding on to her side. What was she supposed to do? Where was she supposed to go? Anyone who looked at her face would know what had happened, without a doubt. She wouldn't be able to hide away from the pity in their eyes. It was embarrassing.

She looked down at her cracked phone. Even with her best friends, she'd have to live with the shame of being the girl whose husband beat her, the one who'd messed up after thinking she had everything she'd ever wanted.

A sob exploded from deep inside, sending a shock wave of pain across her chest as she realised that there was only one person she wanted to see, and she was miles away in Ibiza. At this time of night she'd probably be curled up with a cup of camomile tea, reading a book. Despite their offbeat relationship, Penny would know what to do. She'd been in the same position once before.

Darryl, one of her many boyfriends, had a distinctly mean streak. Effie clearly remembered hearing the shouts, the furniture being toppled over in the next room, the way he'd pinch her mum's arms whenever she'd snap back at him in public. That had been Penny's one and only attempt at normality, living a standard life at Effie's request. At eleven years old, all she'd wanted was to be like everyone else – to have a mum who had a normal job, who wore normal clothes and had a normal boyfriend, like Darryl. After eight months of abuse, of trying and failing to shield Effie from what was going on, Penny had vowed never to do it again. She'd said that if living with Darryl was normal, she'd rather live her life as abnormally as she could. Effie sniffed. She couldn't go to her mum. Penny would be too disappointed that Effie hadn't learned from her own mistakes.

Scanning the bedroom, her gaze swept over the pictures on the walls until she stopped to look at the small frame holding the receipt from the bar where she'd met Oliver. His battery had died, and she'd written her number on the back of it. He'd said the old-school gesture was romantic and she'd agreed, especially when she found out that he'd kept it, even after he'd stored her number in his phone. It was things like that that made a home, or so she'd thought. She'd always wanted a house full of keepsakes, a kitchen table that was always laden with books and papers, a hallway littered with wellies and shoes. She'd wanted a house that felt lived in and warm but the beautiful, smart, respectable home she now found herself in felt positively arctic.

She looked at the bag again and scowled, her sadness slowly being overtaken by fury. Why was *she* packing? Why should *she* be the one to leave? She tipped the bag upside down and replaced her things with Oliver's, randomly pulling things from drawers and the wardrobe. She hesitated when she touched the sweater she'd bought him at Christmas, remembering how perfect that morning had been. It felt like a million years ago as she sat on the bed again, shivering. He'd scared her so much she'd wet herself. Shame crept its way down her back. It wasn't a good place to be in, no matter which way she looked at it.

Her head jerked up as Oliver's footsteps bounded up the stairs, and she stood up, holding the bag as the door swung open. Terror held her in its grip so strongly that she couldn't even breathe, but Oliver said nothing until he looked down and saw the bag in her hand. His eyes flicked from the bag to the heap of clothes on the bed. When he looked back at Effie and the grim set of her mouth, he inhaled sharply and his face crumpled.

'You're leaving?'

Effie didn't say anything. There was nothing she *could* say.

'You can't.' His voice was thick with suppressed tears as he shook his head. 'You can't leave, not like this. You know I didn't mean it.' He stepped towards her, but she backed into the wall.

'You said the same thing the morning after Valentine's Day.'

She thought back to how he'd slapped her and how he'd apologised, saying it was reflex. Not meaning to do something implied what happened was an accident, and while he'd managed to convince her that it was after Valentine's Day, there was no way that what he'd just done could have been anything other than intentional.

'That was different,' he replied. His voice was soft and coaxing, but it made Effie's skin crawl. 'I just—'

'Don't come anywhere near me.' She backed into the wall as he stepped towards her. 'Take one more step and I swear to god, I'll scream.'

He stopped in the middle of the room. The beam of a car's headlights sped past, creating a wave of shadows on the wall as he rubbed the heels of his hands into his eyes.

'I'm not going to hurt you – you know that. You're my world. I can't lose you.'

She tightened her grip on the bag. 'You already have.'

'Effie.' His voice cracked. 'You can't.'

His eyes, so dark and menacing just a while ago, looked back at her with pathetic sadness.

'Give me one good reason why I should stay.' She winced at the pain in her stomach.

'Because I love you. I know I've got problems, but I'll fix them, I promise. I was angry that you'd lied, and work's been getting on top of me. You know I'm not a violent man, Effie.'

She pointed towards her eye. 'So did I do this to myself?'

'You *made* me do that. *You* hit *me*. You slapped me, remember?'

Yes, she remembered, but *that* had been reflex. Punching her in the face and kicking her senseless wasn't, and she shook her head at him, disgusted that he was trying to turn it around.

'Don't you dare blame me. I hit you, but you didn't have to hit me back. You didn't have to kick me like a ragdoll and spit in my face.' Oliver flinched as she hurled her words at him.

'I know I went too far. I don't even know what happened.' His shoulders drooped.

'You went through my phone. You had no right.'

'She texted while you were in the shower. I did call you, but you must not have heard me. It's not like I intentionally went through your messages. I've never done that – I trust you. I love you, you know I do.'

She looked him in the eye. 'So you keep saying. But the thing is, I don't want love like this.'

Oliver sniffed as tears rolled down his cheeks. She'd never seen him like this before, so contrite. He looked like he'd shrunk to a tenth of his size as he stood in the middle of the room.

'Please don't say that. I'll do whatever you want. I'll take anger management classes, whatever it takes. Just please, don't leave me.'

Her head flooded with the memory of him holding her hair and spitting in her face, the way he'd prodded her with his foot.

'You're fucking disgusting.'

Her stomach turned as she tried to stop her chin from wobbling, trying not to cry or show him any signs of weakness.

'Baby,' – he dropped to his knees and looked at her – 'please. I don't know what I'd do without you. Please, don't go.'

'I'm not.'

For a second, Oliver's eyes brightened, and he reached out a hand towards her, but the look in his eyes gave way to confusion as she rolled her shoulders back, ignoring the pain and threw the bag at him.

'You are.'

18.

Effie winced as she dabbed a cotton wool ball doused with antiseptic lotion on the cut under her eye. It stung like hell, but it was nothing compared to the pain she was feeling inside.

He'd gone. He hadn't even put up a fight when she'd thrown the bag at him. It was like he'd admitted defeat as he slowly picked it up and walked downstairs without saying a word before leaving the house. There was nothing he could have said anyway. He must have known after seeing her face that there were no words that could ever make what he'd done okay.

The skin under her eye socket was swollen and split, streaked with dark, dry blood. A deep red bruise had already spread, covering her eye completely. She didn't need to look under her jumper. She knew her side and abdomen were covered in red blotches, like a rash.

Effie threw the cotton ball into the bin. The look on Oliver's face when he'd come into the bedroom . . . For a second, it had flickered with shame and disgust. At least, she hoped that's what it was. Despite everything he'd done, she didn't want to believe she'd really married a monster, incapable of true remorse. The truth was, she hadn't expected it to be so easy to tell him to leave and really mean it. What did that say about their marriage, about her? Was any of it even real? Had she ever really loved him if it had been so easy to tell him to go? And what if he'd really meant what he'd said, about him changing? What if what happened was just a blip, and he really was still the nice, dependable Oliver she'd married? Her head was filled with so many doubts, but all she felt now was numb.

⚬

For the third night in a row, she lay in bed, staring at the ceiling and running through every memory of her relationship with Oliver, trying to pin down where it had all gone wrong. And for the third morning in a row, she watched the sun rise over the rooftops through her window, having reached no conclusion.

Her phone vibrated on the bed next to her. Another voice-mail. She'd diverted all calls, and if the rate of alerts was anything to go by, her mailbox was probably full. She didn't care. She didn't want to speak to anyone. Instead, she listened to her street waking up. She listened to the postman opening and closing front gates until she heard her own letterbox clang, followed by the thud of envelopes hitting the floor. As the hours passed and the sun rose higher, front doors opened and closed as people left for work, and the chatter of children on their way to school floated through the air.

Her mobile vibrated again, and she sighed, sitting up. Maybe it was work. She'd told them she was ill and wouldn't be in for the rest of the week, but it wasn't unheard of for them to call on a day off. She held her breath as she took the divert off, bracing herself for the barrage of missed call alerts from Oliver. As the notifications popped up on her screen, she frowned. Missed calls from Lou, a couple from Mickey, two from the office and fifteen from Izzy, but not one call or text from Oliver. She was about to dial through to her voicemail when it rang, with Izzy's name blinking on her screen.

Effie diverted it before switching her phone off and burying herself back under the covers.

§

Two days later, Effie jolted awake and sat up in bed. She wiped the sweat from her chest and strained her ears, listening for the noise that had woken her from an already restless sleep. She'd never noticed before just how big the house was. It seemed like every room had doubled in size, and noises she'd never heard before filled the house at night. The boiler ticked over loudly, and the wind whistled through the sash windows. She'd taken to closing all of the doors in the house so they wouldn't creak. For peace of mind, she'd had the locks changed on the same day Oliver had left, but even still, being alone was testing her to the limits. After a few minutes of silence, she slowly lay back down.

Stop being ridiculous.

She'd lived on her own for years; it wasn't as if she was scared of living by herself. Effie turned on her side and took a deep breath. She was being paranoid, that was all. The numbers on the digital clock on the bedside table flicked over, and she closed her eyes. She had to shift the dull throb that had lodged itself in the back of her head since the night Oliver had left. She had to sleep, but the sound of rustling outside made her eyes snap wide open.

It's probably a fox. Go to sleep.

But when she heard the noise again, her paranoia became something else. There was someone in the garden, she was sure of it. She sat bolt upright and grabbed her phone from the bedside table. What if it was a burglar? All of the windows and doors were locked, and the alarm was enabled. A burglar wouldn't be able to get in without making a real disturbance, but her skin bloomed with fear as she sat perfectly still.

Calm down. It's nothing. You're overtired, and your mind is playing tricks on you.

If she didn't hear anything else in the next two minutes, she'd pull herself together and try to sleep.

A minute passed. Then two. Slowly, she began to relax and lay back in bed, her heartbeat slowing to a steadier pace. Even if it had been a would-be burglar, he'd have given up and moved on to the next house after seeing no way in. She closed her eyes, took a deep breath and loudly exhaled. There was nothing to be scared of – except for the unexpected vibration of her phone. Her stomach jumped as it buzzed next to her, and she almost let out a nervous laugh. She was turning into a jumbled bag of nerves.

'Seriously, you need to chill the hell out.' She heaved a sigh as she spoke quietly to herself in the dark room and slid a thumb across the screen.

She read the message, and tears pricked her eyes. She turned her phone off and put it in the drawer, but she could still see the message as clearly as if her mind had photographed it.

I miss you. I need you. I love you.

She was sure all three statements were true, and a flash of confusion and anger hit her. Why had he messaged her? Did he really think a nine-word text message was going to do anything to repair what had happened? And why had she felt a glimmer of happiness when she'd seen his name? This was the man who'd made her wet herself through fear. The only thing she should feel thinking about him was hate.

Effie huffed and turned onto her back. She'd meant what she'd said to him. She didn't need his kind of love.

189

19.

'These are some impressive flowers. They were left by the door.' Lou handed Effie a bunch of deep red roses and raised an eyebrow. 'Do you have any idea how worried I've been?'

Effie looked down into the flowers and sighed. 'I know. I'm sorry.'

As Lou stepped past her into the house, Effie took a deep breath. Since Oliver had gone, she'd avoided everyone, and it was only when Lou banged on her front door with relentless vigour that Effie took the first tentative steps to re-entering the world. She looked at the flowers again and put them on the sideboard without reading the card. With their luscious, thick blood-red petals and expensive cellophane and paper wrapping, she knew they were from Oliver, and he had nothing to say that she wanted to hear. She took a quick look in the mirror. Thanks to the Internet, she'd found a plethora of makeup tips to cover bruises, and she'd been experimenting, since she'd have to return to work soon. Still, she took her hair from the ponytail it was in to let it fall over her face.

'How are you?' Effie asked. Lou was looking much better than she had the last time Effie had seen her.

'I'm fine. Nothing's really changed, apart from you dropping off the face of the earth. What's going on?'

'Tea? The kettle's just boiled, and it's a long story.'

Lou nodded and followed Effie into the kitchen. It *was* a long story, and she needed to come up with a cover quickly.

'I'm sorry I disappeared.' Effie looked down as she dropped teabags into two mugs.

'What's up with you? Have you been sick? You don't look so good.'

Effie slowly pressed a teaspoon against one of the teabags. 'I've been better.'

'Where's Olly?'

Effie sighed, knowing there was no way to dress it up. 'He's moved out.'

Lou's jaw dropped. 'No way. When?'

Effie slid a cup towards her. 'Last week.'

'Why? I mean, what happened?'

All Effie could do was shrug. Despite being alone with her thoughts for over a week, she still hadn't come up with an acceptable cover story as to why she was now living alone. *My husband beat me up* was a sentence she never wanted to utter aloud.

'The flowers are from him?' Lou asked, and Effie nodded as she picked up her cup. 'Has something happened with Smith?'

Smith. The sweet smell of sweat and grass filled Effie's nose, and a pang hit her in the solar plexus so hard, her thumb slipped in the handle of her cup.

'Shit,' Effie swore as half the cup of tea spilled down her top, scalding her skin.

She handed her cup to Lou and whipped off her vest. As Lou gasped, Effie stood frozen on the spot.

Shit.

How could she have been so stupid? She didn't look up at her best friend. She daren't. She didn't want to see the look of horror and pity that would no doubt be plastered all over her face.

'Effie,' Lou whispered and put her cup down. 'What the hell?'

She flinched as Lou reached out and touched her skin. She'd grown so used to seeing it over the past few days that, perversely, she'd almost forgotten it was even there. Effie closed her eyes, wishing she could rewind just a few seconds. Lou's seeing the bruise would change everything. It would make it all real. Until now, Effie had been able to at least try to push what had happened from her mind, almost as if it hadn't happened at all and that she'd told Oliver to leave because of something else.

'What happened?'

The entire right side of her abdomen was covered in big yellow and brown bruises. It wasn't anywhere near as tender as it had been, but that was little consolation.

'Did Olly do this to you?' Lou's voice was thick under the strain of tears.

Effie stayed quiet. Why had she taken her bloody vest off? Now what was she going to do?

'Effie? Did he do this to you?'

If she didn't speak now, Lou would know for sure, and everything would be ruined. Lou would make her go to the police and she'd have to sit in a room, telling people all the ins and outs of her life.

'I'll fucking kill him.'

'No.' The sudden intensity in Lou's voice made Effie snap her head up. 'Don't.'

'I'll wring his fucking neck.'

Lou slammed down her cup, and Effie squeezed the vest in her hands. 'Lou, stop. It really wasn't his fault. Honestly.'

Why was she protecting him? Lou was her best friend. They didn't have secrets. Effie looked at her. Lou's face was set with horror, concern and an anger Effie had never seen before.

'So what happened then? And don't tell me you walked into a door.'

'Can I change my top? Then we'll talk.'

Lou looked back at her for a few seconds before sighing loudly as she nodded, and Effie ran up the stairs. As she pulled a fresh T-shirt from the drawer, she ran through excuses in her head. She wasn't protecting Oliver; she was protecting herself. She didn't want the drama that telling the truth would bring, and what did it matter now anyway? Oliver was gone. They were over. He couldn't hurt her again. She headed back downstairs and into the kitchen.

Lou shook her head. 'Please tell me why you have a bruise the size of Australia on your side.'

Effie slid into the chair opposite. 'I fell down the stairs.'

Lou rolled her eyes.

'I'm serious. We were arguing upstairs, and he stormed out. I tried to go after him, and I tripped.'

Effie looked at her, willing her to believe what she'd said. It was half true – they *had* argued upstairs. She'd read somewhere once that if you were going to lie, you should try to incorporate some truth into it, to make it convincing.

'Arguing about what?'

'I dunno, the usual stuff.'

'Usual stuff that made him move out and gave you those bruises? Do you think I was born yesterday? At least come up with something more original than falling down the bloody stairs.'

'It's the truth.'

'Swear it. Swear on my life.' Lou stared at her and shook her head when Effie didn't reply. 'Why didn't you tell me?'

She already knows.

Lou wasn't stupid. Effie knew she could see through her lie. She looked at Lou, and her stomach swirled. Would it really be so bad to admit it? Would Lou really pity her?

Tell her.

They'd been friends since Effie's first day at secondary school. She could trust her.

'There's nothing to tell,' Effie said quietly. 'It's not like he's been beating me up all the time.'

'So he *did* hit you?' Lou slammed her hand on the table and stood up, shaking her head as she paced the kitchen. When she stopped and looked back at Effie, her eyes were blazing with fury. 'It doesn't matter how often he's been doing it; he still hit you. I can't believe you didn't tell me.'

'Lou, I'm fine. Really. Do I look like a battered housewife to you?'

'Quite frankly, yes.' Lou shook her head. 'Effie, you need to call the police. You need to call the police and get his sorry arse thrown into jail.'

Effie sighed. 'No, I don't. I've kicked him out. It's over, and he knows it.'

'And what's to stop him coming back and doing it again? You *need* to go to the police.'

'What's the point? To have some can't-be-arsed police officer come round and ask questions and do nothing about it?'

'It's not like that anymore. They take domestic violence seriously now, Eff.'

Effie shivered at the words. Domestic violence. She was already just another statistic.

'Olly's a barrister. I can't go up against him.'

Lou shook her head again. 'That little shit. He deserves to be locked up until he rots. All you're doing by not going to the police is protecting him.'

'I'm not. I'm just trying to get on with my life.'

'You do know I can report it on your behalf? It doesn't have to come from you.'

'I mean it, Lou. No police.'

Lou took her phone from her pocket. 'Then at least let me take pictures, just in case you change your mind. Think about it a bit more at least. Just because he's a barrister doesn't mean he's exempt from any kind of justice.'

'Why?' Effie's arms instinctively covered her stomach as she pictured seeing shots of her bruised body plastered over a host of social media sites.

'You have to have something to fight with. If he ever does anything like this again—'

'He won't. He's gone and he's not coming back.'

'Just in case,' Lou pressed. 'I still think you should go to the police, but if you won't, then at least let me take some photos.'

Effie slowly lifted the top. 'Okay, but you can't show them to anyone.'

'Of course not. Unless he tries something like this again.'

The clicking of Lou's camera echoed through the kitchen, and Effie closed her eyes. Usually when Lou took photos, they were self-ies of the two of them pulling silly faces and having fun. This time, they were documentation of abuse. How had her life come to this?

∽

Later that night, Effie sat on the sofa, trying not to feel dwarfed in her big house. Lou had offered to put her up, but Effie couldn't quite bring herself to leave. This was her dream house after all. It was just that she hadn't banked on feeling so lonely when Oliver had left. She'd spent nights alone in the house when he'd worked late and once when he'd gone to a conference in Birmingham, but she'd always known he'd be back. Now, it was different. Perversely, she missed his presence in the house. She missed having someone else around.

She draped a blanket over her legs and switched the television over to reruns of *Friends* while she ate a bowl of soup. It was the first proper meal she'd eaten for days, and she greedily wiped the bowl dry with the last of a crusty loaf, feeling oddly calm. Lou finding out had released some of the tension Effie hadn't even realised she'd been holding. Someone else knew, and she trusted Lou to keep her secret, whether she agreed with Effie's feelings on what to do next or not.

She put the bowl on the coffee table and curled up under the blanket. How many times had she seen this episode? Too many, probably, but with the absence of anyone else in the house, its familiarity was almost as comforting as her blanket. When the door knocked, she ignored it. She wasn't expecting anyone, and she was too snug to move. Last weekend, two Jehovah's Witnesses had knocked on their door. It was probably them again, and she couldn't be bothered to politely decline. She ignored the persistent knocking and hoped they wouldn't look through the window.

'Effie?'

At the sound of Oliver's voice, her entire body ran cold and froze, as if the temperature in the house had suddenly plummeted. Her heart stopped mid-beat. The voice she'd heard was muffled, but there was no doubt that it was his.

'Effie. Open up.' He knocked again, but she didn't budge until she heard his key trying to fit in the lock.

There was no way he could get in, but she shot up from the sofa and went to the living room doorway, peering into the hallway. Oliver's silhouette stood on the other side of the frosted glass panes. She saw him press the side of his hand against the door as he tried to peer inside.

'Effie? Come on, let me in. I just want to talk.'

His voice was soft and gentle, like it usually was when he wasn't stressed or angry. It sounded like Oliver. Like her husband. She didn't move as he crouched down and lifted the letterbox, looking inside.

'I know you're there. I can see your feet.'

Her breath caught in her throat as she moved backwards into the living room.

'I just want to talk. Things have changed. I've started an anger management course, and I really want to tell you about it.'

Effie closed her eyes and clenched her fists. She had to stand her ground. She couldn't let him try to explain and twist things around in her head.

'Come on, baby. We don't want the whole street to know our business.'

She heard the letterbox close and after a few seconds, she let out her breath in one long, slow exhale. He was gone. She'd resisted him. Even though her heart ached at the sound of his voice, she couldn't, under any circumstances, let him get inside her head, especially now Lou knew what had happened. It was bad enough to be an abused partner, but it would be even worse to be the abused partner who kept going back for more. She turned around to sit back on the sofa and froze as her breath caught in her throat.

Looking back at her were Oliver's blue eyes, big, round and sad as they peered through the window. Her shoulders sagged as she stared back into them. He didn't move or say anything – he just looked at her. Her spine tingled as she took in the features of his face. She knew them as well as she knew her own.

Remember what he did. Remember how he hit you.

Effie closed her eyes against the tears. How did he do this? How could he make her begin to doubt herself? Her breathing quickened as she waited for him to do something, anything. Why wasn't he getting angry? Why wasn't he banging on the window, calling her all the names under the sun? Why was he making this so damned difficult?

'You're fucking disgusting.'

He'd made her wet herself. He'd beaten her like an unwanted dog.

'I love you.'

Even through the glass, she could hear what he'd said.

'You're fucking disgusting.'

She remembered how he'd spat on her, feeling the warm fluid trickle down her cheek in her mind. Where was *that* Oliver now? Why was the good version of her husband standing in front of her, looking at her like she was the oxygen he needed to survive instead of the uncontrollable monster she'd thrown out? Why was he getting into her head, making the good memories of their marriage play out in her mind like a montage, making her wonder if she'd been hasty in telling him to leave. She shook her head as she found herself wondering what would happen if she talked back or opened the door, and whether everyone deserved a second chance.

Effie opened her eyes and slowly, Oliver raised his fingers to his mouth and pressed them against his lips before touching the window in front of him.

'I'm sorry.'

He looked at her again with those sad blue eyes, turned around and walked away. She heard him walk around to the front of the house and open and close the front gate. When she heard the BMW drive away, she slumped to the floor, hugged her knees to her chest and cried.

20.

Effie put her head in her hands. Her eyes were aching. She hated spreadsheets at the best of times, but this felt like torture. After a week off, she'd returned to work, but all she wanted was to go straight back home again.

'Are you alright?' Nikki asked.

Effie nodded and rubbed her eyes. 'Yeah, fine. Just this thing is making my eyes hurt.'

'I know it's a bit of a mess. I tried, but I suck at Excel.'

'Don't worry about it. Thanks for taking care of it while I was off.'

She threw Nikki a smile, but the spreadsheet she'd carefully constructed no longer made sense. Something had happened to the formulas, and she couldn't see what it was.

'No worries.' Nikki smiled back. 'Are you sure you're better, though? You look a bit peaky.'

'It'll take a while to get my strength back, but I'll be fine.' Effie turned back to her screen and squinted her watery eyes.

'My flatmate had salmonella poisoning too once. I've never seen someone so sick before. It can really knock you for six. You shouldn't have rushed back; I could've covered for you for longer.'

Salmonella poisoning. That was her excuse for being off, and thanks to the lack of sleep, her body really did look like it had been through the wars.

'I had to come back sometime.' Effie shrugged. It was true. As tempting as it was to hide away from the world, she'd had to leave the house.

Since Oliver had turned up, she'd felt trapped, even though he hadn't threatened her in any way. He'd come back once more, left flowers and called through the letterbox, telling her how much he loved her, how much he needed her, how much he'd changed. Afterwards, she'd lain wide awake in bed, already unsettled by the noises of the house, convinced that he was standing outside watching the house, and it was messing with her mind. It didn't make her feel worried or scared. It was worse than that. It made her feel sorry that their marriage had deteriorated in such a bad way and that the person she'd thought was her rock was sleeping somewhere else, in an unfamiliar room in an unfamiliar bed, instead of the one they'd once shared.

Her mind was a whirlwind of confusion, and she was so tired that even her teeth ached. All she wanted to do was sleep, and looking at a screen full of numbers wasn't helping.

'Did you hear about Sketch yet?'

Effie shook her head. 'No. Why? What's happened?'

'XFM have profiled them and are championing their single this week. They've been booked for an interview on Friday and everything. How cool is that?'

'That's amazing,' Effie replied. 'Doug must be over the moon.'

'I'll say. Smith too.'

Effie sighed at the mention of his name. Smith was supposed to be the one with the messed-up life – surrounded by drugs, sleeping with another guy's girlfriend while cheating on his own and getting beaten up to the point of hospitalisation. When had it all changed? Ever since he'd come back, her life had started to spiral out of control while his was steadying out. He had a girlfriend, a nice flat and a good job – a job where he was proving himself. Would he have been like this if they'd stayed together?

Effie pressed her fingers into her eyes. The truth was, it didn't matter. She'd screwed everything up. She'd married someone she thought she knew and ended up on her own, and even if she hadn't, it was too late. Smith was taken, pinned down into a relationship with Mile-High Claire.

She looked at the spreadsheet again and shook her head with a sigh. 'Everything's fucked.'

❧

'Okay, okay, shush.' Doug called for quiet in the office and turned up the volume on his computer. The excitement was palpable as the Archive family huddled around his desk.

It had been the longest workweek of her life. Oliver hadn't turned up again, but all the sleepless nights listening out for him had taken their toll, not to mention trying to appear normal in the office. She was struggling, but at five thirty on Friday afternoon, she'd stayed behind with everyone else to listen to Sketch's interview. There was no doubt as to what this opportunity meant. Rush-hour drive time was one of two peaks for listenership, and all week long Archive's collective energy had been ploughed into advertising and making sure the whole world knew about it.

Effie leaned against the wall and fanned her face with her hand. The blazing sunshine and heat outside would be perfect if she were sitting in her garden, but being in the office was a different story. She looked at her colleagues, all so engrossed by the radio that they barely seemed to notice the sweltering heat.

'This is it.' Doug grinned as Sketch's debut single played through the speakers, and Effie smiled as everyone applauded, clapping their hands and slapping each other on the back. The long hours, the preparations for the launch – even the mind-numbing process of mailing out CDs – it had paid off. She looked at Doug, who was positively glowing. After twenty-odd years, Archive had a band that had made the transition from being an underground success to being on the cusp of a mainstream breakthrough. Next to him, Smith stood with his back to her and his arms folded, his T-shirt pulled taut against his broad shoulders. Even with his back to her, she could sense his pride.

Once the song had finished and the radio DJ introduced the band, the chatter in the office stopped, but Effie felt like she was on the outside, looking in. Her head was thick and fuzzy. When had she last slept for more than a couple of hours at a time? She blinked and pressed a hand to her forehead as the ground gently swayed under her feet. Jesus, it was hot. Her nostrils felt like they'd shrunk as she tried to take a deep breath.

Smith turned his head a fraction, and she moved her hand, pressing the backs of her fingers against the nape of her neck to try to cool herself down, but they felt as hot as the air around her.

'You okay?' Smith whispered, leaning back to look at her.

She nodded. 'Yeah, I'm fine. Just hot.'

He turned back to listen to the radio, and Effie tried to concentrate. What were they talking about? She could hear them speaking, but the words were jumbling up, meshing with the buzzing in her ears like static. She took another deep breath, and Smith turned around again.

'Are you sure you're alright?'

'Yeah,' she whispered back, but she didn't feel alright. Her pulse was loud in her ears, and her head was getting lighter by the second.

'You don't look it.' Smith frowned.

She was about to answer back, but her vision swam, and for a second there were two Smiths standing in front of her instead of one.

'Come on, you need some air.' He turned and put his hand on her arm.

'The interview . . .' she mumbled. Why couldn't she speak properly?

Smith opened his mouth, but she didn't hear a single word of what he said. The inside of her head turned to wool as her legs gave way beneath her, and everything went black.

❧

'Effie?'

Effie slowly opened her eyes, blinking against the bright sunlight. Her head felt oddly disconnected from her body.

'Don't worry – you're alright.' Smith was crouching in front of her, looking into her eyes. 'You fainted.'

'I feel sick,' she replied shakily.

'Here.'

He handed her a glass of water and kept his fingers at the base, steadying it as she took a sip with trembling hands. Slowly, the buzzing in her ears receded, and the brightness in her vision dimmed. She felt the heat of the sun on her arms and looked around. They were outside on the balcony.

'How is she?' Doug asked, stepping through the door.

Smith nodded. 'She's alright.'

'Oh, god. The interview,' Effie groaned.

She'd fainted right in the middle of it. She'd missed it and probably caused a commotion at the same time.

'Don't worry about that,' Doug replied softly. 'All you need to worry about right now is getting better.'

'I'm fine, really. It just got too hot in there.'

Doug frowned. 'The air conditioning is on full blast.'

It was? She hadn't felt it at all. If anything, she'd felt like she was in a sauna, wearing winter clothes.

'Effie, you're not ready to be back at work. You need to go home and rest.'

She opened her mouth to reply, but he put his hand up to stop her.

'No arguments. Rest. We'll make sure you get home okay once you're feeling a bit steadier, and you're not to come back until you're fit and healthy. Understood?'

He sounded like her dad. Or how she imagined her dad might sound anyway. She looked from Doug to Smith, both mirroring the same concerned but firm expressions. Clearly, they weren't going to take no for an answer, despite knowing how stubborn she could be. She sighed and nodded.

'But what about—'

'Nikki can cover you, and we'll pull together. It's what we do.' Doug looked at Smith. 'Take care of her until she's ready to go.'

'Don't worry, I will,' Smith replied with a nod as Doug patted her on the shoulder. They both watched him go back inside.

'Talk about embarrassing,' Effie said and took another sip of water.

Smith shrugged. 'You're sick. It's nothing to be embarrassed about. How are you feeling now?'

Her insides were still trembling, but the disjointed light-headedness was all but gone. 'Better. I just need to sleep.'

'You look like shit.' He grinned.

'Thanks. You know how to kick a girl when she's down.'

'I didn't know salmonella messed with your brain too. You know you always look gorgeous. Even with those massive bags under your eyes.'

She laughed nervously as he brushed the delicate skin under her eyes and swatted his hand away. He'd called her gorgeous, and she drank in the backhanded compliment, even though she knew it was an outright lie. She *did* have massive bags under her eyes, and she knew for a fact that she looked like she'd been dragged up from the bottom of the Thames.

'Come on.' Smith stood up and held his hands out to help her up. 'Let's get you home.'

❧

'If you feel faint, you tell me. If you feel sick, you tell me. If you want me to slow down—'

'I tell you.' Effie nodded. 'I've got it.'

She took the helmet from him and looked at the bike, remembering the urge she'd had to kick it just before she'd argued with Smith. Was she mad? Surely it made more sense to go home in something more suitable, something with a proper seat and doors? Something like, say, a cab? But Smith had offered, and she couldn't say no. It had been so long since she'd been on it, and she didn't want to face a journey home with a chatty cab driver. Smith sat on the bike and put his helmet on before nodding at her to get on behind him.

'Ready?'

Effie nodded and wrapped her arms around him as he set off. With her thighs straddling his, she couldn't ignore the real reason she'd accepted his offer of a ride home. She hadn't been this close to him since before he'd left to go travelling. Flesh on flesh, skin on skin. As he slowly navigated the streets of London, she let herself melt into his back. The taut abs she'd seen in Ireland were right under her hands, and she splayed her hands out holding him as close to her as possible. It wasn't just about attraction. She felt safe. Even though she was probably too fragile to be on the back of a bike and even though the last time she'd been on one had ended in disaster, she felt safe with him. He seemed to be on high alert, watching out for her as he rode along. At every red light, he

205

put his hand on her thigh and turned his head, asking if she was alright.

Was he like this with Claire too? How many times had Claire been in this position with her arms and legs wrapped around him just like Effie was now? Maybe she was imagining it all – Smith's attention to her, his considered riding. He had a girl-friend, and Effie was sick. He was simply being a friend – a friend she thought she'd lost after their argument. She, meanwhile, was sleep deprived and estranged from her abusive, confusing husband. It was no wonder her heart was racing at being in such close proximity to someone who was acting like he actually cared about her.

When they stopped outside her house, Smith killed the engine and took off his helmet. Effie climbed off the bike and looked at him with a pang of uncontrollable, irrational longing. He was made for that bike. In a plain white T-shirt and 501s, he looked just like James Dean. Only fitter.

'Is Oliver home?'

Effie looked at the helmet cradled in his arms and shook her head.

'What time is he usually back? I don't think you should be on your own.'

'I don't know.' She sighed and handed her helmet to him. 'Actually, he moved out a couple of weeks ago.'

A tiny frown flickered across Smith's face, but he didn't press for details. 'So you're alone?'

Effie nodded. 'But I'll be fine.'

'Yeah, right,' Smith said and got off the bike. 'I don't think so.'

She watched him clip the helmets to the back. 'Honestly, Smith, I'm fine. I feel much better. Thanks for the lift.'

'When's the last time you ate?'

'I had dinner last night.'

He folded his arms and leaned against his bike. 'Something other than soup. I know you, remember? If you had it your way, you'd live on nothing but soup and crusty bread. Especially when you're upset.'

'Who said I was upset?'

'Your husband's moved out, and you've been off work for a week. There was no salmonella, was there?'

Effie sighed. 'Since when did you become Inspector Clouseau?'

'I've got many hidden depths, Effie – what can I say?'

'Fine, whatever.' She walked towards the house, but Smith stayed where he was until she turned and looked at him. 'Well, come on, then.'

He unfolded his arms and followed her up the path. Maybe it wasn't the best of ideas to invite him in, but as much as she hated to admit it, he was right. She hadn't eaten anything other than soup and bread since Oliver had left. She could do with a decent meal and company, even if that company made her frustrated and confused in equal measure. Smith closed the front door behind him, and she threw her keys into the bowl on the sideboard. He wandered up the hallway and poked his head into the living room.

'Nice place.'

'Thanks.'

'It's not what I expected,' he replied, sitting on the bottom step of the staircase and pulling the Converse from his feet.

Effie looked down at the stripy socks on his feet. 'Why? What did you expect?'

'Something a bit more . . .' He stood up and shrugged. 'I dunno. Something like your old place, I guess.'

'Yeah, right.' She snorted and led him through to the living room. 'That place was a dump.'

'No, it wasn't. Okay, so it was on a crappy estate, but it was a nice flat. You did it up well.'

He moved around the living room, picking up ornaments, inspecting them and putting them back. He picked up a photo frame from the shelf above the fireplace. The picture inside was of Effie and Oliver on their honeymoon, smiling into the camera. She frowned and watched as he carefully put it back.

'It was kind of bohemian,' he continued. 'A little hippyish. It was cute.'

Effie screwed up her nose. 'I think you're confusing me with someone else. My flat definitely wasn't *hippyish*.'

He shrugged again. 'Okay, maybe not hippyish. I dunno what you call it. Interior design isn't really my thing.'

It was true that when she'd been given her council flat, she'd had to take some of the things her mum had left behind, but she'd slowly replaced them with things that were more to her own taste. It had resulted in a mishmash of old and new, bohemian and modern. She'd been working her way towards refurnishing her cramped flat with nice fittings and classy, colour-coordinated ornaments. Moving in with Oliver had been the final leap to what she'd been trying to achieve. This house represented everything she'd aspired to be.

'So,' – he turned and looked at her – 'food?'

She nodded and they headed to the kitchen. 'I don't even know what I've got in.'

He opened up the fridge and peered inside, apparently as comfortable as if he were in his own house. 'Not a lot, it would seem.'

'I need to do some shopping. I'll just order something in.'

Smith looked at her and opened the freezer door. 'We can do better than that. You're the girl who could make a three-course dinner out of the tins from the back of the cupboard.'

She smiled and shook her head. Before Oliver, she'd had to watch what she spent. She didn't have a choice. She was a savvy shopper, always on the lookout for supermarket deals, and takeaways were a very rare treat. These days, she loaded up her trolley without a second thought for the price.

'Okay, so you've got prawns. We could do those.' He slung the bag of grey prawns on the side and closed the freezer door before opening up the cupboards. 'And risotto rice. Perfect.'

'Are you going to make me sick like you did last time?' Effie asked, leaning against the counter on the other side of the kitchen.

'Don't be silly.' Smith grinned. 'I'm better with prawns than I am with crab.'

She watched as he moved around the kitchen with fluid ease, gathering up everything he needed in silence. She'd forgotten how methodical he was when he cooked. He set everything up to be ready for when he needed it – chopping an onion and some garlic ready for the frying pan, pouring out the exact amount of rice required and putting it in a bowl.

'So what happened with you and Prince Charming?' He kept his back to her as he fried the onions and garlic in butter.

Effie looked at the floor. 'It's a long and very boring story.'

'I doubt that. Nothing's ever boring with you.'

He never missed a trick. Boring was the complete opposite of her situation. 'Thanks. I think.'

'So are you, like, on a break, or are you heading for a divorce court?'

She sighed heavily. 'I haven't thought that far ahead yet.'

'It was you who ended it?' He looked at her. She nodded and he turned back to the cooker.

'What?' she asked, warily. His silence was disconcerting. Smith always had something to say.

'Nothing.' He shrugged. 'It's just you were so adamant about him and how perfect your life was. I'm surprised, I guess.'

'Yeah, well. Nothing's ever really perfect,' she replied under her breath. 'It's funny how things work out, isn't it? I mean, there I was, secure and married while you were single and living it up, and now I'm separated and you're all loved up.'

Smith snorted. 'Me, loved up? I don't think so.'

Effie raised an eyebrow and stared at his back. Now this was interesting. 'How *is* Claire?'

'Fine. We haven't really spoken for a while.'

Effie held her breath and waited for him to continue, but he didn't. Instead, he turned and looked at her with his annoying know-it-all grin.

'It isn't like you to not ask for all the ins and outs. Aren't you going to ask me what happened?'

'It's not really my business.'

Oh, but it is.

'Well, that's new.' He turned back to the cooker, and Effie rolled her eyes. Clearly he was going to make her ask.

'Okay, what happened? I thought you were love's young dream.'

'Nothing happened. It just ran its course.'

'She dumped you?' She smirked at the thought.

'As if.' He laughed. 'Really, it was nothing major.'

'That's a shame. She seemed nice.'

'Pull the other one. You couldn't stand her.'

'That's not true.'

It was harsh to say that Effie couldn't stand her. She'd been jealous, and Claire had known far too much about Effie's feelings for Smith – that was all.

'It was fun while it lasted, but it was never a serious thing anyway, you know?'

Effie nodded, but the truth was, she didn't know. She'd never had flings before, only boyfriends. And now a husband, albeit one she was separated from. She'd always been sure of what she was doing when it came to love. Her relationship with Smith might have been heady, intense and rocky, but she'd known how she felt about him. And she knew how she felt about Oliver, or at least she'd thought she did. Since they'd separated, she wasn't sure about anything anymore. All she did know was that she didn't want to be like her mum, happy to go with whatever came along on a whim. She wanted the real deal, and she'd thought she'd got it. Now look at her.

'Earth to Effie? Are you okay? Are you feeling faint again?'

She looked up at him, standing by her cooker with a spoon in his hand, and shook her head. 'Sorry, I was miles away. I'm fine.'

'I was asking if al dente is okay?'

Effie nodded. 'Yeah. Al dente is perfect.'

'Where do you usually eat? Here?' He looked at the kitchen table, and she nodded.

Smith dished up the risotto and handed her a plate. 'So let's mix it up.'

She followed him through to the living room, where they sat on the floor, eating with their legs stretched out wide and Jeff Buckley playing softly in the background.

'Where did you learn to cook without poisoning people? This is lovely,' Effie said with a full mouth.

Smith shook his head with mock disgust. 'Did nobody ever tell you it's rude to talk with your mouth full? And as for it not being poisonous, you might want to wait a couple of hours before being sure about that.'

Effie laughed and softly kicked his foot with hers.

'It's another benefit of travelling. I took loads of cooking classes, and it saves money instead of eating out all the time.'

'Sounds like you had a blast.'

'Man.' Smith sighed. 'It was awesome. I'd do it all again tomorrow.'

Effie's heart stalled at the mere thought of him leaving for a second time.

'What about you?' he asked. 'What will you do now you're single again?'

'No idea.' She grimaced. 'I haven't thought about myself as being *single*.'

'Travel cures a broken heart, or so they say. It's a distraction at the very least. You used to say you wanted to see the world.'

'I used to say a lot of things.' Effie shrugged. 'It was easy to imagine it when I was younger and Mum would take me away all the time.'

'So what changed?'

'I grew up. And now . . . Well, things are different. Too much has happened to just pack up and leave.'

'You'd be surprised. It's like having amnesia once you're gone. It's hard to dwell on stuff when you're experiencing so much.'

'What was the best thing? Like, what was your highlight?' Effie asked and took the last mouthful of risotto. It really was just what she needed, and she felt a million times better than she had that morning.

'Angkor Wat in Cambodia. It's probably the most awe-inspiring thing I've ever seen in my life. As clichéd as it sounds, being in a place like that made me realise just how small I was in the grand scheme of things. I'm sure you saw the photos I put on Facebook anyway.'

Effie shook her head as a blush erupted on her face. 'We're not Facebook friends anymore, remember?'

'Oh yeah.' Smith laughed. 'That's a pretty dumb state of affairs.'

He took out his phone and whizzed his fingers over the screen. Seconds later, her phone buzzed, and she looked at the notification.

James: Smith sent you a friend request.

She grinned and accepted it before putting her plate to one side. It was churlish to have un-friended him in the first place, pathetic even.

'And what was the worst thing?'

He put his plate on top of hers and crossed his legs. 'Saying goodbye to people all the time. You meet so many cool people, bond with them super quick and then before you know it, they're moving on to the next place. It's inherently transient.'

Bond with them? Images of him *bonding* filled her head. It was one of the reasons she'd un-friended him on Facebook. She hadn't wanted to end up stalking his every move out of jealousy.

He bumped his shoulder against hers. 'Not *that* kind of bonding.'

Effie shook her head. 'Why do you always presume to know what I'm thinking?'

'Because I do. It was written all over your face.'

'Well, that's where you're wrong. What's written on my face is tiredness.' Right on cue, she stifled a yawn. 'I haven't had a proper night's sleep in ages.'

Smith brought his legs up and rested his arms on his knees as he picked at his nails. 'Missing Oliver?'

'It's mostly just trying to adjust to being alone, you know?' She looked at him and then looked around the room. 'This house makes some weird noises at night. It makes me paranoid.'

'You're worried there's a bogeyman hiding under your bed?'

Effie laughed and thought back to the night she'd convinced herself she was getting burgled. 'Something like that.'

'You must be exhausted. On top of not eating properly, it's no wonder you fainted.'

'I know. Thanks for dinner. I really needed it.'

'Anytime.' Smith grinned.

Another yawn welled up inside her, and this time she didn't try to hide it. In the space of a few seconds, anchors had apparently fixed themselves to her eyelids.

'I should get going so you can sleep,' Smith said and went to get up, but Effie stopped him.

'Actually, could you stay? Just for a bit.'

Whoa, where did that come from?

'I might be able to get a few hours knowing someone else is in the house.'

Her tired brain must have short-circuited. What was she doing? Asking Smith to stay was like sticking a finger into a beehive. No good could ever come from it. Except, maybe, sleep. Just a few hours and she'd feel better. They didn't have to go upstairs. They didn't even have to move. She was so tired she'd be happy to sleep right there on the floor.

Smith slowly sat back down and nodded, leaning against the sofa. 'Yeah. Sure.'

Effie yawned again and shuffled closer to him, resting her head on his denim-clad thighs. She smiled, blissfully aware of the heat of his body radiating onto her face. His hand rested on her back, and she closed her eyes.

21.

Effie stood in the garden, holding a cup of tea, and looked at the tiny rosebush in the corner. The beautiful weather had continued throughout April, and even though she didn't know anything about gardening, she knew it was early for rosebuds to appear on the first of May. She looked up at the sky speckled with early morning clouds and the trail of a plane flying overhead. The clouds didn't worry her. She knew they'd soon part and let the sun through, just like they had for the past month.

For the past few days, she'd opened her eyes before her alarm went off, fully rested and wide awake. Smith's visit had been something of a turning point. He'd ended up staying until the early hours of the morning, when she'd woken up. She'd stumbled to bed, and he'd left, and ever since then, she'd started sleeping better, progressing from a few hours to a full night. The occasions when she woke up with cold fear dousing her like a cloak were now few and far between, and she could only put it down to her slowly getting used to Oliver not being around. She still kept asking herself whether her decision to throw him out was right or wrong, but instead of it being a state of constant confusion, it had settled down to long periods of certainty followed by uncertainty. Sometimes, it felt like her mind was a pendulum, swinging steadily, and at the very least it seemed to be giving her brain enough rest time to sleep better.

Oliver's lessening contact was helping too. He'd sent a message, telling her he'd back off to give her some space, and although she hadn't heard anything else, flowers had been delivered for the past three days in a row. Even without a message card, it was clear they were from Oliver.

She sipped her tea and wandered over to the rosebush, feeling the fresh dew tickling her bare feet. If she'd taken it at face value, she'd have thought it was dead with its dry, bare branches, but it wasn't. It was starting to come to life again, having survived the long, cold and dark winter.

She'd settled into a routine, one where she was independent and did whatever she wanted. And while it mainly only consisted of going to work, coming home and getting lost in a film or a book, it was a step in the right direction. She still loved Oliver. A few weeks apart couldn't change that. She still found herself wondering what would happen if she did take him back, which parts of their relationship would need to be worked on and whether they could ever truly get back to where they had been. She'd always told herself that she'd never get involved with a violent man, but here she was. A domestic violence victim. She shook her head. She wasn't a victim – not anymore. Spring was turning to summer, and she was ready to come back to life, just like the rosebush.

As she moved around the house, getting ready for work, she held on to the feeling of happiness she'd woken up with. She sang along to the radio as she dressed, applied her makeup in record time and skipped down the stairs in her yellow, polka-dotted mini-dress and ballet pumps. After one last check in the mirror, she put her headphones in and opened the front door. She stopped just before she closed it behind her. Next to the potted plant was a bunch of posies, the latest offering from Oliver. She picked them up and held them to her nose. They weren't her favourite flowers but he'd already sent roses, orchids, and tulips. He was consistent, she'd give him that. She went back into the house, put them on the sideboard and closed the door behind her to go to work. She hummed along to her iPod on the walk to the Tube station.

Today was going to be a good day.

∾

The morning was spent breezing around the office with a smile on her face, making endless cups of tea for her colleagues and answering the phone in a happy, high-pitched voice. Whenever her mind strayed to the intricacies of separation from Oliver, she pulled it right back again. If she finally decided that they were separated for good, she knew she'd have to think about the logistics at some point because one thing was for sure: she couldn't afford to live there alone, and besides, it was Oliver's place, not hers. She'd changed the locks so he couldn't get in, but technically speaking, he could come back and kick her out whenever he felt like it.

She leaned back in her chair and looked up at the clock. A couple of street food stalls had popped up by the Tube station, and she'd been thinking about pulled pork and black beans all day. She opened up the messenger window on her screen and clicked on Smith's name before typing out a message.

Effie: What are you doing for lunch? Cuban?
James: Can't, I've got a meeting in 30 mins ☹
Effie: Ok, no problem ☺

Effie shrugged and took her purse from her bag, checking that she had cash. It was Smith's loss. Nikki had tried the food at the Cuban stall last week and had raved about it ever since.

James: Fancy a drink after work?

She looked up and saw Smith looking back at her with a grin and a raised eyebrow. She'd treated herself to the *Sex and the City* box set, one of her favourite shows, and she'd received an email that morning saying it had been delivered. She had been planning on curling up on the sofa and starting a marathon.

Effie: Hmm. Not sure. I've got a date with Carrie Bradshaw.
James: Who?

She smiled and shook her head. Smith was awful when it came to TV shows.

Effie: Duh. Sex and the City!
James: As if you haven't watched every episode before! You're really going to blow me out for that crap??
Effie: It isn't crap. It's the best show ever!
James: Watch it when you get home later. Come out, just for one. Everyone else has blown me out.
Effie: It's Monday. Most people just want to get home, not go to the pub.
James: The sun's out. Seems a shame to waste the evening . . .

He was right. It would be a shame to waste the evening on her sofa. As much as she loved *SATC*, she had to stop being a hermit. And anyway, today was a good day. She owed it to herself to make it a great evening too.

❧

'I said I'd come for *one*,' Effie said, shielding the sun from her eyes with her hand, looking up at Smith.

218

'Nobody ever goes out for *just one*.' He sat next to her on the pavement holding a bottle of rosé in a bucket. 'Besides, it makes more economical sense to get a bottle instead.'

'Fair enough.' Effie grinned as he poured out the wine. 'Since when did you drink rosé anyway?'

'A glass or two's nice in the sun, and I didn't fancy a beer.'

She leaned back against the cool, red, glazed tiles of the pub's exterior and stretched her legs out, looking at her feet. Why hadn't she worn sandals like ninety per cent of the women around her? It was a sticky evening, and the heavy London air clung to her skin.

'What *is* that bloody song? You've been humming it all day.'

She hadn't even realised she'd been humming. 'It's from *Despicable Me 2*.'

'Am I supposed to know what that is?'

'It's a film,' she explained, and he stared back at her with a blank expression. She laughed and rolled her eyes. 'Pharrell Williams? *Happy*? You know, the song with all the YouTube videos?'

'Ah, yeah. I know it. Just didn't recognise your version. You're hardly the best hummer in the world.'

She laughed at the mischievous grin on his face and shook her head before looking out at the road. 'I love London when it's like this. When the sun shines, there's no place like it.'

'Yep.' Smith grinned and held up his glass for a toast.

'What are we drinking to?' Effie asked.

'This. You *are* the sunshine today, Effie.'

Effie blushed and shook her head. 'Let's hope I don't burn out.'

'Not possible. At least, I hope not. Without the sun, there'd be nothing else.'

'How intensely profound.' She grinned, feeling her face redden even more.

'It's just nice to see you happy again.'

'It's nice to *feel* happy again.'

They clinked their glasses together, and Smith nodded towards the pavement. 'It's crazy. Summer's the only time of the year you'd ever see anyone sitting on the pavement.'

'It's not summer yet. And we're sitting on a ledge.'

'It's a glorified skirting board. Though after bumming it for months, you don't get precious about where you sit.'

A dozen conversations filled the air around them, creating a constant buzz of chatter and laughter. The pavement outside the pub was packed with men with their shirtsleeves rolled up and women in maxi dresses. The roar of bus engines and cars blaring music from their speakers added to the atmosphere that was the distinct anthem of a sun-soaked London. Effie looked down at Smith's bare arms, tanned from the sun.

'You had more tattoos while you were away.'

'The ones on my ribs?' Smith looked at her and grinned. 'You noticed then?'

The memory of him stretching in the kitchen of the cottage in Ireland filled her head, and she took a long swig of wine.

'Well you *were* half naked,' she said. 'It would have been hard not to.'

Smith laughed. 'I got fed up of people asking about my scar. I didn't really want to have to explain about the punctured lung and stuff. I found a good tattoo artist in Thailand and got it covered up.'

'Can I ask you something?' Effie turned and looked at him. 'Keisha. Why did you do it? I mean, putting us to one side, you must have known it wouldn't end well.'

Keisha's boyfriend was the owner of a club where Smith used to DJ, and he was known as something of a gangster. God only knew what had been going through Smith's mind.

His eyes flickered away from her face. 'To be honest, I didn't really think about it. I didn't really care.'

'You almost died,' Effie replied quietly. Whenever she thought about him laid up in that hospital bed, her blood ran cold.

'Something like that was always going to happen. I mean, come on. I was hardly a poster boy for good living, was I?'

Smith had partied hard back then, and while he claimed not to have sold any drugs, he was surrounded by them all the time. With his bike, chiselled looks and tattoos, he went around scooping up girls like there was no tomorrow.

'I suppose not.'

'I was cocky, restless and earning more money than I knew how to spend. It had to come to a head eventually. I just did it in spectacular fashion.'

And broke my heart in the process.

'I really never meant to hurt you,' he said, playing with the stem of his glass. 'I know it's a cliché, but it's true. I was operating on a completely different level. It sounds harsh, but I didn't think about you while I was doing that stuff. It was like, if I didn't think, it didn't matter.'

Effie drained her wine. That hurt. But she got it. It was easier to pretend things weren't really happening, especially when those things were of your own making.

'And now?'

'Now.' Smith puffed out his cheeks. 'I'm just a Regular Joe. I don't want to be a prick who goes around hurting people. Especially people who deserve it the least.'

Effie blushed at the way he threw her a small smile. Maybe he really had changed. He seemed so much more humble than he had when he'd left. Maybe she'd mistaken his embarrassment at the way he'd treated her for arrogance. In some perverse way, maybe everything that had happened, happened for a reason.

'It's kind of appropriate to have a skull tattoo covering the scar,' she said.

'Skulls signify a lot of things. Death, knowledge, overcoming obstacles.' He held the bottle out to refill her glass. 'So yeah, it's appropriate. I'll get more soon.'

'You'll end up completely covered at the rate you're going.' She tutted but they both knew she appreciated his tattoos just as much as he did.

'What about you? Will you get any more? Though the one you have already is cute enough on its own.'

Effie almost choked on her wine. She'd tagged along with him when he went for a new addition to his sleeve and ended up getting a tiny love heart on her pelvis. The memory of him kissing it after it had healed popped up in her mind, and since his cheeks reddened, she guessed the same was true for him too.

She shook her head and cleared her throat. 'Nope. One's enough for me.'

Smith put his glass on the floor and took out a box of Marlboros.

'You've started smoking again?'

'Nah, but it's sunny, I'm at a pub and I've got a drink in my hand.' He looked at the glass. 'Well, I've got a drink on the floor. It'd be rude not to.'

She held her hand out and grinned. 'Can I nick one?'

'You've quit.'

'So have you, but I won't tell if you don't tell.'

Smith laughed and handed her a cigarette. She cupped a hand around his as he struck his lighter and lit the tip.

'It can be our little secret.'

22.

hocolate, thick socks and *Sex and the City*. It was Effie's idea of bliss, and as the familiar theme tune played out on the television, she sighed contentedly and wriggled her toes, stretching her legs out on the sofa. She was on episode three of her marathon, and her family-sized bag of Minstrels was already almost depleted. After last night's drinks with Smith, she was grateful for the peace and quiet of home. They'd ended up staying at the pub until the sun had set, soaking up every last ray of sunshine, and she'd woken this morning with a slight hangover.

A car pulled up outside, and she turned her head to look out of the window just in time to see the black BMW that, until Oliver moved out, had always been parked up in their driveway. It was the first time he'd come round for days, and she waited to hear him knock on the door, pushing away the dull ache settling in her chest. Alarmingly, as time went on, the confusion had stopped abating and settled into a steady worry about whether she'd been harsh towards him, even though what he'd done to her was inexplicably wrong. She frowned at the silence. What was he doing?

She quietly crept to the living room doorway and peered out into the hallway, expecting to see his silhouette behind the door, but he wasn't there. She stood still for a couple of minutes, her heart steadily pounding in her chest. Had she closed all the windows?

Maybe he was trying to find a way in. She wasn't scared of him. He'd been nothing but repentant, but she only wanted to see him face-to-face on her terms.

The letterbox flipped up, and a small card fluttered to the ground. She caught a glimpse of Oliver's fingers and realised he must have been sitting in the doorway, writing whatever he had. She slowly walked towards the door, her socked feet slightly slipping on the varnished oak floor. The lights were on in the house. There was little point in pretending she wasn't in. She crouched down and picked up the card and read his scrawled handwriting.

Since the flowers weren't enough, maybe this will work instead . . .

She turned it over and frowned. Maybe what will? She looked at the door. Was he still outside, or was that all he had to say? She looked back at the card as the letterbox opened again and another card fell onto the bristly floor mat.

There are no words to express how sorry I am . . .

Again, there was only one line. She sat on the floor and crossed her legs as another came.

I don't expect you to believe me, and if this were a film, I'd be the first to tell you to stay away . . .

She traced a finger over the messy, looped letters. He'd never written to her before. She guessed love letters were passé these days, but she couldn't deny the way her throat was tightening with every card he posted.

But this isn't a film. It's real life. I screwed up . . .

If only it were that easy. If only admitting he'd screwed up could fix everything. She'd been getting on with her life since he'd moved out, and it was getting easier every day, but she'd married for love. She'd married for life. She'd be lying if she said she didn't want back the happiness they'd had in the beginning.

I REALLY screwed up. But I'm fixing it. I'm doing the course, like I said I would.

She hadn't thought he'd been serious about doing the anger management course. It would have meant publicly acknowledging that he had a problem he couldn't control. It must have dented his pride in a big way.

It's working already. I can see why I acted like I did. Why I did what I did. I just want you to know . . .

Effie found herself tapping her fingers on her knee, waiting for the next card. When he posted it, she caught it before it hit the ground and read it. The tears that had been clogging her throat fell from her eyes.

None of it was your fault. It was all mine.

She wiped a cheek and read it again as another card dropped through.

I know you'll say no, but please, give me one last chance, and I promise I'll spend the rest of my life making you happy.

Her heart ached. The part of her that wanted to believe him was taking over, but she couldn't. She'd already made that mistake once before.

I'm sorry.

I love you.

She read the last two cards, posted at the same time and leaned her head against the wall as tears continued to fall down her cheeks. On the other side of the door, she heard him shuffle around before he stood up, his silhouette against the glass. She held her breath and didn't let it out until he turned and left.

23.

Effie opened the front door just as Lou clambered out of the car, sucking on an ice lolly. She was perfectly dressed for the summer in tiny shorts, a vest and flip-flops. The fragile, heartbroken version of her friend had come a long way.

'Do you need a hand?' Effie asked as Lou swung her handbag onto her shoulder.

'Yep,' Lou replied, taking plastic bags from the back seat. 'You can take the foot spa. It's in the boot.'

Effie clicked the latch of the front door down and opened the boot to look at the bags inside. 'Is that *all* booze?'

'There's food as well, obviously.' Lou grinned as Effie took the big box containing the foot spa from the boot. 'We're having a proper girly pamper day. No cutting corners.'

Lou followed her into the house and dumped the bags on the kitchen table. 'Right. Food-wise, we've got baguettes, cheese, salad, breadsticks and assorted dips, plus olives for you.'

Effie put the foot spa on the table. 'Ooh, yum. Thanks.'

'God knows how you eat that stuff. Talk about gross.' Lou pulled a face. 'We've also got strawberries, blueberries and pine-apple. For booze, we've got Pimm's and a couple of bottles of wine.'

'I've forgotten how much you like to boss people around,' Effie replied, putting the drinks in the fridge. 'Let's start with Pimm's.'

'And away from the alcohol and food,' Lou continued, 'I've brought the foot spa, face masks and mani-pedi stuff. I forgot the creams and scrubs for our feet, though.'

'Don't worry about it. Izzy sent me loads of products for my birthday, I'm pretty sure I've got some upstairs.'

'This is going to be sooooo good,' Lou said as she set about chopping up strawberries and cucumber for the Pimm's.

'It is.' Effie grinned. It was the perfect spring day. The sun was shining, the sky was a clear blue and there were two sunloungers waiting in the garden with their names on them. 'So how are things with Mickey?'

Lou shrugged. 'We spoke a couple of days ago. He wanted to hear me out about what happened.'

'And?'

'And that was it. He said he needed to have time to calm down before we spoke, and I guess he has now. I haven't spoken to him since, though.'

Lou turned to face her, holding the jug of Pimm's in her hand. She was smiling, but Effie could still see the pain behind her eyes.

'Do you think there's a chance for you two?'

'Nope.' Lou shrugged. 'I dunno. I keep thinking, if it were the other way around, would I be able to take him back? Would I forgive him? The answer changes on a daily basis.'

Effie could understand that. Could she forgive Oliver? Since he'd posted the notes through the letterbox, she'd reverted to the mental state she'd been in right after he'd left. She could wake up in the morning, convinced that they were over, but by the afternoon, she'd be bombarded by the good memories they'd created and the overwhelming sense of duty to stick to the vows they'd made. She wondered if Mickey was still resolute that his relationship with Lou was finished. Both Lou and Oliver had done something that was unforgiveable in one way or another.

'You still want him back, though?' Effie asked.

'Of course I do. All I can do now is think positive and hope he changes his mind. I'll see him at Smith's barbecue, I'm sure. Maybe I'll have a better idea then.'

That'd be interesting. Smith was having a barbecue for his birthday, and it would be the first time Lou and Mickey would be in the same space since they'd split. Effie hoped for her sake that it wouldn't turn into a car crash.

She took the dips and breadsticks and followed Lou outside as they padded across the garden.

'What about you? Is the douchebag still sending you flowers?'

'Hold on a sec.' Effie went back into the kitchen and dug out the cards he'd posted from a drawer. She took them out to Lou, who was sitting on her lounger. 'He posted these a couple of days ago. I haven't heard from him since.'

She drank her Pimm's as Lou looked through the cards. All she'd had since he'd posted them was radio silence, and it was starting to bother her. Why? She sighed. God, it was all so confusing. She hated him for what he'd done, but at the same time, she found herself missing parts of him. She missed having someone to come home to, to hug when she felt wobbly, to talk to over dinner. She found herself questioning whether her heart was really broken over their separation, even though her head told her it should be. At first, she'd felt overwhelmed by his attempts to win her back. All she'd wanted was to be left alone. She'd got her wish when he stopped, but the initial relief had morphed into a nagging sense of disappointment weighing down in her chest. He'd given up so easily.

Lou handed back the cards with a scowl. 'Pathetic. None of this crap excuses what he did.'

'I know.' Effie nodded.

So why do I miss him?

Maybe he hadn't really meant what he'd written. Maybe it was all a ploy to get back at her for throwing him out. He was confusing the hell out of her. At least when Smith had gone, he'd gone. She wasn't on tenterhooks, waiting to see when he'd be back. It had ended and that was that – until he'd come back anyway.

'I still can't believe it,' Lou said, shaking her head. 'To think I was singing his praises the whole time. He totally pulled the wool over everyone's eyes.'

'I know,' Effie replied.

'He makes Smith look like the perfect guy.'

'Ha!' Effie laughed, sitting back on her lounger. 'When you put it like that, maybe we should just swear off men.'

'No way. I'm going to do everything I can to get mine back.' Lou propped herself up on her elbows. 'Maybe I was wrong about Smith.'

'In what sense?'

'Well, I was always quick to point out his flaws because he hurt you so much, but he's been so different since he came back. When you told me about him bringing you home when you got sick, it didn't surprise me at all. He totally screwed things up, but you were a great couple. And even though he might not be the most reliable and perfect of men, at least he loved you. He'd never have done anything to hurt you, not in the way that Olly did.'

Effie nodded. She was right about that, but a broken heart hurt just as much as being beaten up, if not more.

'You know if you wanted to, you could just reach out and grab him. You know he still loves you.'

'As if. Bringing me home and taking me for a drink doesn't mean he's in love with me, and I'm in no position to be reaching out and grabbing anyone.'

The last thing she needed was complications. Having Smith stay at her place for a few hours so she could sleep was one thing.

Taking it further when she was in a state of flux about Oliver was quite another. And anyway, there was nothing to say that there was anything *to* take further, even if she wanted to. Things had been friendly enough between her and Smith since the day he'd brought her home, and he'd sent her the odd text to see if she was doing okay, but apart from seeing him at work, nothing between them had changed. Certainly not to the extent where she could *reach out and grab him.*

They lay on their loungers in silence, soaking up the sun and drinking their drinks. The distinctive smell of a charcoal barbecue infused the air, and Effie's stomach rumbled. She sat up and tied her hair up in a high bun. The chemical straightening she'd had for her birthday had grown out, and her curls had returned. Since Oliver had left, she hadn't even so much as reached for her GHDs, and now she was left with a huge mass of bouncy curls. She took the lids off the dips and stuck a breadstick into the taramasalata.

'Ah, this is bliss.' Lou sighed and Effie smiled. She couldn't agree more.

∾

'Is this ready to come off, do you think?' Effie asked, trying not to move her mouth too much against the firm set of the clay mask Lou had applied.

Lou peered at her face. 'Yep, I think so.'

The afternoon had passed in a beautiful blur of Pimm's, light food and sunbathing. Maybe it was the booze, but as Effie removed the cucumber slices from her eyes, she could've sworn there was an almost magical haze to the atmosphere. It was like looking at the world through a filtered camera lens. The bushes in the garden were ultra-green and the sky ultra-blue, and the air was dotted with tiny dandelion seeds fluttering in the breeze. She leaned back on her hands and looked up at the sky. It was a day she never wanted to end.

'Do you want anything from inside?' she asked.

'Some of that brie would be nice. And more booze.'

Effie swung her legs to the side of the sunlounger and let her feet sink into the grass. It reminded her of her wedding night, when she'd escaped outside for a moment of solitude and stepped out of her heels. She did her best to disguise the pang in her chest and ignore the confusion about whether the pang was about seeing Smith for the first time after so long or the memory of how happy she'd been on her wedding day. It was hard to believe it was only six months ago. How quickly things had changed. They hadn't even made it to their first anniversary without things falling apart. Effie sighed and stood up, and her knees almost buckled.

'Oh, god.' She gripped the back of the sunlounger. Olly was standing by the back door, looking at her.

'What?' Lou asked and followed the trail of Effie's stare back to the house. 'What the hell is *he* doing here?'

Effie didn't say anything as she looked at her husband. How had he got in? The locks had been changed, and she'd been meticulous about keeping the windows closed, even in the midst of their freak heatwave.

'Did you take the door off the latch when you came in?' she asked as quietly as she could without taking her eyes off Oliver.

Lou swore. 'I didn't realise it was on. I thought it had closed behind me.' She swore again. 'I'm sorry.'

Effie shook her head. 'Don't worry about it.'

There was no point stressing about it now. It had to come to a head sooner or later. It was just a shame it had to be today, on what had turned out to be one of the best days she'd had in a long time.

'Don't, Effie,' Lou said, standing up and putting her hand on Effie's shoulder. 'Don't let him try and win you back.'

'I'm not,' Effie replied. 'But this is his house.'

'So come stay with me, and leave that dickhead here on his own. Don't let him manipulate you.'

Lou threw Oliver a look of pure disdain, but he still didn't budge from the doorway. It must have been obvious that Lou knew what he'd done and was rallying around her best friend, but he seemed to be waiting to be given the all-clear before making contact.

Effie sighed. 'I have to talk to him.'

'Why?'

Effie looked at him again. He looked like a child, worried about whether it was safe to cross the playground. She wanted to hear what he had to say. It was shaky ground, she knew. She was confused; Oliver could turn on the charm when he needed to, and she'd told herself she wouldn't ever take him back, but she still wondered if somewhere, deep down, she still loved him. Having Smith around had turned her head, distracted her and made her question her life, but what she had with Oliver was different. It was bound in marriage. Surely that had to mean something? And somewhere, in a place she'd been trying to keep buried, part of her was wondering if they could try again and make a go of things. Maybe they could go back to the good times they'd had.

'Because I have to,' she said.

'But what if he tries something?'

'He won't. He wouldn't, and I'm not scared of him.'

'But *I'm* scared for you.'

'Seriously, Lou, it's fine.'

'No way am I leaving you with him.' Lou shook her head. 'But if you really want to talk to him – and I have no idea why you would – then I'll wait in the car.'

Effie nodded. It sounded like a fair compromise.

'You come straight out if anything goes wrong. And if you need to, you'll stay at mine. Okay?'

'I will.' Effie nodded. 'I promise.'

Lou hugged her, and Effie watched as she walked across the garden. Oliver stepped outside to let her pass, and she hovered in front of him, staring him down. The look on Oliver's face made it clear that he was embarrassed. And so he should be.

With Lou gone, he walked across the grass and started to speak, but she cut him off.

'I need to go clean up.'

Oliver nodded. 'Sure. I'll wait inside.'

'No, we'll talk out here.'

She didn't want to feel trapped. She wanted to be outside, not surrounded by photos of them to sway her mind.

Okay, Effie. You can do this.

And, she wanted to give the impression of being in control. He'd come into the house without warning, but she wanted this to be on her terms.

You're in control.

24.

Effie looked at Oliver through the kitchen window. Seeing him in a plain T-shirt, shorts and boat shoes, she could almost imagine that things were normal, and he was chilling out in the garden, waiting for her to join him. In a parallel universe, that was probably what was happening. She took a gulp of water and headed outside. It was crunch time.

She pulled her lounger away from his and sat cross-legged. 'How did you get in?'

'The door was on the latch.' He had the good grace to look sheepish. 'I hope you don't mind. I had to take advantage of it. I had to see you.'

His skin had tanned since she'd last seen him, and he looked good. He looked how he had on Koh Tao, beautifully bronzed. But she'd since learned that looks didn't mean anything. He rested his elbows on his knees and crossed his arms.

'You look great,' he said, looking her over.

She had no makeup on, and she was wearing a pair of old shorts and a T-shirt. She'd looked way more glamorous than this.

'What were you expecting?' she asked. 'An emaciated mess?'

Oliver shook his head. 'Not at all. You're strong. I'm not surprised you're doing so well.'

Effie shrugged. All her life, she'd had to be resilient and flexible. This was just another in a long line of tests life had thrown her way. She reached down and picked a blade of grass from the ground.

'What do you want?' she asked, looking down at it and slowly tearing it in half.

'I miss you.'

'I already know that. You've told me a billion times.'

'But I haven't actually *told* you. Not face-to-face. I felt like I had to give it one more try. Just one last shot.' He looked down at his hands. 'I had to.'

'Why? I told you, it's over.'

He looked back up at her. 'I can't accept that.'

Effie shook her head and looked away. Why couldn't he just leave her alone? Why did he have to show her this side of his personality, the sincere, repentant side, after showing her the parts of him that were as destructive as an atom bomb?

'I can't live without you, Effie.'

'You seem to be doing alright so far.' And he did. He looked well. He didn't look undernourished or anguished.

He laughed shortly. 'You couldn't be more wrong. This last month has been like living half a life. I've swayed from wanting to bombard you with texts and calls to telling myself to let you go, but I can't. I know it's the right thing to do, to see you happy. But I can't stay away from you.'

It sounded like he was confused too, just like she was, torn between wanting to keep a hold on the life they'd started together, and doing what was best. How were they even *in* this situation? How did a guy like Oliver, someone who'd been raised to be a gentleman, with every opportunity anyone could ever wish for, be apologising to his wife for hitting her?

235

The image of his face, twisted with rage, filled her head. She saw the blurry movement of his leg as his foot connected with her stomach over and over again and the way his spit angrily hit her cheek, burning like fire. She gulped and closed her eyes. What the hell should she say? The Oliver she'd seen that night wasn't her Oliver. He wasn't *Olly* – the man who spoke like Prince Harry and who had charmed his way into her life. The man she'd seen that night was someone else, a total stranger.

'You have no idea how you've turned my life around. It's as if I was just drifting along before I met you, and then – boom. Everything made sense.' He picked at his nails. 'I'd never felt like that before. I'd never had a moment of clarity like that before, and I know you felt it too.'

When he looked back at her, his eyes were filled with tears, but he blinked them away, which was just as well. She'd been holding her breath while he spoke, and she didn't think she could cope with seeing him cry.

'I knew, right then, what I wanted. I had a house and I had my job, but I hadn't realised how empty I'd felt until you. You made me want to *live*. To think about really settling down, getting married, having kids.' He paused to rub his eyes. 'I'm still doing that anger management course.'

Effie nodded and cleared her throat. 'That's good.'

'I didn't realise how angry I really was. How screwed up I was. The whole thing with Dad's affair affected me more than I really understood, and I let it spill over into us. The things we argued about . . .' He shook his head. 'I tried to control you, insulted you. I *hurt* you. And I never wanted to do that. I only ever wanted to take care of you, and instead I used all of your hurts to manipulate you.'

She drew her knees up to her chest as if they could guard her heart. His apology was so heartfelt that she could already feel the barriers that had come up since the night she'd thrown him out beginning to come down. She tightened her arms around her knees.

'And what I said about Lou . . . it was out of order. The whole thing was utterly unforgiveable, but I know why I did what I did now. And now that I know, I can control it. I can work through it. I have to. I don't want to be that person anymore.'

'What do you want me to say, Olly? You can't just come in here and apologise and expect everything to be okay again.'

'I know.' He nodded. 'I'm taking responsibility for what I did. All I ever wanted was for you to be happy, and I've had to come to terms with the idea that it might not be me who can do that. But if it is . . . if it ever was . . . I really want to try again.'

Effie sucked in her breath. He sounded so honest, so true, so sincere. What if he really *had* changed? What if they could get back to how they used to be?

'I get that it's a huge, huge ask, and I know I've probably killed any trust you had in me, but I had to try. You've changed my life in so many ways. Even now, you're fixing me without even knowing it.'

His voice broke, and when the tears finally fell from his eyes, it was all Effie could do not to lean across the gap between the loungers and hug him. It was an automatic response because, even after everything he'd done – the things he'd said, the physical pain he'd caused – she couldn't bear to see him cry. She kept her hands where they were, refusing to give in.

'You're magical and amazing, and I love you.'

Her barriers started to crash to the ground, one by one. She thought back over the past month. She'd felt like she was finally coming out of a shell she hadn't even known she'd been under. It had been scary and liberating at the same time. She'd operated at her own pace, in her own rhythm, and other people had noticed it too. She thought about what Smith had said, about her being like the sun. She'd half dismissed it at the time, but nobody had ever said anything like that about her before.

'Olly . . .' She shook her head and rubbed her eyes.

'You're my whole life. Please. Just give me one last chance, just one.'

'I think . . .' She looked at him, at his trembling chin and watery eyes, and her stomach flipped over. 'I think you should go.'

'Effie . . .'

'Please, Olly. Just go.'

25.

There were two simple, but non-negotiable rules:

1. He had to continue his anger management course.

2. She could spend as much time away from him with her friends as she wanted, no questions asked.

'One 99 Flake and chocolate sauce.' Oliver handed her the cone filled with ice cream and sat next to her on the bench. The obvious rule of *no violence* was clearly implied.

When Effie had stood in front of him at the altar on their wedding day, he'd smiled at her – a smile of pure, complete happiness and love. He had that same smile on his face now.

She took the ice cream and returned his smile. 'Thanks.'

In all the time they'd lived in Clapham, they'd only been to the Common once before, a few days after she'd moved in. On a beautiful, crisp autumn day, they'd wandered around, wrapped up in thick, woolly scarves and gloves as they held hands, kicking up the crunchy rust-coloured leaves scattered on the ground. The smell of burnt wood had floated in the freezing air, and Oliver's nose had felt cold against hers when they'd kissed. They'd returned home to a sumptuous roast dinner. It was one of those perfect long days when every moment had created new memories.

'What do you want to do tonight?' Oliver asked.

Effie shrugged. 'The cinema, maybe?'

'Good idea. We haven't been to The Picturehouse before, and there are some nice restaurants nearby too. I'll book us a table, if you want.'

Effie licked her ice cream and nodded. It was Oliver who'd suggested they have at least one night a week where they did something together. A *date night*. She'd cringed when she'd realised that's what it was, but she hadn't wanted to say no. It wasn't like she had a problem with the principle; it was just that it sounded so forced. It reminded her of when Oliver had insisted they *try* for a baby.

She looked at him eating his ice cream. He was being so nice that, on the surface, she couldn't find fault with him. After he'd gatecrashed the garden party and she'd sent him away, he'd called round again a few days later to collect more clothes. He hadn't tried to reason with her or begged for another chance. Instead, he'd quietly headed straight upstairs to pack, and Effie had sat on the sofa as he moved around the house, realising that she was counting down the seconds to when he would leave again. Only, it wasn't because she wanted him to go. It was because she'd wanted him to stay.

She hadn't been able to ignore his sincerity when he'd explained himself out in the garden. It was as if she'd seen a side to him she'd forgotten about. She'd seen Olly, the *real* Olly. He'd laid himself bare, stripped away his ego and put himself on the line. He'd explained that his anger and the battle to control it was like a disease. He had to work to control his anger in the same way an alcoholic or a gambler had to work to control the lure of their addiction. It could be fixed. There were men who'd moved on from being abusive to developing loving relationships, and there was no reason he couldn't be one of them, at least, that's what she'd told Lou.

She'd urged Effie not to take him back, not to fall for his spiel, and she'd even come round to try to talk her out of it, but Effie's stubborn streak had stood its ground. She couldn't turn her back on him. For better, for worse – she hadn't said those vows for fun.

He needed her help, and she didn't want to be questioned about her motives for taking him back – not yet. Despite him being a picture-perfect husband since his return, there was a part of her that was still on red alert, and she didn't want to be reminded of the possibility of it all blowing up in her face.

'Maybe we could tackle the garden when we get back?' Oliver said. 'It's starting to look like a jungle.'

It wasn't. With its decking and super manicured lawn, it looked like something from the pages of a home and garden magazine. It was one of the things she loved about the house the most.

'It's too hot to be gardening,' Effie replied.

She leaned back against the bench and stretched her legs out, watching a mother and daughter walk past with a Dalmatian on a lead.

Oliver leaned back too and bit into his cone. 'That's true. It's a beautiful day, isn't it?' He looked at her. 'You've got chocolate sauce on your chin.'

'Bloody stuff gets everywhere.' She laughed and wiped it away with the back of her hand.

'Like rice?' Oliver grinned.

'Yeah.' She nodded, smiling, remembering their wedding day and how they'd clung to each other on the dance floor. 'Like rice.'

'You know, I was thinking. Maybe we should look at flights to Corsica soon. I haven't seen Mum since the wedding, and it might do us some good to get away from it all.'

She'd been so excited when he'd suggested it on her birthday, but now she wasn't so sure. Celeste Barton-Cole was razor sharp. Effie would bet money that she'd pick up on the underlying tension between her son and daughter-in-law, and the fact that they weren't sleeping in the same bed wouldn't help. Effie would either have to face questions about why or give in and take the step she was still reluctant to take. She might have taken him back, but it was conditional, and she wasn't ready to be that close to him again yet.

'What do you think?'

Effie puffed the air out in her cheeks. 'I don't know. It would be nice to get away, like you say, but it might be a bit too soon.'

Oliver looked away and nodded, his jaws twitching as he clenched them together.

'Maybe in a few months?' Effie added.

'I guess you're right.' He looked back at her. 'It's just difficult, you know. I don't want to crowd you and make you feel under pressure, but I want you to see how serious I am about making this work.'

'I know. But the best way of doing that is to let me take things at my own pace.'

'Things are better, though, aren't they? I mean, I know it's early days and everything, but it feels right, doesn't it?'

Effie looked away from his hopeful, cornflower-blue eyes. 'It's just going to take time.'

'They told me that, at the classes. It's really been amazing. It's made me see myself in a whole new light. Crazy how something that happened half my lifetime ago could have had such a profound effect, isn't it?'

'It sure is.' Effie nodded. She could understand that. She was still feeling the effects of her mum leaving, even now. 'You know, I just realised. We were both fifteen when our family shit hit the fan.'

Oliver raised his eyebrows. 'That's right. It's such a pivotal age too. It's a surprise we've turned out to be as normal as we have.'

Effie laughed with a hint of irony. Normal was about as far away as it could possibly get. 'I've never known what *normal* is like.'

'I thought I did,' he replied, draping an arm over the back of the bench and lightly stroking her arm. 'I thought it meant just dealing with it, working, dating, going through the motions. Now I know I was just burying it.'

'These classes sound really good for you. Have you told Izzy?'

Oliver snorted. 'God, no. She's so together in comparison. I just want you to know that it doesn't matter how long all this takes,' he said, lightly brushing a strand of hair behind her ears. 'It won't be easy, but even if it takes the next fifty years to prove it, you'll see. From here on out, I'm going to be a better man.'

Cooking, cleaning, taking the wheelie bins out onto the street the night before collection day – Oliver did it all. If being a better man meant becoming the poster boy for the modern husband, he would have topped the list, and what was more, he did it all before Effie even had the chance to think about doing it herself. Later that evening, she looked at him as he came into the kitchen and washed his hands in the sink, having put the bins out.

'You don't have to do all the housework, you know,' she said, careful not to sound ungrateful. 'Don't get me wrong – I'm not complaining. I just don't think it's fair for you to do all of it.'

'I'm not. You've vacuumed the whole house, changed the beds, done the laundry, shopping and the cleaning this weekend.' He dried his hands as he pointed out the chores Effie had completed on autopilot. 'Anyway, it's part of the programme I've been given.'

'Cleaning is supposed to help with your anger?' She raised an eyebrow.

'It's more that it's a mundane task. It doesn't take a lot of mental energy. I find it kind of therapeutic. I can think.'

'Fair enough.' She shrugged. 'By the way, I'm not around for dinner tomorrow.'

'Oh?' He briefly looked at her before pulling some chicken from the fridge for dinner. 'Going anywhere nice?'

He sounded like a hairdresser instead of her husband. It all seemed so formal, but at least he was sticking to the rules.

'I'm meeting Izzy. She's in town for a meeting, so I said we'd catch up. I haven't seen her for ages.'

'Oh, good. It'll be nice for you two to spend some time together.'

'Yeah.' She nodded. 'It will.'

He'd apologised for what he'd said about Lou, but Effie couldn't help but wonder if his reaction would have been as placid had she said she was meeting with her friend instead. She'd watched his face for any hints of relief when she'd said she was meeting with Izzy, but he had a poker face that was second to none. Smith's barbecue wasn't far away, and Oliver most definitely wasn't welcome. She'd find out if he'd make true on his promises soon enough.

∽

When Izzy texted the address of the place they were to meet for dinner the next day, Effie had looked at the street name in the heart of the West End and assumed they'd be eating in a plush, high-end restaurant. After a long and frustrating day at work, she was looking forward to a bit of luxury, so when she stood outside their meeting place, she frowned, peering through the window. This couldn't possibly be right. She double-checked the details in the text, and when she looked through the window again, she saw Izzy, sitting at a table, waving. Effie raised an eyebrow and stepped inside.

A man smiled at her from behind a glass counter holding raw diced chicken and lamb on skewers as he shaved strips from a lump of doner meat. The smell of frying onions and bacon hung heavy in the air, and Effie excused herself, shimmying past two heavy-set men waiting for their food.

'It's so good to see you.' Izzy stood and hugged her before sliding back into her chair. 'Isn't this place great?'

Effie looked around as she sat down. The chairs were screwed down into the floor, and there were only five tiny tables, three of which were occupied by men tucking into enormous fry-ups.

'I always come here when I'm in the area,' Izzy said. 'Their bubble and squeak is to die for.'

It was the last thing Effie would have expected to come out of Izzy's mouth. For one thing, she barely ever saw her eat anything, and when she did, it was always bland. The first time she'd gone to their house with Oliver, Izzy had grilled a chicken breast with no seasoning and steamed some vegetables. It was nutritious, but it had been like swallowing cardboard. She'd since discovered that it was Tom who did the cooking in their house.

'Bubble and squeak?'

'It's my guilty pleasure.' Izzy grinned. 'There's nothing like a bit of comfort food every now and then.'

Effie looked at the laminated menu. There was nothing remotely wholesome on the list at all. When was the last time she'd pigged out on junk food? Her mouth flooded with the anticipation of bacon, sausage, fried egg and mushrooms. When the waitress came to scribble down their order, she ordered without hesitation.

'How did your meeting go?'

Izzy beamed a smile across the table. 'Amazingly well. I'm not supposed to say anything to anyone yet, but, well, it looks like you'll soon be able to buy my products in Selfridges.'

'No way.' Effie grinned and squeezed Izzy's hand. 'That's fantastic news.'

'I know. The pitch almost killed me, hence the reason why I need some comfort food, and there aren't many people I could bring to a place like this.'

Effie wasn't sure if it was a compliment or not, especially after what Izzy had said at the New Year's Eve party about her not being typical Barton-Cole standard.

'Seriously, you can't breathe a word of my meeting to anyone. Not even Olly. I want to wait until it's one hundred per cent confirmed.'

Effie nodded and crossed her heart. 'I promise.'

It was funny how things were turning out. Oliver and Izzy were close, but it was Effie who was in the middle of them both, holding their secrets. Izzy had no idea about Oliver's anger management classes or why he had to take them in the first place, and he had no idea about her breakthrough Selfridges deal.

'How is my little brother? I'm so pleased you've worked things out.' Izzy clasped her hands together and smiled.

'It's early days, but so far, so good. He's trying really hard. He really seems to want to make it work.'

'Well, of course he does.' Izzy rolled her eyes. 'He loves the bones of you. Honestly, he was devastated, moping around the place. I don't think I could have dealt with it for much longer.'

'Thank you,' Effie said, although she wasn't entirely sure what she was thanking her for.

'Oh, it's nothing.' She waved a hand in front of her face. 'He's a pain sometimes, but he's my brother. He knows he's always welcome – you both are.' Izzy looked over Effie's shoulder and grinned. 'Ooh, yes. Here it is.'

The waitress put their plates on the table, and Effie shook her head with a slightly stunned smile. Izzy's bubble and squeak was piled high next to a portion of cold meat and Effie's own plate held the biggest fry-up she'd ever seen.

'Bon appétit,' Izzy said and picked up her knife and fork. She took a mouthful and sighed, looking up at the ceiling. 'Simply divine.'

It was all Effie could do not to laugh. With her super sharp suit, flawless hair and cut-glass accent, Izzy stuck out in the cafe like an inkblot on a white shirt.

'So, what was it that made you change your mind?' Izzy asked.

As far as Effie knew, Oliver hadn't told his sister the real reason behind the rift in their marriage. She sliced into her sausage, skewered it with her fork and shrugged. 'He came round and we talked.

246

Or rather, he talked and I listened. I guess I just couldn't give up on him. On us.'

She shrugged again, and Izzy nodded.

'Marriage is for life,' Izzy said. 'Even after Mummy and Daddy divorced, they still tried to impress that on us. I think she'd suspected he cheated for a long time, but she let it slide until it got too much. After seeing how their divorce ripped the family apart, I decided I never wanted to be a divorcée, and I expect Olly is the same. Being married isn't easy.'

Effie looked at Izzy as she loaded her fork, and wondered if she really did find it hard. As far as she could see, Izzy and Tom had the perfect life. They had great careers and a fabulous house, took multiple holidays a year and were more than financially stable.

'I'd have thought it was easy for you. You and Tom seem to be in a permanent state of bliss,' Effie said.

Izzy laughed. 'God, no. Don't get me wrong; we love each other, but sometimes he drives me insane. We've tried and failed to get pregnant, he's got promotion after promotion and now he spends more time in the office than at home. My business has taken off better than I could ever have expected, and all my energy seems to go there right now instead of into my marriage.' She shrugged with a smile. 'There's only so much a relationship can take before something has to give.'

'Have you ever separated?'

'Almost. For a long time I wondered if we were really right for each other. There was a year when we seemed to just argue *all* the time, but we made the choice to stay together. I definitely don't subscribe to the thought that there's only one person in the world for someone. I think it's more that you choose whoever is the right person at the time, and then you try to grow together. You either do, or you don't.'

Effie slowly buttered her toast. If Izzy was right, then her conflicting feelings for Smith might make sense, but on the flipside, it could also mean that her doubts about Oliver were because she'd made the wrong choice in marrying him to begin with. She loaded her toast with beans and took a bite. The beans had been cooked rather than just heated up, and the tomato sauce was sweet and thick on her tongue.

'Every couple argues, I guess,' Effie said, 'but you and Tom seem to have it figured out for the most part.'

'We do now, but it took a while to get there.' Izzy put her fork down. 'I know what people think when they see Tom. He's a little podgy around the edges, and he's so absorbed in his work, he barely notices anything else, but what they *don't* see is how dedicated he is. Give him a stable centre to come from, and he radiates it back. I've dated guys before who wouldn't know stability if it hit them in the face. It's a roller-coaster ride, for sure, but roller coasters have to come to a grinding halt at some point.'

Effie nodded. What could she say to that? For a second, she'd almost forgotten it was her sister-in-law she was talking to, but she couldn't very well say that she understood the thrill of being with a guy who had the ability to turn the world upside down, someone who made stability look about as normal as a green sky.

'For what it's worth, I think you're doing the right thing, taking Olly back,' Izzy continued, 'and I'm not just saying that because he's my brother. If you can't work through the bad stuff, then what's the point? You just have to ask yourself if you love Olly. *Really* love him. Strip away everything you associate with him – his job, his family, his social status – everything. If you love him for who he is, the raw essence of him, then you'll be fine.'

Effie frowned as Izzy tucked into her bubble and squeak. She'd never thought about loving the *raw essence* of someone. She wasn't even entirely sure what it meant. She knew she loved Oliver; otherwise, she'd never have married him, but she'd never really stopped to try to break it down to such a detailed level before.

'Are you happy, though?' Effie asked.

Izzy nodded and waited to swallow her food before answering, 'Definitely. Sometimes you have to adjust what your expectations of happiness are, that's all.'

Adjust her expectations of happiness? Why did that sound like such a massive compromise?

'And right now, bubble and squeak is the very definition of happiness.'

26.

ssence: The intrinsic nature or indispensable quality of something which determines its character. Origin: from Latin, essential, from *esse*, 'to be'.

Effie turned the definition she'd read online over and over in her head as she walked up the road to Smith's parents' house. Since she'd met Izzy for dinner, she'd thought of little else. It was like she'd given her a Rubik's cube containing the secret to the meaning of life, and just like the infamous game, it was frustrating the hell out of her. It was making her question *why* she loved Oliver.

Whenever she'd thought about it before, any number of reasons had come to mind. He was good looking, charming, well brought up, wealthy, secure and successful. He'd represented everything she wasn't and everything she'd thought she wanted, but little by little, the veneer had started to slip, and now she didn't know how much of what she thought she knew was real and how much was what she'd wanted to see.

The charm that had made her dizzy at the beginning was the same charm he'd shown when he'd talked her round to giving him one more chance. She didn't doubt his sincerity, but it was much easier to swallow when he knew how to pull at her heartstrings. He might have been well brought up, but he still hadn't been sheltered from the fallout of family drama – a fallout that had triggered deep-seated issues. There was no doubt that he was successful – he was one of the most sought after barristers in London. But he wasn't wealthy; his family was. The material security the Barton-Cole name had given her had meant nothing when it came down to it. It hadn't protected her from him. The more she'd tried to think about whether she loved Oliver's *essence*, the more she questioned if she even knew what it was.

A drop of rain hit her bare shoulder, and she frowned, looking up at the sky. The morning clouds had lingered through to the afternoon, and they were looking greyer by the minute. Smith's flat only had a small balcony, so he was having his birthday barbecue at his parents' house instead. Their garden was beautiful and mature after years of nurturing, and Effie felt a stir in the depths of her stomach. She'd stayed there countless times at the end of nights out with Smith, sharing a bed and longing for him to make a move, until the night he finally did. She looked at the house a few doors up the street. When would this ever end? Why did her mind always revert to Smith when she should be thinking about her husband and their fragile future together instead?

The front door was open, and as she walked up the tiny path, she dug her nails into her palms to steel herself against the stir that was turning into butterflies with every step she took. To say she wasn't looking forward to this party was an understatement. Despite being jealous of Smith, Oliver had merely nodded when she told him she was going, and although she knew it couldn't have been easy for him, she was pleased he was sticking to his word about not questioning her time with her friends. Still, there was a huge part of her that didn't want to go. Not only was she about to surround herself with people who despised Oliver, but she also had to do it while questioning herself about why she was with him in the first place. As soon as she walked through the door, she saw Smith's mum, Yvette, coming down the stairs, with her hair in rollers.

'There she is,' Yvette said, holding her arms out to give Effie a hug. 'How are you? It's been a long time.'

'It has,' Effie replied, folding herself into Yvette's arms. Her hugs were legendary, and she'd always welcomed Effie with open arms when she used to visit. 'I'm good, thanks. How are you?'

'Good. Great, in fact.' Yvette linked her arm through Effie's and led her through to the kitchen. 'It's been so lovely having James back, and we all know how much of a turnaround that is.'

She winked and Effie grinned. It was Yvette who'd told Smith in no uncertain terms that he had to leave when everything had gone wrong. He'd been laid up in his hospital bed, and she hadn't given him a choice. Effie had sunk low into the hard, plastic chair, trying to make herself invisible. It had turned out to be the best thing Yvette could've done if the way he'd been since his return was anything to go by. Effie couldn't imagine what it must've taken for her to say those words to her son, but Yvette was clearly savvy enough to know that he had to either disappear or die.

Effie watched her friends through the kitchen window as they sat in the garden chatting. Mickey and Smith manned the barbecue, and she looked at Smith as he flipped a burger over, laughing at something Mickey had said. There was no sign of Lou, but it was hardly surprising. She was always late for everything.

'We had to put the gazebo up. I've no idea why James insisted on a barbecue when the forecast predicted rain.' Yvette tutted.

Effie laughed. 'You know him. He never takes the easy route.'

'God only knows where he got that from.' The grin on Yvette's face told Effie that it was no secret that he'd got it from her. 'And how are you, my lovely? James tells me you got married?'

'Yep. Seven months now.' Effie nodded.

'Congratulations. I'm so pleased for you.'

She did seem genuinely happy, judging by her smile, but she'd always said what a good couple Effie and Smith had made. Of course, she hadn't seen the crushing heartache Effie had felt when she'd heard that he'd hooked up with someone else, and as far as Yvette knew, their relationship had been a normal one – boyfriend and girlfriend, not girlfriend and non-committal man.

'Where's Dermot?' Effie asked, looking out to the garden again for Smith's dad.

'Supermarket. I think it's fair to say James vastly underestimated the amount of food you generally need for a barbecue, especially with the amount of alcohol he's bought.' Yvette shook her head. 'Right, you go and have fun, and I'm sure I'll see you later when we get back.'

'You're not staying?'

'Oh, heavens no. We wouldn't want to cramp James's style. I'm off to take these rollers out and get beautified. We're meeting up with friends for dinner, so we'll leave you young ones to it.' She kissed Effie on the cheek. 'Have a lovely time.'

Effie stayed in the kitchen when Yvette went back upstairs, and looked out of the window again. They were her best friends, but she felt like turning around and slipping out unnoticed. She turned and looked at the fridge, covered with letters and memos stuck to the door with magnets. On the wall next to it was a cork noticeboard covered with photos. She smiled at a strip of pictures taken of Yvette and Dermot in a photo booth, the pleated burnt-orange curtain bright against them in the background. The first photo showed them grinning into the camera, the second showed them kissing and the third showed them laughing. They looked young, no older than their early twenties. Sean, Smith's older brother, was thirty, and Smith had told her they'd got married before he was born.

Thirty-odd years. That was a long time to be with someone, and when Effie had said her vows, she'd promised to be with Oliver for life, but now? She was sure Izzy had intended to help, but instead, all she'd done was inadvertently burrow the seed of doubt even deeper into Effie's mind.

She looked at a photo of Smith, sitting in a high chair with chocolate smeared around his mouth. Even as a toddler, he'd had a mass of brown curls, and his grey eyes looked bigger than ever. Next to his photo was one of Brendan, the middle son who'd died two years before Smith had been born.

'It'll be twenty-seven years this September.'

Effie turned at the sound of Smith's voice. 'Brendan?'

Smith nodded, and she turned back to look at the photo of his brother, sleeping in his incubator. It was grainy and faded at the edges with age. He'd been born prematurely, with a heart defect.

'I try to imagine what he'd be like,' Smith said. 'I reckon he'd have been super cool. Middle kids always are, aren't they?'

He stood with his head right next to hers, and she turned a little to look at him as he studied the photo. A light coating of stubble coated his jaw. He smelled of charcoal and summertime, and Effie wanted to sink into him and soak it in. Instead, she looked back at the photo.

'Yeah,' she agreed. 'He probably would have been.'

'So.' He looked down at her and stuffed his hands into his jeans pockets. 'How's things?'

Effie nodded and looked back at him. 'They're good. One step at a time, you know?'

He nodded back, but his face told a different story. It displayed the very reason why she'd been nervous about today. The look in his eyes made it clear he thought she'd made a mistake in taking Oliver back, and that was without him knowing the real reason they'd separated in the first place.

'Oh, of course. Happy birthday.' Effie smiled as she handed him the small bag.

'Cheers.' He took the book from the bag. 'Aw, Eff, I've got this already.'

'I know – I remember. Look inside.'

He opened it, and the awkward, apologetic look on his face gave way to a grin. 'No way. A signed copy?'

He ran his fingers over the page and shook his head. *Into the Wild* was his favourite book, and the copy he had was tattered with age.

'Man, that's . . .' He looked back at her and shook his head again. 'It's probably the best present I've ever had.'

Effie grinned and shrugged. 'It's nothing.'

But it *was* something. She'd wanted to get him something personal, something that would somehow convey her gratitude for what he'd done while she was separated from Oliver. It was Smith who had looked after her when she'd fainted, cooked her dinner and made her feel safe enough to stay in the house on her own. She owed him, and she wanted to pay him back. He hugged her, his strong arms around her neck, and she inhaled his summertime scent. She also hoped the gift was a token of an apology. Nothing had actually happened between them, but she couldn't deny that they'd got closer in those few weeks. She couldn't shake the sense that he felt let down now that she'd taken Oliver back.

Smith rested his chin on the top of her head and squeezed her. 'Thank you.'

Maybe today wouldn't be so bad after all.

❧

Every so often, the garden would be transformed from a sunny little haven to a chamber of mental torture. When the sun was out, everyone would spread themselves across the garden, but as soon as the clouds merged and dumped the rain down, they'd huddle together under the gazebo. With the rest of Smith's friends, there was nowhere near enough room for them all, and she could almost feel the air under the gazebo crackling with tension whenever Lou and Mickey looked at each other. Being clumped together must have been as unbearable for the both of them as it was for everyone else.

As heavy pellets of rain lashed the gazebo and bounced up from the grass, Effie looked at her friends. Mickey stood by the barbecue, right at the edge of the shelter provided by the white structure above them. He kept his eyes down, fixed to the ground, with his eyebrows furrowed together and his clenching jaw working overtime. Lou stood on the other side of the barbecue, trying, and clearly failing, not to look at Mickey. For every glance she directed elsewhere, two seemed to focus in on him. She had such a look of concentration on her face that Effie could only imagine that Lou was trying to telepathically send him signals to look back at her. He didn't.

Effie looked up at Smith standing next to her, nursing a can of Red Stripe. 'Great day for a barbecue.'

'I know.' Smith grimaced, took a sip of beer and then shrugged. 'It is England, though. A barbecue isn't a barbecue without the threat of rain. It's tradition.'

'Little bit more than a threat.'

So far, it had only showered, and after a couple of minutes, the sun had come out, dried the grass enough for them to sit on blankets and they'd got straight back to the party. This time, it looked like the sun had disappeared, never to return again. Lou sighed heavily, and Effie turned to look at her.

'Shall we go inside?' Effie asked. 'I'm getting a bit cold. You guys can stay out here and talk about boy stuff.'

'That's a bit sexist,' Smith said. 'What do you even define as *boy stuff*?'

Effie shrugged. 'I dunno. Football, *Top Gear*, beer.'

'So stereotypical. If you must know, I've been wanting to talk about the resurgence of feminism. I read a really interesting article about it recently. It was a theory that feminism was actually a concept invented by a guy to control women. Fascinating.'

'Smart-arse,' she replied and flicked Smith's arm, grinning as she tried to hide her guilt at getting back with Oliver. His ability to bounce back to her playful banter was one of the things she adored about him the most.

'What was that saying again? Don't judge a book by its cover – that was it.' Smith grinned back.

'Does it still count if you've known the book long enough to know the words by heart?' Effie raised an eyebrow. 'Stop being a smart alec. We'll come back out when the rain stops.'

'So basically, never,' Mickey said, looking up and once again locking eyes with Lou. Effie looked at the two of them, both clearly wanting to say something to each other and both hanging back.

'Come on.' Effie took charge and hurried through the garden and into the house, holding the back door open for Lou to follow her. Once they were inside, she grabbed a piece of kitchen paper and dabbed away the rain on her arms.

'Thanks,' Lou said with a sad smile. 'I don't think I could've stayed under there for much longer.'

'I thought you'd agreed to talk?'

'We had,' Lou replied, looking at her. 'He texted a few days ago to say that we should. I just don't know what to say to him. I don't know how to.'

'Maybe getting away from everyone else is a good way to start?' Effie suggested. 'You can't talk while you're surrounded by all of us.'

Lou turned and leaned against the sink, looking at Mickey through the window. 'What if he says no?'

'He won't.' Effie followed the direction of Lou's gaze. He looked every bit as miserable as Lou did. 'He said he wanted to talk, so you should talk. You've spent a year and a half together. Short of Smith, you know him better than anyone else here.'

'Oh, god. I feel sick.' Lou looked out of the window again at Mickey. 'I'll send him a text. Do you think we can use Smith's old room?'

'Don't see why not.'

'Okay,' Lou said and looked up at her once she'd sent the text. 'Sent.'

Effie looked past Lou into the garden, watching Mickey as he took his phone from his pocket. 'He's reading it.'

'Oh, crap. Okay. I'll go up. How do I look?'

'Like you've been caught in the rain and you're shit-scared about facing the man you love.'

Lou nodded. 'All of which are true.'

'Go.' Effie smiled at her and held up her crossed fingers. 'Good luck.'

No sooner had Lou disappeared from the kitchen than Mickey came in, closely followed by Smith.

'He doesn't need an escort, surely?' Effie said to Smith, but he shook his head, avoiding her eyes.

'Claire's lost. I've got to go and meet her.'

Effie's heart stopped as he walked past. 'Claire? But I thought you said—'

He'd walked too far to hear or he'd ignored her, but either way, he didn't reply, and Effie was left standing in the middle of the kitchen with her stomach dropping like an apple from a tree. He'd said they were over, so why was she coming?

From then on, Effie's mood darkened, and by the time Smith and Claire returned, the rain had intensified. She watched as Claire waved hello to everyone and handed Smith a present – a fancy bottle of whisky. Effie scowled and poured another vodka and Coke. Big deal. At least Effie had put some thought into Smith's gift. She sank her drink and poured another, her mood matched perfectly by the grey, dank weather outside.

An hour later, she picked at the barbecued leftovers, trying to abate the effects of the vodka. She didn't even like vodka, but she had to do something to block out the fact that Claire was there. It wasn't that she wanted Smith for herself. It was just that Claire made her uncomfortable. She looked up as Lou came back into the kitchen and joined her by the sink. When Mickey followed her in and threw her a small smile, Effie turned to look at Lou.

'How did it go?' Effie asked. She went to lean against the sink but misjudged the distance, and her elbow slipped from its ceramic surface.

'Whoa there.' Lou steadied her. 'How much have you had to drink?'

Effie shrugged and nibbled on a piece of chicken breast. 'It's a party, isn't it? Isn't this what you're meant to do?'

'Get shit-faced?' Lou raised an eyebrow. 'Yes, but you don't look like you're in the right mood to be getting drunk. How are you getting home?'

'I'll text Olly. Don't worry, I'll be fine.'

Lou followed her gaze to see Claire across the room, chatting to Mickey. 'When did Claire get here?'

Effie shrugged, chewing her chicken. 'Ages ago. She's just come in and stood there looking all smug. What's her game? Why hasn't she mentioned anything about what she heard?'

'I don't know.' Lou took the glass from Effie's hand before she had a chance to refill it. 'Maybe it's because she's a nice person. Not everyone is out to try and screw you over. And why do you care anyway? You're back with Horrible Oliver.'

'I *don't* care.'

'Of course you don't. That's why you're standing here with a face like thunder, all because Smith's brought another girl to his birthday party.'

'Give it a rest, Lou. I'm not in the mood.'

Lou sighed. 'Why can't you just admit you made a mistake and move on? There's no shame in it, and it's got to be better than going back to someone who—'

Effie cut her off by grabbing her glass and the bottle of vodka and walking away. She didn't look back as she stalked out into the garden and leaned against the wall. She poured herself another drink, refusing to cry. This was exactly what she'd expected to happen, but she'd fooled herself into thinking that she'd somehow escaped having to hear what they really thought. She pulled a cigarette from the box in her pocket and lit the tip before angrily expelling the smoke through her mouth and taking her phone from her bag. She texted Oliver with Smith's parents' address, asking him to pick her up sooner rather than later. At least Oliver had really changed. He'd been able to own up to his mistake and to try to be a better person, unlike Smith who only ever played games. She'd had enough, and all she wanted to do was go home, sleep and fast-forward to tomorrow.

Laughter erupted from the kitchen, and she turned her head to look through the steamed-up windows. Through the haze, she saw Smith leaning his head against his arm on the fridge, bent over with laughter. She took another deep drag on her cigarette and flicked it away with pure disgust. She had to stop smoking. She didn't even like it anymore, and Oliver was right – it was a disgusting habit. She'd smoked way too much over the weeks when he'd moved out, and now, standing outside in the rain while her friends joked about inside, she could see how much she was using it as a crutch. Any time she felt angry, confused or bored, she'd reached for her cigarettes. Enough was enough.

'Jeez, anyone would think we're in the Amazon with this,' Claire said, closing the back door behind her.

Effie kept her eyes fixed onto the puddle in the middle of the garden, caused by the rain rolling from the gazebo and down onto the ground.

'I was wondering where you'd got to,' Claire continued, unde-terred by Effie's silence.

Why couldn't she take the hint? Effie sipped her drink, trying her best to project her need to be alone in Claire's direction, but when Claire sidled up next to her, it was clear that she'd failed.

It was like Claire had no sense whatsoever about body language or how to read it. If Effie had approached someone who had her arms folded in defence and who ignored every word she said, she wouldn't hang around trying to make conversation.

'I've been dying to speak to you properly.'

Effie looked at her with raised eyebrows. 'Why?'

Claire shrugged. 'Because you seem cool, and you're the only one I haven't chatted to properly yet.'

There's a reason for that, silly cow.

'Aren't you meant to be thirty thousand feet somewhere? You're an air hostess – always mile high.'

She couldn't help but make a dig and refer to Claire's Tinder profile, but instead of showing any signs of embarrassment, Claire tipped her head back and laughed, a laugh that seemed to take over the entire garden.

'Smith told me he'd shown you my profile. But in answer to your question, no. It was my baby niece's christening this week, so I made sure I'd be around. They've got another on the way, so it's always nice to get home and spend some family time. Smith told me about the barbecue, and I thought I'd come along.'

'That's nice,' Effie mumbled, but she couldn't have cared less. She just wanted her to go away.

'Look, Effie,' – Claire turned to face her and put her hand on Effie's arm – 'I just wanted to say that you don't have anything to worry about from me.'

Effie looked down at Claire's hand on her arm. On what level did she think that was okay? Talk about overstepping boundaries.

'About what?'

'What you said that night at the launch party. About Smith.'

Effie shrugged and moved her arm away from Claire's hand. 'I was drunk.'

'I get it.' Claire nodded. 'It sounded like things were complicated for you, to say the least. I just didn't want you to feel uncomfortable or anything. I haven't said anything about it, and I won't.'

Effie took a gulp of her drink. Thank god for that. Still, she could do without Claire hanging around. Whether she said anything or not was irrelevant – she simply reminded Effie of what had happened that night, how Smith had been inches away from kissing her and how she'd very nearly let him. It reminded her of the way her heart had been crushed when she'd seen him with Claire afterwards.

'I've got to say, though,' Claire said, looking through the kitchen window, 'I can see why you like him. He's a super cool guy.'

Effie rolled her eyes as Claire continued to look through the window. So not only was she trying to make Effie feel better about the admission she'd made, she was apparently cool enough to talk about how she *understood* why another woman was hung up on her boyfriend. God, could she get any more sickly sweet? And the worst thing was that Smith had been right when they'd argued about Claire going to Effie's birthday drinks. Claire seemed like a nice person. Under other circumstances, Effie would have welcomed her in as a friend, but these weren't other circumstances, and to make it worse, Smith had lied to her. He'd said they'd split up, but clearly, the opposite was true. He'd reeled her in and then spat her out, yet again.

'Yeah. He is,' Effie replied.

'Honestly, I don't think I've ever met someone who's done as much crazy stuff as him. Though sometimes he does seem to take things a step too far.' Claire winked.

How much had he told her? Surely he hadn't told her the real reason he'd left to go travelling? Smith wasn't the type to tell his life story to just anyone, and if he had told her, it clearly meant he liked her far more than he'd let on. It was a depressing thought.

'That's Smith. He likes to live dangerously,' Effie said.

Claire laughed. 'I'll say. The thing in Thailand sounded like something from *The Hangover*.'

What thing in Thailand? From what he'd told her, Thailand had been idyllic. How did Claire know more about it than she did?

'I know,' Effie replied, hoping that Claire would elaborate and at the same time, wanting her to keep quiet because she knew by the way her heart was racing that it wouldn't be anything good. She looked at him through the window. 'Did he tell you everything?'

'About the Russian gangsters in Bangkok?' Claire nodded. 'I have to admit, I did wonder who I was mixing with when he told me. I mean, seriously, who gets run out of Thailand by a group of thugs in real life?'

Russian gangsters? And not just any Russian gangsters, but gangsters who could run him out of the country. The alcohol Effie had drunk seemed to leave her body in one fell swoop as she sobered up. She looked at him drinking a beer. He'd lied. *Again.* How many times was she going to be fooled by him? There was only one reason he'd ended up mixed up in something like that. Drugs.

Claire was talking, but Effie couldn't hear a word she was saying, with her pulse beating loudly in her ears. He'd said he came back for her and that he'd changed, but it was all lies. Every single thing he'd said and done since he got back – it was all lies. She pushed past Claire and swung the back door open. As the handle hit the wall, the laughter in the kitchen stopped.

'You lying pig.'

Smith's eyebrows knitted together in confusion as a hush fell in the kitchen. 'Who, me?'

'Yes, you. You're a fucking liar.'

Smith frowned as Lou and Mickey looked at each other, then at Smith and finally at Effie.

'Do you ever tell the truth? Do you even know how to?'

'Do you want to tell me what it is I've supposedly lied about?'

Effie had to grip the glass in her hand to stop herself from throwing it at him. 'Everything.'

She slammed the glass on the side and picked up her bag hanging on the chair.

'What's happened? Are you okay?' Lou tried to take her hand, but Effie shrugged her off.

'No, I am *not* okay. I have to leave. I don't want to be anywhere near you.' She looked at Smith, seeing past his good looks and his stupid grey eyes to the person he'd shown himself to be.

Her chest finally caved under the weight of her tears as she barged past him into the hallway. He put his beer on the side and followed her out, grabbing her hand as she pulled open the front door. Outside, the headlights of Oliver's BMW shone as he parked up outside the house, lighting her way home, and she yanked her hand from Smith's.

'Are you going to tell me what the hell it is I'm meant to have done wrong?'

'You lied.' Effie spat the words from her mouth, hating the fact that she was having to say them, that any of what Claire had said could possibly be true. 'You showed up at my wedding and ruined the happiest day of my life, telling me you came back for me.'

Confusion spread across Smith's face. 'Yes, and? What is it I'm supposed to have lied about?'

Even now, as she stood in front of him, telling him she knew he was lying, he still couldn't bring himself to tell her the truth.

'You know what really hurts? You told Claire the real reason why you left Thailand, and yet you couldn't tell me. Because if you did, you'd have had to admit that you haven't changed at all.'

Smith's shoulders sagged as realisation dawned and he shook his head. 'Effie, I—'

'Effie, *nothing*. You've lied from the minute you got back. Even what you said about you and Claire splitting up – it was all bullshit. I don't want to hear your lies anymore.'

'Eff, if you'd just hear me out—' Smith moved towards her, but she stepped back outside onto the garden path and shook her head, blinking against the tears.

'I mean it. I am done.'

27.

S he turned and ran down the path, onto the pavement, and swung open the car door before throwing herself inside.

'What's going on?' Oliver asked, leaning across Effie to look at the house. Smith had his back to them, shaking his head and talking to someone in the house.

'Just drive.' Effie slammed the car door, but Oliver didn't move.

'What happened? It looked like you were arguing.'

'It doesn't matter. I just want to go home.' She looked at him with tears streaking down her face, her eyes pleading with him to get her away from Smith as fast as the BMW could take them.

He looked back at the house and nodded, putting the car into gear. 'Okay.'

The street lights bounced off the slick pavement, and Effie's tears silently rolled down her face. With the rain still falling, it was as if everything in the world had turned sour, and even the sky was feeling her pain. Smith had lied, and Effie's heart was breaking all over again. She couldn't contain the sobs as Oliver ferried her away from Smith, and after flashing concerned looks her way and repeatedly asking if she was okay, he pulled over.

He reached over and put his hand on her knee. 'Effie? Baby, what happened?'

She couldn't speak, even if she wanted to. Finding out the truth about Smith had killed her inside. It was all a mess. If Smith hadn't come back, spouting his lies, she'd have carried on with her life and been all the better for being ignorant instead of thinking that he'd changed.

'Look at me.' Oliver tilted her head to face his and wiped the tears from her face with his thumb. 'What happened? It was Smith you were arguing with, wasn't it? I saw from the car. What were you arguing about?'

She shook her head and tried to look away, but Oliver held her face where it was. 'Let go of me.'

'Why were you arguing?'

Effie shoved his hand away. 'Just leave it. It doesn't matter.'

'Of course it does. You ask me to come and get you, and you run out of his house drunk and hysterical. What am I supposed to think?'

'I don't *care* what you think. Think whatever the hell you want. You always do – you're all the same.'

'Who's all the same?' Oliver's eyebrows pulled together. 'You're not making any sense.'

Effie tilted her head back against the headrest and looked up, trying to stop the tears in their tracks. She didn't want to have to explain herself. She couldn't. Her head was a jumbled mess.

'Can we please just go home?'

'Not until you tell me what's going on,' Oliver said and killed the engine.

'No questions asked, remember? I can see my friends, and there'll be no questions asked.'

'You can't throw that at me. Look at the state of you,' Oliver said, and Effie didn't need to look at him to hear his voice straining. 'Now tell me what happened.'

She shook her head and half laughed. 'You promised me you wouldn't ask any questions, but it was a lie. You've always lied, both of you. You act like you love me, and then you just lie and make me feel like an idiot. You're all the bloody same.'

The smell of the leather seats was making her stomach turn, and the windows were steaming up. With every breath she dragged in between her sobs, the car seemed to get smaller, and the sobriety that had hit her when Claire had told her the real reason Smith had come back disappeared as her head swam under the effects of the vodka.

'You ruined everything,' she sobbed, holding her head in her hands.

If Oliver hadn't beaten her up, she'd never have kicked him out, and Smith wouldn't have been able to worm his way in, acting like he gave a damn.

'Effie, baby, I've apologised over and over. I'm trying, but right now, you're not making it easy.'

'I don't even know who you are. I don't know your essence.'

'My essence?' Oliver shook his head. 'What are you talking about?'

She looked at him with tear-filled eyes, and he shook his head again.

'You need to sleep this off,' he said. 'You're talking gibberish.'

Oliver started the car again and sped down the quiet street. She was drunk and upset, but she wasn't talking gibberish. She'd spent days thinking about what Izzy had said, and now it was time that she finally admitted it to herself: she didn't know what Oliver's essence was. She didn't know why she loved him or why she'd married him.

I don't even think I love him.

If Izzy's comment had been like giving her a jumbled-up Rubik's cube, then it was suddenly as if she was a square away from solving it. If she really loved Oliver, really *truly* loved him, would she be as cut up about Smith's lies as she was? The truth was, Smith had just hurt her in a way Oliver never could. Even when he'd beaten her up, it was nothing compared to the wrenching pain in her stomach now that she knew the truth about Smith.

She didn't love him.

'It's over.'

The words tumbled quietly from her mouth before she'd even had a chance to think about whether she wanted to say it out loud.

Oliver looked at her with his face set into a blank expression. 'What are you talking about?'

She looked back at him, feeling as if someone had wiped all of the confusion from her mind. Despite the alcohol and tears, she'd never felt clearer about anything.

'I don't know if I love you.'

Oliver stopped the car in the middle of the road. Outside, the rain fell, and for a few seconds, water on metal was the only sound in the world. All at once, the expression on Oliver's face changed from being blank to confused, and Effie knew that it was true. She'd never loved him the way she'd loved Smith.

'You what?' His hand was gripping the steering wheel so hard that his knuckles popped white against his skin.

'I don't love you.'

It was abrupt, but now that she'd admitted it to herself, she couldn't pretend anymore, not even to spare his feelings. Even though everything she thought she knew about the 'new' Smith was based on lies, she couldn't bear to bury her head in the sand for a minute longer.

'You *don't love me*?' Oliver echoed her, his voice dripping with spite like acid. 'What the fuck is that supposed to mean?'

A car pulled up behind, and the driver flashed the headlights at them, but Oliver didn't move.

'You can't stay here,' she said. 'There are people behind.'

'Wait. This is his doing, isn't it?' He looked at her, and she saw the flash of anger behind his eyes. 'I fucking knew it.'

He slammed his fist against the steering wheel, and Effie flinched. Suddenly, she was thrown back to that night when he'd launched himself at her, punching her in the face and kicking her on the ground. There was no way he'd do the same now, surely? Not when he knew that her friends knew what he'd done, and definitely not with an impatient driver behind them. Right on cue, the driver behind beeped his horn. With cars parked on either side of the narrow road, there was nowhere else for them to go.

'I knew it. I knew there was something going on with that little creep, but I told myself you wouldn't have cheated on me.'

'I haven't,' Effie replied, shaking her head, thankful that nothing had actually happened with Smith. At least she could say she hadn't lied, unlike some.

'Well, you would say that, wouldn't you? You *and* Lou? What did you do – swap notes on how to sneak around?'

The car behind beeped again, and Effie's heart raced. The atmosphere was too charged, and she knew better than to trap herself with Oliver when he got angry. She pulled on the handle to get out, but it was centrally locked.

'Can you unlock the door?'

'How long has it been going on for?' he asked, ignoring her as he looked at his hand on the steering wheel. She could tell by the tone of his voice that he was fighting his anger, but she'd seen how quickly he could flip. Tears pricked at her eyes as fear started to creep its way up her back.

'Olly, will you open the door?'

'Why?' He snapped his head to look at her. His face dripped with scorn, and goosebumps prickled Effie's skin. 'So you can go back to your lover boy?'

She kept a hold on the handle as her chest heaved. 'I mean it. Open the door.'

He looked at her with his cold blue eyes. 'Why the hell should I? So you can go back to *my* house and lock me out again?'

She backed into the door, yanking the handle down with a trembling hand. 'Oliver, you're scaring me.'

Effie fumbled for the window control and pressed it down, the cool air and rain brushing against her cheek as the glass wound down. Oliver barely even seemed to notice as he swore.

'I've given you everything, and you've thrown it back in my face. I've begged you like a fucking idiot, and now you're doing this?'

She stuck her arm outside and reached for the handle. As the door unlocked, she swung it open and leapt out.

'Get back in the car.' Oliver leaned over to the passenger seat, but Effie moved away, looking at the car behind, beeping its horn. She looked at Oliver, staring out at her with his red, scowling face, his hand still gripping the steering wheel.

'Will you move your fucking car?' The man in the car behind stuck his head out of the window and shouted at her.

'Get back in the car, Effie.' Oliver's voice was as hard as stone, but as she stood in the road with the rain hitting her skin like bullets, she shook her head. She couldn't. He'd tried hard since she'd taken him back, but the simple fact was, she didn't trust him and now she realised she never could. How could she trust someone she was afraid of?

She slammed the door shut, turned and ran down the street. She needed to get as far away from Oliver as she could, just like she'd needed to get away from Smith. She just wanted to be alone.

The white beam of the BMW's headlights rushed past her, followed by the tail lights of the angry driver behind. Oliver turned right into the next street, and Effie ran in the opposite direction. Up ahead, traffic roared past on the high street, and she ran towards it, the Converse on her feet slapping loudly against the pavement as the adrenalin continued to pulse through her veins. Black wheelie bins blocked the pavement up ahead, so she wove herself between two parked cars.

The headlights of a car lit up the darkness around her as she ran out to cross the street, and she put a hand up to shield her eyes just as the front bumper hit her knees. The metal of the bonnet felt cold against her skin, and the air rushed from her as she slammed into the windscreen.

As her body was thrown up into the air, Effie saw the grey-blue clouds in the sky, shielding the moon, and then flipped over to see the ground rush up towards her. The side of her face thumped against the wet tarmac, and her vision blurred as she looked at the bright red tail lights of the car. She winced at the pain in her head, and everything went black.

28.

Effie's eyelids fluttered. They felt heavy and thick, like she'd had too much sleep, and her mouth was dry. A slither of light burned her eyes as they inched open.

'She's awake. Get the nurse.' A voice echoed in the room as she tried to swallow and almost choked at the tightness of her throat.

'Don't worry, Sweetpea. You're alright.'

Mum?

A warm hand pressed against her arm, and through the blurriness, she saw emerald-green feathers in a sea of grey.

'You're alright,' the voice said, and the familiar scent of sandalwood washed over her. Effie closed her eyes.

୧୨

The next time Effie opened her eyes, she kept them open and blinked against the bright lights as she turned her head as slowly as she could. As her eyes focused, she saw cards standing on a table next to her, along with an array of jagged, coloured crystals. Her cheek brushed the pillow as she turned her head as far as she could. There, on the plastic chair next to the bed, was her mum. She hadn't dreamt it. The green feathers she'd seen were woven into her mum's grey hair, and she looked small, wrapped under a blanket with her head resting on her hand as she slept.

The door to the room opened, and Smith stepped inside holding two cups. An unexpected wave of anger and disappointment swept over her, and she knew, without a doubt, that something had happened with him. When he finally looked towards the bed and saw that she was awake, his face flooded with relief, and he put the cups on the table.

'You're awake. Thank god.' He went to lean over and kiss her forehead, but something made him stop, and he sat on the bed next to her instead. 'You just missed Lou. How do you feel?'

'Thirsty,' she croaked, her throat seemingly lined with rusted razor blades. He poured water from a jug into a cup and held it in front of her, putting the straw in her mouth.

Effie drank warily. Something was telling her he was as on guard as she was. She could tell by the way he was looking at her, like he was waiting for her to say something. He had bags under his eyes, and his skin looked paler than usual. He looked like he hadn't slept for days. She stopped drinking, and he took the cup away, setting it down on the table.

'Do you remember what happened?' he asked.

She shook her head a little.

'You were hit by a car after you left the barbecue.'

Effie frowned. She'd been knocked over? How?

'You left with Oliver,' Smith said, matching her frown with his. 'He came to pick you up, but somewhere between leaving and getting home, you got run over. Do you remember anything?'

'No.' She shook her head a little. 'But Olly must know what happened. Where is he?'

A look flickered across Smith's face. 'He said you'd stormed off from the car.'

'Why would I do that?' Effie frowned.

'You were drunk and upset . . .'

Smith tailed off, and Effie looked out of the window flecked with specks of rain. Rain. It had been raining. She screwed her eyebrows together, willing herself to think back to the barbecue. She hadn't wanted to go; she remembered that. And she remembered giving Smith his present. What else?

The rain . . . standing under the gazebo . . . Lou and Mickey going upstairs . . .

The image of Smith walking past her ran across her mind, accompanied by a sinking feeling in her stomach. She looked at him again.

'I was upset because of you, wasn't I?'

He nodded and she didn't miss the shame flicker across his face. He'd looked like that at the barbecue too.

Claire.

Slowly, the scrambled pieces of the jigsaw that was her memory started to slot back into place.

'Thailand.' She tried to turn away from him and winced at the pain in her ribs. 'I remember now.'

'You left before I had a chance to explain.'

'You don't need to explain. You just need to leave.'

She didn't turn to look at him. She couldn't. As if she wasn't in enough pain already, the realisation of her memory added to it. She remembered that he'd lied and how it had made her heart splinter.

'Effie . . .'

'Just go, Smith. Please?' She winced again at the effort it had taken to raise her voice enough to show how serious she was.

'What's going on? She's awake?'

Penny's voice cut through the air, and Effie turned to see her mum getting up from the chair. Involuntary tears fell from her eyes as her mum sat on the bed.

'Why didn't you wake me up?' Penny asked, looking at Smith.

'It's only been a couple of minutes, and you needed the rest. I wanted to try and talk to her, to find out what happened—'

'I know what happened,' Effie interrupted. Now that she'd remembered why she was angry with him, she couldn't see anything other than the look on his face when he'd realised she knew the real reason he'd left Thailand. 'You lied, like you always have.'

'Maybe you should go,' Penny said, smoothing down Effie's hair as she looked at Smith. 'She shouldn't be upset right now.'

He looked at Penny and then at Effie. God, he was good. He looked utterly crestfallen, but Effie knew it was all for show.

I am done.

Her own voice echoed loudly in her head, and fragments of their argument played out in front of her like a film. She'd meant what she'd said. She still did.

Smith nodded and picked up his jacket. 'Okay, but I'll be back tomorrow.'

'Don't bother,' Effie muttered, wishing she could stop the tears from falling.

As Smith left the room, Effie looked at her mum without blinking, afraid that if she closed her eyes, even for a second, she'd open them and Penny would be gone. She couldn't quite believe she was really there.

'When did you get here? How long have I been out?'

'Three days,' Penny replied and wiped the tears from Effie's cheeks with her thumb. 'Lou called me, and I took the next flight out.'

For the first time she could remember, her mum was there, right when Effie needed her the most. She looked at her again, taking in the soft lines on her face, and sobbed.

'Oh, Sweetpea.' Penny lay down next to her, propping an arm around Effie as best she could before kissing the side of her head. 'You'll be fine. Mummy's here.'

❧

Severe concussion, a fractured eye socket and three broken ribs. If it weren't for the pain in her chest every time she took a breath, Effie wouldn't have believed that the list of injuries Penny recited described her. The 'severe concussion' part had terrified her. She'd had swelling on the brain. That was serious. As Penny had told her, she was lucky to be alive.

Effie sighed as the police officers left. It was beyond frustrating, trying to grasp at the fragments of what she did recall. She remembered the moment before the impact, when the headlights had shone in her face, and she remembered looking at the red lights on the back of the car afterwards. Her shattered memories of that night had slowly come back to her over the two days she'd been awake, but the central piece, remembering anything about the car that hit her, was missing.

Her marriage was over; she knew that much. She saw Oliver's face, hurt and angry as he sat in the driver's seat when she'd told him she didn't love him. She looked at the cards on the table next to her from Mickey, Lou, Smith and her colleagues at Archive. There was even one from Smith's parents. Her mum had read them all out to her, but despite their well wishes, she couldn't think of anything other than that there had been no mention of Oliver since she'd woken up.

Her mobile had smashed in the impact of the accident, and Smith had brought her round a new one. She'd taken it from him without looking him in the eye. She didn't want to make eye contact with him, not when she knew she couldn't trust a word he said. He'd sloped away, and when she put the SIM card into her new phone, she'd been stunned to find nothing from Oliver. He hadn't sent a single text, and she had no voicemails or missed calls from him.

'Why hasn't Olly been?' Effie asked, looking at her mum. She might've told him their marriage was over, but she was still his wife.

She'd nearly died. Surely he'd have come to see her, even if he had accepted what she'd said.

Penny moved a pink crystal on the table closer to Effie's bed. 'Did you know that rose quartz is amazing for emotional recovery? I've got you some clear quartz as well – the master of all the crystals.'

Effie frowned. Why was her mum talking about crystals? It wasn't as if her body hadn't been pumped full of painkillers for the last few days. 'Mum?'

'This one is blue kyanite.' She held up a fragment of dark blue crystal. 'It'll help your bones heal quicker.'

'Mum,' Effie said firmly, 'where's Olly? Why hasn't he visited?'

Penny's face darkened as she left the crystals alone. 'He has.'

'When? Why haven't I seen him?'

If he's been once, then why hasn't he come back?

'When did he come?' she asked again, and Penny sighed.

'Soon after you were brought in.'

'So why hasn't he come back?'

It made no sense that he'd simply disappear, regardless of the last things they'd said to each other. Effie watched her mum's face. Slowly, the realisation of the truth dawned on her. Penny's silence wasn't because she didn't know; it was because she didn't want to tell her the truth.

What could have happened while she'd been lying unconscious? Oliver would've crossed paths with Lou – that was for sure. She knew what Lou was like, especially in an emergency. She would've panicked and lashed out, and she'd bet that Lou would've told Oliver exactly what she thought of him. It was obvious. Oliver was giving Effie a wide berth because his secret was well and truly out.

Penny tucked a strand of hair behind Effie's ear. 'We'll talk about it later, when you're feeling a bit stronger. All you have to worry about right now is getting better.'

Her mum knew everything, and she'd have to tell her about how her life had got into the state it had. Effie's eyes pricked as Penny picked up her book and settled into her chair. At least she wouldn't have to do it straight away.

Effie studied the picture of a man meditating on the bright red cover. As she read, Penny played with the small pendant in the shape of a palm with an eye in the centre, hanging from a silver chain around her neck. Penny had always flitted from things – houses, jobs and men – but the one thing that had always remained the same was her way of life and what she believed in.

What did Effie believe in? She looked up at the ceiling tiles. In such a short space of time, everything she'd thought she'd known and wanted had been turned on its head. At that moment in time, she'd have traded the world to have something in her life that remained unchanged. She'd almost died, and the one person she'd expected to see when she'd opened her eyes had been Oliver. Instead, she'd seen Smith and her mum.

'When can I get out of here?'

'In a couple of days, probably,' Penny replied, turning the page of her book. 'Because of your head injury, they need to monitor you awhile longer.'

'When do you have to go back?'

Penny put the book down on her lap. 'I don't have to go anywhere. I'll stay as long as you want me to. Until you're better, at least.'

Her mum had taken the first available plane and flown across Europe to be there for her and would stay for as long as it took. If she hadn't been able to see it for herself, she'd never have believed it. Effie frowned as Penny went back to her book. Where was she staying? Hotels weren't really her style – not when she liked to be in the middle of nature. She thought about Ibiza, imagining the heat on her skin. It was no wonder her mum would rather be there than in England.

'Mum?'

'Yes, Sweetpea?'

'When I get discharged, can we go to Spain?'

Penny looked up with a smile and nodded. 'Of course, Sweetpea. Anything you want.'

Four days later, Effie was discharged, and as she limped through the hospital doors with her mum and Lou, she took in a deep breath of air. After being in an air-conditioned room for over a week, nothing had ever smelled sweeter.

'Call me whenever you need to, okay?' Lou said.

'I will,' Effie nodded.

'And don't slap me, but Smith said to tell you the same.'

Effie tutted. 'He just doesn't get it, does he?'

'He's worried about you. We all are.'

'She'll be fine,' Penny said, squeezing Lou's arm. 'After some sun and home-made, nutritious food, she'll be back on her feet before you know it. Now make sure you call me the minute you hear anything.'

'I will.' Lou nodded and Effie looked at the both of them.

'Hear anything about what?'

Lou and Penny had engaged in hushed conversations ever since Lou had come to the hospital with Effie's passport and some clothes.

'Is it about Olly? Have you heard from him?'

Lou glanced at Penny before looking back at Effie. 'You know how you said that both his and your passports were in your top drawer?'

Effie nodded.

'There was only yours when we went round.'

'So?'

'Olly's gone. I've been trying to call him to let him know you're being discharged, but I can't get through. The thing is' – Lou looked at Penny hesitantly before looking back at Effie – 'I kind of told him that what happened to you was his fault. I mean, you left with him. You should have got home safely, but instead—'

'It's not your fault he's gone, Lou,' Penny said as a minicab pulled up in front of them. 'It's for the best that he has, or he'd have had me to deal with. Wherever he is, you let him go, Sweetpea.'

Effie frowned as Lou nodded. 'Your mum's right. He's a dick, and he'll get what's coming to him, but you did the right thing by ending it.'

Lou had just about managed to stop herself from applauding Effie when she'd told her about their argument in the car. She'd made no secret of the fact that she thought Effie had made a mistake in taking him back, a mistake that had been proven by Oliver's absence since her accident.

'He should've treated you better in the first place, and not coming back to see how you are . . . after everything he's done to you, that's the lowest of the low.' Lou pulled her in for a loose hug again, careful not to hurt her ribs, and Penny put their bags in the boot. 'Just know that we're all rooting for you.'

Effie looked out of the window of the taxi at Lou as it pulled away, trying to put the confusion and disappointment about Oliver's apparent lack of concern from her mind, and told herself that if she had Penny and Lou rooting for her, then she didn't need anything or anyone else.

29.

Effie stood in the small bedroom, her eyes taking in every detail. 'This is mine?'

'Of course it is. Who else's would it be?' Penny replied, putting Effie's small bag on the floor.

She'd never expected that her mum would have a space set aside for her, let alone a room. The white curtains flapped gently in the breeze coming through the open window, and a double bed was tucked into the corner. Its wrought-iron frame was the only darkness in an otherwise light-filled room. The house they'd lived in when Penny had left had been decorated with deep burgundies and rich violets. Every room was filled with stacks of books and ornaments from far-flung corners of the globe. The cloying scent of incense had hung in every room, penetrating every inch of fabric, including Effie's school uniform. Even after years of being exposed to it, she could never get used to the musky smell. When she'd walked into Penny's bungalow at the far corner of the commune, she'd prepared herself for more of the same, but she couldn't have been more wrong.

With a reception room, small kitchen, bathroom and two bedrooms, the bungalow was small but beautifully decorated. The dark walls she'd braced herself for were instead painted pale green and yellow, and the overpowering incense sticks were nowhere to be seen. Instead, scented tea lights sat on the small wooden coffee table and windowsills. The mountains of books Effie had always had to weave between and step over were stacked on bookshelves. Penny, the queen of clutter, had cleared her life out.

'It's beautiful,' Effie said, looking around at her room.

'You sound surprised,' Penny replied, walking to the window.

'I am.'

It had been a spur-of-the-moment decision to ask Penny to bring her to Spain. There was no way her mum could have pre-planned having Effie over to stay, yet the room was made up. How long had it been like this, ready and waiting for her?

Penny pulled down the mosquito screen and smiled. 'Good. Now, how are you feeling? If you're hungry, I can knock something together.'

'No, I'm okay. I'm still a bit tired. I think it's the painkillers.' Effie sat on the bed and ran her hands across the sheet. She'd slept during most of the flight and nearly the whole drive from the airport to Colinas Verdes.

'You've got extra sheets and blankets in the trunk, in case you get cold.'

'Unlikely,' Effie replied. 'It's roasting.'

'It's hot now, but it still gets a little chilly at night. You'll soon acclimatise.'

She hoped not. Despite her reasons for being in Ibiza, the moment Effie had stepped out into the sunshine at the airport, she'd smiled. After the claustrophobic heatwave back in London, summer had seemingly disappeared behind a deluge of rain, as if things weren't depressing enough already. She looked down at the small bedside table and picked up the wooden photo frame.

Effie looked at the image of the topless woman wearing jeans, standing with her back to the camera, holding a crying baby.

'This is in Norfolk?'

Penny nodded, leaning against the doorjamb. 'It's at Nanny Abbott's. I thought you'd be too young to remember.'

Effie shook her head, thinking about Euphemia Abbott, her great-grandmother. 'I don't remember her much, but I remember her place.'

'I don't expect you would; you were only four when she died.'

She'd seen pictures of her Great-Nanny Effie with her tall, willowy limbs and high eyebrows. If only she could remember meeting the woman she'd been named after – the same woman who had taken in a nineteen-year-old, pregnant Penny. Penny had been offered a place at Cambridge University to read English, but she'd turned it down, opting to travel to the south of France with a group of people she'd only just met instead. Coming back pregnant by an unknown man, an unknown black man, was simply too much for Penny's ultraconservative parents to take. All at once, the smell of apples and wet leaves filled Effie's nose. Her great-grandmother had owned an orchard, and Effie remembered the sweet scent that hung around the house and its small grounds. After her death, Penny and Effie had holidayed there for years, until the orchard had to be sold.

'I've got a whole bag full of photo albums,' Penny said. 'When you're feeling up to it, we'll take a look through them. I've got quite a few photos of her. She was an incredibly strong woman. She seems to have passed the trait down, if Mum's anything to go by.'

Effie had only ever met her grandparents a handful of times, but if one thing was obvious, it was that the Abbott women tended to be on the fierce, matriarchal side – Penny included. Sure, she had her faults and definitely had her own ideas about how to live life, but when Effie was little, Penny had been a force to reckon with. Effie sighed and looked at the photo in her hands. What would her Great-Nanny Effie say if she could see the broken great-granddaughter who shared her name?

She put the frame back on the bedside table and lay down, curling up on the bed. 'That trait seems to have stopped with me. I don't feel strong.'

'Oh, you are. And you always will be,' Penny replied. 'You're an Abbott more than you ever were a Barton-Cole.'

For the next three days, Effie didn't move from her bed. Every inch of her body felt deathly tired, and it was all she could do to stay awake. The only interaction she had was when Penny would come into her room to bring food or open and close her curtains. They didn't speak. There wasn't much to say. Effie knew that when the time came for talking, she was going to have to tell her mum the truth about her life with Oliver, and knowing that Penny had already been told didn't make it any easier. It made it harder.

On the fourth day, she got out of bed. As comfortable as it was, her body ached from being inactive, and she winced at the groaning of her bones when she stood. Her ribs still ached, but she couldn't spend another day looking out of the window and replaying memories in her head. They all led to the same conclusion anyway. After having everything, she now had nothing.

She pulled on a pair of leggings and a T-shirt and slipped outside her room. She'd heard her mum moving around earlier, but she was nowhere to be seen. Effie had learned Penny's morning routine over the last three days. She'd wake up, make a cup of tea and then go out for an hour. Effie guessed it was when she'd practise her yoga.

With the house to herself, Effie made herself a coffee and went to sit out on the porch. A look at her phone told her it was barely nine in the morning, but already the sun was hot on her skin. She slid her finger across the screen and deactivated 'Flight Mode' for the first time since leaving London. There seemed to be little point in having her phone on anyway. Penny had let Lou know they'd arrived safely, and there wasn't anyone else she wanted to hear from. She took a sip of coffee as the notifications popped up on her screen.

Spam emails, notifications of her phone bill, a reminder to go to the doctor's for her pill – she swiped them all away. For the last few days, her life had stopped, but back home it had continued as normal. She propped up her feet on the chair opposite as she scrolled through the instant messaging app, reading the missed messages from Smith and Mickey, asking how she was. She'd reply to Mickey later. As for Smith . . . She shook her head and dialled through to her voicemail, pressing the phone against her ear. She didn't have the energy to deal with him yet.

'Where are you?'

She almost dropped the phone at the sound of Oliver's agitated voice on the phone.

'When did they let you out? I just got back, and they said you've been discharged. Where are you? Please, just call me and let me know you're alright. I'm worried about you.'

The message ended, and she put her cup on the side. She jabbed at the button to delete the message, and put the phone down on the chair. He'd just got back from where? She shook her head. Why was he calling her now, after days of silence? He obviously didn't really care how she was, and it had only confirmed what she'd said in the car. Their marriage was over. She picked up the phone. She didn't want him to contact her and didn't want to hear his voice, trying to charm his way back in, but before she could reactivate 'Flight Mode', an instant message flashed on her screen. It was Oliver.

Oliver: You're online! Where are you??

Damn. She'd forgotten that the instant message app left a date and time stamp every time she went online.

Oliver: What happened? I got back and you'd gone. You have no idea how worried I've been, and nobody's telling me anything.

She shook her head at the screen. What was he playing at?

Oliver: I know you said what you did, but I still love you. Why aren't you messaging back??

Effie closed the app and switched on 'Flight Mode', her heart beating loudly in her chest. Had she imagined it all? Had she actually woken up in hospital, or was this some elaborate dream? He was crazy – he had to be. It was the only way to explain why he was acting like nothing had happened, like she hadn't told him she didn't love him. She put the phone on the far side of the table and stared out into the distance, pushing him from her mind. She had to do what Penny said and focus on getting better, and thinking about Oliver wouldn't help. It would only do the opposite.

She stayed there, unmoving, until Penny returned and stepped onto the porch with a pink, rolled-up yoga mat under her arm. Her hair was tied back, and her skin was slick with sweat.

'You're up,' she said, propping the mat against the wall. She pressed the small towel around her neck against her forehead. 'How are you feeling?'

Effie grimaced and lifted her feet from the chair to let Penny sit down. She rested her feet on her mum's knees.

'That good?' Her mum smiled. 'At least you're up. I was starting to get a bit worried about the painkillers you're taking.'

'They knocked me out, but I couldn't stay in bed forever. My back was starting to hurt.'

'I'll give you a massage later, if you want.' Penny looked at the table and saw Effie's phone. 'What's happening in the outside world?'

Effie sighed and looked at her phone before turning back to her mum. 'Nothing worth knowing about. I wish I'd never turned it on.'

'Oliver?' Penny knowingly raised an eyebrow, and Effie nodded as her body tensed at the mere thought of him.

Instead of asking for details, Penny pressed her thumbs deep into the soles of Effie's feet. 'I was thinking we could have seafood paella this evening. My neighbour, George, said he'd be going into town later. I might ask him to get some mussels and prawns. It'll be a welcome change from soup, no?'

Effie nodded and smiled. 'Thanks.'

The thanks was for more than just the idea of dinner. It was for giving her space to bring up her marital problems when she was ready. Her eye socket was slowly mending, despite the ugly bruise around it, and she'd have to live with the broken ribs until they healed in their own time. She wasn't ready to go anywhere just yet. There was plenty of time for confessions. Penny smiled back and looked down at Effie's feet as she massaged away the tension.

Effie looked out at the grounds. In her head, she'd imagined Colinas Verdes to be dominated by a big, old tumbling-down house filled with transient people sharing everything from food to partners, or groups of tents around a firepit. At the very least, she'd expected to see some dreadlocks, but the people she'd seen from her window, milling around, looked surprisingly normal.

'This place isn't what I expected. It doesn't feel like a commune. It's nothing like the one we stayed on.'

'Oh, the one in Dorset?' Penny smiled. 'There aren't many places like that.'

'Thank god.'

That was the big shared house with no doors. All they'd had for privacy was a bed sheet tacked to the doorframe.

'We don't call this a commune,' Penny said. 'It's an independent community.'

Effie didn't understand the difference, but she knew it didn't fit the image from her childhood memories.

'You were asleep when we crossed the bridge to get here, but technically this is a little island of its own. In reality, you can walk back over to the mainland even at high tide. Sometimes we do, but we're almost entirely self-sufficient. We all pooled our money together to buy the land, and there are thirteen families in all. That's where we grow our fruit and veg,' Penny said, pointing to the east of the land. 'We sell the excess at the weekly farmers' market on the mainland. You've seen the solar roof panels already, and of course everything is recycled.'

Effie nodded, looking at the shimmering panels on top of the bungalows scattered around.

'We've got the communal pool, which is entirely organic, with plants filtering the water instead of chlorine, and a fresh-water creek over to the west. We've strung a hammock up, and it's a nice place to relax and swim in. Not everyone is so keen on the pool.'

Effie had seen the pool from her bedroom, and judging by the croaks she'd heard, it was a magnet for local wildlife. She shuddered. Why on earth would anyone want to swim with frogs when they were surrounded by the beautiful Mediterranean Sea?

'Can't say I blame them.'

'It's not for everyone,' Penny said and went back to massaging Effie's feet. 'But we all share the same vision of how we want to live, and we all work together, sharing things out equally. In that regard, yes, I suppose it is a commune. It's just a modern one.'

Modern was the right word. The community had its own Internet page and, as she'd just experienced for herself, Wi-Fi.

Penny squeezed Effie's toes before clapping her hands together. 'Right. I need to get cleaned up. I've got a client coming in half an hour. Since you're up, you should take a wander around, get to know the place a little.'

Effie was still in pain, but the idea of hanging around while her mum did her reiki freaked her out.

'Yeah, maybe you're right. I might check out that creek.'

Penny frowned. 'I don't think you're ready yet. It's a long walk, and the terrain's uneven.'

Effie rolled her eyes. 'I'll take it slowly.'

'Maybe I could cancel the appointment and come with you.'

'Don't worry, Mum,' Effie said, putting her feet on the floor. 'I'll be fine.'

30.

'You know I didn't want to leave you. I didn't have a choice. I don't understand why you're being like this.'

Effie clenched her jaw at Oliver's voice in her ear. So much for not thinking about him. After walking to the creek, she'd switched her phone on for just a minute, and no sooner had her signal kicked in than her phone had rung. She'd stared at it, debating whether to reject his call, but something had compelled her to answer.

'We can't just leave things like this. I know you didn't mean what you said that night. You were drunk. I bet you don't even really remember it.'

'I remember everything.'

'Good, because Lou's trying to pin the blame on someone, and she's got her sights set on me. I know I'm not her favourite person, but if you'd seen her at the hospital . . .' Oliver's voice strained on the other end. 'She was out of line. You need to put her straight. You need to put her straight and come home.'

Effie scrunched her eyebrows together and shook her head. 'She's right, though, isn't she?'

'That's not fair, Effie. You got out of the car. There was nothing I could have done. But you're still my wife.'

'A wife who was laid up in hospital who you didn't even think to look in on.'

'I did – I told you – but Lou told me to go. And even if she hadn't, I was going away anyway, remember? I told you I had to go to Sorrento for work. I don't have signal there.'

Effie shook her head. 'You told me no such thing, and there's no way you'd have stayed away just because Lou told you to. I was almost killed, for god's sake. Any normal person would have cancelled the trip.'

Was she being unreasonable? She'd told Oliver that she didn't love him, and that hadn't changed, but would it have killed him to at least check up on her more?

'Will you please just come home?' He sighed. 'We can talk this through. Where are you anyway?'

'You don't need to know where I am, and I'm not coming home. I meant what I said.'

'Effie, will you listen to yourself?'

She looked down at the rocky ground. She felt broken, but she couldn't run away from the truth anymore, and she didn't want to. She remembered what her mum had said. She was an Abbott. It was what had made her press on with her walk to the creek despite the uneven terrain, and it was what had made her answer Oliver's call.

She took a breath, squeezing her eyes shut. 'I want a divorce.'

Oliver stuttered down the phone, and she hung up, her hands shaking. He was trying to win her round again, but even if he'd got her to change her mind in the past, this time she wouldn't let him. She clenched her jaw and nodded to herself. She'd made the decision beforehand anyway – she wanted a divorce.

The overhanging tree provided some shade and she lay back, letting the hammock rock her from side to side. She was perfectly alone, and after a while, the buzzing of the cicadas went from being unbearable to oddly hypnotic. She looked up at the azure sky and sighed. In just eight months, her life had changed so much that it was barely recognisable, but at the same time her mind felt so much lighter.

What the hell do I do next?

Her eyebrows furrowed together at the thought, and she turned her head to look at the crystal-clear water trickling across the rocks.

I want to talk to Mum.

The thought wasn't a surprising one. For years, Effie had thought that her mum simply didn't care about her enough, but from the moment she'd opened her eyes in the hospital, Penny hadn't left her side. She had a room set aside for her, and she'd been nothing but loving and supportive. Effie had seen a different side to her, a side she hadn't seen since her early childhood. And now she wanted to find out why Penny had left it all behind. She looked at her watch. If she left now, she'd be back for lunch and the next dose of medication. She climbed down from the hammock and began the slow walk back.

❧

If there was one thing that fitted with the original idea of a commune in Effie's head, it was the firepit, but even that wasn't what she'd expected. The large bowl containing the three-foot-tall flames wouldn't have looked out of place in front of a five-star hotel.

'It's beautiful,' she said, pointing to it as her mum's neighbour, George, poked at the fire.

'Isn't she just? Eighty pounds of American cold-rolled steel right there.' His Texan drawl emphasised each word, and even though Effie had no idea what he was talking about, he sounded immensely proud.

'George is very talented,' Penny said, sitting next to Effie and handing her a cup of tea. 'He does sculptures for Burning Man every year too. He's pretty big in his circles.'

Penny threw him a smile. She smiled at most people here. It was hard not to since everyone seemed so relaxed and happy, but the one she flashed at George was different. Effie remembered the way her mum had pointed out his sculptures, dotted around the place, with a sense of pride, and now she thought about it, her mum talked about him an awful lot – 'George says this' and 'George thinks that'. His neck flushed red as he took the compliment, and Penny's hand flew to her ear, playing with the dangling earring.

Oh, dear god. Were they flirting?

'I'll just go and . . .' George mumbled, pushing his silver-grey hair from his eyes as he stood up. He left the two of them sitting on the wooden slab serving as a bench.

Effie cleared her throat and took a sip of tea.

'What?' Penny asked.

'Nothing.' She shook her head. She didn't want to know about her mum's love life. She'd been overexposed to it enough over the years.

'You're trying to guess whether I'm having sex with George, aren't you?'

'Mum!' Effie spluttered into her cup, and her face blazed red.

'Oh, come on. We're both adults.' Penny grinned.

Effie watched as he ambled his tall, broad frame over to his bungalow. She had to admit, he was handsome, but he was ancient compared to her mum.

'Isn't he way older than you?'

'Ten years,' Penny replied and looked over at him. 'He's nice, though, isn't he? Kind too. I can trust him, and believe me, it's an understated quality.'

Effie looked into the flames flickering in front of them. The crowd that had gathered for dinner had slowly dispersed, leaving only a handful behind. Everyone in the camp knew her by association, and over the last few days, nearly all of them had gone out of their way to say hello and welcome her. They'd all asked how she was feeling and whether there was anything she needed. It seemed that kindness was a universal trait here.

'Yeah.' Effie sighed. 'I guess it is. I don't know who to trust anymore.'

Penny stood up and wrapped the blanket around her shoulders. 'Wait here. I'll be right back.'

The disorientating feeling of not knowing who to trust had rocked her from the moment she'd woken up in the hospital. She looked up at the sky, sprinkled with glittering stars. The twinkling lights reminded her of pictures from a book about the universe she'd had when she was little. Her mum was lucky to be able to see this every night.

Spending time together had been nice. Really nice. Given how little they'd seen and spoken to each other over the last decade and how fraught their relationship was, it should have felt strange to suddenly be in constant close proximity, but it didn't. It was easy and, she imagined, how a mature mother–daughter relationship should be. The problem was that it all felt too good to be true. She still didn't trust her.

Effie turned her head and saw Penny step down from the porch of her bungalow, carrying a large hemp bag. She'd done everything she could to make Effie feel comfortable and at home. She hadn't tried to push her into talking about what had happened with Oliver, but even still. She'd disappeared once, and she could do it again.

'There's something I want to show you,' Penny said, handing Effie the bag as she sat down.

It was heavy as she pulled it up onto her lap. Penny crossed her legs again and turned her body to face Effie's. 'You need the big brown one.'

Effie opened the bag to see a bunch of big books and pulled out the largest one. Through the flickering orange glow of the fire, she saw the embossed golden lettering on the front: 'Photo Album'. This must be the bag of photos her mum had told her about. She opened it, peeling back the sheet of tissue paper. The images were familiar, and she remembered going through them with her mum years ago. She smiled at the photo of herself, sitting on a carpeted floor, her chubby legs splayed out in front of her.

'I remember these,' she said, flicking through the pages.

'Look at the last page,' Penny replied. Effie frowned, picking up on the apprehension in her mum's voice.

She flipped over the heavy cream-coloured pages and looked at the image on the last page. She ran her fingers across the laminated sheet covering the black and white image and turned the album to sit landscape view on her knees. Her eyes scanned the grainy picture of a group of people hanging around a VW camper van, but she didn't recognise any of them. Just as she was about to say so, she looked at it again. She hunched herself over the photo and tilted it towards the fire to get some more light.

'Is that you?' she asked, looking at her mum.

Penny nodded. 'I was eighteen.'

Effie looked at the picture again. She'd always known how beautiful Penny had been. She'd seen plenty of pictures of her mum before, but this one was different. Penny's sandy blonde hair was scooped across one of her shoulders, and her skin was bronzed. She was wearing a tight T-shirt and tiny shorts, standing on top of the van with her arms outstretched. A duffel bag was suspended mid-air, falling into the arms of the man standing on the ground. She had a look of radiance that Effie had never seen before.

'You look great.'

'I didn't have anything to worry about back then.'

That was true. By the time she'd have celebrated her nineteenth birthday, she would've been pregnant already.

'An old friend passed through not too long ago,' Penny continued. 'It was random, as most good things are. She'd heard about this place and wanted to check it out. That's her, Annelie, there.' She pointed to a woman in equally tiny shorts standing by the van. 'We hadn't seen or spoken to each other in twenty-five years, and of all the places in the world for her to come to, she came here. She sent the photo to me when she got back to Sweden.'

Effie went to hand the album back, but Penny shook her head. 'You see this guy?'

The long, curved ring on Penny's middle finger glinted in the firelight, and Effie's eyes followed as her mum pointed to the man waiting to catch the duffel bag.

'That's Gabriel. Your dad. Although he hated the English pronunciation. You'd have to say it the French way, or he'd get moody.'

Her dad? Effie's heart jumped as she looked at him again. He was standing barefoot with his back to the camera, the muscles in his bare back flexing against his brown skin as his arms outstretched to catch the bag. His thick, black dreadlocks hung down to the waistline of his shorts. For years she'd imagined what her dad must have been like. All she'd known was that he was African, and as Penny had told her once, too handsome for his own good.

'I thought you said he was African?' Effie frowned.

'He was born in Cameroon, but he was raised in Paris.'

'How . . . ? I mean,' Effie stuttered, trying to put her feelings into words.

For the first time, her dad was a real person instead of an abstract one. If only the picture had been taken from the front, so she could have seen what he really looked like.

'I know you must've thought I was holding back on information about him, but the truth was, I didn't have much to tell,' Penny said, picking at her fingernails.

Effie had only ever asked about her dad a handful of times and had realised from an early age that Penny was always reluctant to talk about him.

'So what changed?'

'Getting this.' Penny nodded towards the photo. 'What happened with you. Us spending time together. A lot of things.'

'What was he like?' she asked, tracing her finger across the outline of her dad again.

Penny puffed the air out of her cheeks and turned on the bench, stretching her legs out in front of her. Effie watched as she flexed her toes.

'What was he like . . . ?' Penny sighed. 'Honestly? He was a heartbreaker. I knew it from the get-go. He was the most beautiful man I'd ever seen, and strong too, in that quiet kind of way. I'd never met anyone like him before.'

Effie looked at the photo again, trying to see the dynamics between her parents. Penny was laughing at something as she'd thrown the bag down to him, and she wanted to believe it was Gabriel who'd said whatever it was that had put that smile on her mum's face. Gabriel. She tested the word out in her head.

'He was a friend of a friend, and we met him in Marseilles. He was a street performer, doing acrobatics and things like that. Really talented too. He travelled around with us for a couple of months.'

'Not very long, then,' Effie said quietly.

'No.' Penny leaned over to look at the photo. 'But it was long enough.'

'Did you love him?'

'Like mad. It was hard not to love him.' Penny smiled. 'He was exactly what I needed at the time, the complete opposite to everything I'd left behind. He was exotic, daring and adventurous. He was only a year older than me, but he'd travelled through most of Europe already.'

'So what happened?'

'Life, I suppose. We had fun together – don't get me wrong. We shared an experience that I think only comes along once in a lifetime. And yes, before you ask, some of it was chemically induced. But nothing could have kept him in one place. If ever there was a case of itchy feet, he had it by the bucketload. We were a constantly changing group. People came and went. I couldn't make him stay, and I never wanted to. We spoke about meeting up again, once I'd seen a bit more of France.'

'And?'

'I found out I was pregnant. We spoke on the phone, but . . . Well, he was only nineteen. Can't blame him for not wanting to settle down.'

Effie looked at the photo again, and a flash of anger surged through her. He'd turned his back on her. On them.

'I never saw or spoke to him again.'

For a brief moment, she'd thought the point of her mum showing her his photo was to tell her she knew where he was and how she could contact him. She closed the photo album and put it down on her lap. She'd grown up thinking she was the product of a drug-hazed bunk-up. Penny had always been open about what she'd got up to, and she never had any details to share about Effie's dad. Instead, the opposite was true. Even though they'd only been together a short time, she'd loved her dad.

'I'm sorry,' Effie mumbled. She didn't have a clue what she was apologising for, but she did feel sorry.

'Whatever for? Having you was the best thing I ever did. Okay, so it might have been the final nail in the coffin with Mum and Dad, and I had to be a single parent, but I wouldn't change it for anything. Not even a lifetime of being with Gabriel.'

Effie blushed and looked down at her feet. Her mum had never told her that before. She'd always assumed she'd been a burden, getting in the way of the carefree lifestyle her mum had always craved. Wasn't that why she'd left?

'Having you made me a stronger person. I learned how to rely on myself and to trust people.'

'I don't see how it could make you trust people. Surely it would've done the opposite?'

'When you find yourself pregnant by some lovable rogue you hardly even know, you learn to accept help where you find it. Being a single parent isn't easy. You have to let people in; you just do it in a different way.'

'Did you never try to find him?'

'It wasn't like it is now. We didn't have mobile phones or Facebook, and he'd made his decision. The lifestyle he lived wasn't compatible with children. He moved around too much.'

'But you did it,' Effie said. 'Look how many times we went away and moved around.'

'Don't tell me you enjoyed it,' Penny scoffed. 'Because I know you didn't.'

Effie grinned. 'No, you're right. I hated it.'

It had always felt like they were constantly packing and unpacking, making a home in a new place and meeting new people. She frowned and looked at the flickering flames. Her mum was cut from the same cloth as her dad. That was why they'd never stayed in one place for too long, until Effie had started secondary school. Penny always had to be on the move.

'I was born with a strong sense of wanderlust,' Penny said, 'but I did try to calm it down. We stayed in Kennington for ages, didn't we?'

It had barely been four years – hardly ages.

'Is that why you left, because of me?'

Penny shook her head and put her arm around Effie, squeezing her arms. 'Of course not. Why would you think that?'

Effie shrugged. 'You said it yourself: I hated moving around all the time. I must have got in the way.'

'I left because . . .' Penny sighed. 'Well, I suppose I left because you simply didn't need me anymore. You were completely independent. You always had been. You could take care of yourself. You're my daughter and I raised you, but you were never really mine. I don't own you, and I never have. And you were always so vocal about hating the way we lived, I suppose I thought it was for the best.'

'But you just upped and left. How could it have been the best for me to come home from school and find you gone?' Effie fought to keep the anger from her voice as she remembered the day she'd walked back to an empty house to find a wad of money and a note in place of her mum.

'I know, and I've always regretted that. It wasn't an easy decision to make, and I wish I could take it back. If I'd done it differently, maybe you wouldn't have ended up where you have. When I met Oliver' – she shook her head – 'I knew he was a bad egg. I could see how vulnerable you were with him. How much you wanted to be *normal.*'

Penny said it like it was a horrible-tasting thing in her mouth, and Effie grimaced because she was right. The lifestyle Oliver had offered her was all she had ever wanted, her chance at the fairy-tale ending.

'I told myself you'd be fine and could look after yourself, but I know the way we moved around so much and my going away left you with abandonment issues. I just realised it all too late. When Lou told me about him beating you . . .' She shook her head and looked at Effie, wrapping her hands around Effie's. 'I'm sorry, Sweetpea. I really am.'

Effie looked at the skin on her neck, sun-kissed and smattered with dark freckles.

'It's okay,' Effie said, and it really was. For the first time, she didn't feel angry with her anymore. She smiled at her mum, trying to look braver than she felt. 'I'm recovering, and I'm doing it here with you. In a twisted kind of way, it's ended up turning into something good.'

'It has.' Penny smiled back and patted her hand.

Effie looked around. It was a beautiful place, and she could see why her mum loved it here. It was peaceful and calming. She looked at the solar fairy lights strung up in the trees and the small wooden signposts stuck into the ground outside each of the bungalows. Instead of numbers, they all had names, and Penny's was 'Hope'. It felt like the bungalow name had infected her with that very feeling. She felt like everything would work out for the best. It wasn't like last time, when she'd told Oliver to leave. This time, she felt stronger.

31.

London felt a million miles away, and Effie didn't want to think about having to go back, especially now. She'd found out the truth about her dad, and seen him, in a manner of speaking. Not to mention how she'd started the long road to building a proper relationship with her mum. Neither of them were the failing parents she'd thought they were. They were little more than kids when Penny fell pregnant. Of course she wished her dad had stuck around, but as her mum had said, he'd made his choice. Maybe it was better for him to be absent instead of being somewhere he didn't want to be, living a life he wasn't cut out for.

Effie looked up as her mum propped her yoga mat up against the wall. They'd developed a routine where Effie would wake up, make coffee and sit out on the porch until Penny returned from her yoga practice. It was hardly active, but relaxing was just what she'd needed. She'd barely touched her painkillers for the past few days, only taking one when it got unbearable, and her eye almost looked normal. Her ribs still ached, but the doctor had warned her it would be a slow recovery.

When Penny returned, they'd usually sit together, talking about what to have for dinner or whether they'd walk down to the beach after her last client for the day.

'Good practice?' Effie asked, taking her feet off the chair so Penny could sit.

'As always,' Penny replied, wiping her face with a towel. 'It's so damned hot now. I think I'll have to switch to doing it in the evenings.'

She took her phone from the small leather belt around her waist, looked at the screen and laughed to herself before pressing the keys. It was the oldest phone Effie had ever seen, from a time when 3G was probably even barely a concept. Penny laughed again and shook her head.

'What?' Effie asked, taking a sip of her coffee.

'Oh, nothing.'

She raised an eyebrow and grinned. 'George?'

'Nope,' Penny replied and took the cup from Effie's hands. 'Smith, actually.'

Effie frowned as her mum took a gulp of coffee. Since when was Smith sending funny texts to her mum?

'What did he want?'

'The same thing as always.' Penny shrugged. 'To see how you're doing.'

'Ugh.' Effie shook her head. 'Why won't he just give it up?'

'Well, I'd have thought that was obvious, Sweetpea.' Penny handed back the cup and got up from the chair. 'Right, I'm jumping in the shower.'

She picked up her yoga mat, dropped a kiss on the crown of Effie's head and wandered into the house. Effie drained the coffee and scowled, tapping her foot on the floor. What was with him? She'd been explicit – she didn't want to know. There were only so many lies she could take, and he'd exhausted his chances. It wasn't like she hadn't had enough to deal with lately. And anyway, why should it be obvious why Smith was checking up on her?

For the past few days, she'd focused on good things – reducing her painkiller intake because the pain wasn't so acute anymore; going for walks in the fields, with the grass tickling her toes; and dipping her legs into the fresh water of the creek. She hadn't thought about Smith once. She frowned. Okay, that was a lie. She had thought about him, but only because she was angry with him.

Inside the bungalow, the shower was running, and Effie stood up. Penny never closed the door when she showered. She'd only just started wrapping herself in a towel after using the bathroom, and that was purely because Effie insisted on it. They might have grown closer, but she didn't need to see her mum wandering around the house naked. She leaned her back against the doorjamb as Penny showered behind the curtain.

'Why should it be obvious?'

'Why should what be obvious? Could you pass me another bottle of shower gel? This one's finished.' Penny's hand shot out from behind the curtain, holding an empty bottle. 'It's under the sink.'

Effie took it and crouched down, looking into the small cabinet. She grabbed the full bottle and handed it to her mum before going back to her position in the doorway.

'Just now, when I asked why he was texting, you said it should be obvious. What did you mean?'

'I thought you said you didn't want to hear anything about Smith, remember?'

'Yeah, but I didn't know he'd been in touch.' She crossed her arms. At the hospital, Smith had tried to visit, and she'd told her mum in no uncertain terms that he wasn't welcome and she didn't want to hear about anything to do with him. 'What does he want?'

'Like I said, he asks how you're doing and whether you've remembered anything about what happened.'

'How many times has he texted?'

'Every day. Sometimes more.'

Effie's heart sped as she looked at her feet. More than once a day? Her injuries wouldn't change that dramatically from one day to the next. Why did he feel the need to get daily updates?

'I don't get it. He knows I don't want to talk to him.'

The shower switched off, and Penny grabbed the towel from the rail. She stepped over the bath, her feet soaking the mat as a cloud of lavender-scented steam billowed out behind her.

'Yes, but he isn't talking to you, is he? He's talking to me.'

Effie rolled her eyes. 'You know what I mean.'

'Sweetpea,' Penny said, grabbing the brush from the side and raking it through her hair, 'that boy sat with you the entire time you were unconscious. He barely ate, never mind slept.'

Her heartbeat notched up a gear as she pictured him watching her intently as she lay unconscious. 'Did he?'

'Well, of course. If you'd seen what you looked like, lying there all battered and bruised. And unconscious.' Penny shuddered. 'He was terrified you wouldn't wake up again, or that if you did, you wouldn't be the same. We all were. He didn't even go home for a change of clothes. He wanted to be there when you woke up.'

'He needn't have bothered. He probably felt guilty for lying to me all along.'

'Yes, he told me you argued, but, you know,' Penny said, looking at Effie through the mirror, 'you really ought to ask yourself why you're so angry with Smith for lying to you, yet you won't go to the police about the hideous man who beat you up.'

'Because . . . because I just am,' Effie replied, flustered.

Penny sighed and put the brush down. 'If you ask me, you're directing your anger at the wrong person. Smith loves you. If you'd seen what he was like for those three days, you'd know that.'

Effie's stomach fluttered at the thought, but she shook her head. 'He doesn't love me. He never has, not really.'

'Doesn't he?' Penny raised an eyebrow again and walked past her.

She watched her mum pad into her bedroom and shut the door, her mind racing. She thought back to Ireland and the Sketch launch, when she'd finally admitted she still had feelings for him. She couldn't deny there wasn't a huge part of her that wanted it to be true. Even though she was in enough of a predicament as it was with her catastrophic marriage, she wanted Smith to love her, but she just couldn't trust him, and she couldn't allow herself to believe that what her mum was saying was true. She'd spent ages doing that while they were in their not-quite relationship and had ended up getting burned as a result. Why would he suddenly love her now? He might have been jealous that she'd married Oliver, but jealousy wasn't love, and what Claire told her had shattered everything. And even if she hadn't told Effie anything, Smith had lied anyway. Claire was clearly still on the scene.

She sat on the chair and shook her head again. Penny was being ridiculous, looking for a happy ending where there couldn't be one. Effie felt she'd made a mistake listening to Oliver's convincing lies and paid the price. She didn't have the energy or the capacity for more.

∽

'Say that Smith *does* love me. What am I supposed to do about it?' Effie asked, removing her finger from her mouth. She'd chewed her nails down as far as she could. She hated flying, and it wouldn't be like last time when she'd been knocked out by her painkillers for the whole flight.

'What do you *want* to do?'

She looked at her mum as they stood outside the airport. After being on the near-isolated island of Colinas Verdes for three weeks, being thrust back into the real world was disorientating, and there was a part of her that wanted to scuttle back to her mum's little haven. A group of tired-looking teenage boys wheeled their suitcases through the doors next to them, and Effie sighed.

'I don't know, Mum. Smith is just wrong for me on so many levels.'

'And Oliver wasn't?'

'Not on paper.'

'And tell me when that ever counts for anything in the real world?' Penny replied with a stern face.

She rubbed the heels of her palms over her eyes. 'I shouldn't even be thinking about this. I should be in bits about my marriage being an epic disaster. It's not right.'

'What's with all the *shoulds*? I should be doing this, I shouldn't be doing that. It's nonsense. Who cares what people think?' Penny tutted. 'Have you ever thought that you're not cut up about Oliver because he was never right for you in the first place? If you've learned anything from all of this, it should be that you should go with what your heart tells you, not your head.'

Effie looked at the pavement. It was easy to say, but doing it was another matter.

'What is your heart telling you?'

She barely had time to breathe before Smith's face flashed up in her mind.

'I'm scared,' she said quietly.

'Being scared isn't a bad thing. It just means you know how much there is to lose. Loving someone is easy. It's the ego that makes it difficult, and right now yours is bruised. Remember you said you wanted the perfect person?'

Effie nodded.

'He's your perfect person. He always has been, from the moment you two became friends. I've always liked him, and he loves you in a way that bastard Oliver never could.'

'Mum!' Effie laughed. Penny never usually swore.

'Well, he is. If you ask me, that's putting it mildly. A more appropriate word would be c—'

Effie's hand flew to her mum's mouth, clamping it shut before she could finish. Penny swatted her hand away as they both burst out laughing.

'Stop. I can't cope with hearing you swear. It's not right.'

'I thought *I* was supposed to be the parent.'

'Yeah, well.' Effie grinned. 'We've never been conventional, have we?'

Penny pulled her in for a hug and squeezed her. 'I'm going to miss you, Sweetpea.'

Effie's throat constricted, and all she could do was nod. If anyone had told her she'd be hugging her mum goodbye with tears in her eyes, she'd have told them they were mad, but as Penny squeezed her, Effie didn't want her to let go.

'Now you'll come back and visit, won't you?' Penny said, releasing her.

Effie nodded and looked at her with her feather-entwined hair, black vest and bright pink tie-dyed leggings. Nobody else at the airport wore the things she wore or looked the way she did. They looked dull in comparison.

'And promise me you won't go back to that house.'

'I promise. Lou took a bunch of stuff to hers when I was in hospital anyway, and I'll sort the rest out later. There's no need for me to go back there.'

'Good. Let me know when you land.' Penny scratched the back of her neck and cleared her throat. 'Now you'd best be off, or you'll be late.'

'You're not coming to the security gate?' Effie asked, trying not to let her voice break.

'Oh, god no. I'm awful at goodbyes. That's why I never gave you one.' Penny kissed her cheek and gave her one last squeeze. 'Love you, Sweetpea. You're going to be just fine.'

Before Effie could reply, Penny turned and left, walking towards the car park. Effie watched her as she went, trying to control the tears threatening to spill onto her cheeks. When her mum disappeared out of sight, she wiped her eyes and tightened her hold on the boarding pass in her hand.

It was time to go home.

32.

What was he doing here? Effie slowly walked towards Smith as he leaned against a pillar with his hands in his pockets. Despite the sinking feeling of disappointment and anger that seemed to go hand in hand with her feelings about him, she couldn't help the fluttering in her stomach. Why did he have to be so damned good looking? His sunglasses were perched on top of his head, and a dark stubble ran across his cheeks and jawline. In a white T-shirt, jeans and Converse, he looked exactly like the version of himself Effie always reverted to in her head.

'The wanderer returns.' He grinned as she stood in front of him. 'You look great. Really great.'

The fluttering went into overdrive as her anger suddenly deserted her. The time away had left her with a deep tan, and the healthy food had made her skin glow. She was sure nobody could have guessed she'd been laid up in hospital only weeks ago, but, god, she was pathetic. One compliment from him, and she was melting like butter on a hot knife.

'Where's Lou?' she asked, narrowing her eyes.

'Something came up. She couldn't make it.'

Since when? She'd texted Lou to make sure she'd be able to meet her, and up until last night there hadn't been a problem.

'But you could?' she asked.

How convenient.

'I didn't want you to get the train alone.' He leaned over to take her suitcase, sending his familiar smell towards her.

'I would've been fine,' she said. 'It's a lot more comfortable than a motorbike, and I've got luggage.'

'I've hired a car.'

'Oh.'

He put his hand on the small of her back to prompt her to start walking, and she flinched at the warmth of his hand on her cotton vest. Smith didn't do cars. Had she ever even seen him behind the wheel of one before? As impractical as the motorbike was, she couldn't forget how it had felt being on it last time, having his body under her hands, between her legs. She frowned and inched away from him, forcing him to drop his hand. She was being ridiculous, thanks to Penny and her silly notions, and the close contact between them wasn't helping.

As they walked out of the terminal towards the car park, a group of girls passed them, wheeling huge sports bags on trolleys. Effie fought to keep herself from scowling at them as they shot Smith appreciative looks. They weren't even being discreet about it, but he barely seemed to notice. She dropped her sunglasses down onto the bridge of her nose. It wasn't like she could blame them – he looked great.

'Did Lou say why she couldn't make it?' she asked as they waited for the lift. She wasn't buying his story for a minute.

'Nope,' he replied as the doors opened and people wheeling trolleys spilled out, 'but she told me about you and Olly not working out. I didn't want you to turn up here with no one to meet you.'

A loaded silence fell between them as they were carried up three floors. She felt stronger after being in Ibiza, but it would have been disheartening to step off the plane with nobody waiting for her. She needed her friends more than ever now.

'Thanks,' she said and smiled – a genuine smile. 'I appreciate it.'

'It's nothing.' He shrugged.

She followed him out of the lift and watched him as he stuck the ticket for the car park in the machine. She looked at the entry time and saw that he'd got there almost an hour ago. He swore as the machine spat his ten pound note back out at him, and she hid a smile. His nostrils had a tendency to flare when he was agitated.

'We're just over here,' he said once he'd finally paid.

'Nice wheels.' Effie looked at the grey VW Golf as Smith unlocked it. It matched the colour of his eyes, and she feigned interest in the alloys instead of Smith's biceps when he lifted the boot.

'It's not bad. Still prefer two wheels to four, though.' He smiled at her as she opened the passenger door and got in.

Smith slipped the car out of its space and left the car park with ease. She might never have seen him drive a car before but he seemed just as at home in one as he did on his bike. She watched as he changed gears, his thigh rising as his foot left the clutch like it was second nature. As they turned out of the airport and joined the motorway, Effie settled back in the chair, slipping her feet out of her flip-flops. Lindy, a woman who lived a couple of bungalows down from Penny, had given her a pedicure and painted her toenails turquoise. There was something about the colour that made her feel summery and refreshed.

'So how was Ibiza? Looks like it did you some good.'

'You know what? It was really nice. I spent a lot of time with Mum, and we talked a lot. Things are better between us now.'

'That's good. It was long overdue.' He nodded and tapped his thumb against the steering wheel in time to the music on the radio.

Effie turned her head, looking out at the fields passing by in a blur. In the distance, a plane was coming in to land.

'It's really nice there,' she said. 'Not what I expected at all. I almost didn't want to come back.'

'I'll have to see it for myself sometime.'

An image of Smith in Colinas Verdes popped up in her mind, as vivid as if it were reality. She pictured him swinging in the hammock by the creek, with his long legs stretched out, and digging up the vegetables, his skin glistening with sweat.

Smith cleared his throat as he switched lanes, overtaking the car in front. 'Speaking of coming back, there was another reason I came to pick you up.'

'What?' Effie replied warily, looking at his profile.

'The thing with Claire, at the barbecue.' He quickly looked at her with a flicker of apprehension on his face. 'You never gave me the chance to explain.'

She frowned. He was smart. She'd bet that Lou didn't have a reason for not being the one to meet her. He was doing what he'd done in Ireland, putting her in a situation where it would be just the two of them, where she couldn't get away from him. The skin on the back of her neck tingled as she remembered his unique method of warming her up on the beach, and even if she could have got away from him now, there was an overwhelming part of her that didn't want to. He looked at her again, and she sighed.

'I didn't let you because I didn't want you to.'

'But you just took her word over mine.'

'Why was she even there in the first place? You said you'd split up.' She couldn't keep the jealousy from her voice, and judging by the way he looked at her, he'd picked up on it too.

'Because she's my friend.'

Yeah, with benefits.

Effie shook her head and stared straight ahead. Penny was wrong; his *friendship* with Claire only confirmed that. She hadn't imagined the way they'd grown closer while she'd been separated from Oliver, had she? He'd told her they'd split up. And even though she'd taken Oliver back, she hadn't fully realised how dull her feelings were for him in comparison with those she had for Smith until the barbecue.

'You still lied,' she said, keeping her eyes fixed on the car in front.

'Yeah, I did.'

'See?' She shook her head at his matter-of-fact reply and crossed her arms. He'd admitted it: she'd been right.

'I lied, but not to you. Not once.' The sincerity in his voice made her turn her head.

'But you just said—'

'I lied to Claire. Well, not *lied*, exactly. Travelling was one of the things we spoke about a lot when we first matched on Tinder. She's been around the world, I love to travel – it was inevitable.' He shrugged. 'I told her I'd left for a year, and she asked why I'd come back so soon. I could hardly tell her the truth, could I?'

'Why not?'

'Really?' He raised his eyebrows at her. 'If you were chatting to a guy, and he told you he left Thailand to try and stop his ex's wedding, would you bother seeing him again?'

Effie's heart stopped. 'But that's not why you came back. You told me it was because you had to see it for yourself.'

Was he lying again? Maybe he'd spun so many that he couldn't keep track anymore. She looked at him as he pulled his eyebrows together and clenched his jaw. His neck had flushed red. Her breath became shallow as she realised he was blushing. He wasn't lying.

'You came to stop my wedding?' She looked at him, but he didn't respond as he dropped the car back into the middle lane. Effie shook her head. 'But you were hours late for that.'

What would have happened if he'd been on time? Would he have barged into the ceremony and demanded it be stopped like a scene from a film? Her stomach flipped at the thought, but it wasn't from imagining the disruption he'd have caused. It flipped because she was imagining what would have happened if she'd changed her mind and walked out of there with Smith, not Oliver. If she'd never become a Barton-Cole.

'Smith?'

He sighed and dropped one of his arms to drive one-handed. 'Mickey told me about the wedding a couple of weeks beforehand. He said you were happy and that Oliver was a nice guy, but I got it into my head that I had to come back and stop it, so I booked a flight. I flew in the night before and stayed with him. I saw the invite at his house, so I knew where to go, but when the morning came . . .'

Smith stopped talking, and Effie looked, with her heart in her mouth, at his hand resting on the gearstick.

'I couldn't do it. The way things were between us when I left . . .' He shrugged again. 'I told myself you'd be better off with him, whoever he was. I told myself he'd be better for you than I ever was.'

'So why did you come at all?' she asked, remembering the way he'd stood in front of her on the lawn, all suited and booted, looking at her in her wedding dress.

'I told you, I had to see it for myself.'

He'd wanted to stop the wedding. Why would he have wanted to do that if he didn't love her? It couldn't have just been jealousy that drove him to spend hundreds of pounds on a flight back at short notice.

'So, you see, I couldn't say that to Claire. I'd have looked like I was still hung up on you.'

Are you?

She wanted to ask the question so badly she had to clamp her lips together to keep them closed.

'So you told her you got driven out of Thailand by gangsters instead?'

Smith chuckled. 'Not quite. She embellished a bit. I'd met a couple of Russian guys, and they were cool. We went on a few trips together, but it was only when we went to Krabi that I realised the trips we'd been on were to shift MDMA.'

Effie shook her head. Trust Smith to end up surrounded by drugs. Some things never changed.

'They asked me if I wanted in, but I'd left England to get away from all that. I told them so, and after that, they were just off with me. Mickey emailed me a couple of days later about your wedding, and, well, it seemed a good time to leave. I told you I'd changed, and I meant it.'

It sounded plausible enough. More plausible than being chased out of the country by gangsters anyway, and it also meant that he really hadn't lied about why he came back or about trying to turn his life around.

'So you were trying to impress her.'

'I guess. Pretty pathetic, isn't it?' Smith grimaced. 'It wasn't even worth it in the end. Nothing really ever happened between us. She's hung up on some other guy she met at Christmas anyway, and even if she wasn't, I simply wasn't ready for anything to happen.'

Effie's heart rammed, trying to leap out from her chest.

'She really is just a friend, with no added extras,' he said, looking at her.

A smile fought its way onto her face, and she looked outside the window to hide it. Now that she thought about it, she'd never seen them kiss or hold hands. She'd never seen anything in the way they'd acted together to mark them out as a couple. When he'd taken her home after she'd fallen ill at work, he'd told her they hadn't spoken for a while and that it was only casual. Had she really got it all wrong? Had he been in love with her all along? She wanted to believe it, but he'd told her in Ireland that he didn't want her. He'd told her he wanted to be just friends.

'I shouldn't have come back,' he said, and the glow in Effie's chest was swiftly extinguished. 'There wouldn't have been a barbecue or an argument if I hadn't. You wouldn't have ended up in hospital.'

'Don't say that.' She shook her head.

The idea that he might have stayed away made her cold inside. Yes, they'd argued, and her life had spiralled out of control, but that would have happened anyway. It wasn't Smith's fault that Oliver was violent, and even though she'd ended up with broken bones, she was happy Smith had come back.

'I'm glad you came back.' She looked at him. 'I'm sorry I was pig-headed. I should've let you explain.'

'We don't like to make things easy, do we?' He smiled and she laughed back at him. That was the truth. *Easy* was a word that could never describe their connection, but maybe that was what she liked about it.

'It's nice to have you back, and it's not a moment too soon.' He grinned and shifted the gearstick, slowing down for the roadwork ahead. 'Lou will be stoked, and it means she'll have someone else to call to dissect what's happening with Mickey.'

'What is happening? Are they back together?' Effie's eyes brightened at the thought of her best friend getting the one thing she wanted the most.

'Not quite, but they're getting there. All I know is, I can't handle another hour-long phone call, and it doesn't help when I'm getting it from both sides.'

Effie laughed at his obvious lies. It was simply in his nature to help the people he cared about, and if that meant taking an hour-long phone call every day from both Mickey and Lou to talk about the same thing, he'd do it, no questions asked. It was one of the things that made him who he was.

By the time they pulled up outside Lou's place, they'd fallen back into the friendship they'd had before the disastrous barbecue. He'd gently teased her when she'd hooked up her phone to the car's Bluetooth and played her pop playlist. It was her guilty pleasure, and she'd listened to it every day at the creek in Ibiza. Meanwhile, she'd teased him about his bike, telling him she preferred the car, when actually the opposite was true. Now she knew he hadn't lied and that maybe Penny was right, she wished she'd been able to sit close to him, her arms wrapped around his waist with her thighs gripping his.

'So,' he said, turning to face her as she took off her seatbelt. 'I guess I'll see you back at work. Are you sure you're ready to come back?'

'It's been weeks, and my doctor's certificate runs out soon. I'll see how I go, but I've got to start sorting my life out sometime.'

He followed her out of the car and got her bag from the boot.

'If you don't mind my asking . . . what happened with you and Olly? You only just took him back.'

She looked down at the pavement. She wanted to tell him; it was clear Lou hadn't told him the real reason. It would be wrong and downright hypocritical to lie to him now she knew he'd been honest with her, but she didn't want to think about what Oliver had done. She looked normal, and despite the odd stab of pain in her ribs, she *felt* normal. Things had been sorted out between her and Penny, and her and Smith. She didn't want to ruin the mood by telling him the truth.

'It's complicated,' she replied as Lou opened the front door and excitedly waved at her.

'Fair enough.' He nodded and looked over at Lou. 'I'd better leave you two to it.'

Effie stood in front of him, and his eyes flicked down to the ground. Were they supposed to hug goodbye? What did they normally do? She tried to remember, but her mind drew a blank. Why was this so awkward? Smith leaned forward to hug her as she turned her head to kiss his cheek and her lips ended up somewhere between his mouth and chin. Her cheeks burned as he awkwardly patted her back, and she pulled away, keeping her eyes firmly on the ground. Talk about embarrassing.

'See you later. And thanks for the lift.'

She scurried away from him and headed towards Lou, who was standing in the doorway with her lips clamped together and pulled tight as she held back a laugh.

'Don't,' Effie warned, but she couldn't keep the grin off her face.

Lou let the laugh out and wrapped her in a tight hug, and Effie heard the Golf's engine start. 'I'm not saying a word. It's ace to have you back.'

An hour later, Lou put the plastic container that had held her special fried rice on the coffee table. 'So, basically, Mickey and I are hanging out in a kind of friends situation. It's nowhere near a relationship, but I'm grabbing it with both hands.'

'That's great.' Effie smiled. 'It's got to be a good sign.'

Lou grinned. 'It is. It feels like we're heading in the right direction.'

Effie put her container on top of Lou's and sat back in the sofa. They'd ordered takeaway and gone through the mountain of food, catching up. In the time she'd been away, Lou and Mickey had been talking often, working their way through what had happened, and she looked happy. Ecstatic, even.

'Have you been on any dates together?' Effie asked, rubbing her full stomach.

'Not really. I mean, we haven't spent any real time alone together, but it's been nice. You can see for yourself soon. There's that open-air cinema thing later this month. He said he'll try and get some tickets if you're up for it.'

'To see what?'

'*Back to the Future.*' Effie grimaced, and Lou matched it before laughing. 'I know. It's so not my thing either. If it were up to me it'd be *Dirty Dancing*, but they've sold out.'

'Let's face it, it's not really about the film, though, is it?'

Lou blushed. 'Will you come? It'll take the pressure off.'

'Of course.' Effie nodded. 'Although if this is you under pressure, I have to say, it suits you. You look great.'

'So do you. You look happy.'

'I am.' Effie smiled. 'It feels weird to say it, given what happened, but maybe it was all for the best.'

'Have you heard anything from him since you said you wanted a divorce?'

Effie nodded. 'I've had to keep my phone switched off. He keeps texting and calling. Izzy too.'

She'd ignored her sister-in-law's calls, just as she'd ignored Oliver's, and she felt bad for it. She liked Izzy, and it didn't feel right to block her out, but she couldn't speak to her. She didn't want to have to be the one to tell her that the brother she loved so dearly was a monster. Let Oliver be the one to tell his family and friends why their marriage had ended.

'You know you can get his number blocked,' Lou said. 'Just tell them he's harassing you.'

'I'll get a new number. It'll be quicker and much less hassle. That way I can just give the new number to the people I want to have it.'

'And would that include a certain James Smith?' Lou grinned. 'Seriously, you two were like a pair of teenagers outside.'

'God, don't. It was beyond embarrassing.' Effie buried her face in her hands.

'He looked just as awkward as you did, so don't worry about it. At least you got to clear the air.'

Effie looked back up at Lou and frowned. 'Did you duck out of picking me up on purpose?'

'Yep, and you can thank me later,' Lou replied, tucking her feet under her on the sofa. 'He told us about what Claire said to you and gave us his version. You had to hear him out, and you're as stubborn as anything, so, sorry – but not really.'

'It's fine,' Effie replied, rubbing the skin that, up until a couple of weeks ago, used to be covered by her wedding ring. 'I should've listened to him in the first place. Thanks for not telling him by the way, about . . . you know.'

'There's no way I was going to unleash that bit of information.' Lou shook her head. 'He'll go ballistic if he finds out.'

'I know.'

'So what happens now with you two? I mean, let's face it: it's not like you're going to rebound from twat-face, is it? Not if you didn't love him properly in the first place.'

'Nothing's going to happen. I don't even know how Smith really feels about me.'

Lou rolled her eyes. 'Oh, for goodness sake. Are you blind? Did he not tell you the reason he came back?'

'No, I'm not, and yes, he did, but he also told me he wasn't interested when we went to Ireland. You sound like Mum. He's been back eight months, and a lot can change in that time. Look at my life.'

'You're wrong,' Lou said, shaking her head, 'and me and your mum are right.'

'Has he actually told you he loves me, in those words?'

Lou frowned. 'Well, no, not exactly. But he doesn't have to. It's obvious.'

Effie pulled the small cushion to rest on her lap. 'I'm not going to take the chance on a maybe.'

'But you love him. You pretty much said so yourself at the Sketch launch.'

'I know.' Effie nodded. 'But I've got so much stuff to think about right now. I've got to get better, change my number, find out about a divorce, somehow get my stuff back from the house and find somewhere to live. I can't put my energy into something that might not work out. Not when it comes to Smith.'

Coward.

She frowned, remembering what Penny had said at the airport, but surely it was better to protect herself right now than to be exposed. Imagine how mortifying it would be if he turned her down. They'd only just got their friendship back to a good place. Maybe it was better to just leave things as they were.

Lou leaned over and squeezed Effie's knee. 'I know it's over-whelming, but you just need to take one day at a time, like you told me, remember? Make a list, and we can go from there. And you know you can stay here as long as you like.'

'Thanks.' Effie smiled.

'That said, I still think you're wrong about Smith, but I hear you. You need to sort things out first, and he's not going anywhere. One day at a time.'

33.

'H'ow did you get on?' Lou asked.

Effie held her phone to her ear and sighed, closing the door behind her. 'It was a waste of time. I can't get a divorce because we've been married less than a year.'

'What about an annulment?'

'Nope. I don't qualify.' She put her handbag on the sofa and sat down. 'If he'd given me an STD on the other hand, there'd be nothing stopping me.'

'Seriously? You mean battery isn't a good enough reason to split from your husband, but being given chlamydia is?' Lou asked with more than a touch of sarcasm.

Effie sighed again. She'd spent all morning at the local Citizens Advice Bureau, having secured an appointment, and after thinking she'd have to wait for weeks to get one, she'd taken it as a good omen. She'd expected to hear good news and had stepped out of the house full of optimism. The day after getting back from Ibiza, she'd got a new number and mentally crossed it off her to-do list. She'd wanted to do the same with the start of divorce proceedings, as she was eager to try to get her life in order. The idea of waiting another three months before she could start the process to dissolve her marriage made her feel grey inside.

'The good news is, I could get legal aid after November because of the violence.'

'I don't understand. Surely if you went to the police, this could get expedited? We have the photos we took too, remember?'

'I'm not going to the police,' Effie replied, kicking her shoes off. 'I told you already. It happened ages ago, and it'll be my word against his.'

'No, it won't. They take it seriously now.'

'Lou . . .' Effie ran a hand through her hair. 'He knows the law inside out, and his dad was one of the best QCs in the country. I'd be stuck with a solicitor through legal aid. I wouldn't stand a chance, and I don't want the ins and outs of our relationship to become public. And even if I did go to the police, it wouldn't change the facts. We've not been married long enough to divorce.'

'So what are you going to do?'

'I'll have to wait it out until then, I guess. There's not much else I *can* do.'

Effie scowled. She should never have married him in the first place.

'He doesn't know you're at mine, does he?'

'No, thank god. He doesn't even know I'm back in the country.'

'Well that's good,' Lou offered, raising the tone of her voice in an attempt to cheer Effie up.

'I know. I just wanted to get the ball rolling, you know?'

'It's just three months,' Lou replied. 'It'll fly past, and come the fifth of November, you can be the first in line for a solicitor.'

'Don't worry, I will be.'

'That's my girl. Twat-face won't know what's hit him when the time comes. Serves him right. Listen, I've got to go, but I'll be home by six. We'll talk more then, okay?'

Effie nodded. 'Okay. I'll see you later.'

She hung up and rubbed her hands over her face. The optimism she'd come back from Ibiza with had disappeared in the space of one morning, and as she inhaled, a sharp pain made her catch her breath. She'd thought her ribs had almost healed. The doctors had said it would take around six weeks, and she hadn't needed to take her painkillers for ages.

Tears loomed in her eyes, but it was more from disappointment than pain. She took a deep breath, clenching her teeth as her ribs protested. She couldn't fall apart, not now. Her appointment was a setback, but it was only three months. She could do it. Come Monday, she'd be back at work, and the days would pass more quickly. Oliver couldn't contact her anymore, and he didn't know where she was. She could keep it up until November. She just had to keep focused.

❧

'One smoked-chicken and sun-dried tomato panini and a bottle of water.' Smith put the paper bag down on her desk as he perched on the end of it.

'Thanks.' Effie sat back in her chair and smiled at him.

'How's it going so far?'

'Good.' She nodded. 'I've got a mountain of emails to get through, but it's nothing major.'

Her first morning back at Archive had passed quickly. After walking into the office to see her desk covered with balloons and a welcome back banner, she'd spent more time catching up with her colleagues than working.

'It feels more like a Friday than a Monday,' she said, tearing the wrapping from her panini.

'We're happy to have you back,' Smith replied, leaning over to take one of the doughnuts from the box she'd brought in. 'Nobody else can work that spreadsheet like you do.'

'Thanks. It's how I make myself indispensable.'

'You don't have to make a spreadsheet for that.' He grinned and took a bite of the doughnut. 'Did Lou mention the open-air cinema thing? Mickey got the tickets this morning. It should be fun.'

She shook her head with a smile. 'Did nobody ever tell you it's rude to talk with your mouth full?'

'Blame my parents.' He took another bite, bigger than the last one. 'Shit.'

Effie laughed as a blob of raspberry jam dropped from the doughnut onto his jeans, and handed him a tissue. 'Serves you right.'

He took it from her and scooped it away.

'What do you think about him and Lou?' she asked, unscrewing the lid from her bottle. 'Do you think they'll get back together? Has he said anything to you?'

'Are you scoping out information for Lou?' He raised an eyebrow and scrunched the tissue up in his hand. 'Because if you are, you're not getting anything from me.'

'No,' she lied. 'As if.'

'Good.'

'It's just that she's really nervous about it. It's the proper first date they'll have been on since they started talking again, right?'

'Yeah, but we'll be there too. It's not like it'll be an intimate kind of thing.'

'I suppose.' She took the panini from the bag.

Smith was too astute for his own good. She'd promised Lou she'd try to sound him out, but Smith wasn't budging, and his view that it wouldn't be intimate unexpectedly stung.

'Okay, fine. All I'm going to say is, it's looking hopeful.'

'Really?' Effie grinned.

'He loves her. She loves him. It's only a matter of time, right?'

He looked her in the eye, and she blinked. Why had that sounded like it was about much more than Lou and Mickey?

'It's all about the long game.'

327

He grinned, took another bite of his doughnut and went back to his desk. As she watched him, a wave of warmth started in her stomach and spread throughout her body in seconds. She turned her chair so he wouldn't be in her line of sight.

The long game. Was that what he was doing, waiting until the opportunity presented itself to . . . what? Kiss her? Tell her he loved her? Assuming that he really did love her, of course. She wondered what would happen if she were the one to make the first move, and then she bit into her panini, determined to think of something else. She was in no position to do that, no matter how much she wanted to. And besides, she still wasn't sure that he was for real. Smith was competitive, and if he was looking at this as a game, she'd end up being a pawn. He'd told her himself, he wanted to be Just Friends.

She picked up her small desk calendar, flicked through to the fifth of November and drew a circle around it. The red ink looked stark against the white background. Smith wasn't the only one with a long game to play.

∽

A few days later, Effie sat on the grass in the park close by their office and took her salad box from a brown paper bag.

'Hang on,' Smith said and pulled out a paper napkin from his bag. 'Here.'

She took it from him and pulled her sunglasses down from her head, looking around them. She sighed dreamily as she lifted the lid on her salad box.

'Do we really have to go back to work?' she asked.

He smiled and crossed his legs. 'Yep. But not for another forty-four minutes.'

'Ooh, lucky us.' Effie drizzled the lyonnaise dressing from the small sachet over her salad. 'Forty-four minutes isn't that long.'

If she could, she'd lie back on the grass until the sun went down. She hadn't banked on missing the Clapham garden, and Lou's tiny balcony was no comparison. For now, snatched moments in the park would have to do, and if she had to share it with half of London, so be it. She looked around at the dozens of other people squeezed into the little patch of green between her office and the Tube station.

'Had enough of being back already?' Smith asked and bit into his baguette.

Effie shook her head and looked at him, his jaw flexing as he chewed his food. 'Not at all. It's just such a beautiful day, it's a shame we have to be stuck in the office.'

'I'll play hooky if you will. We can escape for the afternoon.'

She laughed at his cheeky grin. 'You're a bad influence, Smith.'

'I don't even try to deny it.'

She stuck her plastic fork into her lettuce leaves. Since she'd returned to work, the days had flown past, exactly as she'd hoped. She'd settled straight back into her routine with ease, and everything was as it had been before, with three notable exceptions.

The first was obvious. Instead of leaving her marital home each morning, she left from Lou's flat. It had been two and a half weeks of unashamed fun. They ate together almost every night and had breakfast together in the mornings. The evenings had been spent watching old films, both of them with their feet propped up on the sofa as they wore face masks or painted their nails. Even though Effie was camping on the sofa, she wouldn't have traded it for her luxury memory foam mattress back in her marital home for anything.

Secondly, Oliver was still firmly off Effie's radar. She'd half expected him to turn up at her office at some point, pleading with her to take him back, but he'd clearly accepted that they were over, because she'd heard nothing. And she wasn't surprised to realise that she didn't care. If anything, it only made her resolve even stronger to go for a divorce when the time came.

'Okay, I've got a question for you,' Smith said, holding his baguette with one hand and sticking his hand into a bag of crisps with the other. 'Imagine there were only forty-four minutes left to live.'

Effie grimaced. 'Jeez. This sounds like a fun conversation.'

'Maybe there's an asteroid racing towards us, or the ice caps have melted and a massive tidal wave's going to kill us all. What would you do?'

'Apart from panic and cry?'

Smith nodded and tipped his head back, dropping a few crisps into his mouth. How could anyone eat salt and vinegar crisps and a tandoori chicken baguette at the same time? Through the dark lenses of her glasses, she watched as he washed it down with a mouthful of Coke and thought about his question.

The third and most obvious difference to her life before was Smith. If he was playing the long game, then he was the star player. Every day, he'd get to the office with an extra hot latte for her in addition to his Americano. They'd started lunching together when his schedule allowed it and fallen into a pattern of 'I'll pay this time, you pay next time.' At the start of her second week back at work, the Northern Line had messed up on her way home, and she'd ended up being stuck in a tunnel along with a seemingly inhumane number of other commuters for twenty minutes, all packed together and sweltering in the August heat. Smith had offered her a ride home the next day, and ever since, he'd brought his spare helmet as a matter of course. He looked out for her as much as he could, so much so that she knew they were attracting strange glances in the office. She could only imagine what their colleagues thought was going on, but the fact was, nothing had changed. Fundamentally, they were the same as before. Just Friends. There'd been plenty of opportunities for him to make a move, to get to the final stage of his game, but he'd placed himself firmly in the friend zone.

Nearly every memory she had of the time since she'd come back from Ibiza had him in it – at the airport, in the car, on his bike. If the world was going to end in forty-four minutes' time, she wouldn't care what she did. As long as she did it with him.

She looked at him again as he squinted his eyes against the sun. Her salad had suddenly taken on the consistency of cardboard, and she struggled to swallow it. Her mum had told her about positive thinking, saying that the more she thought about something, the more likely it was to come true. She hadn't bought into it, but what if her mum had been right? She'd wished for Oliver to leave her alone, and he had. Maybe if she'd wished for Smith to make a move, instead of wondering about his motives, he would have.

'So?' he asked.

'No idea,' she replied with a shrug and put her salad box on the ground. Her appetite had disappeared.

'Oh, come on. There must be *something* you'd want to do?'

'I don't know.' She rubbed her hands and shrugged again. 'The usual, I guess. Say my goodbyes and stuff. What about you?'

'I'd like to think I'd do something profound, but let's face it – that's unlikely.' He laughed. 'I'd probably go up on a roof somewhere really high and play some good tunes. It'd be cool to see everything happen from a height.'

'Rather you than me. I wouldn't spend my last few minutes on earth scaling a tall building.'

'You're going to die anyway; you might as well do something you've been afraid of your whole life first.'

'You get your kicks in some weird places, Smith.' Effie laughed. 'Wouldn't you rather spend it with people you love?'

'Of course, but it's only forty-four minutes. It's impossible to get everyone together that quickly, and transport would be all kinds of crazy.'

She shook her head, laughing. He'd clearly thought this through, right down to the last detail.

'And you'd be there.' He shrugged. 'So it'd be all good.'

Her laughter stopped abruptly. Thank god, she was wearing glasses, or her eyes would have given her away. She was sure they were as wide as saucers.

'I would?'

'Well, yeah,' he replied as if it was the only obvious answer, and he smiled.

It was so genuine that she couldn't *not* believe that what Penny and Lou said was true. She fanned her face with her hand, grateful that the redness creeping up her neck could easily be put down to the heat.

'I dunno, though,' he said, leaning in close so their shoulders touched.

He looked up at the sky and then turned his head to face her. He was about to kiss her – she was sure of it. Her heart raced in her chest.

'Don't know about what?'

Why had she ordered salad with onions in it? And why was she wearing her sunglasses? Should she take them off? She wanted to see his eyes properly, to look at the grey irises, flecked with dots of blue.

'Can't see any asteroids. I think we're safe.' He smiled, and she swore it had more than a hint of regret to it. 'Shame.'

34.

For the rest of the afternoon, Effie had been able to think of nothing else, so much so that she'd almost wished there *were* an asteroid hurtling towards the earth. She'd sat at her desk, looking at the digital clock in the bottom corner of her screen, counting down the minutes to the moment she'd be able to get on the back of Smith's bike for him to take her home.

Could he tell that she'd been willing him to kiss her? He'd handed her the helmet with a knowing look, as if she'd left herself wide open, and she tried not to hold on to him too tightly for the drive back to Lou's. She'd grown used to being on the bike and his way of riding, and the truth was, she could easily sit on it without having to hold on to him at all. Instead, she kept her hands loose around his waist, all too aware of how close she was to the one part of him she really wanted to touch. He kept up the habit of putting his hand on her thigh and turning to check on her when he stopped at a red light, and unless she was completely delusional, she was sure his grip was firmer and higher than it usually was.

By the time they got to Lou's, her top was stuck to her back, and she didn't know whether it was from the heat of the sun or her body going into overdrive over the tension she was sure she'd felt between them all day. He turned the key and killed the engine as he put his foot on the ground to stabilise the bike.

'Wow, it's hot,' she said, passing the helmet to him. She was certain her hair was stuck to her head where it had been under the helmet, and with the curly ends being windswept, she must have looked a complete state.

He took the helmet from her and removed his. 'It is.'

Effie bit down on her lip. God, this was going to sound so lame. 'Do you want some water or something?'

'Or something.' She saw the hint of a smile on his lips. 'Sounds good.'

The blush almost burned her skin as he climbed off the bike. Why was she so nervous? This was Smith. It wasn't like they hadn't been in this place before. Why were her insides shaking as they walked up the stairs to Lou's flat?

He followed her in and exhaled loudly. 'Ah, this is nice. My place is like an oven, even with the windows open.'

He flopped on the sofa, his legs splayed wide, and Effie left him to go into the kitchen. She stood by the sink and gripped the edge of it, feeling the cool steel under her palms. *Or something.* That was pretty clear, wasn't it? She never could tell with him. It was why it had taken them so long to get together in the first place. She could never work out whether he was simply flirting or stating his intent.

'Lou not around?' he asked.

Effie cleared her throat and opened the fridge to pull out a carton of juice. 'No. She's facilitating some kind of event up in Newcastle. She won't be back till tomorrow.'

Would she have invited him up here if Lou had been around? The honest answer was probably not. Lou's flat didn't have much room for privacy. The last thing she needed was an audience to watch the 'will they, won't they?' drama between them. She filled two glasses and walked the two paces from the kitchen to the living room.

'I hope it's cold enough.'

He took the glass and drank a sip. 'It's perfect, thanks.'

She hovered next to the sofa for a second before sitting on the other end, and they drank in silence. Their swallowing seemed to echo its way all around the flat, and she felt every bit as awkward as she had when he'd dropped her off the day she'd got back from Ibiza.

'So what are you up to this evening?' Smith asked a little too loudly.

'I don't know. Flat hunting online, probably. I might Skype with Mum too.'

He put his glass on the table. 'How is she?'

'Good.' Effie smiled. 'Really good. She's getting ready for her annual trip to India.'

'Lucky her. I've always wanted to go there.'

She looked down into her empty glass before putting it next to his. 'Do you want some music or something?'

Before he could reply, she dove into her handbag, looking for her phone, grateful to have something to do other than wonder about what was going on. She wasn't imagining it – something had changed. She connected her phone to the Bluetooth speakers and looked back at Smith.

'Okay. *I've* got a question for *you.*'

'Shoot.'

She sat facing him with her back against the arm of the sofa and put her legs up in front of her. 'If I were to put your music on shuffle, which three songs would you be most embarrassed about playing?'

'That's easy.' He shrugged. 'None.'

'Bull. We all have guilty pleasures when it comes to music.' She grinned, feeling much more at ease. As long as they kept talking, there wouldn't be any awkward silences to be filled. 'We could just put your music on now and find out?'

'Oh, you're good.' He grinned back and crossed his arms, fixing his face with a look of concentration. 'I've got some ABBA on there.'

Effie stifled a laugh.

'Come on, it's not fair if you're going to laugh. Besides, ABBA was pretty cool. What else?' He frowned and thought for a few minutes. 'Destiny's Child, Survivor. And . . . I dunno. Cutting Crew, probably.'

'I don't know them,' she replied, putting her glass on the table.

'Sure you do. "I just died in your arms tonight"? It's an oldie.'

Effie burst out laughing as the bars of the song came into her head. 'In all the time I've known you, I've never had you pegged as a power-ballad type.'

'What?' he said, grabbing the small cushion and resting his hands on it as he pretended to sulk. 'There's nothing wrong with it now and again. It's a guilty pleasure, like you said.'

She tried to catch her breath, but when she looked at him, she fell back into a fit of giggles. He always seemed to surprise her.

'You're so mean.' He laughed and moved towards her on the sofa with the cushion in his hand, and for a split second, his beautiful face morphed until she saw Oliver in front of her, not Smith.

Effie instinctively turned, curling herself up into a little ball, just as she had that night in the hallway in her house, but instead of Oliver's foot connecting with her stomach, the cushion Smith was holding whacked against her arm. The sound of her glass clunking against the carpet as the cushion knocked it off the coffee table rang in her ears, and a shot of cold fear ran down her back as she froze. She didn't move when Smith stopped hitting her with the cushion.

'Oh, come on,' Smith said, but she stayed where she was, not daring to look up. 'If anyone's going to start sulking, it should be me.'

She flinched as his hand touched her back, but it was tender, not angry.

'What's wrong? You're shaking like a leaf.'

The tender care in Smith's voice made her slowly turn her head. 'Effie?'

He was crouched on the floor, right by her side, and he kept his hand on her back as she slowly looked back at him. Tears were already streaking down her face. There was no way she could disguise them.

'Jesus. Are you alright? Do you want some water or something?'

Her heart was thumping in her chest, and her body was trembling with misplaced fear, but she still caught the irony of him echoing the words she'd said earlier.

'I'll be right back. Don't move.'

He crossed the living room in three strides, and Effie put her head in her hands. It wasn't like she had anywhere to move to anyway. What the hell? Why had she freaked out like that? She hadn't thought about Oliver for what felt like ages – why had that memory come at her like a sledgehammer? She heard the tap running in the kitchen, and what seemed like less than a second later, Smith was crouching in front of her again.

'Here.'

Her hands trembled as she drank, and he held the bottom of the glass, just as he had after she'd fainted at work. God, she was ridiculous. How many times was he going to have to take care of her? His eyebrows were strung tightly together as he looked at her, his face full of concern. How could *he* have triggered a memory like that? She'd never once felt unsafe with Smith.

'Fuck.' He shook his head and looked at the cushion on the floor. 'I'm sorry. I don't know what happened, I—'

'Don't worry about it,' Effie replied, holding the glass in her hands. She didn't want him to talk about it. She wanted to rewind and erase it from history.

'What happened? Look at you, you're shaking.'

'Nothing. Honestly, I'm fine. I just freaked out.'

'About what?' He shook his head again and looked back at the cushion.

Don't. Please don't.

She could see his mind working. She could almost hear the cogs of his thoughts clicking into place, and when he looked back at her, she avoided his eyes.

'You were scared.' He kept his stare fixed on her. 'Why?'

His eyes scorched her skin like laser beams. She couldn't tell him the truth. It would go from being a manageable situation to a catastrophic one. Smith wasn't the violent type, but she knew there was no way she could tell him the truth without things escalating.

'Effie.' His voice was firm, and he took her chin in his hand, turning her head to face him.

Don't cry.

She had to hold the tears in. Her body shook with the sheer effort it took not to let it betray her need to keep quiet.

'Did he . . . ?' He looked down at the floor, and she saw the muscles in his jaw twitching. He looked back up at her and frowned. 'Did Oliver . . . ?'

She shook her head and mentally clenched every muscle in her body to stop the shaking. There was too much at stake. If Smith got involved and things got messy, he'd end up in prison, or worse. There was no way he could go up against Oliver any more than she could.

'No.' The lie fell from her mouth, and she held her breath.

'Tell me the truth, Effie.' He sat next to her on the sofa and put an arm around her shoulder. 'Did he hurt you?'

His voice faltered under the weight of his question, and the fear that had shaken her quickly ebbed away as she looked at him. His hand was warm and soft on her shoulder, and she could feel the racing of his heart against her arm. It almost matched her own, and she knew then, as she felt the rapid pulsation of his heartbeat, that Penny and Lou had been right. His reaction said it all.

'Do you love me?' she asked.

He frowned and shook his head a little, blindsided by her question. 'What? Effie, you just shrank into the sofa because I hit you with a cushion. This isn't the time to—'

'When we were in Ireland, you said you were glad I stopped you from kissing me.'

'I was. Because I didn't want you to do something you didn't want to do.'

'So you did want to then?' She looked him in the eye as he nodded. 'I need to know how you really feel. Do you love me?'

His heart raced even quicker. It wasn't fair on him to switch the subject like that, but she needed to know. He looked back at her for a few seconds, seconds that felt like hours.

'You know I do.'

His voice was low, quiet and unsure, and Effie's heart swelled at the four words he'd just said. He loved her. Never in all their time together had he said it, or even anything close. She looked at his beautiful, confused face and took her index finger, tracing it along his eyebrow and cheekbone, down to his lips. Had he stopped breathing too? His pupils were fully dilated, and he was so utterly still. Her finger grazed against his lip, and the cotton of his T-shirt quivered as he sucked in a short breath. She leaned forward, and his eyes flicked down to her mouth.

Every cell in her body came alive as their lips connected. Her heart fluttered, her skin flushed with heat and desire coursed right down to the depths of her belly. What started as a tentative kiss intensified as he parted her lips with his tongue and put his hands either side of her head, cupping her face. She melted as he pulled her closer, kissing her with complete confidence in a way that had always made her knees weak. Memories raced through her head as he moved his hands to her hair, and her scalp tingled with pleasure as he grabbed a handful of it, holding it in his fist. It was the one thing he would do that was guaranteed to heat things up between them, any time, any place. She remembered the way he'd done it when they'd kissed for the first time at Notting Hill Carnival. He'd pinned her to the wall, her hands roaming across his back as crowds of revellers partied around them.

She slipped her hands under his T-shirt, eager to do more than just remember. His skin was hot as she ran her palms up the length of his back, feeling the curves of the muscles either side of his spine. Her hands found their way to his chest, rising and falling quicker with every breath he took as he kissed her even harder. He flinched as her fingers trailed down his chest and over his abs, finding the fly on his jeans. He was kissing her so hard, her lips burned, but she didn't break away as she leaned back on the sofa, pulling him down on top of her by his jeans. She opened her eyes just as he did the same.

'Effie,' he mumbled between kisses, but her fervent kisses silenced him.

He was there, kissing her, with his hands scorching her skin as they trailed across her body. He'd said all he'd needed to say and all Effie had needed to hear.

She was done talking.

35.

This is driving me nuts.' Smith nipped Effie's earlobe and dropped more kisses into the crook of her neck.

It had been five days since they'd kissed in Lou's flat, and as he ran a finger down the length of her spine, she stifled a moan, remembering how it had felt to finally have him after so long. She hadn't fully realised until then just how much she'd wanted him, and as they'd lain on the floor, naked, with their limbs entwined, she'd fallen asleep with a smile on her face.

'Tell me again why we have to keep this quiet?' he asked.

'Because it wouldn't be fair on Lou and Mickey to steal their thunder.' She looked up at him as he sighed and put a hand on the wall behind her. 'And we're supposed to be chaperoning.'

'I'd rather take you home and skip it altogether.'

She hooked her fingers into the front of his jeans and pulled him closer. 'It's only for a few hours.'

He sighed again and looked down at her. 'And then we can go public? I can't handle being around you and not being able to touch you. Not now.'

He dropped a kiss on the tip of her nose, and she grinned.

'I promise.'

The open-air cinema screening was later that evening, and Lou and Mickey would be on their first official date. Or, to be more accurate, their second first date. Lou had spent all of last night pulling clothes from her wardrobe, wailing that she had nothing to wear. Effie had never seen her so panicked, but Lou's nerves about their double date provided a great distraction, and she hadn't picked up on the goofy grin Effie had been wearing for days. The only thing that seemed to be keeping her from having a breakdown altogether was knowing that Effie and Smith would be there to act as buffers. It wouldn't be fair to turn up and announce that they'd finally got together and have Lou and Mickey end up as gooseberries.

He kissed her again, and she had to stop herself from giving in to what he wanted. Since they'd woken up on Lou's living room floor, they hadn't spent more than a few snatched moments together. Mickey was living at Smith's, and she was living with Lou. Until they got back together, there was nowhere for them to go, and it was killing her just as much as him. He'd covered her body in kisses that went from being heart-stoppingly tender to downright filthy in turns, and when he'd lain on top of her, she'd realised that nobody else would ever have really stood a chance, whether she married the person or not. Nobody else was like Smith, or even close, and she wondered why she'd stayed away from him for so long. Even when things were at their best with Oliver, there was simply no comparison. Nobody else could hold her in a way that was so gentle and fierce all at the same time. She'd had a taste of him after far too long, and she was impatient for more. They only had five minutes of their lunch break left, and neither one of them had so much as mentioned the idea of eating. She grazed his bottom lip with her teeth as they kissed, and he stopped.

'You are . . .' He shook his head and exhaled loudly.

Effie smiled up at him. 'What?'

'Fucking Amazing. With a capital A.'

It was a surprise her lips hadn't fallen off with the sheer amount of kissing she'd indulged in. They felt raw, and she was steadily working her way through her tub of lip balm, but it was so worth it.

'I reckon we can spare ten minutes,' he said, tearing his lips away from hers as they stood on the pavement outside Lou's flat after work.

Effie shook her head and laughed. 'No, we can't. Lou's going straight from work, and I promised I'd meet her for a quick drink for some Dutch courage first. You need to take the bike home anyway.'

'Screw the bike. I'll leave it here, or I just won't drink tonight.' He leaned in to kiss her again, but she ducked away, grinning.

'Behave.'

'I would, but you make it so damn hard.' He crossed his arms and leaned against the bike, grinning back at her. 'Fine, have it your way.'

'Go take your baby home.'

He grabbed her and pulled her in for another kiss, unbothered by the people walking past.

'I'll see you there.' He pulled on a curl before tucking it behind her ear.

Effie nodded. 'With bells on.'

Her cheeks hurt with the permanent grin that had fixed itself onto her face, and she pulled at them as she walked away from Smith to head upstairs. When she opened the front door, she heard the distinctive roar of his engine as he left to take the bike home, and she looked up at the clock. Thanks to their pavement kissing, she was running late, but she simply smiled. She was certain that tonight would go the way Lou wanted it to, and she couldn't wait to see her face when she told her about Smith. The night ahead held possibilities, and all of them were good.

She threw her bag on the sofa and took her shoes off before pulling a pair of jeans and a vest top from her suitcase and laying them out. She grabbed a butterfly clip and twisted her hair up, pinning it back from her face as she hurried to the shower. There'd be no time to wash it now – not unless she wanted to leave the house with a full-on Afro.

Effie hummed as she showered. She felt giddy, almost bordering on hyperactive. When she thought about everything that had happened between Smith and her, and Oliver and her, it seemed impossible that she'd ended up happy at all. But she was. Deliriously so. She was aching for him already, and he'd only just left. She turned the shower off and shook her head, the grin still fixed to her face. She felt like a lovesick teenager.

In less than twenty minutes, she'd showered, dressed and applied the least amount of makeup she could get away with. Considering they'd be sat outside in the heat, she didn't want to end up sweating and leaving with half of it down her face. And besides, there was little point in wearing anything beyond eye makeup these days. The constant kissing meant lipstick was definitely out of the question. A quick glance at her watch made her relax a little. She'd made the time up and wouldn't be more than ten minutes late at most. Considering that Lou was often late herself, she could probably afford to move a bit slower. She smiled as she checked her reflection one last time. She couldn't move any quicker if she tried. She had way too much energy to burn.

She pulled the front door to the flat open and stepped out into the hallway, bumping straight into someone coming up the stairs. Her bag dropped from her hands, and the contents scattered across the carpeted floor.

'Oh, god. Sorry,' she said, closing the door behind her and crouching down to pick up her things. 'I wasn't looking where I was going.'

The embarrassed smile slowly fell from her face as she looked at the hand holding her purse out towards her. She looked at the fingernails, pale pink with perfect half crescents by the cuticle, and the long fingers on the end of a strong, male hand. The platinum band across the third finger made her breath catch in her throat. It matched the one she used to wear. Her eyes flicked down to the shiny brogues on his feet and the smart, tailored navy trousers on his legs. He stood up slowly, taking her purse with him.

'Hello, Effie.'

She swallowed as Oliver's voice bounced off the walls around them, and closed her eyes. It wasn't him. It couldn't be. He didn't know she was staying at Lou's. They hadn't spoken since she was in Ibiza – how could he?

'You've ignored me for weeks. The least you can do is say hello.'

Her legs shook as she slowly stood up, trying to ignore the way the entire world had shifted right beneath her feet.

'Oliver.'

'Hey, baby.' He smiled, and she just managed to hold back the wince at the sound of him calling her *baby*. She wasn't his baby, and she hadn't been for a long time.

'What are you doing here?'

'I came to see you, obviously. One of your neighbours let me in as he was leaving.' He held her purse out to her, and she stared at it without moving. 'Take it.'

Her hand shook as she took it from him.

'I had to see you.'

His blue eyes were as cold as ice as he looked her up and down, and a wave of revulsion rocked her to the core. How had she never noticed the way they stared so intently before?

'I—'

'Shh.' He put a finger to her lips, and Effie closed her eyes, shuddering. After the sweetness of Smith on her lips, Oliver's touch made her feel sick to her stomach. 'You don't have to say anything.'

He dropped his finger, and she stood perfectly still, barely breathing.

'I thought we could talk.'

'I can't. I'm on my way out. Lou's just behind me.'

Oliver tilted his head, looking at the door behind her and raised his eyebrow. 'No, she isn't. If I've understood correctly, she should have left work by now, and I *think* she'll be on her way to Old Street to meet you.'

Effie opened her mouth to reply, but nothing came out. How the hell did he know that?

'Facebook.' He shrugged with a smile. 'I've had to keep tabs on you somehow.'

'But—' She shook her head, confused. She'd blocked him on Facebook when she was in Ibiza.

'Lou really should check her privacy settings.'

The air rushed out of her, and she looked down at the floor. Lou had updated her status about their plans, and Effie had seen it just before she'd left the office. Even though there was no way Oliver could have seen her name tagged in it, Lou had referred to her *bestie*. It wouldn't have been hard to put two and two together.

'I had to make sure you were alright, for one thing,' he continued, his voice oddly neutral and lacking any emotion whatsoever. 'I mean, you haven't contacted me at all, and at first I was worried. When you said you wanted a divorce, I thought you were having some kind of mental breakdown, but then I drove by your office last week, and lo and behold, there you were. Looking perfectly fine and not so mentally confused after all. Which made absolutely no sense, seeing as you didn't come home.'

'I told you I wouldn't.' She kept her eyes on his feet, not wanting to look back at his face. 'I told you I want a divorce.'

He gave a wry laugh. 'I thought you were joking. I know you don't seriously think you could go up against me.'

So what did he want then? Why was he standing outside Lou's flat, blocking the stairs? There was nothing he could ever do or say that would make her go back. Not for anything in the world.

'If you think I'm divorcing you so you can shack up with that little shit, you'd better think again.'

Her head snapped up as his voice hardened, and she looked at him as he screwed his face up.

'I've seen you two together.'

He made a noise somewhere between a groan and a sob, but it was so full of jealousy and anger that Effie instinctively stepped back, her hand finding the waist-high lock on Lou's door.

'You're my *wife*. How could you do this to us? To *me*?'

She heard the throb of her pulse in her ears as Oliver shook his head. The vein in the middle of his forehead bulged angrily, and she quickly looked down at the floor. Her keys were right by his feet. The last time she'd seen that vein, he'd kicked her to pieces in their hallway. Her breath quickened as she looked past him to the stairs his body was blocking. Could she slip by him, if she were quick enough? Lou's flat was on the first floor. If she could make it downstairs, she could get help.

'Look.' He turned his palms face down and took a deep breath before slowly letting it out again. 'I get it. You were angry with me because I shouted at you in the car, but I forgive you.'

Forgave her? For what? She hadn't done anything wrong.

'Let's just put this all behind us and go home. I'll even overlook this *thing* with you and Smith.'

Effie shook her head, looking past him at the stairs again. She needed to get away from him. He was delusional, and despite his efforts, she could hear the fury in his voice. It was exactly the same as it had been in the car after Smith's barbecue. She'd picked up on it early enough to get away from him then, and she had to do the same now.

'I'm not going to let you leave here without me.' His voice was clear, and with his cut-glass accent, the threat sounded even more menacing. He stared right at her. 'Understand?'

The sound of the letterbox for the communal door downstairs opening and closing distracted him for a second, and he turned his head to the stairwell.

Go! Now!

Effie bolted, trying to knock him out of the way as she made for the stairs, but he caught her wrist, just as she was about to put her foot on the first step.

'Let go of me.' She tried to shake him off, but his grip was vice tight, and he yanked her back, pushing her up against the wall.

Her heart rammed in her chest as she panted, with his face merely inches away, towering above her. His eyes had gone from being ice cold to blazing with anger, so hard they'd almost turned a darker shade of blue. His forearm pressed against her chest, pinning her to the wall.

'Olly, don't!' she cried, trying to wriggle free, but his grip was so strong she could barely move. He was pressed up against her so tight that she couldn't even lift her leg to knee him in the balls – the most basic self-protection manoeuvre there was.

'Why are you being so difficult?' he asked, shaking his head as if they were having a normal conversation. 'Can't you see how much I've missed you?'

Effie trembled, racked with fear as he buried his face into her hair and sniffed at her. She should scream. He'd said a neighbour had let him in – someone would hear her. But before she had a chance to, Oliver crushed his lips against hers. She tried to push him away, to get him off her, but his weight was too strong, and he didn't budge.

She fought against him as he used his free hand to hold her chin in place, and she sobbed, trying to keep her mouth closed. Her stomach quivered as he pushed his rough lips against hers even harder than before, and he let out a moan.

Oh, god. No. Please don't.

His moan sounded wrong. It sounded like there was an edge of sexuality to it, and she sobbed even harder as she realised that he wasn't going to stop. She pushed her hands into his stomach, trying to drive him away. It was like pushing against a brick wall, but she had to do something – anything – to get him off her. He barely flinched as he continued trying to get her to kiss him back. Instinctively, she opened her mouth and bit down on his lip, feeling the flesh between her teeth as the tangy, iron-like taste of blood filled her mouth. Oliver yelped and dropped his arms, his hands flying straight to his mouth.

'You fucking bitch. You bit me!'

He'd barely finished the sentence before Effie shot down the stairs. Tears streamed down her face, stinging her eyes and blurring her vision. She could hardly see as she gripped the handrail, taking the stairs two or three steps at a time, stumbling as she went. Her breath was ragged, her heart pounding, and she could hear Oliver's footsteps, heavy and even as he followed after her. As she reached the bottom of the stairs, she saw the communal door at the end of the hallway. She just needed to get outside, and she'd be fine. There was no way he'd risk anything out in public.

She turned to look behind her and tripped over a bicycle leaning against the wall. She scrambled forward, pulling herself up off the floor, but Oliver grabbed the back of her neck and fell on top of her. The air whooshed out of her in one breath with the impact, and it didn't come back as she tried to wriggle her way from underneath him. He grabbed her shoulder and turned her over before sitting right on her stomach with his hands gripping her neck.

Effie snatched a breath, but his weight was too heavy, and his thumbs were pressed too tightly into the hollow of her throat.

'You fucking bitch. I should have turned the car around and finished the job.'

Spittle flew from his mouth, hitting her face, and her eyes widened. It had been Oliver who had run her over. Terror filled her as she thrashed beneath him, trying to scream, but nothing came out of her mouth as he dug his thumbs in harder. She stretched her arms out, trying to claw at his face, but she couldn't reach.

Oliver looked down at her with a scornful smile, as if her efforts to free herself were amusing him. 'You can't just decide you don't love someone and run off, Effie. We made vows. What was I supposed to do – just let you run away from me? How many times do I have to teach you that actions have consequences?'

Her heart beat loudly in her ears, tears ran from her eyes and she cried silently, panicking at the pressure building in her head and lungs.

Her mum, Mickey, Lou – she saw their faces and struggled even harder, trying to reach Oliver's face with her hands. She couldn't let him take them away from her, but her vision was blurring and the edges of her sight were tinged with red. The floor was cold underneath her, and she was suddenly thrown back to that night, lying on the wet tarmac, looking at the tail lights of the car that had run her over. Only now, she knew it was Oliver behind the wheel – the man who'd sworn to protect her in front of family and friends. He was going to kill her. He'd tried once and failed, and now he was going to try again, and there was nothing and nobody to stop him.

Smith's face filled her head. She saw his beautiful eyes and heard his hearty laugh. Smith, who loved her. She'd only just got him back. The pressure in her head reached tipping point, and she realised that she hadn't told him she loved him back.

I love you, Smith. I love you, I love you, I love you.

If she could've said it out loud, she would have, just so that Oliver would know he hadn't won. That she wasn't his and never had been or would be, whether she was alive or not.

'Effie?'

She heard Smith's voice as her arms dropped to the floor. Despite Oliver's thumbs pressing into her throat, a small smile flickered at her mouth. Nobody could ever say her name like him, and if she had to die, she wanted the memory of his voice to be the last thing she heard. She closed her eyes. She had no more fight left in her, and her lungs couldn't take any more. She stopped resisting, and the pressure disappeared.

Was she dead?

She gasped, drawing in a breath so sharp it made her gag. She turned on her side, doubled over as her forehead pressed to the floor while she coughed and dragged in as much air as she could in turns. She was alive. Her throat was burning, and her brain felt like it was spinning in her head, but she was alive. She pulled herself up onto her elbows, shaking as she looked up, trying to work out what had happened, just in time to see Smith tussling with Oliver on the floor by the stairs.

'Smith?' she choked out. He was there. She hadn't imagined it.

He didn't hear her tiny voice as he punched Oliver in the face, right in the jaw. The sound of bone connecting with bone echoed loudly, and Effie tried to drag herself forward, but her body was too heavy and her ribs ached.

'Smith, don't.'

He landed three more blows to Oliver's face as the communal door opened, and a young woman Effie recognised as one of the upstairs neighbours walked in. The woman stopped mid-stride, her face aghast at what was happening.

'Call the police,' Smith shouted, pinning Oliver down to the ground. 'Now!'

The woman nodded and scrambled through her bag as Effie hauled herself up to sit against the wall. She coughed again, wincing at the raw burn in her throat as the neighbour frantically jabbed at her mobile phone and Smith turned his head.

'Effie.' He leapt up, leaving Oliver sprawled on the floor, and shot over to her, almost tripping over his feet. He fell to the floor next to her and pulled her into his arms, kissing her face over and over again. He looked at her, his eyes darting across her face and his hands in her hair as he checked her over. 'I thought you were . . . Thank god, you're okay.'

He pulled her back into him, his strong arms holding her close as she sobbed.

'You came back.'

'Of course I came back.' He squeezed her and kissed the top of her head. 'I wasn't going to miss being with you just to take my bike back.'

The adrenalin pulsing through Effie's body fought its way up through her throat in a shaky, misplaced laugh. If he'd carried on home, she would have died. The young woman looked at them, with the phone still pressed to her ear, as she gave the police their address, and when she hung up, she looked from Smith and Effie to Oliver, lying on the ground, and back again.

'They're on the way,' she said as Oliver turned on his side to hawk and spit. 'I'll get some water.'

She raced up the stairs, and Oliver sat up, holding his nose. His light blue shirt was stained with blood.

'If you even so much as *think* about moving . . .' Smith snarled at him.

'Smith, don't,' Effie said, squeezing his arm.

'He tried to kill you.'

'I know, but you can't go at him again. I mean it, Smith. Please.' Effie's voice trembled.

Oliver wasn't going anywhere, not with Smith blocking the way out. The police were on their way, but she knew that before the night was out, he'd have a top-drawer lawyer to represent him. She couldn't let Smith do anything more that might see him land in prison. She could almost see the anger at Oliver pulsing from Smith's body, but she held on to him tightly.

'Please, Smith. Let the police deal with it.'

His jaws clenched as he turned to look at Oliver again, and Effie willed him not to go back and finish what he'd started. She could see the fire in his eyes as he looked at the man who had tried to kill her, but she interlocked her fingers with his. Smith looked back at her and nodded.

'Fine, but I'm not taking my eyes off him.'

Just as he'd said he would, Smith glared at Oliver right up until the moment the police arrived. Effie stood next to Smith with an itchy wool blanket around her shoulders, watching as two officers read Oliver his rights and slapped the handcuffs on his wrists. She felt lighter with every breath she took. It was finally over.

'You know I'll probably get arrested too, right? I don't want you to panic.' Smith hooked his hand around the back of her head and kissed the top of her forehead.

'Why? You didn't do anything wrong.'

'I'm sure he'll have something different to say about that.'

Oliver threw her a look of pure disgust as he was led outside onto the street and into the shimmering blue lights of the police sirens. She held on to Smith tightly, praying the police wouldn't come back for him. He'd only been defending her, but this was exactly what she'd been afraid of, what she'd been trying to protect him from.

'Hey.' Smith kissed her again and pulled her in for a hug. 'We'll be fine. I promise.'

The flickering of the lights lit up the hallway in an eerily calm glow. The neighbour was talking to an officer, telling him what she saw. Surely she'd say that Smith was the good guy in all this? Effie burrowed her head into his chest, sucking in the scent she'd thought she'd never smell again.

'I know what I'd do if I only had forty-four minutes left to live now.' She looked up at him, and he smiled.

'A near-death experience will do that.' He tucked her hair behind her ears. 'So, what would you do?'

Effie reached up on her tiptoes and wrapped her arms around his neck, letting the blanket fall to her feet as she kissed him, her hands delving into his hair. He kissed her back, holding her close to him as the flashing blue lights lit up the space around them. She broke away from him and looked at his beautiful grey eyes. Even when she'd looked into them on her wedding day, she'd known, deep down, how she felt.

'I love you.'

'Took you long enough.' Smith grinned. 'Tell me something I don't know.'

He laughed and pulled her back in close to his chest, squeezing her in a hug as she wrapped her arms around his waist.

'I love you too,' he murmured.

Effie smiled, clinging on to him, and didn't let go.

SIX MONTHS LATER

Effie sat in her seat and looked out of the rain-speckled cabin window, letting out a long breath. Why did it have to rain, today of all days? She turned to look at Smith as he put their hand luggage in the overhead locker, and she saw the taut strip of flesh on his abs as his T-shirt rode up. One look at the line of hair leading from his belly button to his jeans made her cheeks burn.

'You okay?' he asked, sitting next to her and taking her hand.

'Yep. I just wish it wasn't raining.'

He laughed and kissed her knuckles. 'We'll be fine. It's just rain.'

'Ladies and gentlemen, welcome onboard Air India Flight 9W121 from London to Delhi.'

Effie listened to the captain's distorted voice through the tannoy and looked at Smith. 'What's the flight time again?'

'About nine hours,' Smith replied.

A flight attendant made her way up the aisle, checking that the overhead lockers were securely closed.

'I hope I'll be able to sleep.'

Smith leaned over and kissed the space right under her ear. 'We could always try the mile-high thing. That might tire you out.'

She grinned and playfully whacked his arm. 'Shush. People can hear you.'

'So?' He shrugged. 'Once we're up in the air, we're free.'

Effie looked out of the window again at the bright lights of Heathrow's terminal building. They were free, and she felt it too. Now she could see how much Oliver had manipulated her, trying to turn her into something she wasn't, from the clothes he'd bought her to his suggestions about how she should wear her hair. She'd been trying to run away from herself for so long, ashamed at being abandoned by her mum and hurt by what had happened with Smith, that she had been an easy target. It had taken being beaten and almost killed to make her see what Smith, Lou and her mum had said all along. She was fine as she was. Better than fine, in fact.

She choked back the tears in her throat. Her heart had wrenched in her chest when they'd hugged Lou and Mickey goodbye by the security gate. After Oliver's arrest, Lou hadn't wanted to let Effie out of her sight, feeling guilty for having arranged to meet her instead of coming straight home from work. It was only because of Smith that she'd reluctantly let someone take over babysitting duty, not that Effie needed it. The minute her soon-to-be ex-husband had been led away in handcuffs, she'd felt freer than she had for a long time.

'You're worried about Lou, aren't you?' Smith asked, and she looked back at him with her chin wobbling and nodded. She always had been bad at goodbyes. She must have inherited that from Penny.

'She'll be fine. Besides, she's got Mickey.'

Lou and Mickey getting back together was the one thing that had made leaving so much easier. When Smith had called to tell them what had happened, they'd both raced back to Lou's and had been almost inseparable since.

'I know. I'm just being silly.'

He tucked her hair behind her ear. 'No, you're just being you. And I love you for it.'

Effie smiled. No matter how many times he said it, the sheen never wore off. He loved her, just as she was. What they had now was completely different than it had been before. He'd been her rock for the last few months, holding her shaking hand when she'd been called in to give her statement to the Crown Prosecution Service against Oliver. His being a top barrister had meant nothing – not when there was photographic evidence of his violence. And since he'd confessed to running her over, his car had been forensically examined, uncovering proof of repairs made to the bodywork. He'd been formally charged and given conditional bail, and from what Effie had heard, things had gone south for him. The air of respectability he had carried around was shattered, and his clients were falling over themselves to take their business elsewhere. Izzy had left her voicemail after voicemail, telling her how horrified she was, how she'd never be able to forgive Oliver for hurting her. Effie hadn't returned her calls. She wanted nothing more to do with Oliver, and if that meant breaking ties with his sister, then so be it. Not even the tiniest part of her felt sorry for him.

The captain announced the closure of the aircraft doors, and Effie buckled her seatbelt. Smith switched his phone to 'Flight Mode', and she took hers from her pocket to do the same. She smiled as she saw the text message on her screen.

Have a safe flight, Sweetpea. Can't wait to see you both and will be waiting at Arrivals. And remember, when you get here, take a deep breath. Your first breath in India is something to be remembered. Love, Mum.

'Should I be worried?' She laughed, showing the message to Smith.

'I'd be lying if I said I hadn't been to some places with a funky smell.' He grinned as she grimaced, and then went back to flicking through the guidebook he'd bought after checking in.

If anyone had told her she'd ever go to India, she'd have thought they were crazy. She'd seen it on the television and in films, looking at the pictures of extreme poverty, slum children and dirt, but Penny had always painted a very different view. After everything that had happened, Effie had wanted to get as far away from London as possible, and when Penny had invited them over, she'd accepted without hesitation. And if she didn't like it, it didn't matter. India was just a pit stop on the way to their final destination of Sydney – the place where Smith was supposed to have finished his year-long trip.

She leaned over and looked at the photograph of the Taj Mahal in his book. 'Will we be able to see it, do you think?'

'We can do whatever you want.' He grinned and kissed the tip of her nose as the air bridge connecting the plane to the airport slowly retracted. 'We've got nothing but time.'

THE END

ACKNOWLEDGEMENTS

Domestic violence is a subject that's close to my heart, so I have to first of all thank the many, many survivors – both men and women – who've shared their stories with me personally and online on anonymous forums. A huge thanks goes to Caroline Batten, the best writing buddy a girl could wish for, and Adele Walklett for support over the last few weeks of writing. A big thanks goes to Janny Peacock, Sam Curniffe and Thandi Davis. Thank you also to Natasha Fonseka for providing Celeste Barton-Cole's name.

The process of writing *Love You Better* was enormously helped along by my lovely Wattpad followers, and I have to say a huge thank you to them for pestering me for new chapters and for their feedback – especially to Maia, an absolute star.

I would also like to thank my editor, Sophie, for sharing the same vision for the book. All the probing and feedback has only made *Love You Better* even stronger, so thank you!

Finally, thanks go to you, the readers, and everyone who's supported me since the release of *Together Apart*. It's been a whirlwind, roller-coaster ride, and I've loved every minute.

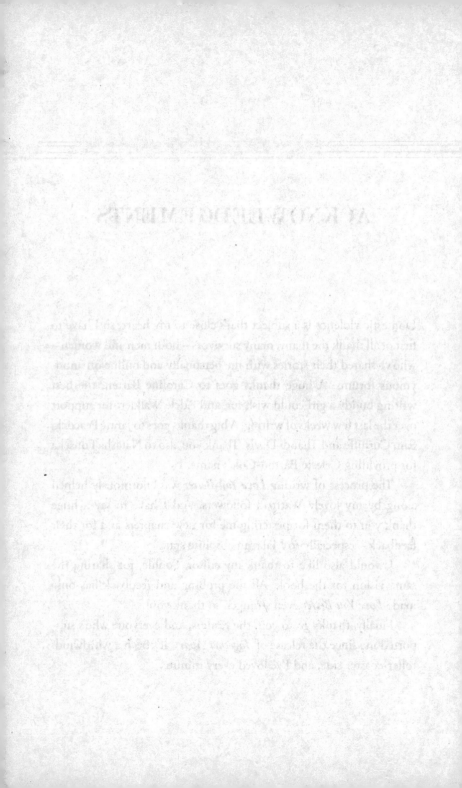

ABOUT THE AUTHOR

Natalie K Martin is a lover of books, music and chocolate peanuts. Originally from Sheffield, Natalie is based in London and loves all things French. In January 2014, she decided to leave her job and travel to India where she published her debut novel, *Together Apart*. Since her return to the UK, her feet have been itching to go somewhere else.